A Scandal in Stresa

An Elspeth Duff Mystery

Ann Crew

Copyright © 2014 by Ann Crew

A Scandal in Stresa is a work of fiction. Names, characters, and incidents are the products of the author's imagination. Any resemblance to actual persons, living or dead, is entirely coincidental. The existing landmarks in Italy are used fictionally. The Kennington Stresa and Umberto Primo hotels, Elspeth's home on Loch Rannoch, and Tay Farm do not exist, nor was there a storm on Lago Maggiore on the eighth of October 2004.

Cover photographs of Stresa rooftops and the promenade with Isola Bella in the distance by Ann Crew © 2004

Author's photograph by Ian Crew

ACE/AC Editions
All rights reserved.
ISBN-10: 1494924234
ISBN-13: 9781494924232

Library of Congress Control Number: 2014900444
CreateSpace Independent Publishing Platform,
North Charleston, South Carolina

anncrew.com

elspethduffmysteries.com

Also by Ann Crew

A Murder in Malta

Praise for *A Murder in Malta:*

"Each main character has a rich backstory with enough skeletons in closets to provide grist for a number of future novels.

An often compelling . . . excursion through exotic locales featuring unusual, complex characters." —*Kirkus Review*

To Dave with thanks and love

Part 1

The Approaching Storm

Prologue

Two shots were heard ringing out loudly and unexpectedly at a few minutes before four o'clock on Monday afternoon the fourth of October two thousand and four. They echoed down the narrow streets of Stresa and brought merchants, shoppers, tourists and residents out into the drizzle of rain that had just begun.

Carlo Bartelli, the Italian ex-Minister of Cultural Affairs, and his secretary flung themselves to the floor of the back seat of the large Alfa Romeo that had brought them from Rome. They both had been trained on how to react in case of an attack, but their movements were more instinctive than learned. The first shot penetrated the windscreen on the driver's side of the car and embedded itself in the leather upholstery of the driver's seat after leaving a narrow red slit across his left arm.

The second shot killed Marco Celli instantly. The bullet entered his right eye and exited through the back of his neck. The projectile made such a small hole that it hardly disfigured his handsome face, so that the embalmer had little challenge in making an open coffin possible.

The next morning the popular press argued fervently about the incident. A large car had been seen hastily leaving the scene. Some said the shots had come from the car. Others said the car had been hit and one of the occupants had slumped forward. No one recorded the number plate of the car, and there was disagreement on its make and model.

The only thing everyone agreed on was that at the sound of the shots Marco Celli had spun around and plunged to the ground. Marco was unaccompanied in the street when he fell. His detractors later said that his last thought must have been filled with sorrow because his adoring fans and the paparazzi were not there to see him die.

1

Silvia Trucco did not expect the shots and, lying on the floor, grabbed tightly to the seat, so that she would not be thrown against Carlo Bartelli, her employer. Her heart pounded, and she prayed to the Virgin. Not this too, she thought. Why this? It does not make any sense. We do not belong in this nightmare.

Silvia Trucco was afraid. She had been since receiving the phone call three days before. As Carlo's personal secretary, she had taken the call in Carlo's private office suite looking out over the Tiber and beyond to Michelangelo's dome rising above the jumbled rooftops of Rome.

The man's voice on the phone was rough and muffled. He spoke in broken English and asked for *Signor* "Baltelli." Silvia pleaded his absence although Carlo was in the next room.

"Tell him. If he want see daughta again, he get one million eulos and bling it to Lago Ma-jo-lay, Localno, Sui-za-lan," the voice said in broken English. He apparently could not enunciate the rolling tones of the name of Lago Maggiore or of the Swiss city of Locarno. Had it not been for his mentioning Switzerland, Silvia would not have understood. "You not tell police or daughta die. Like I-laqi we cut off head. I call you next Fliday, tell you whele take money."

"How will you reach us?" Silvia could barely get out the words.

"Give me mobile numba."

Her voice scratched out her personal number.

"Fliday eleven in molning." Then the voice rang off.

Silvia sat still, smelling fear on her body, and listened to her heart banging in her chest. She was aware that she was holding in her breath. She let it out slowly.

At first she thought the call was a hoax and dismissed it as she had many others, but this one felt different. Constanza Bartelli, Carlo's daughter, on assignment in Nepal for her American left-wing newspaper, had stopped sending her frequent, short, and affectionate email messages to Silvia over three weeks before. Constanza's last email had attached a copy of her article to the paper and a note reading: *I think this is one of my best pieces yet. Knowing the situation in Kathmandu and the corruption in the royal palace, my sympathy is with the rebels here in a land often neglected by the rest of the world as well as its own monarchy. In such a beautiful place, the people are in such need. With love, C.*

Silvia waited until she could get her emotions in check and knocked on the door that connected her outer office to Carlo Bartelli's inner one. He was on the phone talking rapidly to one of his protégés, a young artist who had just received a large commission for a public building in Vicenza. Carlo was congratulating him when he looked up and saw his secretary's face.

He hung up and said, "Is it Constanza?"

"*Sì*, Carlo. This time I think it is for real."

Silvia, from long practice, had turned on the voice recorder when the phone call came in. Carlo was a stickler for exactness, and he preferred his calls recorded rather than noted. She had brought the tiny machine with her and hit the play button for Carlo to hear the mysterious caller's threat. Numerous playbacks did not change it.

Carlo drummed his pen on his desk as he listened, and then he flung the pen across the room. "One million euros is nothing as long as she is safe. But we have no details. Lago Maggiore, Locarno, Friday? Where is the sense in that? Isn't Constanza in Nepal? Didn't you tell me she was trekking into the mountains to interview one of the Maoists guerillas?"

"She sent me a copy of her last article in an email on the tenth of September. I forwarded it to you, but let me go get a another copy."

"No, let me read it on my computer," he snapped. He turned to the flat screen in front of him. Silvia watched him go over the article again and again.

"Silvia," he finally said, "we need to get to Lago Maggiore as quickly as possible. Do you know a hotel there?"

"I believe Lord Kennington has one in Stresa."

"Call Eric Kennington personally and book us there for Monday. See if he can arrange a security guard for us and also a motor launch. I want to be able to travel easily around the lake, and I don't want to be bothered with the treacherous roads along it."

*

Maria, *la duchessa d'Astonino*, was worried about her daughter's wellbeing. The threat to both the duchess and her daughter came from the figure standing vigilantly by the lamppost just as he had at this time for the last four days. The duchess narrowed her eyes with loathing. The sound of the gunshots rang in her eardrums. She gasped as she saw the large Alfa Romero swing around the corner. One shot entered the windscreen of the car and sent it swerving across the road. The driver, who appeared to have been wounded by the bullet, engaged the powerful engine, righted the car, and sped up the hill and out of sight. And, then on the ground, she saw Marco Celli's body. She did not move. She suddenly felt gloriously gratified and set her jaw in utter hatred. So, she thought, Marco Celli has been hit. His body twitched and then lay still. She prayed he was dead because, if he were, he no longer could hurt her Vittoria.

She remained standing and staring at the body for a long time and turned away as the crowds gathered below. She returned to her bedroom. Surveying her wardrobe, she picked out a purple designer dress that brought out the warm tones of her olive skin. Then she retired to her dressing room to complete her preparations for the evening ahead.

Toria Albi, Maria's daughter, who had earlier complained of a headache and taken a tranquilizer, was still asleep in her bedroom on the other side of the suite. The duchess did not tell her about Marco's death until several hours later, when a local television news program flashed a picture of Toria's ex-husband across the screen. Toria rushed from the sitting room of their suite into her bedroom. Her mother, now resplendent in violet, followed to ease her daughter's enormous sobs.

"He is not a loss, Vittoria. He abused you. Your denials won't change that. He wanted me dead to get me out of your life. That is why he stood there everyday trying to frighten us. How did he know we were here? Did you tell him? Did not I use every connection I had, even phoning Lord Kennington himself, to get these rooms for us without anyone knowing? Had your stepfather not been a man of such prestige, I am sure Lord Kennington would not have taken my call."

"I don't care, Mamma. You always hated Mario." Toria, who had thrown herself on her bed, flounced over on her back.

"No, I did not like a man who gave you black eyes," her mother spat out.

"They were accidents and easily covered by sunglasses and makeup. He did not like me to answer back when he had had too much to drink."

"No man has the right to hit my precious daughter, especially not as bad an actor as Mario."

"Mamma, his fans adore him."

"What fans? A few love-starved females here in Italy? Did he ever go to Hollywood they way you did? No. You are good, *mia cara*. He is, was, trash and only had his coarse good looks to recommend him. The world of cinema will not notice that he is dead."

"I will notice he is dead!"

"Then you are more of a fool than I thought, Vittoria, just like your father."

2

Late Tuesday morning in London, Lord Kennington handed Elspeth Duff down from the high-ceilinged taxi. He marveled at the beauty of her Italian black leather three-quarter-length coat, buttery to his touch, and admired her fine woolen gray trousers, her skillfully draped Parisian scarf, and her black low-cut boots. Lord Kennington was a collector of fine things to embellish his hotels, and Elspeth Duff was among them.

"Are we having lunch here?" she asked, straightening up and gazing at the great covered space of Covent Garden and at the bustle of the crowds within it. The rain had stopped, but the dampness of the air held the pungent smells of the marketplace, muddy cobblestones, and bustling humanity. A myriad of small shop windows displayed wares to members of the British shopping public and curious foreign tourists.

Puddles abounded. Lord Kennington sidestepped one of them in order to protect the high polish of his bespoke shoes. Shoes always distinguish a gentleman, he had been told by his mother, who had great ambitions for him.

"Whenever I am near here," he said, "I come and visit the places where the flower sellers used to be. I miss the stalls now that they have gone. Just being at Covent Garden takes me back to a much simpler time."

He insisted having fresh flowers daily in all of his luxury boutique hotels, and here, as a boy, he had first fallen in love with opulent floral displays.

He took Elspeth's arm with pleasure. He hoped that by getting her out of the Kennington Organisation corporate offices in the City of London, he would set a mood where he could make the proposal that she might not otherwise be inclined to accept. The rain had begun again, and he raised his twelve-spoke umbrella over her. Taking care that she stay dry, he navigated her down the narrowness of Henrietta Street, passed the sandwich boards that lined the cluttered pavement and drew her up and through the old-fashioned glass and metal doorway of a restaurant that announced its true British fare.

Lord Kennington had chosen the restaurant with deliberation. The small and trendy place had food that, although traditional, catered to the lighter palates of the twenty-first century. The interior welcomed patrons with bare wooden tables, set with brightly colored cloth napkins and substantial flatware. The walls were punctuated with memorabilia, old clocks, children's toys, and theatrical posters from the past.

Lord Kennington had booked a corner table for its privacy. After holding out one of the slat-backed chairs for Elspeth, he removed his mackintosh and sat across from her, so that he could look at her directly. He brushed away the menu and ordered steak and ale pie for them both without asking her preference.

"They serve an excellent St. Emilion. Would you like to try a glass?" he asked.

Elspeth raised her left eyebrow, which was naturally more arched than her right one. "Perrier and lime, please, Eric. I suspect you have business rather than pleasure in mind."

"Elspeth, having lunch with you is always a pleasure."

"It's always a pleasure for me too," she answered with a half smile.

Lord Kennington hoped her response was not only tactful but also truthful. They had dined together before but always in the executive dining room of the Kennington Organisation offices, which looked out over the River Thames from the twentieth floor.

As they waited for the food, they chatted, exchanging reminiscences of cases she had handled in the past. She sat with her hands together and one thumb nervously rubbing the other until the meal was served. As they both cut into the succulent pie's crispy crust, its layers as thin as tissue paper, the pungent suet-filled aroma broke the tension between them. She smiled after her first bite with the delight of someone sampling long forbidden food.

"Now Eric, to what do I owe the honor of this delicious meal, and why couldn't be it discussed in your office?"

Because it was early in the day, the custom in the restaurant was still sparse enough that their conversation could be completely private. Their closest neighbor was the boyish bartender dispensing goblets of wine and tumblers of soft drinks, the small halogen spots above the bar highlighting his practiced gestures.

Although he might wish it differently, Lord Kennington silently applauded Elspeth's need to keep things on a business level. He knew that was why he entrusted her with some of the less savory and more difficult aspects of running his business. Reluctantly he gave up the social pretext of the meal.

"I want you to find an assassin," he said.

Elspeth drew back slightly, closed her eyes and swallowed hard. A look of deep sadness crossed her face. After a long moment, she composed herself, and she said, "As simple as that? Just where and how do you want me to do it?" Her voice, belying her earlier expression, was flippant.

"Where? In Stresa in the Italian Lakes Region. I will leave the how to you."

"Am I to find an assassin to kill someone or am I to find one who already has killed someone?" Now Elspeth seemed amused.

Lord Kennington did not understand Elspeth's fleeting discomfort at the mention of an assassin. He sensed he had touched on some tragedy in her life that she did not want to share. He found Elspeth's quirky humor even more enigmatic.

"I want you to find out if an assassin murdered the right person," he said.

Elspeth pulled a piece of warm bread from the breadbasket and paddled a large chunk of butter onto it with undue concentration. Then she cleared her throat. "I am not sure how to do that. Finding assassins is a bit beyond my usual duties." She hesitated. "Can't you simply ask the police to deal with the matter?"

Lord Kennington shook his head slowly and ran his hand along the side of the beak of his nose, over his clean-shaven cheek and around his long jaw. How much should he share with her?

After pausing, he said to her, "An important friend of mine may have been the assassin's target. I promised I would protect him."

"May I suggest that one of the younger members of the security staff would be more appropriate? Someone with physical skills I don't have."

"Yes, I thought of that, but I need your brain and your presence at the hotel. Someone senior."

"At the Kennington Stresa? I had heard it might close." Elspeth did not share the source of her knowledge, but Eric suspected his business partner, Pamela Crumm.

"Not yet," he said. "I am planning a major renovation of the hotel, but I can't do so if any scandal drives guests away. Yesterday afternoon a murder took place just outside the hotel. Two people were shot at; one was killed. As you know, Pamela reads the international popular press. A photograph she found in one of today's tabloids showed our hotel in the background. I do not want any attention brought to the hotel, particularly not at this time."

Elspeth abandoned her bread and looked up at him with deep cobalt blue eyes whose intelligence always disconcerted him. Damn, he thought, such an appealing woman should not look so intently at a man that way. It unnerved him.

"How does the murder affect the hotel or the security of your friend? I don't understand. Surely the location was coincidental," Elspeth said.

"No, actually, it probably was not. Both of the people who were shot at had links to the hotel."

"Is one of them your friend?"

He lowered his voice, knowing his baritone tended to carry. "From time to time I am asked to provide rooms to people in my acquaintance who want their presence at a hotel kept confidential. For better or for worse, I was approached twice in the last month to harbor two such parties at the Kennington Stresa. One is my friend, a former minister in the Italian government and who wishes to conduct what he called private negotiations, and the other was a film star and her mother. They were trying to hide from her recently divorced husband, who supposedly was stalking them. Both the ex-husband and the ex-minister were shot at; the ex-husband died. A bullet grazed the arm of the ex-minister's driver, but still he was able to pull the car away from the scene of the shooting. The papers have not yet discovered who was in that car, but Marco Celli's photograph has been plastered across the front pages of the Italian popular press and also was on page six of the *Star*."

"Who is Marco Celli? The ex-husband?"

"Yes. His ex-wife is the film star, and her mother is *la duchessa d'Astonino*."

"The Duchess of Astonino. Is she someone I should know?" Elspeth asked.

"No. She is not someone anyone should know." Eric's grimaced at the thought of the duchess and her coercion of him.

"Is she a real duchess?"

"The title is real. *Il duca d'Astonino*, the duke, died at age eighty-five several years ago. The duchess is much younger."

"Why is there a problem?"

"She is the mother of Toria Albi."

Elspeth took another bite of her steak and ale pie, and chewed it slowly, before making the identification. "The Italian film star?"

"Exactly."

"I don't have Pamela's encyclopedic knowledge of the celebrities of this world, but can I presume that the duke was not Toria Albi's father?"

"He was not. Pamela tells me that the duke's real fascination was with the daughter, but there was over sixty years difference in their ages, and *la mamma* would not tolerate it. She married him instead. He got to be with the daughter, and she got the money and position."

Eric Kennington looked across at Elspeth's chiseled cheekbones, sharp nose, and determined chin. So satisfactorily

British, he thought, remembering she was Scottish and not English. She was aging with such perfection.

Chastising himself for focusing on Elspeth's looks, Lord Kennington scowled at his pie dish as if to command it to be bottomless. Disappointed not to find another morsel of beef, he continued. "Toria Albi has just divorced husband number three, who happens to be the now-deceased Marco Celli. Celli publicly threatened to kill *la duchessa*, whom he accused of engineering the divorce. Last Thursday the duchess rang me from Italy and pleaded that I give her and her daughter safe haven at the Kennington Stresa. Incognito."

"If I remember Toria Albi's physical endowments correctly, I wonder if she could be completely incognita," Elspeth said. "If they were in hiding, how did Marco Celli appear on the scene outside the hotel?"

He smoothed his hand over his expansive pinstriped waistcoat. He was glad it had not been soiled in his pursuit of the steak and ale pie. He emptied his glass of wine and waved to the waiter for another. At her request, he ordered a coffee for Elspeth.

"Now you see one of the problems I want you to find the answer to," he said.

"I am beginning to understand," she said, "and what of the ex-minister? Why is keeping the secret of his stay at the hotel so important?"

"Both before, during, and after Carlo Bartelli was Minister for Cultural Affairs, he and I worked together on numerous occasions. He helped me find art for my hotels in Italy, and I helped him promote up-and-coming Italian artists. His confidential secretary rang me and asked if I could provide a place for him to stay while he was conducting what she called 'private matters.' She would not tell me anymore, but there was a certain tension in her voice that made me think something was disturbing Carlo. Both his wealth and influence put him in a position to be instrumental in affairs that even now affect both the government and cultural affairs in Italy, and he often acts in an ex-officio capacity. This would be enough for him to want privacy, but, from his secretary's tone, I concluded that the negotiations he is anticipating are worrisome to him personally."

"Could the shots have been meant for him and not Marco Celli?"

"Possibly," Lord Kennington conceded.

"Then Mario Celli was in the wrong place at the wrong time for the wrong reason and was not the real target of the assassin?"

Lord Kennington raised his bushy eyebrows and shook his head doubtfully.

"I sense you already have a plan for my stay in Stresa. I hope I can carry it out, Eric. I am still not sure why you have chosen me."

"I cannot afford to have anything happen to Carlo Bartelli. He is a friend but also someone so well known in Italy that to have harm come to him at one of my hotels would be disastrous. Your primary concern must be to discover the identity of the murderer and make sure he does not endanger anyone at the hotel again. You won't be alone; I am setting up a whole team there, with you at the head."

"Have you chosen the team or do I get some say?"

"Both."

Elspeth took a sip of her coffee and considered for a moment. "I have worked with Will Tuttle before. He is quick-witted and likeable. As I remember, he is a master in kung fu and always carries a camera. He also can charm people with his innocent manner, but I'm not too sure he can speak Italian."

Eric concurred. "Good choice. I can have Pamela arrange for an interpreter. If he is as engaging as you say, I want him to deal with Toria Albi."

"Whom else do you have in mind, Eric?"

"Sandro Liu."

Elspeth puzzled at the name. "I haven't worked with him. Is he new to the security department?"

"Yes, fairly new. Just like your Will, he is enormously talented. He speaks six languages fluently, including English, Italian, French, two dialects of Chinese, and Burmese."

"Tell me more about him."

"Sandro, as you would assume from his surname, is Chinese. His family lived in Burma, where Sandro was born. During political troubles there, his family was killed by the military, and Sandro was smuggled out the country by an Italian priest. Liu was ten years old at the time. The priest's family adopted him, raised him in Livorno and gave him his Italian Christian name. He is very earnest and, like Will, skilled in martial arts. He was in the intelligence service of the Italian navy for several years and is a master helmsman, which may be useful for an assignment on a lake."

"I look forward to meeting him. He sounds suitable, if a little overly qualified. And the others?"

"Of course, one is the manager of the hotel in Stresa, Franca Donatello. She will be a vital member of the team. I won't describe her to you because I want you to make your own judgment of her. She can be a bit temperamental at times but keeps a tightly-run hotel."

Lord Kennington held his newly replenished wine glass up to the bright lights at the bar and considered their reflection before he outlined the final step in his plan. He knew what he was about to propose to Elspeth was out of the ordinary, but his success had often come by his ability to demand the unique.

"One other thing," he finally said. "I want outside people on the team who are not members of our security staff. I'd like you to choose someone in your acquaintance who can be a presence in the hotel, a guest who will appear to be unassociated with any investigation, but who can report back to you."

"I don't understand, Eric."

"I would prefer someone with a title—a real one."

"One that can be found in Debrett's?"

"Certainly."

Elspeth held her coffee cup in midair. "Why?"

"To play the role of an innocent guest and to be an ear. Someone who can sit in the lounge and strike up conversations, or linger about and watch what is going on there."

"Do you have any of my 'titled' friends in mind?"

"Not exactly. I understand you have an increasingly close relationship with Sir Richard Munro."

Elspeth nodded, but she did not look pleased. Lord Kennington took pains to keep track of his top employees' personal lives, Pamela Crumm often being his source.

"Richard and I, as you may know, are childhood friends."

"Is that where it ends? I have often asked myself why you haven't remarried, Elspeth. God knows, you are attractive enough."

Elspeth flushed but did not reply.

Assuming he had paid her a compliment rather than causing her discomfort, Eric Kennington continued, "Elspeth, you must know people of consequence in Scotland."

"Good heavens, no. Not at all. I left Scotland when I was eighteen. Did Pamela put that idea in your head?"

Eric Kennington ignored her remark. "Surely you have family friends who have a title but might be feeling impoverished enough to accept an all expenses paid holiday at a luxurious hotel in the Italian Lakes Region?"

"What are you suggesting?"

"This. I am sure that you can convince Sir Richard to go to Stresa for some rest and recreation, particularly if you are there. He was helpful to us in Malta and probably can assist us in Stresa as well. I also need a titled woman of an age similar to that of the duchess, someone who could strike up an acquaintance with her without attracting suspicion. From my few dealings with the duchess, I think she may be difficult." He let out a short huff.

"Do you think she is likely to cause a stink at the hotel?"

"I wouldn't have put it exactly that way. Really, Elspeth, your years living in America have made you quite direct and some of your language is hardly refined."

Elspeth chuckled. "You are not the first person to say so. Richard Munro made the same remark recently."

His lordship was not deterred. "Pamela has told me that *la duchessa,* when left to her own devices, plays the duchess in all respects. She is demanding, self-aggrandizing, and quite insufferable. My fear is that she may wish, as you say, to make 'a stink' about Marco Celli's death. Pamela's reports also say that she is subdued by the presence of real aristocracy."

"Therefore you are seeking the help of an impoverished gentlewoman of aristocratic lineage and a proper title to distract her."

"As for finding the perfect person, I rely on you. Surely you must have at least one useful relative or friend," Lord Kennington said.

"Biddy," responded Elspeth without hesitation.

"Biddy?"

"Yes, my cousin, Lady Elisabeth Baillie Shaw. My uncle had the dubious distinction of being one of the most poverty-stricken members of the nobility of Scotland. He inherited the much-encumbered earldom of Tay and did little to relieve his family's obligations during his lifetime. Biddy is his daughter."

"Tell me about her."

"Biddy and I grew up together, although we are quite different. She always disapproved me, I think. I didn't care a bit about my roots or the fact that I had a many times great-grandfather who betrayed the clans and supported the Redcoats in seventeen forty-six. He was given a title for doing so. When we were growing up Biddy was all flowery and good; I was a terrible tomboy."

Lord Kennington tried to envision Elspeth as a child but failed. Elspeth was always beautifully dressed and carried herself with the deportment of the grandest of French women. He could not imagine her climbing a tree or skinning her knee.

"What happened to her?"

"She married Ivor—Ivor Baillie Shaw. He came from a family who had earned their money in trade, much to my grandmother's disapproval, and enjoyed enough inheritance to bail out the Tay 'estate', which actually is little more than a farm. Biddy and he lead a happy existence on the farm and had three marvelous children. Ivor died about a year ago."

"Where did that leave Lady Elisabeth?"

"Saddened. Ivor was a wonderful person. We all adored him because he was witty and completely uncomplicated."

"Is Lady Elisabeth a grieving widow?" Eric Kennington asked.

"Yes and no. Biddy, when young, was a bit fey, but she has grown wiser with age. When Ivor died, neither her brother, the current earl, nor her children wanted to live on the farm. So Biddy was left to run it, which, quite unexpectedly, she has succeeded in doing."

"Why did she come to mind for an assignment in Stresa?"

"She could use a holiday, and she does have a flair for the dramatic. Because she was pretty, at school she was always chosen to play the part of the heroine."

"Could she play a part now?"

"Perfectly."

"I assume you will have no difficulty persuading her to go to Stresa."

"I should think none at all," said Elspeth, although from her expression Lord Kennington was not quite sure if she truly believed so.

"Then I want you to go to Scotland this afternoon and convince her to be in London tomorrow to see Pamela. I'll have one of our planes take you to Edinburgh this afternoon and then meet you tomorrow morning to fly you directly to Milan. A car and driver will take you to Stresa from there."

His task completed, Lord Kennington cut the meal short and rang Pamela Crumm on his mobile to have her make the necessary arrangements for Elspeth.

"Oh, and Elspeth," he said after signing a chit on his account, "find the assassin before the police or press do—and keep everyone safe. I want no harm to come to any of my guests, and, above all, I want no bad publicity."

3

Elspeth's legs were beginning to cramp. She had driven without stopping from the small airport in Dundee because she wanted to get to her parent's house before dark. Being October, the days were now shortening into the darkness of the Scottish autumn and winter. As she entered the familiar cathedral of trees that covered the road going from Pitlochry toward Kinloch Rannoch, cold descended into the open car and wind rushed around her. She pulled into a lay-by that offered stunning views of Loch Tummel below and the highlands beyond. Several black-faced sheep bleated at her arrival and then turned away from her, disinterested. Twilight was crossing the loch, obscuring the fringe of yellowing alders, copper-colored larches, and dark conifers, faintly mirrored at the edge of the loch's smooth surface. The last of the sun touched the whisper of the snow on the tops of the high peaks beyond and rimmed their edges with a cold white line. Elspeth took in a long cleansing breath and got out of the car to put up its ragtop. How wonderful it was to be back in Scotland even for a brief moment.

She steered the convertible down the narrow road toward Loch Rannoch, through the tight bends, across the tiny stone bridges, and along the single-track road bounded by mossy dry stonewalls and wire sheep fences. She rounded the last curve of the familiar road that brought into view the rambling and ivy-covered stone house with its gabled roofs and multiple chimneystacks, a place she once called home. She sighted the still vibrant but stooped figure of her father, waiting impatiently in the garden above the gates and pretending to prune an old apple tree that sometimes blossomed but no longer bore fruit. Elspeth slowed the car and paused to punch in the code for the gate. Not for the first time, she noticed her father's increasing age. He raised his hand in greeting.

Neither the house nor her parents' manner changed with time, Elspeth thought, as she explained the reason for her visit.

"Biddy?" her mother said with theatrical tones. "Why Biddy?"

Elspeth's father, characteristically thoughtful and, unlike her mother, generally supportive of Elspeth's schemes, responded positively to Elspeth's suggestion, "I can see every reason why Lord Kennington would want Biddy." Although his eighty years had wizened his face, his mind had suffered no decay.

Elspeth looked across the sitting room filled with chintz, battered Persian rugs, and some quite good watercolors, at her mother, who stood in the kitchen door holding up a wooden spoon as if it were the scepter of the realm. Her face was a web of creases and was filled with an astuteness that was no longer deceived by life but was only amused by it.

"Who will care for the animals?" her mother said. Fiona Duff had been brought up at Tay Farm. Despite its mismanagement in her childhood, she knew that one could not simply pack up and leave for a holiday if one lived on a farm.

"Robbie MacPherson can manage for a day or two, but the farm cannot be run without someone in charge," Fiona said definitively.

"Mother, Lord Kennington, or rather Pamela Crumm, will have thought of that. She probably has already selected a suitable caretaker. Besides, Biddy won't be away for more than a fortnight. No great harm can be done to the farm in that time, especially with Robbie about. I think Biddy will jump at the chance."

As a child, her cousin Biddy had dreamed of far off places filled with rich and famous people. How strange that it should be Elspeth who actually fulfilled that dream, and not Biddy, who still lived where she was born.

Biddy Baillie Shaw, however, was not as cooperative as Elspeth had hoped. Fiona Duff had invited Biddy for a late dinner, and she arrived shortly after eight in a mud-spattered Land Rover of unknown vintage. She entered the house without knocking, and the Duff's two Labradors rushed to welcome her with tails waging and wet noses seeking her hands in an accustomed greeting. Biddy shed her tartan shawl and pulled off her boots. As she greeted her aunt and uncle, she searched through her canvas tote for her shoes. She came across the room to hug her cousin, whom she had not seen for several years. The roughness of the wool of Biddy's cardigan cut through the silk of Elspeth's blouse and brought tears to Elspeth's eyes, not from physical pain but from the old closeness of her relationship with Biddy and unchanging quality of her family's life. What would life have been like had her fiancé Malcolm not been murdered? Elspeth wondered. Would she be a mirror image of her cousin, all tweeds and dogs and Wellington boots? Would she have thrived as a solicitor in the firm of Duff MacBean and MacRoberts in Pitlochry if she had been granted different choices from those real life had offered her? Elspeth put these thoughts aside and allowed her love for her parents and cousin to flow over her. How stable their lives had been and how unlike her own.

They took their places among the cushions of the armchairs that had given comfort to the Duffs as long as Elspeth could remember. Settling the dogs down and stirring the wood fire, James Duff offered them sherry. Accepting, Elspeth noted it was finer than his usual. Fiona settled in only briefly, and then rose and took her glass into the kitchen to make final preparations for the meal. After several minutes of family chatter, Elspeth put forward Lord Kennington's proposal.

"I can't do that, 'Peth. I know nothing about murders or murderers. That's your job," Biddy cried.

"I assure you my job routinely involves making arrangements for the security of high-muck-a-mucks, coping with family emergencies of the rich and famous who at Kennington prices think they deserve special attention, and dispatching highly placed swindlers who try to defraud the hotel or the guests. Murder is a rare occurrence."

"What about the murder in Malta? Now this one in Stresa? Besides, I don't speak any Italian except perhaps *buongiorno, ciao* and *grazie*. How can I encourage the friendship of an Italian duchess or turn into a spy in the lounge?"

Dressed appropriately, Biddy would indeed look the part of a titled middle-aged widow who might stay at the Kennington Stresa. She carried herself like a gentlewoman and had the natural assuredness of the British gentry. Biddy shared Elspeth's high coloring but had always been thought pretty rather than handsome. Her light brown hair was peppered with gray rather than skillfully tinted and streaked like Elspeth's. Biddy had it cut for practicality rather than for fashion. She had also inherited the family's intensely blue eyes, sharp nose, and direct manner that was polite but could be demanding.

A Scandal in Stresa

Elspeth should not have been as startled as she was at Biddy's reluctance to go to Italy. Even as a schoolgirl Biddy had been slow to take up a new adventure, and therefore Elspeth suggested Biddy have another glass of sherry and tried to think of other ways to persuade her.

"To begin with, *la duchessa* is only a duchess by marriage and definitely will be impressed with the daughter of a Scottish earl, probably to the extent that she will eschew speaking Italian at all. Lord Kennington assures me that the duchess speaks passable English. Also, the guests in the hotel come from all over the world and many of them do relax for hours in the lounge. Your doing so will not seem out of the ordinary. You needn't consider yourself a spy." Elspeth hoped she sounded convincing.

"You know about this sort of thing more than I do. I don't claim to lead an international jet-set style life but do find a full day's occupation at the farm." Biddy sounded defensive but then smiled. "Lives on Loch Tay probably have as many twists as those at the Kennington hotels, just on a less exalted scale," Biddy said.

Elspeth suspected this was true.

"My life is less glamorous than you think, and often is hard work with long hours," Elspeth replied. "Sometimes even the good food, comfortable beds, and exceptional service do not make up for the demands Lord Kennington makes on me." Elspeth bit her lip, wishing she had not said this.

"Is that what I should expect?" Biddy cried, "Long hours and hard work compensated for by good food and a comfortable bed? The farm offers better than that. What about clothes?" Biddy asked, suddenly shifting her posture. "I can hardly appear at a Kennington hotel in my country rags."

Elspeth sensed that Lord Kennington's seductive offer was not completely lost on her cousin.

"Of course tweeds wouldn't do. The hotels are heated for the comfort of Americans and other less hearty souls than we Scots, but I have already discussed this with Pamela Crumm. The Kennington Organisation will provide you with a wardrobe that is suitable. Pamela suggested that it might not be extensive, but that it would be of excellent quality and sufficiently lightweight to suit the climate inside the hotel in Stresa. I can throw in some Hermès scarves and jewelry." Elspeth did not mention that her own clothes probably would not fit her heartier, thinner, and taller cousin.

"Does the Kennington Organisation have that much money that it can throw it away for little or no good?"

"It won't be thrown away. The small amount spent on clothes for you will be offset in a very short time if guests can continue to flow happily into the Kennington Stresa. Like you, none of them take positively to the thought of murder, especially when one has occurred at the hotel's doorsteps. All you need to do is strike up an acquaintance with the duchess and find out what she knows about Marco Celli's death. After that you can enjoy all the hotel has to offer." Elspeth made no mention of ex-Minister Carlo Bartelli.

"Is the duchess difficult?" Biddy asked.

"She may be but don't worry. We handle difficult personalities on a daily if not hourly basis. All Lord Kennington wants you to do is to make friends with the duchess. The duchess has a reputation for being outspoken, and we want to keep her attention diverted away from going to the press about the murder."

"He wants me to do that?" Biddy sounded doubtful.

"Biddy, you can do this. Haven't you always wanted dramatic roles? You can play the part perfectly." Elspeth beamed enthusiastically at her cousin.

"Scottish amateur dramatics is one thing but subduing an unpleasant duchess is another." Biddy's innate stubbornness came out.

"I can't image that she will be the least unpleasant," Elspeth prevaricated.

"You always used that tone when you were about to do something that Aunt Fiona, Grandmother Tay, or the school would disapprove of, 'Peth."

"Did I? I don't remember. Would I lead you astray?" Elspeth said with the slightest of smiles, hoping her expression would convey pure innocence.

"You did—often."

During their childhood Elspeth had disdained her cousin's reluctance in joining in on some of the more adventuresome of Elspeth's schemes, which often ended in trouble for them both. Rather than Elspeth admitting this past behavior, she tried another argument.

"Have you ever been to the Italian Lakes Region?"

"No. Ivor and I took the children to Venice and Tuscany about ten years ago, but, other than that, I haven't been to Italy at all."

Elspeth had only passed through the Lakes Region once, on a hurried car trip from Geneva to Rome, but she extolled the area's virtues, as if she were an expert. "The Lakes Region is incredibly beautiful. Lake Maggiore sits deep among the Italian Alps and is steeped in history as far back as ancient times. There are wonderful gardens, villas on islands, and breathtaking views. You will not regret a fortnight there.

Besides you will be staying in very luxurious digs. You will be pampered, Lady Elisabeth."

Biddy cocked her head and looked doubtful. "I have a feeling, 'Peth, that you are leading me into some mischief I will later regret."

Elspeth took a deep breath and hoped it would not be so.

Sunlight broke through the window of Elspeth's bedroom and woke her without the necessity of the satellite-controlled alarm clock she had set out on her bedside table. She glanced at the clock and calculated she had another half hour to snuggle in the memories of the days she had spent here on Loch Rannoch in her childhood. Dear Mother and Daddy, she thought, how precious they were. Their own preoccupations with life had allowed Elspeth in childhood to wander alone onto the braes above Loch Rannoch, Loch Tummel, and Loch Tay and discover her own feelings about life and love and, later, to drown her grief after Malcolm's murder. This room, this home, this dear place had shaped Elspeth more than she had ever imagined before.

She thought of all the people in the world who had not had this stable core, even her own children, who had been raised in the milieu of Hollywood and then been subjected to the growing distance between and finally the divorce of their parents. How lucky I am, she thought, that for all the strangeness of my life's journey, I can always return to this place. She suppressed the thought that her parents might not always be here.

She regretted that she could not drive over to visit Biddy's farm on Loch Tay before she left for the airport. She had wanted to say more to Biddy than last night's conversation afforded, but there would be time in Stresa to do so, she hoped.

She smiled at the recollection of her cousin. While growing up, they had been such opposites. Biddy had been soft, feminine and pretty and, except in the presence of Elspeth, had been quite confident that people admired her. Elspeth had been a bookish and independently-minded tomboy who cared little for attention.

Then there were those heavenly days at Cambridge with Malcolm, six short months that woke her mind to all the possibilities of the intellectual world he introduced to her and opened her heart to all the pleasures of his intense love. Instead of dealing with these last memories, she decided to rise and be on the road early. Although the Kennington Organisation plane would wait for her, she did not want to be late.

4

Elspeth stretched out in the reclining seat of the Kennington Organisation private jet and pondered how best to handle Lord Kennington's request that Sir Richard Munro be used to dissuade the duchess from raising problems at the Kennington Stresa. Wasn't Eric Kennington presuming a great deal? How had he put it, that Richard and she had a close relationship?

Lord Kennington's suggestion that she invite Sir Richard to Stresa presented a larger problem for Elspeth. Richard, indeed, was a childhood friend but one that caused complexities both past and present.

Elspeth's cousin and Biddy's brother, Johnnie, the current Lord Tay, had brought Richard home with him to Tay Farm after their first year at Oxford. Richard, then and as now, was tall and lean with angular features. The word distinguished came to people's lips, even when he was a young man. Richard had acquired the sobriquet of "Dickie" at Oxford, not only because of his given name but also because, even when young, he had an uncanny resemblance to Lord Mountbatten of Burma. This likeness had grown with age, but Richard had insisted to all his adult acquaintances that he should be called Richard, despite any similarity with the royal earl. Now only Elspeth, Johnnie, and Biddy called him Dickie as far as Elspeth knew.

A Scandal in Stresa

Elspeth's current relationship with Richard was causing her more anxiety than she liked. Yes, Richard was a friend she had first known when she still was at school. She had met him when she was fifteen and considered any member of the opposite gender to be, at best, like her cousin, Johnnie—a companion for making mischief and a foil in contests of wits. Richard had not been that, however. He was naturally somber and steady, thoughtful but not whimsical, and more often avuncular and highbrow than madcap and merry. Yet Richard often saved the day when Elspeth and Johnnie caused roguery that demanded amends to be made in the end. For two summers they had become a threesome, and a bond formed among them that even now was not entirely broken.

It was Richard, a new recruit to the Foreign and Commonwealth Office, who had come to Cambridge at the end of Elspeth's first year and taken charge of her at the lowest point in her life, after the police told her that her fiancé, Malcolm Buchanan, had been murdered outside of Girton College. On the news, Richard had escorted Elspeth to her home by Loch Rannoch, where she drowned herself in months of grieving for Malcolm. In the ensuing years, Richard had become her escort when she needed one, not only during her last two years at Cambridge, but also afterwards, when she had joined New Scotland Yard and lived in London.

He had proposed to her twice, and both times she had gently refused him. On her second rejection, Richard withdrew and married the younger daughter of the Earl of Glenborough, who was once high commissioner in New Delhi and had great influence in diplomatic circles. Elspeth knew it was not a love match, but Lady Marjorie opened doors for Richard that Elspeth never could. Richard rose quickly through the ranks of the FCO, finally became high commissioner in several of the more important ex-colonies and received his knighthood in due course. Elspeth subsequently heard that many wags in the FCO attributed Richard's advancement to the influence of Marjorie's family, but Elspeth knew Richard's success came as a result of his ability to smooth over difficulties and facilitate accord between parties who previously had been unwilling to compromise. Marjorie died painfully and slowly two years before. Richard had resigned from the FCO to take care of her in her declining months. After her death, he had asked to return to the diplomatic service and be given an assignment in a quiet corner of the world, where he could live in semi-retirement. The high commissioner's position in Malta usually went to a more junior member of the FCO, but, when Richard heard it was available, he applied for the post. Out of recognition for his long service, the FCO had granted his request.

Elspeth's life had taken a completely different path, less planned and more chaotic. Although it diverged completely from Richard's life, they had met on occasion and remained friends. At those times an unspoken tension always existed between them, but, as they both were married, she chose to let it be there and remain unresolved.

Then, six months ago, they had met in Malta. Richard was widowed and Elspeth divorced, and they both were free to pick up a relationship that had floundered in the past but might flourish in the future. Elspeth suspected that Richard wanted her to replace his wife, but Elspeth also knew that she never could and had no desire to do so. She had twice been deeply involved with men in her life. The first was with her fiancé at Cambridge where their relationship had ended in tragedy. The second was with Alistair Craig, her husband of more than twenty years, where the marriage had ended in separation and then divorce. Elspeth's final jump into independence five years before had freed her of needing men in her life, and she was determined to keep it that way. Until meeting Richard in Malta, she had been content.

In Malta something unspoken had happened to Elspeth, and, as hard as she tried to deny it, it would not leave her in peace. She had stood looking out the window of Richard's office at the British High Commission in Ta'Xbiex, and she had known that, in an instant, her relationship with him had changed from friend to something deeper. She did not put a name to it for fear that doing so would commit her to something she did not want in her life. She could not ignore it either, so she had decided to enjoy Richard's company but steer clear of commitment to him. She found it a satisfactory condition, but she realized it was also an avoidance of the truth. This often bothered her.

Their lives diverged after Elspeth had ferreted out the murderer in the unfortunate incident at the Kennington hotel in Valletta in April. Elspeth returned to London and resumed her duties at the Kennington Organisation; Richard remained at his post in Malta. When they both were in London, they would see each other for dinner and the theater, the ballet, or the opera. They spent idle Sunday afternoons walking in Kensington or Kew Gardens or, on rainy days, at the V&A, the Tate Britain, or the British Museum. Elspeth became comfortable with their new relationship, although she sensed he wanted it to be more. Soon they relaxed in each other's company. They laughed a great deal when they were together, in remembrance of past acquaintance and enjoyment of the current moment. Richard was charming, and Elspeth allowed herself to be charmed, but she always held him at a distance because she did not trust that she could handle their relationship becoming closer.

Consequently, she was challenged by Lord Kennington's insistence that Richard come to Stresa to assist in subduing the Duchess of Astonino. It invaded her private relationship with Richard, and she was not pleased. Still, she had often given in to Eric Kennington in the past and normally found that his reasons for assigning more sensitive cases to her bore some intelligence.

As the plane reached Malpensa Airport outside of Milan, Elspeth brought her thoughts back to her current assignment. Would it be as complicated as she feared? She was accustomed to working alone and did not relish being the leader of a team, its members both known and unknown to her.

5

Elspeth wanted to see where Marco Celli had been killed and the corner where the ex-minister's car had taken the bullet. She asked the driver of her car, a large and luxurious Peugeot, to stop when she sensed they were getting near the hotel. The driver confirmed that, although narrow, this was the most direct street from the center of Stresa to the hotel. She climbed out of the car and asked him to follow closely behind her. This proved a futile request as several ant-like cars immediately crowded behind him and protested with raised voices and tinny klaxons at his formidable blockage of the street. Elspeth waved him on and strode out on her own with a gait that would have won the sharp disapproval of her Aunt Magdelena Cassar, who saw that Elspeth learn the fine art of ladylike progression before she entered Cambridge.

The light of the afternoon sun raked the faces of the three and four story, green-shuttered buildings that cascaded down the hill to the lake and unkindly emphasized their many pock marks and patches, the product of centuries of use and abuse.

The hard leather heels of Elspeth's boots hit the uneven pavement with a drumming rhythm as she trotted up the steep grade, but soon she slowed in order to avoid the shopkeepers opening their large doors and lifting their iron grates to let in the afternoon's customers. She glanced in the shops and wondered if these were the last sights Marco Celli had seen, or was he too intent on staking out a spot where he could watch the duchess and her daughter in the hotel?

The cobblestone street was devoid of any hint of the events surrounding Marco Celli's death or vestige of the shots that had punctured Carlo Bartelli's windscreen. Elspeth looked up at the rooftops. Many were heavily tiled, some had small balconies set in the hip roofs, and most were decorated with satellite dishes pointing south through the gap in the Alps. Elspeth envisioned the assassin laying in wait on one of the top-story balconies among this electronic forest, as a tiger would crouch in the grass waiting for his prey.

Elspeth had never made an in-depth study of the criminal minds of murderers and, looking up at the various locations from which the shots that killed Mario might have been fired, she tried to imagine what the assassin had felt: smugness, anger, fear, revenge, a drug-induced high or even personal terror. The white-collar crimes she normally investigated were almost always motivated by greed, but she could not fathom committing murder for this reason alone. Ill-gotten gain is more easily achieved by other means. The only murder she had handled in her career was the result of a long-standing sense of betrayal. A murder's motivation had to be powerful, but in this case what was it? She wished she had paid more attention to the psychology of violent crime when at Cambridge.

A miniscule fenced-off park lay across from the circular drive into the hotel, and, when she skirted the iron pickets and light poles encircling the tranquil foliage, Elspeth thought this might be where Marco Celli had spun around and died. If the police had outlined the shape of Marco's body on the pavement, it no longer was there. She turned to the hotel itself, whose façade blended with its neighbors, and, other than the discreet brass signage and the two liveried doormen, one might have presumed that the building belonged to a slightly more prosperous tenant than others nearby. She straightened her scarf, spread her hand down the supple arm of her leather coat as if it would give her courage and gave a stern moment's reflection on her task ahead. She hoped Eric knew what he was doing when he asked her to find the murderer before the police did. The moment of doubt passed quickly, and Elspeth marched up the drive to the bronze-studded wooden doors that led into the hotel.

Elspeth saw an Asian man lingering under the porte-cochère of the hotel. Despite his ethnicity, he blended so well into the atmosphere of the hotel that none of the guests going in and out took notice of him. Of medium height and slender build, he was dressed in the Italian manner, his clothes dark, modish and casual, and his black straight hair styled short. His body language parodied the carefully studied, nonchalant gestures often adopted by Italian young men. He straightened as he sighted the large Peugeot come around the corner and hurried to greet its occupant. He opened the door before the doorman could and stared into the empty interior.

"Are you looking for me?" Elspeth said behind him. "You must be Sandro."

The young man stood back and, seeing Elspeth, straightened his body as if coming to attention.

"I am Sandro Liu. Ms. Duff?"

Elspeth grinned at his military bearing. "Yes, I'm Elspeth Duff."

"*La signora* Donatello has asked me to show you into the hotel," he said.

With great formality, he escorted her through the doors into the lobby, where Franca Donatello, the manager of the hotel, was waiting for her. Franca nodded her head up and down as she pumped Elspeth's hand. *"Benvenuta!* Welcome!" In doing so, her many layers of multi-colored clothes whirled about her diminutive, ovoid frame, her numerous bangles clinked up and down. She rushed them through the lobby. Elspeth barely had time to glance at the floor-to-ceiling windows that drew her eyes fleetingly over the tiled rooftops of the city and beyond to the glory of the lake and boldness of the mountains rising above it. Lord Kennington obviously had chosen this as his opening statement to his guests, the natural beauty far surpassing the murals or artwork at his more urban hotels. Of course there were flowers everywhere, which Elspeth knew were picked early that morning and flown in from the extensive Kennington Organisation gardens in Morocco. The blooms had been arranged in large, heavily ornamented vases of Baroque persuasion.

Franca gestured Elspeth and Sandro past the pilastered marble reception desk and into her inner sanctum in the staff area of the hotel. She invited Elspeth to settle into a high-backed wooden chair with intricately stitched petit point cushions on the back and seat, which although imposing were remarkably comfortable. Franca indicated that Sandro should remain standing. He spread his legs and clasped his hands behind him. Elspeth noted that the chair that Franca chose for herself had an extra cushion and a matching footstool on which she planted her short, stout legs. The room, which looked out to the city and hills to the south rather than to the lake, had a florid grandness to it, trumping any other manager's office Elspeth had seen before. A large, ornately carved wooden table served as Franca's desk with an equally old-fashioned chair behind it, again with a footstool. Tapestries adorned the walls and a shallow fireplace with brass andirons held large birch logs ready for lighting. The only touch of modernity was a sleek laptop that was open on Franca's desk, the connecting cables discreetly snaked into what looked like a highly polished bronze umbrella stand with a bas-relief of entwined serpents and olive trees. Elspeth felt she had gone back to the Renaissance with a twist of the twenty-first century imposed on it. She could not see any telephones and assumed they were hidden somewhere in the interior of the desk.

Franca Donatello, despite her petite size and flamboyant dress, reminded Elspeth of the painting of a ruthless Italian prince on the cover of a copy of Machiavelli's treatise on governance that she once had owned.

Franca's soft, low voice rolled melodically over her words. "Elspeth," it came out sounding like Elspetta, "Why are you all coming here?"

Not expecting the question, Elspeth drew back and, looking into Franca's black eyes, saw challenge.

Franca continued, "It is my opinion that Lord Kennington has overreacted to the situation here, and I do not think you are needed. The police have been investigating the incident, of course, and a police *commissario* has questioned me. I told him that it is not possible for him to come into the hotel again. Marco Celli did not die in the hotel, so I do not want police here. I also do not want a security team from London in my hotel."

Elspeth adjusted her posture in her chair as if doing so would alter what she had just heard. She bristled and then eased and smiled without condescension. The power play was a passing one, and Elspeth was not too sure who had won.

"We cannot afford any bad publicity. Surely you know that," Franca said.

Elspeth tempered her tone. "Lord Kennington has, as always, directed us to be discreet."

Franca tapped her toe on her footstool. "Why so many of you?"

"Generally I work alone, but Lord Kennington told me that, with both ex-Minister Bartelli and the Duchess of Astonino here as guests, he wanted to have a security detail assigned to each of them."

"*Il ministro* I can understand but *la duchessa*?" Franca spat out the latter title.

"Lord Kennington would not have sent us here without good reason," Elspeth countered.

Elspeth looked over her shoulder at Sandro Liu, who was standing stoically near her chair. Addressing Franca, she said, "Lord Kennington personally picked Sandro Liu to be detailed to the ex-minister. Will Tuttle from London will be arriving later today and will help with the duchess and her daughter. I've worked with him before. You will find him polite and unobtrusive."

"*Sì.* I know about them both. I approved Sandro. You worked with Will Tuttle and say he is OK. Well then, I must accept him. The security office in London also told me that Lord Kennington has invited two other people to act informally as members of your team, a Lady Elisabetta Bailiesha and a Sir Ricardo Munro. Now I have five people to deal with."

"Lady Elisabeth and Sir Richard are to be observers only. Lord Kennington was quite clear on that point."

"What is your role?"

To wrestle the roomful of personalities with this Italian she-devil snipping at my heels, Elspeth thought. "To be Lord Kennington's eyes and ears," she said. "He feels personal responsibility for his friend Carlo Bartelli's safety, and he does not want the duchess to become a difficulty."

"Then I will leave it all to you." Franca's tone was dismissive.

"Thank you," Elspeth said, wiping the tips of her fingers across her cheekbones to alleviate her tension. "Now tell me about the police. Do you know if they questioned any of the guests when they were outside of the hotel?" she asked.

"Not to my knowledge, *signora*," Franca said stiffly.

"Did the police think the shots came from the hotel?" Elspeth asked.

"Marco Celli twisted as he fell. The police said there was no way to tell where the shots came from."

"What about Carlo Bartelli's car? Do the police know where it was when the shots were fired? Do they know that one of the bullets pierced the car's windscreen?"

Franca shrugged her shoulder. "The car sped from the scene, and the police did not say they knew anything about it. I did not bring it up. No one was seriously hurt in the car, and the incident has not been reported."

Elspeth wondered about Franca's deception. "Can that be considered withholding evidence?"

"Of what, *Signora* Duff?" which became Duffa. "No one has asked, and there is no evidence that the shots were meant for anyone but Marco Celli. The car just drove by at an unfortunate moment."

"Can you be sure?"

"No, but why tell the police that *il ministro* is here when Lord Kennington has asked that his presence be kept quiet?"

Elspeth inwardly blushed at the thought of how many times she had delayed giving evidence to the police but conceded that discretion in such matters was a part of the job Eric Kennington expected of his staff.

"Franca," Elspeth said, "Lord Kennington asked me to talk to Carlo Bartelli and to the duchess and her daughter. I want to do so in due time. First, I want you to tell me what you heard and saw when the shots were fired."

"I heard nothing. I told that to the police." Franca pushed down the sides of her mouth in disgust. "In Italy we try to avoid the police. Sometimes they draw conclusions too rapidly. The press also follows the police. I want them both away from the hotel. The Italian paparazzi are ferocious, and the death of a film star, even as bad a one as Marco Celli, attracts a lot of attention. I do not want the hotel seen or mentioned in the tabloids," Franca said.

Franca rose, walked slowly to the window and continued, "We are on the edge of the city, and therefore pedestrian traffic does not usually come up our hill unless someone is coming to the hotel or one of the small businesses or residences along the way. Marco Celli may have known that Toria Albi and her mother were here, or he may just have heard a rumor. He may have been coming to the hotel, but there is no evidence that he was. You see Marco threatened *la duchessa* publicly, but he may have been in Stresa for other reasons."

"Have the police found any other reason?"

"I do not know. They have not shared that with me. I have denied any knowledge of Marco's actions before he was hit by the bullet. I have said that he was probably an innocent victim."

"Is Stresa usually a safe city?"

"*Sì*. One must be cautious after dark, but there is no big crime here. Mainly it is the young people. Usually it is small theft for drugs and alcohol or a woman. Then there are the family fights."

"But not murder?"

"I do not remember a murder ever. There is some smuggling of contraband across the lake, mainly to and from Switzerland. Most police activity here involves activities on the lake, not in neighborhoods like this one or in the tourist areas."

"And Carlo Bartelli came around the corner at an inappropriate time," Elspeth said.

"Sì."

Franca stood at the window with her back to Elspeth. Elspeth looked across at Franca and then back over her shoulder at Sandro. It would be convenient to believe them, but Elspeth was not sure they were telling the whole truth.

Sandro glanced sideways at Franca, who turned and responded with an almost imperceptible lowering of her eyes. Elspeth could not grasp what the exchange meant.

Keeping her doubts to herself, Elspeth excused herself, pleading the need to go to her room and freshen up after her trip. She trusted Lord Kennington's instincts and doubted he would have set up a security team for the Kennington Stresa unless he had information that he did not want Franca and Sandro to know.

Franca confronted Elspeth as she rose. "You do not believe us, do you?"

"I cannot be sure," Elspeth said honestly. "I hope you are right."

Franca walked across the room and opened the door to Elspeth. "Lord Kennington instructed me to give you a suite in one of the towers because it will give you a place to work where you will not be disturbed. The rooms are small, but they will have to do."

She gave the suite number to Elspeth and, opening her palm toward the door, dismissed her. Sandro stayed behind.

One of Elspeth's windows looked out to the east and to the Alps beyond. The clear sky was beginning to fade as fog crept up the mountain faces and engulfed the snow patches at the top. Elspeth opened the doors on to her small balcony and breathed in the Alpine air, which was icier than that in Scotland. Her Highland sensibilities were attuned to the weather and told her it might be fair again tomorrow, but that rain was also close at hand. She found a heavy shawl, one she put in her case at the last minute, and walked out on to the balcony. The light breeze from the lake danced through the city streets, and its arrival on the balcony made assassination seem an absurdity.

Unfortunate timing, she thought, or was it? Why had both Marco Celli and Carlo Bartelli been at the scene of the murder? Why was Eric Kennington so concerned? Finally, why had he asked her to head up a team of people whose compatibility and loyalty to her remained in doubt?

6

One bullet and then two and then three and then some more, but three was as far as four-year-old Silvia could count. The ugly chatter of the guns reverberated across the hard walls of the ancient room. Sister Lucca spread the wings of her habit over the child. The nun's vast body, now filled with the peppering from the Nazi soldier's machine gun, protected all but the young girl's lower back. Years later Silvia remembered feeling Sister Lucca's heaviness and the warmth of the spilling of her blood spreading out from her corpse over Silvia's small body. Silvia's legs, dulled by the shattering of her lower spine, never felt anything again.

Silvia Trucco had shared that memory with only one person, Carlo Bartelli, but not until fourteen years afterwards, when, with the aid of a pair of oversized crutches, she had struggled up three flights of stairs of the crumbling building where Carlo had set up his first office. She could not afford a wheelchair, and there was no lift. She was a waif-like eighteen-year-old, but she looked younger and offered mediocre secretarial skills, a willingness to accept the few lire he offered in wages, and a request that she start as soon as possible. Carlo later told her that he had imagined his first secretary would be voluptuous, able to type sixty words a minute without mistakes, marry him and give him five children. He added that he had never regretted that Silvia had found him first.

She heard Carlo Bartelli turn on the television in their suite at the Kennington Stresa in time for the news. He pushed the mute button on the remote and went out on the balcony where Silvia was watching the fog growing over the mountains.

"Come in, Silvia. It is getting cold."

The news presenter was pointing to a map of Iraq and then a picture of a hostage, gun to his head. As she wheeled herself back into the room, Silvia did not look at the flat screen.

"I see that the latest bulletin on the murder of Marco Celli is coming up," Carlo said. "No one has shown our car. Let us have faith we will not attract the attention of the press and focus our prayers on getting Constanza home."

The television cut to the image of Marco Celli and then that of Toria Albi. Silvia and Carlo did not need to turn up the sound to make the connection.

"He said he would call Friday." Silvia's throat hurt as she said the words she had said so often before.

"At least then we can begin to negotiate with him. Make sure that your mobile phone is charged, so we can get a clear signal."

She nodded. "You talked to Lord Kennington a few moments ago. What arrangements has he made for you?" she asked.

"He promised a launch that we can take around the lake and a pilot."

"Will I be able to board?"

"I insisted that you could."

Silvia adjusted the wool rug she had put over her legs and turned the wheel of her chair so that she did not have to look at Carlo. She could see the lake from where she sat. "This chair is especially light. Titanium," she said as if addressing the air. "The most maneuverable they make, they told me at the shop, which may have been why they charged me so much. Scoundrels." She rotated her chair back toward Carlo. "Still, it will be easy to lift on board."

"Silvia, you should not come. It will be dangerous."

"Would I stay here, afraid for myself, if Constanza is in danger? Our beautiful Constanza?"

His face softened. "I know you would not."

"Tell me more about Lord Kennington's arrangements," she requested.

"He said he was sending a security team here to help us."

"Does he know about Constanza?" Silvia asked.

"No, I respected our promise to the caller to tell no one until we can be sure Constanza is safe."

"It's been five days now. Do you really think he will call?"

"For a million euros? What do you think?" Carlo growled.

"Have you thought who he might be?"

"When Constanza went to Nepal, what did she tell you?"

"I have told you everything. I have thought over her last day in Rome with me. She was so excited. Because of her paper's communist contacts in Nepal, she thought that she might have a chance to talk to some of the clandestine leaders who had come from China to participate in the Maoist movement."

"Yes, you have told me that, but did she mention any names?" He had asked this many times before.

"No, none that I recall. I do remember that at one point she claimed that she might even be able to get into China or Tibet to follow the origins of the Chinese who help the insurgents."

Carlo paced back and forth, glancing now and then at the news presenter, and waved his hands up and down in the air in frustration.

"Did you put a freeze on Constanza's account?" he asked. She nodded again.

"I never know what Constanza is about. She storms at me that I am a stodgy conservative who prefers the good life in Rome and shouts that her mother is a despicable slave of *la dolce vita*, and that we don't understand the plight of the world's neediest," he said.

Silvia smiled gently. "I think it's her form of loving you."

"Not true. She only thinks of herself, like her mother. Her focus is different, that's all. Damn her. I love her, and she uses me. For all you say the two of you have a special bond, she uses you too." Carlo slammed his fist on the back of the sofa. "Is she manipulating us again?"

"With Constanza, one never can know. The man sounded more serious than any of the others."

"*Mio Dio*, Silvia. Why is my daughter so complex? I prefer my wife, who spends my money and asks for nothing else."

Silvia lowered her eyes, turning away from Carlo's bitterness and pretending to look at a twenty-something woman on the television screen mutely promoting an age-defying face cream.

"Have you called Giulia?" Silvia asked.

"Called her? She doesn't even know I am out of town, and she probably thinks Constanza is in California."

*

Elspeth had just entered her suite when Eric Kennington's call came. She described her arrival at the hotel but did not share her observations about Franca Donatello or Sandro Liu.

"I want you to get to your job immediately," Eric barked. "Carlo Bartelli rang me a moment ago, and he wants every bit of protection possible. I also want the launch readied for his use at any minute."

"Launch? What launch?" Elspeth did not remember a launch being mentioned before, only that Sandro was a sailor.

"The one Sandro Liu is to pilot. Have him get it fully operational and kept that way."

Elspeth had seldom heard such a harsh tone from Lord Kennington before. "Of course," she snapped, feeling falsely used.

"Have you found out anything yet?"

"I just arrived half an hour ago. I hardly . . ."

"Contact Carlo immediately and get Liu ready. Carlo won't tell me anything. He said he did not trust the phones, but I think he will share with you now that you are there. I need you to do everything you can for him. Don't hold back. There is no time for dillydallying."

Elspeth wanted to retort that she never dillydallied on assignment, but thought better of it. "Eric, your wish is my command," was all she could think to say. She hoped she said it without any trace of annoyance, although she wanted to club him with her handset.

"I want a report by the end of the afternoon. I have Will Tuttle and an interpreter arriving later in Stresa today. Will's booking in as a member of a theatrical surveillance team who is scouting good sites for a Hollywood film and possibly stars to feature in them. This will be a good entrée to the duchess and Toria Albi. It will cover his having another person in tow. Get Will on to the duchess's case the minute he arrives. I don't want her even to consider going to the press with her thoughts about the murder."

Elspeth clenched her teeth and counted silently backwards from ten to one. Finding neutrality somewhere down the list of numbers, she changed the topic.

"Eric, do you have any indication that the press has found out that Carlo Bartelli's car was hit by one of the bullets?"

"Pamela's been watching this from here. The presence of the car was noted in one of the more serious papers, but the scandalmongers have not yet picked it up, thank God. Keep them away from the hotel at all costs, what ever it takes."

"What did the more serious papers say?"

"The Reuters' Italian desk mentioned that a large saloon car was seen in the area at the time of the shooting but has not been identified. Luckily AP and CNN haven't reported it."

"Let's hope it stays that way," Elspeth replied. "Franca has spoken to the police but is forbidding their access to the hotel."

She could hear his approval. "Franca is a bit of a martinet. That's one of the reasons I approved her promotion to manager. You'll find that quality useful. Set her on the press if they become intrusive."

Elspeth bristled. "Eric, who's in charge here, Franca or me?"

"You're in charge of finding Marco Celli's murderer; Franca is in charge of the hotel."

"What if there's a conflict?"

"You work it out between yourselves. I don't want to hear about it."

Eric's tone was biting enough to make Elspeth blink. She was not accustomed to his displeasure.

"Use all your charm; that is why I pay you as much as I do," he said caustically.

"Only for my charm?" Elspeth hoped her tone was quizzing, but she couldn't be sure Lord Kennington would take it that way.

Eric Kennington suddenly laughed. "I think you already know the answer to that question. Now let me patch you through to Pamela. She has news of your cousin's arrival in Stresa."

When he rang off, Elspeth blew her breath and waited for her friend to come on the line.

Pamela was chuckling. "Has he been brow beating you, ducks?"

Elspeth imagined Pamela sitting at her large cherry desk in her office next to Eric Kennington's, pushing her round spectacles up her prominent nose and adjusting her expensively handsome clothes across her small body.

"He's a bit testy this afternoon. *The Guardian*'s Italian desk rang him about the incident outside the hotel. He denied knowing anything about what happened. You know how Eric hates the press unless it is promoting his latest project," Pamela said.

"I'm still a bit shaken by his tone just now. I hope we ended on an even note."

"Don't mind him today. Tomorrow you will be back in full favor."

"Should I worry about Franca Donatello?" Elspeth asked.

"No, you are clever enough to handle her."

"She needs handling?"

Pamela did not reply and changed the subject.

7

Will Tuttle was one of the first to make his way off his flight to Milan and up the skyway into the cavernous hall of metal and steel at Malpensa Airport. Following the signs, he wound his way round to the baggage area, found a trolley and collected his bags. He steered himself and his belongings out of the customs area. His eyes cast over the band of anticipatory faces standing at the barrier, some with signs and many with smiles, but he could find no one waiting for him. When he was well beyond the crowd, a voice addressed him in English, not only English but English that was both educated and feminine. He turned in the direction of the voice.

"Hello," she said, "you must be Will. I'm Amanda Bell. My friends call me Mandy."

Mandy Bell looked directly into Will's eyes. Few women in his acquaintance could do that, but Mandy's twinkling eyes were on a level with his.

"Welcome to Italy."

Will had not expected Mandy and, from her reaction, his face showed it.

"Didn't Ms. Crumm tell you I was English?"

Will closed his mouth, conscious that it had dropped open at the sight of this tall and beautiful young woman.

"No. I'm sorry. I must have stared at you. Hardly a polite thing to do."

Mandy grinned. "Not to worry," she said. "Most people gawk. There are very few six-foot-three women in Italy and fewer with green eyes and auburn hair. At least the freckles of my youth have faded almost into imperceptibility. I have a car waiting outside. Ms. Crumm warned me that you were tall, and therefore I tried out each of the rental cars to find one we both could fit in. I bribed the policeman at the curb to let me leave the car there while I came in to find you, but I think we should be quick about it or the car may be towed."

Will laughed and instantly liked this outrageous girl. She was neither the demure Italian female nor serious male student he had expected.

A silver BMW with Milan number plates stood idling by the curb, and the policeman near it put on a silly grin when Mandy appeared. She blew him a kiss across her long fingers and helped Will load his bags into the back. Since he was posing as a film executive, he was traveling much more heavily than he usually did; one case would not suffice to maintain his cover story as a Hollywood talent scout.

Mandy Bell drove with flare, mimicking at times the outrageous gestures of the drivers around her, and, blithely negotiating the traffic from the airport to the *autostrada*, talking gaily as she did so. Will had been in Italy several times before and knew about the ways of Italian drivers, but there were many moments when he wished that Mandy would emulate them less.

"Don't worry," she said to him, "I've taken several of those defensive driving courses. My father insisted after I totally destroyed his favorite Jaguar."

Will tried not to speculate on how much she had retained from these courses.

"Are you studying Italian at university?" Will asked, hoping to divert her from her intense involvement with the other drivers on the road.

"No, my mother is from Italy. I grew up speaking Italian at home. I'm studying archaeology at University College London and am on leave this term. My parents asked me to join them on a trip to Egypt, where my father is on a fact-finding mission for the British Museum. He's studying the possibility of terrorist threats to archaeological sites along the Nile. He is Sir Collingwood Bell, the archaeologist, by the way. Have you heard of him? I returned to London last week, and I don't begin my studies again until January. Lord Kennington met Daddy and Mummy several years ago at the Kennington Cairo and, when Daddy contacted his lordship recently, Lord Kennington suggested that I might work for the Kennington Organisation during the rest of my break. I never thought that would mean a trip to the Lakes Region and a stay at a Kennington hotel. Daddy says I am quite lucky considering the difficulty students have finding part-time jobs these days."

All this information was rattled out in rapid bursts with Mandy turning to Will and waving her right hand to emphasize several points. She passed a long line of cars at breakneck speed and brandished her fist at a lorry that did not pull over to let her by. She pulled onto the shoulder and passed him on the right.

Will hoped that her luck—and his—would continue at least until they got to Stresa. He gripped the right-hand side of his seat and hoped Mandy would not see it. Once they had left the *autostrada*, traffic thinned, and Mandy slowed her pace somewhat.

"It's not far now," she informed him as she pelted down the narrow streets into Stresa. "We should be there in time for tea."

A Scandal in Stresa

Will found Elspeth Duff in her suite. She lead him into the luxury of her small sitting room, and, from the evidence of a laptop on the sofa, briefcase on the floor, and, scattered files strewn on the marble topped coffee table, she had been at work.

After offering him tea, which he refused, she motioned him to an armchair that was free of debris. Before returning to the sofa, she drew the heavy brocade curtains further back and allowed the afternoon light to fill the room. The mountains beyond her balcony were now almost completely obscured by clouds. The west rays of sunshine struck the lake and projected slowly moving patterns of silver ribbons on the water as the wind blew across it. From where he sat Will could see out the long windows. He wished he had brought one of his cameras with him. As they settled down to business Will told Elspeth how much he was looking forward to working with her again.

"Will," Elspeth said, pinching the narrow bridge of her nose where her reading glasses had left an indentation, "our challenge here is delicate. Lord Kennington wants us to work independently from the police investigation of Marco Celli's death. Murder is too dangerous for amateurs, you and I among them, and this assignment makes me uncomfortable."

"They briefed me a bit in London, but I'm not fully aware of what he wants us to do. I agree that working outside of the police may prove . . ." he cleared his throat to search for the best word, "may prove challenging."

"Since my arrival this morning, I have been trying to figure out ways that you and I can provide security for the hotel residents without bringing ourselves to the attention of the police. Murder investigations are not really my expertise nor do I suspect that they are they yours. I have been scribbling some notes about strategy, if one can scribble on the computer."

She waved toward a stack of papers on the table beside her. "I brought some files with me with background material on Marco Celli and Toria Albi and have downloaded more from the internet. I've come to the conclusion that we need to move in closely to Toria and her mother. I've been trying to flesh out a plan. Here's what I have so far. See what you think."

They worked for the better part of an hour, setting up various scenarios and then finding reasons why they would not work. Elspeth finally blew out her breath with frustration.

"Damn. What I won't do for a simple investigation concerning a touch of petty larceny by a little old dear from Kent or credit card fraud by a perennial cheat whose name and address change on every visit," Elspeth said.

"May I make a suggestion?" Will asked. "Both times I have worked with you, I have always admired your clear thinking."

Elspeth cocked an eyebrow at him. "Meaning?"

"At its most basic level murder really is a crime of passion, no matter how rationally thought out."

"What are you getting at?"

"If you will forgive me for saying so, I think you are trying to find a logical way to deal with an illogical act."

Elspeth did not reply immediately. Instead she took the papers off the coffee table, patted them together and laid them in a neat stack.

"Have you ever personally known anyone who was murdered?" she asked.

"Unfortunately, yes, I have, in India, where two friends and I were traveling after we came down from Oxford. I went off to photograph a bird I'd never seen before, and they went off to watch a riot. They were killed; I wasn't." He spoke his next few words with a swallow. "One never quite recovers."

"No, one never does."

Will caught the disembodied tone in Elspeth's voice, the brief shuddering of her eyes, and the tightening of her jaw muscles. He puzzled at what pain might be behind it. She did not enlighten him.

"Elspeth, they told me in London they were sending someone out to deal with the duchess, and I was to deal with Toria Albi."

Elspeth's humor returned. "Will there be a problem dealing with her?"

A blush crossed Will's face, and he cursed his fair skin, which seldom covered his emotions. "I look forward to it," he said with a chuckle.

"It may be more difficult than one would think. The duchess, I understand, hovers over her daughter like a mother hen. I want you to meet the hotel manager. She may shed more light on the situation."

She picked up the house phone and called Franca Donatello.

When Franca opened the door to her office to Elspeth and Will, she said, "I will be leaving the hotel shortly for a personal engagement and can only spare you a few moments. Is this Will Tuttle?"

She turned to Will and took his hand in hers, shaking it slowly up and down several times. "*Benvenuto*, Will." She smiled politely, but her eyes remained cautious as she looked up at his face. She barely acknowledged Elspeth's presence.

"My pleasure," said Will, who did not understand the Italian but assumed from Franca's tone and gestures that she had greeted him in some way. "I want to be as helpful as possible." He hoped he had said the right thing, although he could not read the mood in the room.

Franca indicated with a sweeping gesture that Will should sit at one of the high-backed wooden chairs gathered around the unlit hearth. Without invitation Elspeth took a seat in one of the others. Franca sat down at her desk and gazed hostilely at Elspeth but expectantly at Will.

"I've been asked by London to find out all I can about Toria Albi, and I thought it best if I started with you," he began. Elspeth had coached him to use "I" rather than "we" and warned him that Franca might be antagonistic.

Franca leaned forward, her multiple strands of beads clattering at her ample chest, and cocked her head. "Since you must know, I have been watching the behavior of both Toria Albi and her mother since they first arrived. I am always careful when high-profile people stay here, particularly ones as eye-catching as Toria Albi. I want to make sure nothing will distress the other guests. I have no complaint against the duchess, who has been acting so inconspicuously that I doubt any of the other guests even know she is here. The duchess for the most part stays in her rooms and only has come out occasionally for a meal. Toria Albi, however, has taken to slipping out the back door everyday and spending an hour or two away from the hotel. The floor staff have told me that this is usually during the time her mother is napping after *la colazione*—lunch."

Entranced by Franca's flamboyant gestures despite the straightforwardness of her words, Will decided he would prefer to have *la colazione* rather than lunch, but he did not interrupt.

Franca continued, "For the first few days she came back with trinkets she had purchased, but recently she has come back with nothing but a, how do you say, smug expression on her face. *Signor* Will, find out if Toria Albi was in contact with Marco Celli before he was shot. I am not the best person to understand all the small things about *l'amore*, but I think she probably was seeing him."

Elspeth broke in. "Are you saying Marco Celli was in Stresa because he knew Toria and the duchess were here? Surely not. Hadn't Toria divorced him? Weren't she and her mother trying to hide from his threats?"

Franca turned to Elspeth, stared at her for a moment as if her remarks were out of place and then lowered her eyes. "I think that *la duchessa* is always trying to shield her daughter, and she is the one who wanted them to hide, not *la Toria*."

"The protective mother?" Will suggested.

"More like the manipulating mother," Elspeth said sotto voce.

Franca did not look in Elspeth's direction. "Yes, I think so, or, if she was not guarding her daughter from Mario Celli, then perhaps from another man."

Will had little knowledge of Italian women, or women in general, for that matter. He had a brief affair at Oxford, but it ended sorrowfully for him, and since then he had not met another woman who could ease that pain. Instead he had devoted himself to his work and to vigorous physical exercise: hiking, Nordic skiing, kayaking and kung fu. He wondered how a wife could find pleasure in meeting with her ex-husband after a divorce. He shook his head in disbelief.

"*Signore,* do not be surprised. Women, no matter how badly treated, often go back to their spouses, particularly here in Italy where marriage is still viewed as a sacred thing," Franca said.

Elspeth protested. "This was her third marriage."

"*Sì*, but if you had read our country's press," Franca said, the implication being that Elspeth should be able to but could not read Italian, "you would know her mother arranged the first two. I think that *la signorina* Toria chose to marry Marco Celli because she thought she had finally found her true love."

Elspeth turned to Will. "It sounds as if our work is cut out for us, Will. It will be important to find out where Toria Albi has been spending her afternoons while the duchess was resting. It wouldn't shock me at all if the duchess has a glass or two of wine at lunch and doesn't know of her daughter's waywardness. Of course you'll need to be as cautious as possible. Report back to me anything you find out. Thank you, Franca, for your time."

After they left Franca, Will straightened up and asked, "Whew, what was all that tension about?"

"I don't know, Will, but I want to find out. I know Franca dislikes our presence, but we cannot succeed if she resents our being here."

"Why would she be resentful? Aren't we here to support her?"

"One would think so, but we, or rather I, may also be a threat to her position here. Perhaps she has something to hide. If you have any thoughts about it, let me know. I am as baffled as you are. I don't usually ruffle people on such short acquaintance."

Will believed her.

Released from the discomfort of the interview in Franca's office, Will found Mandy. She was sitting on one of the white iron benches among the urns of red begonias on the public balcony and was wrapped in a woolen cape and doing *The Telegraph*'s cryptic crossword puzzle. She had solved only two of the clues. As Will was not a words man, he was of little help and instead suggested that they stroll down into Stresa. Will felt that understanding the city would help him in the coming days to maneuver without the aid of a map.

Mandy seemed eager to put her crossword aside. "My mother loves Stresa, and I spent several summer hols just outside the city with her, two of her sisters, and their children, my Italian cousins. We all had a great romp. Stresa hasn't changed much, at least not in the main part of town. I'll show you around."

Will accepted her guidance. They wandered along the waterfront promenade and then back along the row of shops until most of them closed for the evening. They found a lively open-air restaurant in a square off the waterfront and were seated at a table with decorative wire chairs and brightly colored table clothes. After a light meal and a glass of local wine, he cried off further activity for the evening. He wanted to return to the hotel, check his email and refine the plans Elspeth and he had concocted for the next day.

They climbed the hill toward the hotel together in comfortable silence. He bid Mandy good night and, ascending one flight, unlocked his guestroom door. He crossed the room, drew the curtains open and saw the waning moon through the gathering clouds. He settled into one of the chairs near the window, took out his laptop and went to work. Several ideas came immediately to mind. He went to bed, however, thinking not of Toria Albi but of Mandy's green eyes.

8

Biddy Baillie Shaw stepped down from the early London train from Scotland onto the platform at King's Cross Station. She looked around for Pamela Crumm among the people who were gathered at the gate but could find no one who matched the deep, crisp voice that had arranged her trip to London. Biddy wheeled her small case behind her and marveled at how little fatigue she felt after the journey in the first class coach, a luxury she never allowed herself on the infrequent trips she made to London. When a voice addressed her, she spun around and, to her amazement, found a small woman, beautifully outfitted in a tailored suit, luxuriant silk scarf, and big round spectacles set solidly on the prominent nose of her large head. The voice matched Pamela's.

Biddy, whose main mode of transport in Scotland was her ancient Land Rover, relished the smell of the leather seats and the comfortable interior of Lord Kennington's Jaguar as Pamela and she made their way to the Kennington Mayfair. While the driver wound through the treacherous maze of London streets, Pamela outlined their activities in preparation for Biddy's trip to Italy.

Before Biddy's departure, her life became filled with an opulence she had never before experienced. Included were a night at the Kennington Mayfair and shopping for clothes and accessories at small boutiques where Pamela was known. A

A Scandal in Stresa

fashionable haircut at the hotel corrected the deficiencies of Biddy's hairdresser in Perthshire, but Biddy balked at coloring. Through all of this Pamela gave Biddy a general review as to her tasks at the Kennington Stresa. Like most women, Biddy loved being pampered and listened only marginally to the risks she might encounter in Stresa. She cared more that the clothes Pamela chose would not be suitable for the Scottish Highlands afterwards, but Pamela insisted they would be just right for the Kennington Stresa in October and were necessary for the role that Biddy was to play there. Pamela's taste never faltered, and Biddy gave in to its impeccability. She finally convinced herself that, although the fineness of her new possessions would have no place among the farmhands at Tay Farm or the elderly ladies of the Scottish kirk in Kenmore, her new wardrobe should be enjoyed for the moment.

Over breakfast the following morning, Pamela broke Biddy's fantasy. "I'm sure that Elspeth told you a bit about the murder outside the hotel, but I've asked her to tell you more when you arrive. You must play innocent when you get there and appear to be pleased at surprising Elspeth with your visit," Pamela instructed Biddy.

Biddy nodded obediently.

"Tell Elspeth everything you learn. She will convey it to me."

Looking out over the splendor of the Kennington Mayfair breakfast room, Biddy nodded again but could not imagine that anything so vile as a murder could touch the magnificence of surroundings of any Kennington hotel.

*

Except for the arrival of Will Tuttle, the day had not gone well for Elspeth, and she was glad when she finally could retire to her suite. The scent from a large vase of roses wafted across the room. She threw open the door of the mini-bar to see if it would offer any relief but found only the healthy food she always requested when staying at a hotel. The packet of crisps she had bought at the airport in Dundee would have to do. Settling into one of the easy chairs, she unzipped her boots and wiggled her toes, which had been continually encapsulated since that morning in her bedroom at Loch Rannoch. If only all relief could be attained so instantaneously, she thought. Her confrontation with Franca Donatello and unpleasant discourse with Eric Kennington had left Elspeth ill tempered. She decided to order dinner from the room service menu, but not before she found some solace from the day's trials in the fat and salty morsels in her hand.

Elspeth took out her laptop, plugged into the data line the hotel provided in each room and opened her email. She skimmed the work related items and then pursed her lips when she saw that earlier in the evening Richard Munro had sent a message.

The confusion of her feelings toward Richard in the last six months washed over her once more. Until she had met Richard in Malta, she thought of her affair with Malcolm at Cambridge as the sparks from a roaring flame, her friendship with Richard the lingering embers of a comfortable fire. Seeing his email, she was vexed by her new feelings. Why couldn't she just enjoy his regard for her and let that be? Why, when she was wary of it, did she want to kindle the same feelings toward Richard that she had for Malcolm before he had been killed thirty-five years before? Richard had none of Malcolm's flair, none of his mercurial magic. Now in her fifties, why would she once again want to make herself vulnerable to the joy and pain of loving a man? Elspeth cursed her newly destroyed sense of contentment, that agreeable state she thought she had finally achieved when she left her husband and went to work for the Kennington Organisation. Damn Dickie, she thought, but knew her apprehension was of her own making, not his. If only she could wrestle the whole conundrum from her mind. Slowly, she turned her attention back to her laptop.

Richard was not the sort to send off emails of a few pithy words. Instead he composed them as he might write a carefully crafted personal note suitable more in Edwardian times than the twenty-first century. Elspeth was of the opposite school and often engaged in short emails with her children and family. She was always hard put to answer Richard's messages. She wanted to keep the tone neutral, not to spill out her feelings for fear of where they might lead her, to be pleasant but not needy, and to maintain her relationship with Richard at a cool and manageable distance.

> *My dear Elspeth,*
>
> *I am delighted to be coming to Stresa and will ring you with my travel arrangements as soon as they are finalised. Diplomacy in Malta at the moment is benign, and my committee in Brussels does not meet again until next month. I saw your Aunt Magdelena last week when I sailed over to Gozo, a pleasure since she only makes rare trips to Valletta. It is always a delightful event when she plays Chopin or Liszt for me, which she did. Do you remember that wonderful Sunday afternoon last May when we all lingered at her home, bathed in her music and hoping that afternoons like that that could go on for ever? I think of that afternoon often.*
> *Affectionately,*
> *Dickie*

Elspeth wondered what memories Richard had of her on that afternoon. She responded with a less courtly note than his, simply thanking him in advance for letting her know when he was arriving.

Elspeth rang Pamela, who was still in her office.

"I just met your cousin and think she will be perfect for the job," Pamela said. "She reminds me of you a bit. She does have a mind of her own."

"Eric said he wanted an aristocratic Scotswoman, and he got one. We Scots have never been completely tamed by the English."

"You seem quite tamed, m'friend, at least most of the time."

"By my own choice and also by years in Southern California where, as they say, 'anything goes.' Where rebellion is the norm, there's no purchase in pushing its edges."

"After meeting Lady Elisabeth, I think she'll serve the Kennington Organisation well," Pamela said. "I have outfitted her to look like a wealthy gentlewoman who travels frequently and therefore lightly, which will be an excuse for her wardrobe being expensive but limited. She's assured me that the clothing I have bought for her would not be at all suitable for Loch Tay. Don't you have central heating up there?"

"Biddy has central heating at her farm but seldom uses it except on particularly cold winter mornings and evenings. When we were growing up, there always was a roaring fire in 'the hall' as my uncle called it. It really was just a large kitchen, but the space was constantly filled with children and dogs and locals of all sorts. In the mayhem, one didn't notice what one was wearing as long as it kept one warm."

Pamela tsked at the thought, and Elspeth expected her London-bred friend would not enjoy the heartiness of Highland life even in modern times.

Pamela reverted to business.

"Lady Elisabeth is flying to Milan tomorrow, and I've arranged for your car and driver to be at her disposal. I've made sure that Franca Donatello has given Lady Elisabeth one of the better suites. If she is to entertain *la duchessa*, the props need to be correct. She should be in Stresa in time for tea."

"Am I to know that she is coming or should I be surprised?"

"Be surprised," said Pamela, and she rang off.

Elspeth then checked to see if she had any new email messages. Richard had not yet contacted her about the exact time of his arrival in Stresa. She was disappointed and then tried to put her feelings away.

Attending to brief emails from her daughter Lizzie in East Sussex and her son Peter in San Francisco, she shut down her computer, stretched out on the sofa and gathered her thoughts. For all of Eric Kennington's good intentions, the team he had put together was not coalescing, and Elspeth needed to figure out why.

Franca Donatello troubled her the most. What had happened during their first interview? Her greeting had been warm in the lobby, but, at the mention of the police, she had bristled. Why was Franca so adamant at keeping the police at bay? Had Elspeth been right when she had speculated with Will that Franca had something to hide? How could Elspeth find out if this were true?

Sandro Liu's distance puzzled her as well. Sandro was new to the Kennington Organisation and had not worked with her before; would this have explained his diffidence?

She felt uncomfortable trusting him completely. She could not justify this feeling other than that it came from an innate sense that she had learned to rely on over the years.

She thought of Will Tuttle, a basset hound by nature, if there could be a six-foot-four, fair-haired basset hound. Elspeth had in the past liked his doggedness and felt she could rely on him when the other members of the team might let her down.

And Richard Munro and Biddy Baillie Shaw? Why had Lord Kennington included them?

She was looking forward to a quiet evening in her room and ordered green cannelloni with ricotta and Parmesan cheeses and a wilted bitter green salad from room service. Shortly after eight, seven London time, she rang Lord Kennington, but, as she hoped, he had left for the day. She left a message saying she planned to meet with the ex-minister in the morning. She was relieved that she did not have to weather another of Lord Kennington's irritable moods. She did not know if *The Guardian*'s Italian desk had become disenchanted with the story connecting the unidentified car in Stresa with Marco Celli's demise, but that was the least of her concerns. Finding the link between the assassination, the duchess, and Carlo Bartelli was more vital. She pulled out a copy of the plan that Will and she had developed and began to pencil in some notes. She would need to talk to Will in the morning.

Elspeth slept fitfully as she often did when starting a new assignment. At half past two she rose, blaming her disquieting dreams to the rich pasta she had heartily enjoyed from the room service menu just hours before. She preferred sleeping with the curtains open, as she loved the morning light, but, now, before turning on any of the lights, she drew the curtains so that no one could see in. She turned on one of the Chinese porcelain lamps on her bedside table and fetched her laptop. Elspeth opened her web browser and typed in *"la duchessa d'Astonino."* She scrolled down the choices offered and soon found what she was looking for, the biography of the current holder of the title.

> *Maria Vittoria Gotti, born in Palermo on 17 November 1948. Educated at l'academia di San Pietro e San Paolo, Palermo. Married Giancarlo Arcangelo Albi on 15 June 1967 in Palermo. Only child: Vittoria Maria Albi, born 25 December 1972. (See Toria Albi.) Giancarlo Albi died in a fatal car accident in May 1994, shortly before the film debut of his daughter in La Vita, directed by . . .* (The film credits went on, with many links to related web sites. These, Elspeth thought, she would pursue later.) *Constant companion of her daughter through out her film career, Maria Albi lived in Rome, Hollywood and Milan before meeting il duca d'Astonino (See Antonio, il duca d'Astonino, b. 17 August 1919 in Milan) at a charity event at his villa in 1997. They were married six weeks later, and la duchessa divided her life between her daughter's film career and running of la villa d'Astonino. Her second husband died in March 2002 of gastric distress, and the duchess resumed her role as companion to her daughter and manager of her career.*

The biography ended there, but it contained enough information to give Elspeth some cause for thought. Toria was born on Christmas Day five years after Maria's marriage to Giancarlo Albi; there were no other children. He died in a car accident. Elspeth would have Pamela find out more Toria's father. What was the "gastric distress" from which the duke had died? Elspeth decided that Maria Gotti was not, as the upper crust might have put it, of the "first water."

Now sleepy, Elspeth printed out the page from the internet on her small printer and folded up her laptop. She slept quietly the rest of the night in the darkness of her room. She did not waken until nine, when the insistent ringing of the phone by her bed brought her to consciousness.

9

Elspeth broke off from briefing Will Tuttle about her morning call with Lord Kennington because she knew Carlo Bartelli would be waiting for her upstairs. She found the service lift at the back of the hotel offices and pressed the button for the third floor. The doors opened on the second floor, rather than the third, and Elspeth faced a room attendant backing her cart into the cab. The starched navy blue uniform worn by all the Kennington hotels' cleaning staff fit comfortably over the slim figure of the young woman and set off the blackness of her hair, which was held back in a short brimmed hat that was a modishly modified version of the ubiquitous American baseball cap. She appeared startled when she bumped into Elspeth and apologized with a soft *mi scusi* and a questioning look. All members of the Kennington Hotel staff were required to speak passable English, and therefore Elspeth confidently spoke to the young woman. Elspeth explained that she was from London under the direct orders of Lord Kennington. She then jumped at an opportunity to question the room attendant before releasing the door and rising to the third floor.

"Did you clean Suite 201 this morning?" This was the suite where the Duchess of Astonino and Toria Albi were staying.

"*Sì, signora.* At first there is a 'Do Not Disturb' sign that hang on the door, but later it is gone, and the old *signora* ask me to come in and clean the room."

"Tell me about her." Elspeth wanted to see how observant the maid was.

"She appear to just get up from the bed. She yawn."

"What was she wearing?"

"A robe, *molto bella*. Red and blue and green silk with flowers and dragons like the Chinese."

Elspeth prodded her further. "Did she say anything to you?"

"Only she go to have a bath and that I return later to clean the bathroom."

"Did you go back?"

The young woman frowned at Elspeth's doubt. "*Sì*, I just go now."

"What is your name?" Elspeth asked.

The room attendant relaxed. "Laura." She pronounced it in the Italian way, sounding all the vowels. La-oo-ra.

"Laura, is there anything unusual about suite 201?"

Laura shrugged her shoulders. "*Sì e no.* Yes and no. *La signorina* is very not neat. She throw the clothes everywhere. Her mamma is opposite, very neat. She put everything away and keep her suitcases always locked. I hear *la mamma*, how do you say, scold *la signorina*, but *la signorina* say she make the money and other people can pick up her things. *La mamma* say if *la signorina* is not more careful she not make money anymore."

"Did they have this argument when you were in the room today?"

"*Sì, signora.* Many guests not notice us when we come in a room. These two women they are the same."

"Laura, I want you to listen carefully to everything that is said when you are in the suite and report it to me but not to anyone else, not even *la signora* Donatello. It is very important. The old *signora* is right. If the *signorina* is not more careful, she may be in trouble. Laura, do not tell anyone else about this conversation."

"*Sì, signora.*"

"Do you know who the two women in Room 201 are?"

"*Sì*, I know Toria Albi. When we come to work here, we not allowed to tell anyone who the guests are, but you come from London, and I break the rule."

"Thank you, Laura. I already know who they are, but you are right in not telling anyone. I think most people would recognize Toria Albi. The other woman is *la duchessa d'Astonino*."

Elspeth released the doors and let the lift rise slowly to the third floor. She left the cab and let Laura descend back to the laundry area below. Elspeth mentally filed away what she had just heard. Although the plan was to leave Toria Albi and the duchess to Will and Biddy, Elspeth thought that Laura's information might come in useful at a later time.

*

Carlo Bartelli looked at Elspeth through the peephole of the door to his suite and then cracked the door, but, as a precaution, he left the night chain in place.

"*Signor* Bartelli," Elspeth said. "I spoke with Eric Kennington earlier this morning, and he asked that I stop by to see that you have everything you need. My name is Elspeth Duff."

Suspicion vanished from Carlo's eyes, and he closed the door in order to unfasten the chain. Opening the door once more, he looked both ways down the hallway, which was empty, and motioned Elspeth to come into the room.

As Elspeth entered, Silvia Trucco came forward in her chair. Pamela Crumm had warned Elspeth about the chair but not the exquisiteness of the woman who sat in it. Silvia's face had the haughty beauty of her Renaissance forbearers and, except for the fashionable haircut suitable for an aging woman of the early twenty-first century, Silvia could have posed for a portrait by Ghirlandaio or even da Vinci himself. She had long, straight features, high cheekbones, thinly arched eyebrows, and an enigmatic expression.

Silvia extended a manicured hand to Elspeth and said in a beautifully low voice, "Welcome, Ms. Duff. Carlo and I are grateful you are here." Unlike Carlo's, Silvia's English was unaccented.

Elspeth turned to Carlo Bartelli, who, after re-chaining the door, looked across at his secretary and gave her a brief smile that was filled with admiration and trust.

"Yes, we are grateful. Silvia and I have been dealing with a matter of great personal concern for the last week, and finally we have agreed that we must seek help. That is why I called Eric Kennington. He assured me that you would be able to help us and would tell no one our secret."

"I will try, *signore*," Elspeth said. "Eric must have told you that my role in the Kennington Organisation is to assist guests in difficult situations. I also have a highly trained staff at my disposal."

Carlo drew back and ran his hand through his cropped grey hair. "*Signora*, we do not want to share with anyone but you. We are taking a great risk in telling you, but we need your help, and Eric promised us you will keep everything completely confidential." He pressed his fingertips together, and his wary eyes slid down his long nose, contemplated his hands and then came back up to Elspeth's face.

Elspeth hesitated before speaking, choosing her words carefully. "You have my full assurance that I will not share any information you want kept secret. I promise that. I'll have to give some direction to my team, but they don't need to know the details as to why."

Silvia wheeled her chair into the center of the room and offered Elspeth a seat on the sofa there. Silvia turned to Carlo, who stood rigidly with one hand on a side table and the other on the back of one of the armchairs, as if in indecision.

"Carlo, we must trust Ms. Duff," Silvia said. "We need her support and have no other choice right now. Too much is at stake."

Carlo breathed in and out slowly. "*Signora*, I trust Silvia more than anyone else in my life. She has seldom given me bad advice and, yes, very much is at stake, perhaps even the life of my daughter."

Silvia nodded when Elspeth glanced at her and asked, "Do you have any children?"

Elspeth replied simply "Yes, I have two, a son and a daughter."

"Do you ever worry about what they are doing?"

"Sometimes, in the rare moments when they decide to tell me if anything is bothering them."

Carlo walked around behind Silvia's chair and put his hand on her shoulder in a gesture of comfort.

"I have a daughter named Constanza, who is what you call in English a 'free spirit.' She was given the finest education here in Italy, but she chose to go to America for university, to Berkeley, California." He spoke the last two words as if they were one, and an anathema at that. "She became a radical and an atheist." He spat out this last word. "It is a disgrace to my family and a disgrace to God. Now she works for an online communist newspaper. She describes herself as their special foreign correspondent."

Elspeth was not sure how to reply and simply said, "We raised our children in California, and I know how young people there take on causes."

Carlo shook his head angrily, and Elspeth winced, hoping that she had not sounded too flippant.

"Constanza has done more than that," he cried out. "She has put herself in great danger many times. For the last few years she has been traveling worldwide and contacting one left-wing organization after another. Under her own name she has written stories for dissemination all over the globe via the internet. Constanza is a beautiful woman and also a rich one. Any simple search on the web could connect her name with mine. Worse, if she had her way, she would give all her money, and mine too, to what she calls the struggling masses of the world."

"How old is Constanza now?" Elspeth asked.

Silvia answered. "She is twenty-nine."

"Where is she now?"

"We don't know," her father said. His eyes were filled with tears. "Every hour we pray to the Virgin for her safety."

Elspeth looked up at him. "Is this the reason you have come to Stresa?"

"Yes," Silvia said softly. She rolled over and placed her hand over Carlo's. "Last week we received a phone call from a person who asked for one million euros ransom to free Constanza. Carlo is ready to turn over the money. He thinks it is a small amount to pay for our beloved Constanza's release."

"Did that person identify himself? I am presuming it was a man."

Carlo shook his head to and fro and ran his hand through his hair again. "A man, yes, but he did not give his name. He simply said he would be here in the Lakes Region and would let us know where we are to bring the money. He said he will call us tomorrow."

"Do you have any idea who this person might be? Did you have any communication from Constanza after the phone call?" Elspeth asked.

Silvia looked at Carlo, as if asking permission. He nodded.

"Six weeks ago Constanza visited us in Rome," she said. "She and I have always had secrets together. She said that she was going to Nepal, although she made me promise that before she left I would tell no one, particularly not her father, who might forbid her from going. She was excited because, as she told me, she might be able to contact one of the Chinese insurgents who was working with the Maoist rebels in the mountains."

"Did she?"

Silvia and Carlo exchanged glances.

Carlo spoke first. "Soon after she was there, she wrote an article for her paper from Kathmandu before going up into the Himalayas. She sent this to Silvia with a brief note that she would soon be filing an even better story. That was her last email."

"When did you receive that?"

Silvia answered this time. "Three weeks ago. I can pull the email off my computer if you wish and get the exact date."

"Yes, I'd like to see it," Elspeth said. "Please give me the web site address for her newspaper. I also want to know more about the phone call demanding the ransom. Did the man say anything that might let you know Constanza's whereabouts? Is she here in the Lakes Region too? More importantly did the man say she would be set free if you paid the ransom?"

After a long moment Carlo broke the silence. "The voice on the telephone was accented. All of his 'r's were pronounced like 'l's. Therefore we assumed that he was Chinese or perhaps Nepalese."

"Did you record the call?"

"Yes, I record all the important calls I receive that are meant for Carlo," Silvia said.

"May I listen to the recording? I don't know if I can hear anything on it that you don't already know, but, if you have a copy, listening to it might make me understand a bit better."

"I left the tape in our safe in Rome, but I have a good memory and can probably tell you what the caller said word for word," Silvia said.

Elspeth knew that would have to do for the moment, although she wished for more. Background noises on tapes often revealed as much as the words themselves.

"Did either of you call the police?"

Carlo began to fidget, waving his hands about in negative gestures. "No. The caller said not to. Our *carabiniere*, the national police, are not always efficient. I cannot take the risk. My daughter's life is worth more than a million euros to me."

"You said that he will contact you tomorrow. Does he know that you are here in Stresa?"

"No. Silvia only gave him her mobile phone number."

"Are you sure your mobile works here in the mountains?"

"Yes. As soon as we arrived, Silvia called my bank in Locarno and several contacts I have here in the mountains. There was no problem with the reception."

"The waiting must be agonizing for you. *Signore*, I don't wish to pry, but where is Constanza's mother? Does she know about this?"

Pamela had already told Elspeth that Carlo Bartelli and his wife, Giulia, had a distant relationship.

"No, *signora*. My wife is a very nervous woman, and I believe that it is best not to tell her about this until my daughter is safe."

"*Sì*," Silvia affirmed.

Elspeth could feel the solidarity between Silvia and Carlo, a kind that few married couples ever achieve. A nervous wife would only complicate things.

"I am here to give you any assistance you may require while staying at the hotel," Elspeth said. "Will you let me know what happens when you hear from the caller tomorrow? I'll personally see to it that our staff is completely at your disposal. As Eric may have told you, one of our security staff, whose name is Sandro Liu, is in the hotel and will be available for any of your needs, including piloting the hotel launch. He's an experienced seaman, having grown up near Livorno where his stepfather is a fisherman. Sandro also has many other skills both physically and in security matters that may prove useful to you."

"Thank you, *signora*, but Silvia and I feel the less people who know about this the better."

"Would you prefer I say nothing to Sandro?"

"For the moment, yes, although we will accept his help with the launch.," Carlo said.

"Of course. I'll simply tell him to assist you in anyway you ask."

Silvia nodded and then said, "Liu is not an Italian surname."

"No," Elspeth confirmed. "He was adopted as a boy. His parents were Chinese, and his stepparents thought it proper that he keep his real surname. There is just one more thing that I must ask you. Do you think that the shooting on Monday that killed Marco Celli has anything to do with Constanza?"

Carlo said, "Silvia and I have spoken of that many times in the last few days. No one other than Eric knew we were coming here except perhaps *la signora* Donatello, who arranged for the room and dispensed with our registering downstairs. Our arrival was more dramatic than either one of us liked, but there has been no mention of our identities in the press. I think we were caught in an act that was not of our making."

Elspeth turned to Silvia. "Do you agree?"

"I hope it's so. *La signora* Donatello tells us that the police are investigating, but they have not mentioned us. She also said she will not tell them we are here unless they ask her."

"Lord Kennington," Elspeth shared, "has a policy that every guest in his hotels have the right to total privacy. Please be assured that this is so in your case. In the meantime, I'll put Sandro on alert. Call me for any reason." She gave them her room extension and mobile number.

Having been sufficiently thanked, Elspeth withdrew from their suite and made her way to her rooms, where she picked up the phone and called Sandro's room. He answered on the first ring.

10

While she waited for Sandro to come to her suite, Elspeth went out on her balcony and looked toward the lake and Alps, their union belted by mist. The high peaks jutted through the clouds, and their tips were mirrored in the unmoving water below. The oscillating buzz of the late morning traffic, the smatterings of shouts from men repairing cobblestones in the street below, the distant roar of the motorway above, and the cheerful chatter of two room attendants on the balcony below lent a touch of humanity to the unrelenting forces of nature. Elspeth felt the rain in the air. She shivered, not from cold but from fear.

Out there somewhere, someone planned to extort a million euros from Carlo Bartelli and possibly harm his child. Elspeth thought of her own children and wondered what, as a parent, her reaction would be if someone demanded a ransom for their wellbeing. Would she cave in the way Carlo seemed to be doing? She wrapped her arms around her body and was grateful she never had to make the choice. What bothered her, however, were the contradictions between the contempt Carlo had expressed for his daughter, the tears that came to his eyes when he spoke of her, and his willingness simply to pay what had been asked.

Elspeth drew in deep breaths of the sharp and still mountain air and slowly exhaled, hoping it would calm her, but doing so did not relieve her anxiety. She went to the edge of the balcony and looked out over the city and the lake. With every sense of normality, cars came and went up and down the street below, and small craft and ferries plied their way across the expanse of water beyond. Everything and everyone appeared to be oblivious to extortion and murder. She had great sympathy for Silvia Trucco, who had made no attempt to conceal her great love for Constanza, more love than Constanza's mother seemed to have. Elspeth, however, was not satisfied that Carlo and Silvia's narrow escape from the assassin's bullets had been entirely coincidental. What if the person who had shot Marco Celli really had wanted to warn Carlo and Silvia that they were being watched and scare them into not talking to the police?

In Elspeth's job, working with the police was always delicate. Four years working at Scotland Yard when she was younger had given her enormous respect for law enforcement, a respect she still retained. In the intervening years, when she had conducted small private investigations in Southern California before joining the Kennington Organisation, she had used the police judiciously and found even the hard-bitten cops of the Los Angeles area were both helpful and useful when needed. Yet both Franca Donatello and Carlo Bartelli not only eschewed the police forces effectiveness but also were highly resistant to ask their assistance. Elspeth had never dealt with the Italian police, but news articles she had read about them spoke of their competence, particularly in the spate of kidnappings across Italy recently. Why then both Franca's and Carlo's hostility? Did they know about kidnappings that never reached the press? Did either one have connections or a past infraction of the law that they did not want the police to know? Or did they have other secrets they wanted to hide?

Elspeth felt she needed more support than Lord Kennington had given her. Her team, as he called them, were, at best, amateurs when it came to the enormity of the crimes of kidnapping, extortion, and murder. She felt that if she expressed this doubt to her employer, he would have curtly replied that he did not ask her to apprehend the murderer but simply to identify him and make sure the identification did not adversely affect the smooth running of the hotel. It had sounded simple over lunch in London. A few well-directed enquiries to make sure no one in the hotel was involved. Now Elspeth saw greater danger. Her best hope would be to confine the team's activities to the hotel, but she already was afraid that they were being lured beyond the walls. Certainly Sandro Liu would be, if he were to pilot the launch for Carlo and Silvia. Elspeth needed to find out more about Sandro and to dispel the uneasy feeling she had experienced in Franca Donatello's office.

When the knock came at her door, she put her growing worries aside and decided to focus on Sandro Liu. She needed his cooperation and discretion, but as yet she was not sure of either.

Sandro stood at the door, his eyes challenging Elspeth. Now is the time, thought Elspeth, to establish the leader of the pack, and so she adjusted her stance from welcoming to commanding.

"Come in, Sandro. We need to talk."

She watched him as he walked in, noting his hands jammed in his pockets and his nonchalant posture.

"Of course, *signora*," he said with what Elspeth took to be a smirk.

Insolent puppy, she thought. He reminded Elspeth of her son's dog who refused to obey. Her ex-husband, Alistair, had consulted a dog psychologist, who charged exorbitant fees that had turned out to be less of a waste of money than Elspeth had originally supposed. The master, the dog psychologist had said, needs to take control. Alistair, who was not in the least interested in anything but his career, had not listened, unlike Elspeth who had. She had heeded the advice given. The dog was never a problem again.

"Sit down, Sandro. I need to talk to you in confidence and give you your assignment. This is not to go beyond this room, not even to Franca Donatello."

He slouched in the chair she offered him. Elspeth was unsure what sort of protest this represented and wondered what Sandro would have done had his commanding officer in the navy been in her place.

"We have not worked together before, but I want you to know that I work under the direct orders of Lord Kennington. He told me that he picked you for this assignment because of your sailing skills as well as your background with the Italian military. He also said you are relatively new to our security staff and will need observation. He will be relying on you to perform to what he calls 'Kennington standards'." Elspeth was making this up as she went along, but Sandro shifted his posture and sat upright as she spoke.

"Lord Kennington pays enormously well, but he expects the highest of service from his employees. He always tests new ones." Elspeth wondered if she was overdoing it, but she had definitely caught Sandro's attention.

She moderated her tone because she wished to retain control of the investigation and did not want to alienate Sandro. She preferred working with her subordinates rather than dictating to them. "Tell me what you have been doing for the last few days. I understand you arrived on Monday evening, just after the Marco Celli incident."

"I am sorry I missed it," he said. "Marco Celli's murder, I mean. It would have made my stay a bit more interesting."

"Have you discovered anything that relates to the murder since you have been here?"

"No, Franca said to lay low and keep to my own business, worse luck. It would have been terrific to go see if I could find out anything about the murder. Franca was very firm."

"What have you done then?"

"I have had nothing really to do since I arrived. Of course I have checked out the launch, which is what London told me to do. I've taken practice runs crisscrossing the lake. I've spent most of my time in the exercise room or just sitting around the hotel. Franca keeps telling me that, after you arrived, I would be asked to do more."

Again Elspeth felt Sandro had put up a challenge. "I'll have something for you to do tomorrow, but, for now, I want you to check the launch again, in a different way. One of your passengers is confined to a wheel chair. I want you to make sure that every accommodation is made for getting the chair in and out of the boat. I'll let you know when you are needed tomorrow, and I want you to be available the instant I ring you. I don't know exactly what time that will be, but I expect it will be in the late morning or early afternoon."

She dismissed him without feeling that she had gained an ally.

Shortly after Sandro left, her phone rang, and she heard Franca on the other end of the line. "*Signora* Duff, the police have arrived in my office, and I think you should be here when I talk with them."

Elspeth was surprised when Franca met her at the door to the lift and warned her that the police wanted to interview the staff of the hotel and possibly some of the guests.

They entered Franca's office together, where a tall, smartly uniformed policeman stood looking out the window. Franca introduced him as *Ispettore* Pietro Luchetti of the Municipal Police.

Elspeth eyed the policeman. Secretly she found him handsome and suspected that he might even be flirtatious when off-duty. Fresh from establishing her role with Sandro Liu, however, she was still filled with a sense of authority and spoke directly to the point.

"*Ispettore*, this is quite unusual. I understand that you wish to question some of our guests. Our guests pay high prices to stay at the Kennington Stresa in peace. There has been no crime committed here that I am aware of."

"*Signora*, we investigate the murder of Marco Celli." The policeman's English was understandable but accented.

"Do you have any evidence that has made you think someone in the hotel is implicated?"

"No, *signora*."

"Then we cannot tolerate your questioning our staff or guests," Elspeth said, using her most commanding voice. She hoped that it might intimidate him. "I have direct authority from the Kennington Organisation in London, in fact from Lord Kennington himself, to keep our guests protected from any unpleasantness.

"You want justice, no?" he said shyly.

Although apparently having gained the advantage, Elspeth suppressed a smile.

"If you have real evidence that something happened here, then we will be cooperative, but we cannot allow you to come into our hotel and make demands without sufficient reason," she said.

She assumed that murder investigations in the Stresa area were rare, but the policeman had the air of one who would pursue the truth with a determination that might defy the stonewalling tactics of a foreign woman, however well placed she might be in the Kennington hotel hierarchy.

Franco Donatello intervened. "*Ispettore, la signora* Duff represents the owner of the hotel and the interests of all the innocent people who are staying here. A shooting," she avoided the word murder, "outside of the hotel is very bad for our business. No one wants to come to a place where they do not feel safe on the streets. The mayor comes here often to enjoy our restaurant. I suggest you go to his office and speak with him about the atmosphere that we maintain here."

Listening to Franca, Elspeth acknowledged to herself that the petite Italian had a better pulse on how to handle the local constabulary than she did. Silently she doffed a hat to Franca and hoped the new spirit of cooperation between them would last.

The policeman spoke to Franca in rapid Italian, which Elspeth could not understand, but the gist was obvious. He was asking for her help.

Franca shifted into English. "You must understand that *la signora* Duff represents *il barone* Kennington in London. She does not understand what happens here all the time, and how you at the police are always willing to help us with small crimes that sometimes happen at the hotel. We will come to the police station this afternoon after lunch and talk to *il commissario* Ponchetti, but it is better that you leave here now."

The policeman raised his head in dignified defeat, took his hat from the table next to his chair, bowed to both the women and made his exit.

"Brava, Franca," Elspeth said appreciatively. She had learned many years ago to be grateful when a member of the Kennington staff had handled a situation more delicately than she could have.

"I have known *il commissario* for many years. He has helped me many times. Still, I think we must be careful with him and meet him at his office, not here in the hotel. I also want to know what he is doing about the shooting of Marco Celli. Will you come with me?"

Hoping her request was an olive branch, Elspeth looked directly at Franca. "Will you trust me to join you?"

"Do I have any choice?" Franca replied without a smile.

11

At half past twelve when Will and Mandy arrived at the glass doors leading into the dining room, they found it already filling despite it being early for Italians to take lunch. Will watched the maître d' greet men and women clothed in Italian sartorial splendor. His familiarity suggested their repeated custom. Many ordered the "usual" drink before listening to the specialties of the day and chatted the way business associates do rather than as friends. Several exchanged polite nods of acquaintanceship with other patrons.

An overly friendly waiter, who introduced himself as Francesco, greeted them at their table. "*Buongiorno*, good day, *Signorina* Bell," which of course became Bella. "Also *Signor* Too-til-a, we are pleased to welcome you. I make sure you have a quiet table with a good view of the mountains."

Both Mandy and Will smiled at the emotive flourish of the waiter's arms as he drew out Mandy's chair.

After they were seated, Will put his hand lightly on Mandy's forearm and thought that she was indeed remarkably *bella*, just as Francesco had said. Will hoped he did not blush. He was glad when faces turned away from him to admire Mandy, who was oblivious to their attention. She instead was gaping openly at the room around her.

The dining room's east wall was lined with French doors, which were draped in creamy damask curtains. The high glass doors opened onto a large terrace used for dining during the summer months and afforded a full panorama of the lake and Alps beyond. The unstable weather, however, had bought the diners inside to enjoy the ambiance conjured up not by Nature but, Will knew, by the creativity of Lord Kennington and his interior designers. The high ceilings were coffered with white and gold moldings. Pinpoint spotlights hidden among the ornately carved ceiling panels cast a subtle radiance at each carefully placed table. The deep carpet with a mauve, blue, and lavender pattern was edged in deep indigo, and the highly polished legs of the cushioned chairs reflected the carpet's colors. For lunch the tablecloths were colored lilac and the napkins ultramarine, although the mountains through the closed doors, not the table settings, claimed dominance despite the growing cloud cover.

Will was thankful for the location of their table, but he wondered if its prime spot had anything to do with rumors that he was a talent scout from Hollywood and therefore worth special attention.

Will and Mandy's table had flowers, deep pink asters, which had been put in a small china vase. Will was accustomed to this personal touch, a signature gesture of the Kennington hotels, but Mandy gushed rhapsodically about it.

"Will, this is so splendid! This feels like the real Italy with all the Italian love of the arts and beauty. I once ate in a hotel in Cairo like this, luckily not the Kennington hotel, and the next day it was blown up by a bomb."

Will laughed outright at Mandy's non sequitur. "Let's hope this hotel fares better than that one. Lord Kennington would not be pleased if his creation, much less his guests, were destroyed by a bomb."

A Scandal in Stresa

Francesco offered the menus with an exaggerated sweep and expounded in a clear tenor voice the virtues of the specialties of the day. Mandy ordered melon with figs and prosciutto, pasta with wine and pine nuts, and a grilled fillet of beef with mushrooms and capers. Will settled for a scampi risotto and a green and red salad on the side without a second course. He wondered how she could eat so much and stay so slender. He thought her figure flawless. Francesco served with the training of a dancer, offering Will the wine as Mandy bit into her first course. Mandy let out a sigh of contentment.

"Another hour in the gym but well worth it," she said. "I never get food like this at university, between the mush my flatmates and I cook and the food in the local establishments. Besides, the food on Daddy's digs is inedible, since he insists on having an Egyptian so-called cook who once saved his life. Mummy has no inclination toward the culinary arts, having been raised in a household with two cooks. This is pure heaven."

The two ate without speaking, savoring the delicate combination of rich sauces, subtle flavorings, and fresh ingredients. Their silence was comfortable and allowed them to observe the other diners. Francesco continued to be attentive, and whenever possible he turned his profile to Will. Both Will and Mandy declined selections from the tray of sweet confections and fresh fruits that Francesco navigated to their table. The meal ended sooner than Will would have wished.

Will watched for the duchess and her daughter, but they did not appear.

Will was just considering rising when Franca Donatello came in to the dining room. She crossed the room and in doing so swirled past and welcomed many of the diners by name. Finally she stopped at Will and Mandy's table. She motioned to a nearby waiter to bring her a chair. Will was uncertain how to react to Franca. Should he acknowledge his previous acquaintance or simply play the innocent? Should he introduce Mandy Bell, although he was sure Franca already knew who Mandy was. He chose simply to smile pleasantly and say nothing.

"Are you pleased with your meal?" Franca asked with warmth; the rancor she had shown toward Elspeth was now gone. "Our lunch chef is new. He comes from Milano with the highest of recommendations, but I need an unbiased opinion."

Mandy introduced herself and raved over the meal and the room. Will looked on without comment and sensed Franca had joined them for some purpose other than seeking a critique of the hotel's new chef.

Franca spoke more loudly than was necessary. "Mr. Tuttle, will you and your lovely interpreter join me in my office. I have a message to share with you that has just come from your studio in Hollywood." Will wondered why the ruse because it was not clear why "his studio" would not have contacted Will directly.

Franca waved to Francesco, who promptly attended to her. "Mr. Tuttle's lunch is courtesy of the hotel," she said. "See that it does not appear on his bill."

Francesco bobbed with delight. With an absurdly broad grin, he bowed deeply to Will and raised his head grandly. "Thank you, signor Too-til-a; I am Francesco, Francesco Perini," he said, his wet teeth gleaming. "I am an actor."

Will tried not to laugh.

*

In a small conference room at the back of the hotel Elspeth stood thinking about the interview to come. Her fingers touched the edge of a side table adorned with a large vase of flowers, less fresh than those in the public areas. Yesterday's flowers were still good enough to grace staff areas. Franca came in with Mandy and Will. Franca left the three of them in the room alone. Elspeth came forward and held her hand out to Mandy in welcome.

Mandy took the extended hand tentatively, as if she was unsure who Elspeth was, and turned to Will for guidance.

Will rescued her. "Elspeth Duff, Amanda Bell. Mandy, Elspeth is in Stresa under personal instructions from Lord Kennington. I report directly to her, and she is the one who will be calling the shots for us for the next few days. Ouch, I didn't mean the pun, although actually that is why we are here. Our task is to find out who fired the shots that killed Marco Celli."

Amanda turned toward Will, curiosity filling her face. "We are not really looking for a promising location for a film, and you are not really a scout for a film company? As nice as you are, Will Tuttle, I should have suspected that you are not really the Hollywood type. Are you a detective?"

Will chuckled. "I suppose in some ways I am, although that is not my title. I'm with the Kennington Organisation security department. Elspeth works independently from our department and is usually on special security assignments for Lord Kennington's office, but we have worked together in the past."

"I see," said Amanda, although her face still registered doubt. "Where do I fit in this picture? I thought from what I was told by your London office that I would be interpreting for you."

Elspeth motioned them to seats around the circular, inlaid mahogany conference table, polished to a high gloss, and adorned with crested cream-colored note pads bearing the Kennington seal and the motto "Comfort and Service." With her fingertips Elspeth squared one of the pads in front of her before answering Mandy.

"Mandy, would you like to join us in doing something a bit more than translating? Will and I talked about this earlier, and he seemed to think you might be amenable to doing so."

"What do you have in mind?" Mandy's eagerness was palpable.

"I have plans for Will this afternoon," Elspeth explained. "He won't need a interpreter. While he's busy, I want you to go into the lounge off the second floor corridor and wait. Take a book or a laptop or whatever is natural for you and settle in. Then I want you to watch if there is any activity around suite 201. Make notes on anything you see or hear and especially the time."

"That seems an easy assignment. If that's all, I'm your person."

Elspeth smiled at Mandy. "Watching is not always that easy," she said. "Make sure you can last for several hours without, as the Victorians put it, any 'necessaries.' Don't get distracted by your book or computer and miss something. Believe me, it isn't as easy as it sounds."

Mandy threw back her auburn head of hair, her green eyes laughing. "Just try me. I'll show you I can."

After Will made his excuses, Elspeth was left alone with Mandy. Elspeth could see her puzzlement and immediately stepped in to explain.

"I am glad we are finally meeting because Lord Kennington has praised you highly. I'm glad you are willing to help us," Elspeth said.

"Did Lord Kennington suggest that I should come here to play detective? I am studying archaeology, but I am not sure than qualifies me. Most of the subjects I investigate have been dead for thousands of years and really don't mind if you need time off for the necessaries. Am I supposed to find a present-day criminal?"

Elspeth shook her head. "Quite the contrary. I need you and Will to help me create a network of safety here. Hotel security is in some ways unique. Our chief purpose is to make all the guests feel there is no need for security. Unlike today's airports and public buildings, we can hardly screen guests who come in the door, particularly when they are paying the prices the Kennington hotels demand. When I first started working for Lord Kennington five years ago, security meant tracing bad credit cards and people who slipped out without paying their bills, but now all that has changed. As the world tightens its security measures against terrorists, our role in hotel security has evolved as well. Now we're more concerned with preventing public disturbances than dealing with petty theft or fraud. Many people now have a heightened sense of anxiety, particularly in a foreign country. It's our job to alleviate their fears."

"Having just returned from Egypt, I'm well aware of all the security measures these days. My friends told me I was insane to travel to Cairo, but Daddy said we probably were safer now than four years ago. Actually we met with more courtesy than usual. The Egyptians are hurting for lack of business."

"I met your parents at a reception in Cairo several years ago and enjoyed hearing about their search for Egyptian antiquities. I've always wanted to go on a dig. Perhaps someday," Elspeth said wistfully.

"I've lived on digs many times in my life. Life in the Egyptian desert was deadly dull when I was a child." Mandy rolled her eyes and groaned.

Elspeth grinned. "Have you ever heard of the film star Toria Albi?"

Mandy screwed up her face for a moment and then burst out laughing. "Big lips, big hair, and prominent frontal features."

Elspeth suppressed a chuckle at Mandy's description. "So you know her. Good. Do you know anything about her other than her physical features?"

"I see her picture in the tabloids on occasion, but, as a university student, I am supposed to be above that sort of thing. I must admit a fascination for the way tabloids distort the truth. I often think that the hieroglyphics on the walls of tombs probably do the same thing."

"Have you ever heard of Marco Celli?" Elspeth asked.

"The one who was shot outside of the hotel several days ago? Will told me about him at lunch and asked what I thought. My comment to Will was 'raw sex.' I've seen several of his films, which are abominable."

"So you know about him too. That helps. Toria Albi married Marco Celli a few years ago, and the marriage has gone sour. *La Toria*, as the tabloids call her, sued him for divorce, but, before the divorce was final, Marco threatened to kill her and her mother as well."

"Charming," said Mandy, with a grin

"Do you know about Toria's mother?"

"Not really, but may I assume that she is a typical clinging stage mum?"

"A bit more than that. Toria's mother is a force unto herself. She almost single-handedly assured Toria's success, and in the process she elevated herself to the grand title of *la duchessa d'Astonino* by marrying the duke under somewhat dubious circumstances."

"How did she do that?"

"I suspect by using her daughter."

"How could I have guessed."

Elspeth liked this outspoken young woman. She reminded Elspeth of her son Peter, who often voiced a level of cynicism that sometimes distressed but often amused his mother.

"The next time you are inclined to dawdle on the internet," Elspeth said, "I suggest you Google Toria Albi, Mario Celli, and *la duchessa d'Astonino*. You will be entertained in a lurid kind of way."

"Am I to assume that all of this has something to do with why you asked me to perch in the second-floor lounge?"

"Intelligent woman. By now you have undoubtedly figured out who the mysterious guests are in suite 201."

"Toria and the duchess." Mandy's smile was conspiratorial. "And then we have Marco Celli lingering outside the hotel when he was shot."

"That is Lord Kennington's worry, and mine as well."

"A murder connected with the Kennington Stresa will not do," Mandy said, in a voice that mocked an erstwhile school head.

"Precisely," said Elspeth in the same tone.

"It is Will's and your job, and now mine, to see that it does not," Mandy said.

"Mandy, I want you mainly as an observer."

"Count me in," said Mandy. Elspeth heard the glee in Mandy's voice that comes with youth rather than experience. She hoped that Will's confidence in Mandy would prove well founded, and that Mandy's enthusiasm would not lead her into any danger, but Elspeth's hopes were not filled with assurance.

*

"Detective, huh?" Will was still chuckling when he left Elspeth and Mandy. If Mandy had any idea of what he was about to do, she would have questioned his honesty. Will had outlined his upcoming task, and Elspeth had agreed to it. He wanted to find out what the police might see if they investigated the hotel and then propose to Elspeth how any incriminating evidence that he discovered might be hidden, at least for the time being.

He went to his room to collect his gear including his small camera, note pad, and measuring tape. He decided to start his search at the bottom of the hotel and proceed up through all the public spaces. Elspeth had limited him only in forbidding him to enter any of the rooms of guests in residence. The underground car park, the back offices, the kitchen, the reception area and shop, staircases, exercise and breakout areas, conference rooms, dining room, tearoom, storage areas, even the roof tops, and any other nook and cranny were fair game. Will was to photograph and document anything he found that appeared suspicious and submit everything for Elspeth's review. In the meantime Elspeth was to keep the police at bay.

Before leaving London, Will had been given a reduced-sized set of blueprints for the hotel, which he now spread out on a clipboard and secured with binder clips. He feared that a guest who was staying at the hotel and saw him enter the hotel in his role as a Hollywood scout might recognize him. Therefore he donned a Kennington Organisation blazer and a large pair of aviator glasses and parted his hair in the middle. His height might have given him away, so Elspeth urged him to stay away from anything that would immediately let the guests compare his height to a tall object. If confronted by anyone in the hotel staff, he was to have them call Franca Donatello.

Will began in the car park. He showed his security badge to the attendant, who assured him that the lunch crowd had now dispersed and that for the next few hours there would be little activity in the area. The space housed about thirty cars. Will moved meticulously from one to the next, noting any anomalies that might attract attention. He found none. He finally got to a dark corner where a car was wrapped in a protective tarpaulin. Glancing to see if the attendant was looking, Will peeled back the cover and discovered a large black Alfa Romeo with a bullet hole piercing the windscreen. He looked and saw that the bullet had landed in the leather upholstery. The hole there was tinged with a dark red crusting of blood. Will took up his camera and recorded this discovery. He noted the number plate and carefully replaced the cover.

Will moved up the staff lift to the service corridor. Finding nothing there except cardboard boxes of toilet tissue and a cart filled with towels, he went into the storage area only to see orderly rows of paper products and cleaning supplies. The linen closet was next, smelling of cleanliness and arranged by room number and bed size. Everything was in order.

In the staff lounge and locker rooms, Will saw that the morning staff members were changing into street clothes, and he decided to return when the afternoon shift had settled into their duties and the rooms would be empty.

He proceeded to the public areas of the ground floor. Several guests were using a conference room off the lobby and watching a soap opera on the television. Will sidestepped the space.

The business center was empty, so he limited his search to the physical parts of the room. A Kennington hotel note pad on a table had some impressions on it from someone writing there. He took the top sheet from the pad and attached it to his clipboard for later analysis. Otherwise the room seemed innocent. Two overweight men, sweating profusely at their tasks, occupied the exercise room. Crossing the lobby, which was empty except for the receptionist, Will took out his clipboard and tried to look efficient and uninterested in anything happening there. Several people were sitting reading newspapers in the lounge. The shop was empty.

Little by little he checked off room after room. All reflected the Kennington Organisation touch, tastefully opulent but without ostentation. Nothing could have attracted the police unless they appreciated pure luxury.

Purposely avoiding the second-floor lounge where he knew Mandy would now be watching, Will made his way to the roof. Patches of sunlight through the clouds did not warm the wind that was coming off the lake. He wished he had something heavy under his blazer but did not want to venture back downstairs. He shivered as he swiveled three hundred sixty degrees to take in the view, first of the mountains and lake and then of the rooftops around him. If Marco had indeed been shot from above, the murderer might have stood here or on any of the roofs nearby and carefully taken aim.

He could not see any physical link between the rooftop of the Kennington Stresa and its neighbors. As he walked over to the edge to look at the street below, the sun appeared and reflected off of something shiny by the parapet. Exploring this further, he found the casings of three fired shells. Brilliant! he thought. This was real evidence, something that probably should not be hidden from the police. Before getting out his camera, he laid out a small measuring stick to establish scale, and photographed the casings from every conceivable angle. Feeling extremely uneasy, he pocketed his camera and beat a retreat. He must contact Elspeth immediately and make sure roof access was denied to anyone before the police could come. Then he remembered that the press had reported two shots, not three. They must have been wrong. One casing was a short distance from the others. Had it been shot at a different time?

Elspeth's mobile phone said she was not available, would he please leave a message. She already had told him she was going with Franca to the police.

Feeling he needed some support, even visually, he took the lift to the second floor, but when he got to the lounge Mandy, despite her protestations to the contrary, was no where to be found.

12

The bells on a church tower nearby rang the half-hour, making Elspeth aware the afternoon was advancing. She had an appointment to meet Franca Donatello in less than thirty minutes to go to the police station. Not yet having lunch and feeling light headed, she rang room service, ordered a cheese and vegetable panini and some tea. Then she pulled out her mobile. She found the number for Scotland Yard, which she had stored on an earlier assignment. The telephone operator at the Yard vetted her before putting her through to Detective Superintendent Tony Ketcham. She explained her need for credibility with the Stresa Municipal Police, and Tony assured Elspeth that he would ring them immediately.

Elspeth snatched up the panini that room service had brought her minutes before. She took several large bites of it as she prepared notes for her meeting. Biddy Baillie Shaw never would have imagined that her cousin existed on grabbing rare meals when she was on duty. Elspeth did not have time to finish her sandwich before getting ready for her visit to the police. She pulled a comb through her hair, added a simple gold necklace under her silk scarf and applied a hint of expensive Parisian scent. One never knows, it might help, she thought.

She took the service lift down and found Franca waiting in the car park below, standing by a hotel car and tapping her foot slowly. She only acknowledged Elspeth's arrival with a nod to the driver. Elspeth checked her watch and saw she was not late. The driver opened the rear door for her, and she bent in because the car was smaller than most of the Kennington Organisation's cars but probably more appropriate for the narrow roads in Stresa. Franca chose to ride in the passenger seat next to the driver rather than alongside Elspeth. As they made their way down the hill, Franca spoke to the driver in rapid Italian, although the short distance to the police station hardly merited instruction. The drive lasted less than two minutes and they arrived well in time for their three o'clock appointment. Had Elspeth been left to her own devices, she would have walked but did not say so. She chose to tread lightly with Franca until discovering the source of her animosity and finding a way to deal with it.

There was little pretension to the municipal offices that housed the police. The boxy, apricot-colored three-story building sat back from the street but barely far enough to allow for a miniscule police car to be tucked in between terra cotta pots blocking the entrance from the road. Franca instructed the driver to pull over and let them out. A man in a goods van behind them raised an irritated protest by sounding off his horn and making angry gestures. Ignoring this, Franca took her time to alight. She flicked her head arrogantly at the driver of the van, raised herself to her full five-feet-two and marched in through the double doors. Elspeth followed, amazed at Franca's contempt.

The receptionist greeted Franca by name and with a broad smile picked up his handset. After a brief conversation, he pressed a buzzer and indicated that they should proceed through a wooden gate by his desk into the interior of the police area. Without formality Elspeth and she were escorted onto a lift and up to the first floor. On arrival, Franca motioned Elspeth toward a door that stood ajar.

The door flung open and round, a dapper man in police uniform came rushing through it. Hardly taller than Franca, he threw his arms around her with a torrent of Italian words, obviously of endearment.

"Come in, come in," he said in English. "You must be *Signora* Elspeth Duff." He struggled with both names. He held his hand out and pumped Elspeth's up and down.

"Come in," he said again. "This is my office." He gestured to two straight-backed chairs that were positioned in front of his neatly arranged desk. A file, which Elspeth could see was labeled *Marco Celli,* lay squarely positioned and open to a picture of the late actor.

"Sit down, sit down," the policeman said. "It pleases me to have you here." His head bobbed several times.

Elspeth had expected the *commissario* to be a person of greater stature and hoped her face did not show this. She thanked him and sat down in one of the chairs. Franca stood for a moment eyeing the *commissario* and after a long pause said something in Italian. The *commissario* made a quick bow as if in acknowledgement to Franca's command. Franca took her seat but perched on its edge, her short legs barely reaching the floor. She flung one of her scarves around her neck, her bracelets jangling, and she grimaced as if she had a sour piece of citrus in her mouth. The *commissario,* oblivious, strutted around behind the desk and took his seat, which must have been elevated, as he appeared taller after he sat down.

The *commissario,* firmly ensconced in his heightened chair, lowered his high tenor voice. "Now, *Signora* Duff, I think you are here to talk about the death of Marco Celli."

"You're kind to see me, *commissario*. I, of course, have no official position, although I am sure Franca has told you the concerns we have at the hotel."

"*Sì, signora*. Franca and I have worked together many times, and we are very close friends." He turned and gave a knowing look at Franca, who sat stonily looking out the window.

Elspeth watched the body language between the two of them, his giving off infatuation, hers broadcasting warning. What did Franca want to hide? An affair with the *commissario*? Was that the cause of her hostility toward Elspeth when she mentioned the police? Or was it simply Elspeth's interference at the hotel?

The policeman continued. "I have just received a call from a colleague at Scotland Yard in London, a distinguished detective superintendent." The *commissario* did not attempt to pronounce Tony Ketcham's surname. "He told me, *Signora* Duff, that you once worked for Scotland Yard and were a very good police officer. I am honored to have you here in my office."

Tony's introduction gave Elspeth the advantage for which she had hoped. She put her hands prayer-like to her chin and smiled a calculatedly demure smile.

The *commissario* beamed.

"Franca tells me you have been with the Stresa police for many years," Elspeth said, "and you have helped her when there were the situations at the hotel that needed police intervention. I look forward to working with you on this current matter."

"Also I," said the *commissario*.

"I realize that you must be well on the trail of the person who shot Marco Celli. My intention is not to interfere with your investigation. I only wish to ask a few questions, so that I may report to my employer, Lord Kennington, about the murder outside his hotel. He gave me two orders: one, that we should cooperate with you but, two, to see that you do not disturb our guests unless absolutely necessary. I am sure you understand."

"Of course, *signora*." He puffed up his body, but a shadow of worry fled across his face. He cleared his throat. "I am reading the file from the coroner right now."

"Forgive me for not understanding Italian," Elspeth said. "Perhaps you can tell me what the report says." She hoped that Eric Kennington would appreciate her "charm."

"Because you are from Scotland Yard, I will share a little of the information. The report says only one bullet hit the head of Marco Celli. It went through his eye and came out the back of his neck."

Elspeth quickly gathered her thoughts. She wanted to divert the policeman's mind from the idea that the bullet, which from his description had probably been fired from above, had come from the hotel.

"If Marco was looking down, the bullet may have come from someone hiding nearby on the street," she suggested.

"Or from a car that went past," the *commissario* said. "One person who saw Marco said he was waiting on the street. When he was shot, a big car went by. My sergeant asked if the shot came from the car. No one said 'yes' or 'no,' only 'maybe.' One person said there were two shots; another person said only one. But, only one bullet hit Marco, so maybe there was only one."

"What sort of gun was used? Do you know yet?" Elspeth asked.

"The bullet was from a Beretta hunting rifle. There are many of these in Italy."

"Aren't rifles rather long?" she asked.

A Scandal in Stresa

"Yes, this one is about a meter long," he answered.

"Then it would be impossible to shoot it from a car. More likely it came from the street," Elspeth said, hoping her ruse would work.

The *commissario* sighed. "The gun has not been found. My men are still looking, but we will find it."

During this exchange Franca said nothing. Finally she broke in. "Aldo, do you even know where the gunman fired from?"

The *commissario* slowly shook his head. "One witness said she saw Marco Celli look up after the shot, and then he twisted and fell. Another, who likes American crime-scene television, looked at her watch and gave us the exact time. Now we know when he fell, exactly at three fifty-three in the afternoon. Another said he saw a large black car with black windows that came very fast around the corner and then disappeared up the hill. Maybe it was a Mercedes or perhaps an Audi. Nobody remembers the details or took down the number plate."

Three days had passed since the crime, and the police seemed no closer to the truth, Elspeth thought.

"If there was more than one bullet, have the other bullet or bullets been found?" Elspeth asked.

"Not yet, but, if they exist, we will find them soon. I have a very good lead."

A small bead of sweat was forming on Aldo Ponchetti's brow, which led Elspeth to think he was farther from the truth than he wished. She suspected he was out of his element but did not want to surrender his authority at the municipal level to the *carabiniere*, the formidable national police.

"I know that the investigation is in good hands here, and you will find the killer soon," Elspeth said ingenuously. "May I ask one more question?"

"Certainly, *signora*."

"Did the postmortem reveal anything else about Marco Celli?"

The *commissario* laughed. "Only that he had eaten mushroom risotto, a veal scaloppini, and asparagus for lunch and that he recently had sexual relations. He was a great, how do you say in English, ladies' man?"

Franca snorted. "Then perhaps, Aldo, he died happy, but why would someone want to kill Marco Celli? He was not a great star."

The *commissario* looked disconcerted and flipped through the papers on his desk.

"I have just received new information about Marco Celli. He was filming a picture in Roma. He left there last Thursday and did not come back to the set on Monday. The director said Marco was very distracted for the last few weeks. Marco was very sad about his divorce from Toria Albi."

Elspeth feigned puzzlement and innocently said, "Why would that bring him to Stresa?" She was fishing to see if the policeman had any hint that Toria Albi was in Stresa as well.

"We have questioned the hotel where Marco was staying. Several times he came in the back door with a woman."

"Which hotel is that?"

The *commissario* identified a large resort hotel on the waterfront, the Umberto Primo.

"Have you identified the woman with Marco Celli?" Franca asked. "Is she a local woman? Could she, or her husband, have shot him?"

"My men are investigating," he said stiffly. "We do not yet know, but we have some clues." The *commissario's* assertion sounded unconvincing. Elspeth was relieved.

A Scandal in Stresa

Franca and Elspeth found the hotel car parked in front of the police station, barely allowing passage of cars around it. The hotel driver rushed to open the back door of the car. This time Franca walked round to the other side of the car and took the seat beside Elspeth. Franca gave hasty instructions to the driver in Italian and then turned to Elspeth.

"Aldo is a fool," she said. "When he was young, he wanted to be a brilliant detective. He spent five years in Milano in the municipal police but later came back to Stresa. He said he wanted to return home to the lakes, but rumor said he had failed in a big case and came home instead of accepting a demotion. Who will ever know?"

"Have you known him a long time?" Elspeth asked.

"We took our catechism together as children. When he was younger, he was more handsome." She smiled into the distance. "His wife is sickly and seldom leaves home. He wanders on occasion."

Elspeth did not ask if Franca had been the object of one of his wanderings but suspected that the relationship between Franca and the *commissario* had at one time been more intimate.

"Do you believe that a local woman might have killed Marco?"

"Marco Celli?" Franca asked, as if Marco's name had been mentioned for the first time. "Who knows? He liked many women from what the paparazzi say and, for some unknown reason, many women seemed to like him."

"Does the *commissario* know Toria Albi and her mother are at the hotel?"

Franca shrugged. "He did not ask."

"And you did not tell?"

"Why should I? Toria would not have killed Marco."

"Are you sure?"

"*Sì*, Elspetta. You have not met La Toria, but she would not kill Marco. I am positive of that."

They rode along in silence. Elspeth leaned her head back on the headrest and thought that right now she needed someone as an ally.

When they got back to the hotel, her wish was granted. That ally was in the person of Lady Elisabeth Baillie Shaw, who was standing at the reception desk.

13

Silvia Trucco moved restlessly in her chair and fidgeted with the fringe of her blanket, although she knew that Carlo hated her doing so. The afternoon ground forward. There was nothing to alleviate the tedium until a knock came at the door. Carlo was resting in his room, and Silvia, hearing the faint sounds of his deep breathing, knew he had fallen into fitful sleep. She moved silently to the door and opened it against the chain. A uniformed member of the concierge's staff addressed her by name.

"Are you *Signora* Silvia Trucco?"

Silvia hesitated but then acknowledged her identity.

"I have an overnight express package for you," he said and slid a packet through the gap in the door.

Carlo woke at the sound and, coming into their sitting room, drew in his breath.

"What do you have?" he asked.

He took the packet and looked at the address: *Sra. Silvia Trucco, Kennington Stresa Hotel, Stresa, Italia.* His face drained of color. The return address was the FedEx office in Geneva. Knowing the thoroughness of Swiss regulations regarding the contents of international shipments, he did not expect anything dangerous. He ripped open the heavy paper jacket and drew out a green bound notebook tied together with a cotton ribbon. Its cover was water stained, and its edges dog-eared. Both he and Silvia had seen notebooks like this many times before. When on assignment, Constanza habitually carried them for note taking. His hand trembled as he untied the ribbon and rippled through the pages, the first half of which were inscribed with the neat round handwriting the nuns had taught Constanza. Silvia shook the express envelope, and a lined index card fell out. In a spidery handwriting she did not recognize was written in English: *We telephone you tomorrow morning eleven o'clock.*

"Blessed Virgin," Carlo muttered and turned the card over to Silvia. "How do they know we are here?"

After reading the card Silvia closed her eyes. She leaned her body over her lifeless legs and put her face in both of her hands. "Constanza, *mia cara*," she whispered. "Carlo, who wrote this card? The man on the phone?"

Carlo approached Silvia's chair and knelt before her, taking her long, fine hands in his. Her hands were shaking.

"I do not know. How can they know we are here? We have told no one," he murmured.

"I can think of no way, unless Constanza told the man of your preference for Kennington hotels."

Carlo's face showed the first signs of hope in a week. "Then that would mean she is alive and perhaps near here, in Geneva perhaps."

False hope would not bring Constanza back to them, Silvia thought. She turned his hand over in hers and looked up him, her mind filed with doubt.

"Or we may have been followed from Rome," she said almost in a whisper. "Could those shots really have been a warning to us that they know where we are? Perhaps we were wrong to tell Ms. Duff that there was no reason to suspect the shots were meant for us."

Carlo stood wearily. "I could not bear it, Silvia, if both Constanza and you were in danger."

Silvia, who had endured more suffering in her life than Carlo ever would, said, "Let's not imagine the worst. Come let us read what is in Constanza's journal. Perhaps it will provide a clue to where she is and if she is safe."

They opened to the first page.

> *11 September: (continued): Now I have all my provisions, native dress, hat and boots because they have warned me against the rains. Even though the monsoons are supposed to be over, I can use them higher up against the snows if I go that far. I feel ready to start. I am leaving my other things here at the hotel in anticipation of my return. I have rented a taxi to take me to the edge of the rebellion area, but even big bribes will not get me further. Plan to stay in (illegible) tonight.*
>
> *12 September: Bed miserably hard, no hot water, and I feel cast off into the sea without a lifeline. This may be my break. The taxi driver told the hotel owners here I was looking for Wei Ling-dao. They muttered together furtively when they heard this. This morning a man came and said he would take me to Phaplu for a very big sum of money. We bargained and I gave him a hundred US dollars. He smiled too much, so I knew I had been cheated.*
>
> *14 September: Three days without hot water or a shower. I smell like a yak, but I am closer to Wei. My guide turned me over to another guide who speaks less English but says he knows the camp of Wei and his comrades. Glad for Nepalese clothing, which makes me*

less conspicuous. Mamma would laugh at me; Silvia would agree with me, comfort over fashion. Today we are on horseback in a caravan of sorts. One old woman speaks a little English. She was in service to a British family in Kathmandu many years ago. She said Wei came to this area six years ago from Tibet. Now people forget he is Chinese and think only that he is their leader, a commander in the war for the people. She says Wei is a powerful man with many followers. When the guide came near us, she stopped talking. I rode alone after that and am sore all over. We climbed under the shadow of the high mountains all day.

15 September: Heavy, humid rain last night. I slept in a small yurt with my guide and a woman, who I think is his wife. She eyed me hostilely, so I did not try to speak to her. We stayed in camp this morning until the winds stopped blowing and the rains cleared away. Today I am even more tired, filthy, and constantly damp. These people have so little and only share with me because the guide tells them to. So much for the $100, which probably will buy guns not food.

16 September: My guide told me this morning that Wei's camp was near and that he would leave me there. We traveled until mid-afternoon with no break for lunch. Finally we stopped, and just as I was finishing a small bowl of gruel and some off-tasting meat curry that left me hungry, the guide took me aside and said another guide would take me to Wei's camp. This new guide speaks no English. We traveled until the sun was low in the sky, when a heavily armed Nepalese on horseback met us. My new guide talked rapidly to him, and he motioned for me to go with him. We traveled until the sun was setting and finally came to a heavily guarded group of yurts. A sentry gestured that I was to get off my horse and follow him. We went into a large yurt that was filled with smoke, and I was told to sit in a dark area away from the fire. Wei appeared through the entrance and demanded that I be brought to him. He speaks broken English and told me to leave the camp if I wanted to stay alive. I appealed to him that it was dark and I had neither a horse nor a guide. He motioned to a guard, and I was taken to another yurt where six women, several in rough uniforms with rifles at their sides and sashes filled with long bullets. No one spoke to me. I was shown a place to sleep, a thin mattress covered with yak skins. One woman took pity on me and offered me a thick bowl of stew and a cup of hot water. It tasted better than anything I have ever eaten before. Chez Panisse move over.

17 September: This morning after breakfast of a sweeter gruel than the day before, one of the women soldiers took me back to the yurt where Wei had been the night before. He was waiting for me. He said he had changed plans and I was to travel with the camp. I told him who I was and whom I represented and asked if I could interview him. He said he would think about it. I am very excited that I may actually get this interview.

19 September: I have not had a bath since leaving Kathmandu. I am beginning to itch all over, but I am now used to the smell. The others smell the same, rancid. I travel on horseback behind Wei every day, but no one speaks to me. I am aware that Wei is watching me. We are traveling down to the plain. We stopped in a small town where there was electricity and where someone had an old computer and modem. Wei spent about an hour on the computer, sending emails, I think.

20 September: Wei came up to me when we had stopped for our midday meal and told me that he had discovered who I am and that my father is very rich. He is demanding €1 million. I told him that I would not cooperate; that I was in Nepal to interview him and that my father had disowned me and would not give him the money. They have seen me writing in this

The notebook, which was written in English, stopped abruptly. On the last page was scribbled in Italian in a shaky hand: *Silvia, pericolo.* Silvia, danger.

When Silvia finished reading, she turned tearful eyes to Carlo and smiled wryly. "How like Constanza to be defiant."

"*Sì*, how like Constanza." He did not smile in return.

14

Amanda Bell, having been warned about the tedium of surveillance and having taken care of all the "necessaries" she could think of, decided to take her laptop with her into the second-floor lounge. She selected one of the love seats whose position afforded a view of the lake and mountains through tall windows that lined the hallway beyond. Heavy curtains were drawn back from the windows by gold braided ropes looped over hooks in the shape of open-mouthed gargoyles. The walls of the lounge were painted a pale peach color and rose over four meters toward an ornate ceiling complete with heavy cornices and gilded stucco bas-relief of florets, braids, and flourishes. She could see the door to Suite 201 without facing it directly. Mandy sat for a moment studying her surroundings and decided that life in a Kennington hotel far surpassed that of life in a tent in the Egyptian Valley of the Kings.

She opened her laptop and made a show of being occupied. She checked her email and decided none demanded an immediate response. Mandy recalled Elspeth's admonition to be diligent, so she let her computer go dark. The afternoon sky grew somber with the clouds covering all but the lower portion of the Alps, which caused Mandy to reach over and turned on one of the porcelain lamps beside her seat. The bulb was subdued and shed a warm glow across her space.

Mandy's mind wandered to Will. She decided he was worth getting to know better. She had sensed he was inexplicably shy, but he was one of the few tall men she had met who had caught her immediate fancy. He was unpretentiously handsome and spoke intelligently on a number of subjects, none of which centered on Mandy's alluring qualities. "Brazen hussy," her father would have said. Mandy suspected Will Tuttle was the sort with whom she needed to be a bit brazen in order to direct his attention away from their job together.

She was just beginning to settle in comfortably when the door to suite 201 flew open and a young woman came rushing out, obviously in a state of acute consternation. The large sunglasses she wore did little to hide her identity.

Toria Albi flounced petulantly toward the lounge and, seeing Mandy, pulled back. She paused and rather myopically stared at Mandy. Throwing both arms in the air, she said in English, "Do you hate your mother?"

Mandy was not prepared for this unanticipated appearance of the object of her surveillance and was not sure what the appropriate response should be. Therefore she responded in Italian, "Is your mother making trouble for you?"

Toria Albi looked surprised. "Oh, are you Italian? I thought you were an American."

"My mother is Italian," Mandy responded, "but my father is English. I suppose I am both." She hoped this would not end the conversation. Apparently she had said the right thing because Toria dropped down in an adjacent love seat with a motion that was somewhere in between comedic and emotive. She turned her full attention to Mandy.

"Then you will understand my desperate situation," Toria said in the seductive tones that entranced her fans.

Having been granted this unforeseen opportunity, Mandy decided to take advantage of it. Toria reminded her of a flatmate she once had who spoke in similar hyperbole, and, consequently, Mandy understood that Toria might be in need of a sympathetic ear.

"I despise my mother!" Toria said in unaccented American English. Toria's venom seemed real, not scripted.

Mandy, remembering what Elspeth had told her about documenting the time of events, glanced at the large wristwatch Toria was wearing, a gold man's watch with a band too large for her wrist. It was a quarter past three.

"Why do you hate her?" Mandy asked.

"Me? I'm a grown woman. I'm famous. I make a lot of money but she treats me like a child. *Come una bambina.* I hate her!"

Mandy was sufficiently English that she felt disquieted by Toria Albi broadcasting her feelings so loudly in a public space. Mandy twisted in her chair and cleared her throat. Toria did not notice.

"Perhaps," said Mandy, "you would like to talk about it somewhere a bit more private."

This caught Toria's attention. "*Sì, davvero,* you are right. I must be discreet and not say what I feel in public. I must consider my press. She says that to me all the time."

Mandy sensed Toria's poison again but was not certain of the reason behind these words. Toria, however, was amenable to moving to a more secluded space.

"I am not doing anything this afternoon," Mandy said, hoping that she sounded innocent. "Would you like to come to my room? It's one of the smaller ones, but it's comfortable."

Toria looked around her and saw a guest emerging from the lift at the end of the hallway. She put her hand to her face, a gesture meant to hide her identity, although Mandy suspected it failed to do so because of Toria's other physical attributes. The guest, however, did not take notice of the two women in the lounge and entered a room down the corridor without glancing up.

"My room is nearby. Do come," Mandy said, hoping she sounded companionable. Mandy was unaccustomed to entertaining celebrities and was grateful when Toria accepted.

"*Sì*. That would be nice," Toria said and rose tragically from her chair as if in great angst. No actress in early silent films could have done better.

As Mandy stood up, she was surprised that Toria Albi, who was wearing low-heeled sandals, was almost as tall is she, and their eyes met evenly. Mandy had heard that many female film stars were tall, but she had not expected Toria Albi to be so. She took Toria's arm and led her to her room. They met no one on the way.

Mandy had traveled much of her life and had been trained by her mother to keep her hotel room in immaculate order. She was thankful now for that lifelong habit. Out of her window she could see the garden across the street. Although she had some difficulty opening it, Mandy had left the window ajar, making the room cool. Toria, who was scantily dressed, shivered as she came into the room, and therefore Mandy closed the window. Two comfortable chairs sat around a small fireplace. Mandy turned on the electric fire, which looked like a real wood one.

"The English side of me can offer you tea and the Italian side some wine," Mandy said.

Toria Albi stood near the reddening pseudo-logs in an effort to warm herself, although the electric flames as yet gave off little heat.

"Do you have coffee?" she asked. "My name is Vittoria. What is yours?" Despite her statuesque posture, her voice was meek.

Mandy hazarded a guess that few people treated Toria in a simple manner and that Toria was unsure how to respond to Mandy's straightforward act of offering sympathy and refreshment without fawning.

"Amanda. Amanda Bell, but I'm called Mandy."

"Thank you, Mandy, for asking me here. I thought I would go crazy if I didn't get away from my mother, but I had nowhere to go."

The childlike declaration of abandonment in her voice filled Mandy with sorrow. Life at the top, or close to the top, of stardom obviously was distressing Toria Albi, at least for the moment.

Having a resourceful mind, Mandy said, "Let me ring room service, and we will have some of that wonderful coffee they serve in the restaurant."

Mandy suggested they order coffee from the hotel kitchen for two reasons. She wanted to treat her guest well, but she also wanted someone else to know where Toria Albi was.

By the time room service brought the coffee and slices of freshly baked chocolate torte, which Mandy had ordered on a whim, Mandy and Vittoria were deep in conversation. Toria calmed down considerably, tucked herself into one of the armchairs and wrapped a brightly colored and heavily woven Egyptian cotton shawl that Mandy had given her around her shoulders.

"Are you here on holiday?" the film star asked, as if the prospect of a simple holiday was beyond her reach.

"No, I am between terms at university and am working as a interpreter for an Englishman who is in the film industry in California. He's here to find a suitable spot for screening a new film about the Second World War in northern Italy," she said. She must remember to tell Will that she had embellished his cover story, so Will would not say the film was a drama set in Roman times.

Toria unwrapped her shapely legs, which she had curled under her, and came to attention, suddenly star quality. "What sort of film? An American one?"

Mandy nodded shamelessly.

"Working in American movies is better than Italian films," Toria confided. "I like working for American directors."

Mandy could think of no reply, so she sat silently, sipping her coffee, and watching the fire, which now was warming the room.

"Are you happy, Mandy?" Toria suddenly asked.

"I never really thought about it. I suppose I am."

"I have not been happy for a long time, a long, long time." Toria spoke in a hush, tears filling her thickly mascarred eyes and slipping down her heavily made up cheeks.

"Vittoria, how very sad for you."

"You see I've just been divorced, and now my husband is dead."

Mandy decided that it was best to feign ignorance. She took a bite of cake and waited for Toria to continue. Because Mandy had never had a husband, she wondered if she could offer Toria any solace.

Toria began to cry in earnest. "My mother said I should be happy because he's gone. But I'm not happy because I loved him, but Mamma did not allow me to be sad. It's terrible."

"Both divorce and death must be dreadful," Mandy said, hoping she sounded concerned.

"Let us talk about other things."

Vittoria Albi closed down and, although she stayed in Mandy's room for another hour, their conversation never reverted back to the tragedy of Toria's current life. As she left the room, Toria looked at her new friend.

"May I come again?" Toria asked. "I feel safe here."

"Come again tomorrow or call any time." Mandy wondered if Toria Albi had ever had a real female friend. She then took unmitigated advantage of the situation. "Let me introduce you to my boss. He might recommend that you have a part in the new film. Or should I pretend that I do not recognize you? Oh, Vittoria, please excuse my boldness," Mandy said without compunction. "I've really enjoyed our chat. Please come again. You're always welcome . . . as a friend."

Toria flung down Mandy's shawl, gave Mandy an exaggerated hug, and exited through the door, once again as if from the stage of a melodrama.

"*Sì*. I would like that," she said in parting.

As the door closed, Mandy put her hand to her face and smiled at the success of her duplicity. She also came away from the encounter with a real feeling of compassion for the film star, who played to her public image with accomplishment but, at the same moment, seemed an innocent and lonely child.

15

Emerging from the private car that had brought her to Stresa, Biddy Baillie Shaw went through the large wooden door that a doorman held opened for her and went toward the reception desk. She saw a woman in the lobby talking with Elspeth. Her cousin must not have seen Biddy and disappeared behind a door marked "Private." The woman rushed toward Biddy and introduced herself as the hotel manager to "Lady Elisabeth" in loud tones. Several people turned their heads, acknowledging that aristocracy had arrived.

Biddy Baillie Shaw, who had lived at Tay Farm all her life and was a farmer by inclination as well as occupation, was taken back. In her mind she envisioned everyone at the Kennington Stresa as tall and slim, and as stylish as Elspeth. Pamela Crumm's physical smallness had been her first disappointment, and Franca Donatello was her second. Franca did not look like a hotel manager but rather like a gypsy who should dance around a campfire.

"*Benvenuta*, Lady Elisabeth," Franca said, using her title again, "we have been looking forward to your visit."

Franca instructed one of the porters to tend to Biddy's luggage and swept her around the reception desk and into an ornate lift that could have been designed in the studio of Charles Beardsley but looked much safer.

A Scandal in Stresa

Biddy and Franca arrived on the third floor of the hotel, and Franca ushered Biddy along a wide hallway with elongated windows at the end that opened out to a grand view of the red tile rooftops of Stresa. The heavy clouds beyond accented their color. Biddy drew in her breath at the scene. The inexpensive pensions on side streets where her husband, her three children, and she had stayed on their visit to Italy had given no hint that such breathtaking surroundings could exist. So this was Elspeth's world, Biddy thought. She tried to look as if she were accustomed to such things, but the slight gape of her mouth must have told Franca otherwise.

"At Ms. Crumm's insistence, I have put you in one of our better suites," Franca explained as she opened a guestroom door, "because it will serve your purposes here. Your rooms are directly above the duchess and her daughter's suite, and your balcony overlooks theirs. You will be able to see them if they venture outside, but it will be difficult for them to see you unless you lean quite far over the railing and they look up. This sitting room is bigger than those in most of our suites. We hope you will bring the duchess here, and she will be impressed by the size and grandeur that rivals her own quarters. Lord Kennington told me that you, Lady Elisabeth, are to appear extremely wealthy. I have tried to make it appear so."

A large basket of fruit, cheese and wine sat on one of the side tables, and a superfluity of fresh flowers spread across the room. Franca led Biddy into the bedroom where long windows looked out to the lake. A high bed was filled with pillows in such profusion Biddy wondered how one might sleep with all of them. It did not seem right to throw them on the floor.

Continuing her tour, Franca opened the door to a magnificent bathroom, complete with a large marble tub with gold claw feet. Mother of pearl and gold fixtures adorned two sinks. The sink surround, the floor, and the wainscoting were cream-colored marble. Multiple fluffy towels on heated racks lined most of one wall. Biddy suspected that the towels were changed once a day if not more often and thought their abundance unwarranted. How often could she have a bath?

"Will it do?" Franca asked.

"It is truly splendid," said Biddy with more enthusiasm than a really wealthy guest who was used to Kennington hotels might show.

"I will leave you to freshen up, and room service will bring your tea if you pick up the phone and punch in six."

The manager was just leaving the room when she said, "I will tell Ms. Duff that you are settling in and not to disturb you."

The command was so sharp that Biddy looked around in surprise. Biddy could not imagine her cousin would jump to Franca Donatello's orders; it was not in Elspeth's character.

After Franca left, Biddy sank into one of the large sofas and let out a sigh of contentment. She threw off her new and uncomfortable high-heeled shoes and for the shortest instant regretted not having brought her country shoes to slip into, although the latent mud on them would be offensive in a room like this.

*

As she turned away, Elspeth heard Franca proclaim Biddy's title to the world. Elspeth thought irreverently that Biddy was off and running and did not even have a chance to go to the loo. Elspeth wondered if Biddy had seen her at all. Biddy had never been to a Kennington hotel before she had been fêted by Pamela in London and undoubtedly was caught up by the Kennington Stresa's magic and probably had no eyes for her cousin.

Elspeth made her way up to her suite to wait for a call from either Biddy or Franca. Elspeth wanted to see her cousin but did not want to cross Franco Donatello one more time. Besides she needed time to assimilate the events of the day and check in with the members of her team.

When Elspeth came out of the lift, she found Mandy Bell perched on an intricately embroidered bench outside of her rooms. Mandy held a fashion magazine without turning the pages. As Elspeth approached, Mandy came rushing forward, hardly able to contain herself. Elspeth invited Mandy into the suite and made her sit down to give her a chance to compose herself before she delivered the news that made her breathless.

"I never have spoken to a film star before," Mandy burst out as she deposited herself in a most ungainly fashion in one of the armchairs. "Toria Albi is incredibly accessible, in fact almost vulnerable. Do you know that she loved Marco Celli, and it was her mother who engineered the whole divorce?"

Elspeth let Mandy spill out her news. Now the team had an inside track to Toria, and Elspeth planned to use it to her advantage. Elspeth thanked Mandy, who left the suite with excitement in her eyes.

Elspeth finally rang Biddy and arranged to meet her at eight for dinner in the main dining room. Biddy was waiting at a table by the windows when Elspeth entered. From afar Elspeth admired Biddy's new finery and suspected Pamela's hand in it.

When she had a chance to eat in the Kennington hotels' dining rooms, Elspeth always acknowledged Lord

Kennington's personal touches. The sprightly spring colors of the luncheon linens gave way to white damask tablecloths and starched white napkins in a fold devised by Lord Kennington and named after him. The silver was real, and the flowers had been changed since the midday meal. Here, as in all his hotels, lighting subtly changed over the evening.

Biddy looked dramatically blasé, her eyebrows arched a little too high for veracity, and, to Elspeth's mind, was blatantly overdoing it. Elspeth reminded herself that she had asked Biddy to act a part, one she had never experienced in real life, but Biddy could have been less emotive. Elspeth hoped no one noticed. She stood a moment and surveyed the dining room before going over to their table, but, to her disappointment, the Duchess of Astonino had not come down from her room.

As Elspeth crossed the room she heard Biddy's name on one couple's lips, but no one else noticed. She greeted her cousin with an affectionate smile and, selecting a seat with her back to the dining room, slid into the softly upholstered chair that the waiter held out for her.

"Elisabeth, how delightful to have you here," Elspeth said for the audience. "How wonderful that you should finally decide to come to Stresa."

Biddy opened her mouth to speak and then checked herself. "Quite charming for a small hotel," she said.

Elspeth wondered what Biddy's initial thought could have been but did not ask.

They took the proffered menus, which were engraved on heavy stock and handed to them with gracious gestures by their two waiters, one for each diner. Both women ordered the specialty of the evening, a chicken scaloppini with mushrooms, herbs and a wine sauce, preceded by crab ravioli in a light tomato cream sauce. The headwaiter suggested a wine, which Elspeth accepted with a brief nod.

When the waiters left, Biddy, with Scottish frugality, leaned over to Elspeth and said in a whisper, "There were no prices."

Elspeth smiled. "Lord Kennington does that purposely, but, if you have the audacity to ask, they do have menus with prices. Have no fear, you will never need to know what they are because everything is being taken care for you."

The cousins drifted into familial chatter, laughing at old stories, each of which they remembered differently.

"How odd," Elspeth said eventually, "that you and I are in some ways strangers. Our meetings in Perthshire have always been so filled with family events that I cannot recall when we ever sat down and talked, just the two of us. There is so much we have never said to each other."

"You are right, 'Peth. It's an unforeseen benefit of my trip here to have time alone with you."

Elspeth bit her lip, unsure of how to proceed. "I have never asked about Ivor," she said hesitantly, not knowing how Biddy was coping with her husband's death and hoping she would not cause Biddy distress.

"Dear Ivor." Biddy's eyes were filed with love not sadness. "Even to the very end, we had an incredible life together, never losing the passion emotionally or physically that we first had. Do you remember the day you caught us in the hayloft of the barn?"

"I still have the scar on my back where I fell off the ladder when spying on you, and the two of you had to rush me off to the village nurse in Kenmore."

"We always kept the love we found that day, and the love stays with me even now. It was something very unique and has made going on possible. He died quickly, you know, within ten days. He was there and then suddenly gone. For a long time, I expected him to come back through the kitchen door, as if nothing had happened."

Elspeth thought of Tay Farm, which had been so much a part of her childhood. The farm was nestled in the pastures that touched the southern side of Loch Tay in the Scottish Highlands. The rambling farmhouse had been expanded into a manor house by Elspeth and Biddy's three times great-grandfather, the fifth Earl of Tay, but it had fallen into disrepair during their grandfather's time. The current Earl of Tay, Biddy's brother Johnnie, had no interest in the farm and had willingly given its care over to Biddy and Ivor Baillie Shaw on their marriage.

Biddy continued, obviously happy to discuss Ivor and the farm, "The farm became part of us and still every day I find his spirit there, when I enter the barn, or feed the chickens, or tend to the sheep. You look startled, 'Peth, that I am not the forlorn widow. I miss his physical presence, yes, particularly during the long nights in the winter, but he is there with me all the time. When I deal with the books, work with the farm hands, or arrange for the sale of the lambs, he is there as well, speaking with me, laughing, and loving me. I feel sustained by him every hour of the day, although often at night I wish he really was there, and that we could share a drink, eat together and then go upstairs together. Am I being too frank about our relationship? Life on a farm is always fairly basic."

Elspeth was glad for the intervention of the waiters bringing the ravioli, as Biddy's words bit deeply into her own failures in life, her lack of an enduring loving relationship with a man, and the solidity of a permanent home. Biddy, dressed in Wellington boots, disreputable corduroys, and one of Ivor's old waxed jackets, driving a decrepit Land Rover and delighting in tending to her animals, had been given a gift that had eluded Elspeth all her life.

Elspeth was surprised by Biddy's frankness but, because of it, was aware that Biddy was no longer the silly girl of their childhood. Her love of Ivor had changed her and made her a person of more depth than Elspeth had expected. Elspeth liked Biddy better for it.

During the pasta course, they chatted about their respective children, a topic where Elspeth felt less bothered by the comparison between her life and Biddy's. All five of their children had been launched successfully into adulthood much to their respective mothers' relief and delight. Conversation flowed easily, the ravioli was served seamlessly, and the second course proved as delectable as the first.

Biddy took her first bites of the chicken and, after declaring it up to expectation in an affected tone for the room to hear, returned her attention to her cousin. "Now, 'Peth, I will hold you to your word, and you will share everything, I hope."

Elspeth was puzzled. "Share what?"

"What happened between you and Alistair?"

Elspeth swallowed abruptly. "Nothing happened, and it happened less and less. Finally there was nothing there."

Biddy looked up at her cousin, and Elspeth evaded her eyes.

Elspeth set her jaw and hoped to make things sound better than they actually were.

"We just drifted apart. Alistair's career had become so important that it finally consumed him. He was in great demand both in Hollywood and on sets in the most exotic places around the world. When he was home in California, he would leave at four in the morning and then stay on set until late into the evening to be available for any change in the script or retake of a scene. He would make sure everything was ready for the next day's shooting or would talk with the actors at the end of the day, advising them how they could improve their fighting techniques if he saw a flaw. Then there were the parties, often silly, drunken, drug-filled events that I abhorred. There was no place there for me. I wasn't one of them nor did I want to be."

"Oh, 'Peth, Ivor and I never knew. You should have asked for help."

Elspeth drew her head up and looked into Biddy's eyes, which were the same cobalt blue as her own.

"Would that have been like me?" she asked.

"No," admitted Biddy.

"I count my life quite successful, you know," Elspeth bristled and then conceded, "except perhaps in the realm of men."

Biddy sat quietly and finally reached out and touched her cousin's hand, which was kneading a bit of warm herbed bread into a glutinous mass.

"Is it still Malcolm?" Biddy said almost inaudibly.

Biddy and Ivor had been married the summer Elspeth came home from Girton, a constricted form of her former self, mourning the loss of her first love, Malcolm Buchanan. Elspeth had not gone to their wedding, instead endlessly wandering grief stricken by the burns and on the braes that surrounded her family home on Loch Rannoch.

Elspeth held the tears in her eyes as best she could. "Damn, Biddy. Why can't I let it go?"

Biddy held on to Elspeth's hand. "To everything there is a season, and a time to every purpose under the heaven . . . a time to mourn . . . a time to love and a time to hate," quoted Biddy. "I don't think you have really taken the time to mourn, 'Peth."

"Haven't I? I think I mourn just about every day and for what? You didn't know I was so maudlin, did you?" Elspeth smiled at her own irony.

"They never found out who murdered Malcolm, did they?"

"No, I think it would be easier if they had, and then I would have had my time to love but also my time to hate."

"Elspeth, you should find someone else to love."

"Should I? At my age? Who?"

After bidding her cousin goodnight Elspeth returned to her room, had a long hot bath, found a favorite pair of silk pajamas and prepared for the night. She lay sleepless for a long time. Finally she rolled her body into a ball and tried to forget.

16

The dampness of the air gusting up from the lake brought a blush to Elspeth's cheeks and helped to hide the signs of her restless sleep the night before. Although seldom up at such an early hour, Elspeth had not been content to lie in bed once she was awake and no longer could keep her mind still. A sleepy doorman acknowledged her exit from the hotel, leaned back against a pillar of the porte-cochère and closed his eyes. Nothing this morning was amiss at the doorway of the Kennington Stresa.

Elspeth preferred walking to jogging and debated which route to take. She realized that, but for her short ride to the police station with Franca the day before, she had not left the hotel since she had arrived. The morning's level of visibility made close-by objects more tantalizing than the unseen. Elspeth made her way across from the entry to the hotel to the small park she had noticed when she arrived. She skirted the puddles in the street and placed her feet carefully on the cobblestones. The metal picketed gate to the park was unlocked and screeched at Elspeth's intrusion. No hand seemed to have tended the park in recent days. A rusty rake had fallen between an iron bench and a statue of a piping faun that had lost one of its horns.

Elspeth stepped over a pile of wet leaves and reached out to touch a clump of rose hips that hung from a thorny and almost leafless branch. This reminder of past beauty attracted her. Had she not bent over to touch the seedpods, she would have missed the fresh hole in the sturdy base of the rose bush. She crouched down and examined her find. A bullet had entered into the thick lower trunk of the old bush at an angle. Elspeth traced the wound in the tree. When tracked back to its origin, the bullet's trajectory suggested that it had been fired from the north wing of the Kennington hotel. So this is the final resting place of the third bullet, the one not mentioned in the press, she thought. Had the bullet been fired before Marco Celli was killed in order to test the trajectory and, therefore, not heard together with the other two? She must ask Will where exactly on the roof he had found the casings, which he had told her about after she returned from the police station.

Elspeth kicked some of the wet leaves around the base of the rosebush and hoped that the next shower would obliterate the evidence of her cover-up. She jumped as she heard the squeal of the gate.

Will Tuttle, in jogging gear, sweating slightly and carrying a large digital camera, made his way toward her. Elspeth let out a short breath, visible in the cold air.

Will held up his camera and said merrily, "I always carry this on my morning run. I find in the early hours I can catch the effects of the light bathing the old buildings in a city center before the business of the day has begun. I find pathos not only in the deserted streets but also hope in the anticipation of the day ahead."

The ordinariness of his voice calmed Elspeth. Fumbling for words, she said, "You enjoy your camera, don't you," although the answer was clear.

"Completely. It makes me pay attention to the details. You've no idea how often I've used this habit in my work. This morning I looked up at the rooftops of the hotel and wondered about the assassin."

"I hope you use the word assassin only with me."

"Elspeth, I become more and more convinced that the killing was both carefully planned and brilliantly executed. From what you've said, the police remain clueless. Do they even suspect who the bullets were meant for?"

"Marco Celli, of course," Elspeth said, more from hope than conviction. "But, why would the murderer choose the rooftop of the hotel, and how would he get there? If things were carefully planned, how would the killer know that Marco would appear outside the hotel that afternoon?" Elspeth frowned and puffed out another frosty breath.

"Are you ruling out the large car that reportedly went through the cross-section when Marco was killed? *The Guardian*'s Italian edition reported one."

Elspeth made a quick decision, although she would have preferred to keep Will in the dark. "I must swear you to secrecy. You saw proof of where the second bullet went in the car park. It's of critical importance that no one else knows, not even Mandy, Franca, or the police—at this point anyway. The life of a young woman who does not deserve to die is at stake. I urge you to forget the large car or that it has anything to do with the shooting and the murder of Marco Celli."

"Of course," he said.

Elspeth did not mention the location of bullet number three.

"Did you find Marco Celli's hotel on your morning jog?" she asked, changing the topic.

He nodded. "I think so. Several fans were laying flowers," he said. "Why do young women do such silly things?"

Elspeth did not answer him but instead said, "Now let's set in motion the plan for you to take Mandy to Marco's hotel to ask about its suitability for your film. You might enquire if any film stars have stayed there. Who knows where the conversation will lead, particularly if you let Mandy unleash all her many allures."

Will laughed out loud, and the dozing doorman straightened up and looked out into the mist.

Will left the garden, but Elspeth lingered. After several moments of reflection, she turned and retreated into the hotel in order to avoid sinking into self-doubt. She hoped Richard's upcoming visit would revive her spirits.

*

Amanda Bell woke slowly and was aware of the lingering musky scent of Toria Albi's perfume in her room. Mandy thought of the strangeness of Toria's words the afternoon before. "May I come again? I feel safe here." They were small and tender words and filled Mandy with the girlhood feelings she had had for several emaciated kittens in an Egyptian bazaar. She still remembered that her father had said that kittens had no place on an archeological dig.

She chose clothes that might be suitable for the interpreter of a Hollywood scout: a mini skirt, white silk blouse that revealed a bit of cleavage, a short green jacket, and large emerald-colored earrings. While she dressed, she wondered how she could make contact with Vittoria again. Elspeth had suggested that Mandy could propose an outing to her new friend, a place close by where they might have some privacy to continue talking. Recalling her childhood excursions with her Italian family, Mandy thought of Villa Taranto. The villa's extensive gardens would be an excellent venue for filming and was one that a Hollywood scout would probably visit on his tour of the Italian Lakes, although it did not exactly fit in with Mandy's vision of a film set in the Second World War. In the end, she did not care because the grounds offered secluded places where they might talk privately. If Will came with them, would the film star persona of Toria emerge, or would she cling to her new friendship with Mandy?

Mandy called Will's room and found him there. He said he was just returning from his run and had briefly seen Elspeth. They arranged to meet at nine for breakfast.

When Will took his place beside Mandy at her table, Mandy was puzzling over how to approach Vittoria if she and her mother appeared in the breakfast room, but the likelihood of that was slim. Mandy was not prepared when Vittoria, alone and with a large silk scarf wrapped around her head, walked into the dining room and came over to Will and Mandy's table.

"Amanda," she whispered in English, "I enjoyed yesterday so much. Let's do it again. My mother will be down at any moment, and I will not be able to talk when she arrives. Meet me in the business room off the main lobby at two o'clock. My mother would never go there. She has arranged for a private table for breakfast. I must go so she will not see us."

The duchess, or at least Mandy assumed the small, purple-clad woman with large dark glasses was the duchess, appeared at that moment. Toria Albi turned and followed her mother to a table in an alcove that was not visible to most of the other guests having breakfast. Mandy could see only the duchess's back and one arm. She was aggressively gesturing toward her daughter.

Mandy called Will's attention to the duchess. "Look at her. Is she a dragon lady or what? Let's listen in."

Will frowned. "I can't see them, and besides they're speaking in Italian."

"Oh," Mandy said and screwed up her face. "I forgot you don't understand. I go back and forth between the languages without thinking. Sorry, Will. I'll try to stay more focused on my role as your interpreter. Do you want to know what they are saying?"

Mandy could only marginally hear the conversation between Toria and her mother and translated what she heard for Will. Their words centered on what was appropriate to eat for breakfast and an admonishment to stay inconspicuous. Mandy speculated that if they truly wished to stay inconspicuous they might have donned less of a disguise. Most guests were dressed for a casual day's touring, not in large headscarves, dark glasses, or funereal clothing.

*

Elspeth asked Franca Donatello to instruct the headwaiter in the breakfast room to call if the duchess and her daughter came down to eat. Elspeth was waiting with Biddy in her suite. They planned to make their entrance into the breakfast room and to be seated within view of the duchess. After the call came, Elspeth and Biddy went downstairs and walked together into the room. After they were seated, Will came over to their table and greeted "Ms. Duff" and "Lady Elisabeth" in tones that were designed for the duchess's hearing. The duchess turned her head toward Biddy, who acknowledged the look with a brief smile. This time Biddy did not overplay her part. The bait had been cast.

Elspeth and Biddy returned to Biddy's suite after breakfast. Biddy flounced on a sofa. "So that is the duchess. She's much smaller than I supposed." Biddy sounded as if she were describing a dead fish rather than an Italian duchess and film star's mother. "Besides, with her shrouded in all those widow's weeds, one really had to take notice. Who wears that sort of thing nowadays? Rather silly, I think. Ivor would have laughed buckets at me if I had!" She began to snigger.

"Biddy, be kind. You'll have to acknowledge her widowhood when you make her acquaintance. That's your job."

"There had to be a rub in this whole assignment," Biddy croaked through laughter. "All right, 'Peth. I'll be on my most proper behavior, I promise. I'll make sure Grandmother Tay's ghost approves. Do you have any suggestions on how I can make the duchess's acquaintance?"

"Here's my plan," her cousin said. "The duchess now knows you are here, and I could not help but notice that she kept looking your way at breakfast. Now that Marco is dead, she must be relaxing her vigilance and be more willing to venture out of her suite. I suggest you plant yourself in the main lounge. You can write postcards, read tour guides or simply enjoy a cup of mid-morning tea. I hope you don't wash away in tea by the end of the morning. You know Eric has his tea especially grown in Sri Lanka and India and imports it to all his hotels," Elspeth said as if in consolation.

"Do you think she will come down from her suite? Am I such a good lure?" Biddy sounded doubtful. "Perhaps we will meet in the loo if I continue to drink tea, good as it is."

Elspeth chuckled and silently hoped that Biddy would not be in the ladies' room when the duchess appeared. "I need to return to the office now, so must be off. Good luck, Biddy."

"Do I need it?" Biddy looked cast adrift.

"No, probably not. Unlike other languages, English really lacks a pithy way to say 'may things fall in your favor.' That's what I meant."

A Scandal in Stresa

Leaving Biddy and before visiting Carlo and Silvia, Elspeth decided to go outside and look up at the rooftops that Will had described to her earlier.

The morning mist had now risen, and the sun came and went at its own pleasure. The entrance to the hotel was still in shadow, and there were new puddles on the pavement, vestiges of a recent shower.

Elspeth walked outside to where she could see beyond the hotel. The protective balustrade of the hotel's roof stood stolidly against the sky. She circled the building, going down the street to the rear entrance of the car park below and back up alongside the outdoor terrace, but no apocalyptic revelation presented itself. Dissatisfied with her surveillance but anxious to be available for Carlo and Silvia when the call came from the kidnapper, Elspeth went back into the hotel. She saw Biddy in her finery sitting in the lobby perusing a large foldout map and ignoring a cup of tea. Biddy winked as Elspeth passed.

17

Carlo was dressing in his room when the room service attendant arrived with breakfast and handed him a note from Elspeth Duff. *The launch will be at your service all day long. Ring me on my mobile, and I will send instructions to Sandro Liu. In the meantime contact me if you need anything else,* it read.

Silvia found the note reassuring. She propped it in front of Carlo's coffee cup and willed herself to be still. The next few hours would pass slowly, but neither she nor Carlo wanted to be distracted by other things. Silently she prayed to the Virgin for Constanza's safety and release. The prayer gave her a momentary sense of serenity.

At breakfast Carlo and Silvia sat in silence. Their attempts at passing the time by talking failed. She not could keep her mind focused on anything except the hour. Time slows down when one is waiting, she thought. Her mobile phone lay on the coffee table between them, the digital time display slowly changing second by second. They had decided that Carlo would answer the phone, rather than Silvia, although she had taken the initial call from the man. Silvia had set her phone so the conversation would be recorded.

They watched the large numbers on the phone roll over to 11:00:00 and waited. Slowly the seconds and minutes passed until the screen read 11:05:00. Silvia had seen Carlo use this tactic before in business transactions and understood that if the kidnapper wanted to gain advantage, he would call later than the designated time.

"Be patient, Silvia. He will call," Carlo said.

Silvia nodded. Her hands were trembling. She shoved them under the blanket that covered her knees, but she knew Carlo had seen them.

Carlo waited and answered the phone on the fourth ring. His hands, like Silvia's, were unsteady, and he had trouble punching the button for an incoming call; he pressed on the speakerphone. His voice was dry when has said *"Pronto."*

The voice on the other end was hard to understand even if there had been no static. The words were in English but the accent was heavy. In her mind Silvia translated the l's into r's.

"Mister Bartelli. Your daughter safe and returned to you if you pay one million euro. Tomorrow at one o'clock in afternoon you go to big house of Borromeo on island in Lake Maggiore. In garden you go to small house where birds live. Put money in box and leave it back of building. You go away very fast."

Carlo closed his eyes as if trying to make sure he understood. Finally he asked the ultimate question, "When will I see my daughter?"

There was long pause on the other end. "You do what I say. No police. Only you. No other people."

"I want to speak to Constanza. I want to know that she is alive." Carlo's voice sounded commanding rather than pleading.

"She alive now. Tomorrow she alive if money OK. We watch you now. No police. Alone only." The voice and the static ceased. The connection went dead.

Carlo said *"pronto, pronto"* into the phone several times. His anxious eyes met Silvia's.

In a hushed tone she said, "At least she is alive."

"If he is speaking the truth," Carlo said handing her the mobile. "Here, take this. See if you can write out what he said from the recording." He grimaced and shook his head.

Silvia took the phone and played back the recording. She listened to it several times before attempting to write out what the voice had said. Finally she took out her laptop and after several tries recorded the conversation fully. Silvia printed out the conversation on the travel printer she had brought from Rome.

Carlo took the copy as if it were a lifeline to his daughter.

"Is this real, Silvia? Not just something Constanza cooked up?" he said as she handed him the transcript.

"Yes, Carlo, I think it is real. If Constanza had been in control, if she were trying to get money from us, the voice would have allowed her to speak, to plead with us." Silvia hunched down in her wheelchair and shook her head.

"Do you think if she did not speak it means she is dead? My beautiful Constanza," Carlo asked.

Silvia put a reassuring hand on his. "No, Carlo, not our Constanza. I can't tell you why, but I don't think she's dead. If she were, how would the caller know we are here in Stresa, and why send Constanza's diary to me rather than you? Only Constanza could have known I would be with you."

"I think we need help now. Do you think I am wrong to ask Ms. Duff? I feel I can trust her."

"Have we any other choice?" Silvia said.

Carlo reached for the phone.

18

Will had had only a day in London to prepare for his assignment in Stresa and had used that time to gather the props for his shallow cover as a Hollywood scout. He produced business cards on his computer, hoping they would at least pass a cursory examination. They read:

will@touchmarkca.net

William C. Tuttle
Greystone Scouts
A Division of Touchmark Productions

100 Touchmark Boulevard, Suite A
Universal City, California 91608

Will had made certain a search on the internet would reveal a website that would give a message saying the site was "down for updating; please try again later." He had a friend who could do that sort of thing. Will thought he needed the card to establish his credentials, at least superficially.

Will laid out a gray suit and unfolded a heavily starched dark blue shirt from its wrapper. He dressed carefully and tied a boldly checked, multicolored tie he bought on a whim in the States earlier that year. He took special care with his cropped sandy hair, using gel and fashioning several short spikes. He rummaged in his case for a pair of narrow wire-framed glasses. Putting them on, he admired his transformation in the mirror. He smiled at himself, winked and hoped Mandy would take notice.

In the lobby, he found Mandy, folded into a comfortable chair in a nook by the door and reading a glossy fashion magazine. When she saw him, her smile assured him that she approved. He sat down across from her and attempted to look serious.

She cocked a skeptical eyebrow at him, and he broke into a grin. Our assignment is going to be more difficult than I expected, he thought to himself, with Mandy being such a distraction. She was dressed for the outdoors in a three-quarter-length, coffee-colored leather jacket that barely allowed her skirt to show below. She had tied back her luxuriant auburn hair with a green scarf that matched her eyes and her earrings. Her long legs were wrapped in dark brown tights, and her high-heeled boots thwarted any misconception that she was trying to disguise her already tall height.

Will directed the taxi to the Umberto Primo Hotel, the opulent Victorian structure that sat opposite the promenade along the lake where Will had seen the fans. During the short taxi ride, Will outlined his strategy.

Mandy caught on immediately, and, by the time the taxi entered the cobblestone drive lined with lawn and multi-colored flowerbeds, she said she was ready for action. Mandy took the portfolio Will supplied for her and put on the thin, oblong-shaped horn-rimmed glasses that she had in her handbag. She approached the concierge's desk, and, by plan and with many hand gestures, explained in rapid Italian who

Will was, or was posing to be, and the nature of their business. The concierge took up a desk phone and called the manager.

Having reconnoitered the outside of the hotel on his morning jog, Will was not surprised that the exterior Victorian embellishments were echoed on the inside. The lobby's high ceilings were filigreed and dotted with large glass chandeliers, moldings festooned bas-relief garlands, and walls covered in red damask. Enormous gilded mirrors with sconces for candles, vestiges of a grander era, looked as if they were still hanging where they had been placed in the eighteen nineties. Unlike the Kennington Stresa, the furniture in the lobby looked imposing but uncomfortable. Nobody was lounging there except the odd businessman. A couple sat stiffly on an ornate settee and was engaged in a hushed disagreement. The Umberto Primo Hotel suited Will's mission exactly. Had Marco Celli chosen a less flamboyant venue, Will's cover story might be less plausible.

The manager, dressed in a tight-fitting black suit and a pinned-on smile, emerged through a hidden door and rushed toward Mandy. He stood half a meter shorter than she, shod as she was, and bounced up and down on his toes as he welcomed her in a string of excited words. Mandy looked down at him through her glasses, responded with tones of importance and motioned toward Will. Will thought Mandy was overdoing it, but the manager did not notice. He came over and pumped Will's hand exuberantly.

"As Miss Bell may have told you . . ." Will started. Mandy began a simultaneous translation.

"*Prego, signore*, please. I speak English. Your charming assistant will not need to translate."

Mandy impatiently tapped a pen on her portfolio. "Mr. Tuttle is a very busy man," she said.

Will made eye contact with Mandy and hoped she would pick up his signal to modify her act, which he felt bordered on farce.

With the slightest of nods toward Will, she spoke again. "Is there a room where we might speak to you less publicly?"

Now that the arguing couple had disappeared and the businessmen had gone, the lobby was deserted and would have served Will's needs perfectly, but the manager directed the concierge to bring coffee to a small sitting room just off the public space.

"Miss Bell," Will said before following the man into the smaller room, "with the manager's permission, survey the lobby for me and see if it will meet our needs."

"Of course, Mr. Tuttle."

"Especially see if it would be appropriate for the scene between Alec and Merle."

"Yes, of course."

The manager adjusted his black tie and cleared his throat. "Alec Baldwin and Merle Streep?" he gasped.

Will put his finger to his lips. "I think we need to talk about your terms first."

*

Will followed the manager out of the lobby, and the rest of their conversation was lost. Acting on the instructions Will had given her in the taxi, Mandy lingered behind and approached the concierge.

"Bully," she said in Italian. "You know these Hollywood types. They think they are only slightly less important than the Holy Father."

The concierge looked around furtively to see if the lobby was still empty. Seeing no one, he relaxed.

"Do you really work in Hollywood?" he asked.

"When we aren't traveling. Mr. Tuttle's job is to find places to film scenes on location in upcoming movies. We're looking for a grand hotel here in Stresa where celebrities and film stars might stay. This place may work."

Mandy opened her portfolio, gripped her pen, and made sure her jacket fell open revealing her half-buttoned blouse. The concierge's eyes widened with pleasure.

"We have celebrities here from time to time. In fact, last week the actor Marco Celli was here."

Mandy took off her glasses and opened wide her green eyes. "Really? Not the one who was murdered? Did you see him?"

"Often."

"Was he as sexy as the tabloids say?"

The concierge chuckled. "I'm the wrong gender to comment. The ladies, well, they found him very attractive."

"Did he have a lady with him?"

"Not staying with him, but in and out." The concierge made a motion with his hand like a swinging door.

"I suppose after his divorce . . ." Mandy let her words hang in the air.

"I hardly would call it a divorce. You see, one of the ladies in and out was La Toria."

Mandy was genuinely surprised. Toria Albi had spoken yesterday of still being in love with Marco, but she had not mentioned seeing him in Stresa.

"You are shocked, *signorina*. I would think this would not raise an eyebrow in Hollywood."

"Hollywood is not a Catholic place," Mandy extemporized.

"Perhaps La Toria learned a thing or two when she was there."

"Are you sure it was Toria Albi?"

"Absolutely. I have . . ." He cleared his throat, "I have admired her since I was a boy. The headscarf and dark glasses hid nothing. She would come in the backdoor near our staff break room and go up to his room. Several hours afterwards, she would tiptoe out. It definitely was her. She came only in the afternoons. In the evening there were others too, but not always the same ones."

"Then he did live up to his reputation."

"Definitely. What staying power! I should have been exhausted with that schedule." He grinned at Mandy, who drew a long face.

"Have the police been here? Do they know?"

"Yes, they've swarmed all over the place and questioned us all."

"I suppose the other women were desperate housewives," Mandy suggested.

The concierge snorted. "More like traveling businesswomen wanting their night away from home."

"Are you sure?"

"When we stand here all day long, little escapes us. You see, we are invisible to the guests, unless they need something. This job is perfect if you like watching people. The women, *ha*, many are so beautiful." He rolled his eyes up with pleasure filling his face. "*Signorina*, like you."

"I am here on business and should not be gossiping. Now tell me about the hotel," Mandy retorted, feeling she had elicited more personal attention from the concierge than she had originally planned.

He turned back to his desk, rustled through some papers and brought out a three-fold pamphlet. "*Sì*, we are both workers. What a pity." His voice changed, becoming stilted.

A Scandal in Stresa

"The hotel has quite a long history, back to the days of the railroad and the grand tours. Here, this should explain it."

Mandy took the brochure.

"Mr. Tuttle will be out shortly, and I'm sure he will want to take photographs."

Having extracted the information Will had wanted, she left the concierge and wandered around the cavernous lobby. She found a chair in front of an ornate marble-topped writing desk and opened her portfolio. After looking round the room, she started making notes. She recorded her conversation with the concierge as completely as possible while pretending to assess the appropriateness of the interior design. She looked up occasionally at the concierge who grinned at her each time. She did not reciprocate. When Will reappeared, she slapped the portfolio shut and rose to meet him. She was glad to end her charade.

*

Will suggested that they walk along the lakeshore before going back to the hotel and waved off the doorman's offer to hail a taxi for them. A passing shower had crisped the air, and numerous couples strolled along the promenade. Water dripped from the large leaves of the hydrangeas that bordered the walk, and gulls circled down from the top of one of the memorial statues to look for fresh grubs in the neatly tended gardens. Will tucked Mandy's arm under his, and, humming a drinking song hailing the virtues of both love and wine, he propelled them out of earshot of the hotel.

Laughing, he said, "You looked quite uncomfortable in there. Did he make a pass at you?"

Mandy chortled. "I think he would have liked to, but probably his job, wife, and children were more important."

Will covered her hand with his and walked on happily. They skirted several small puddles in the brick paving before Will stopped and leaned up against the heavy marble balustrade that lined the lake. He was instantly sorry he had because it was still wet from the rain. He flushed, hoping Mandy would not notice.

"Tell me what you learned in there?" he asked.

"I wrote it down as accurately as I could." She tapped the portfolio under her arm and smiled at Will. "I'll let you read it when we are back at the hotel. Basically, our friend Marco was leading a flagrant and non-celibate life, including afternoon assignations with his former wife and evening flings with many willing women travelers."

Forgetting the wetness of the back of his clothes, Will turned to face Mandy, "What sort of women?"

"He indicated they mainly were businesswomen. Is it important, Will?"

"Maybe. The police must have made a list of the guests, and they may be investigating them now. Are you sure he didn't mention any morning activities?"

"I'm not terribly well-versed in these things," Mandy said. "I haven't . . . er . . . had any first-hand experience with, how would you put it, multi-partnering." Her face reddened furiously.

"Thank God for His many blessings," said Will, taking her arm again.

They decided to walk along the back streets that lead up the hill to the Kennington Stresa. As they approached the cobblestone drive to the hotel, Will realized they were standing near the spot where Marco Celli had died.

"How does all we learned today put Marco outside the Kennington hotel at four o'clock in the afternoon on the day he died?" he asked pensively.

"Watching Toria?" Mandy suggested without any indication she knew the significance of the spot where they stood.

"I don't think so. They already seemed to have an arrangement. What else could have brought him here?

Why, he thought, was someone up on the roof waiting to shoot Marco? It did not make sense unless the bullets were not meant for him but instead for the occupants of the large black car.

19

Although Will was pleased that Mandy had arranged an assignation with Toria Albi, he had misgivings about his part in it. He felt his pose as a location scout for Hollywood was flimsy. He had only visited one studio on a brief visit to Los Angeles when he was in school in America and was more awed with the size of the studio than with its functioning. He wondered how much he could bluff to make his assumed role believable to a film star. After returning to the hotel, he sought out Elspeth Duff, who he knew had previous connections to the world of American cinema.

He found Elspeth in her suite, but, on seeing her, he hoped he had not disturbed her. Her face was drawn, and she looked worried. After offering him a seat, she did not sit down with him but instead went to the window and looked out, as if the view to the mountains would give her an answer she was seeking. Will noticed a half-drunk cup of coffee on a beautifully set tray on the sideboard. She obviously was preoccupied, but she listened to what he had to say. She was not surprised at the information he gave her about Marco Celli or his doubts about the intended victim of the shots from the roof. He then broached his upcoming meeting with Toria Albi.

She smiled sympathetically at his lack of ease.

"Will, believe me, most of the people peripheral to the filmmaking industry act as if they are more important than they really are. Location scouts can be real authorities, friends of the producer, someone who wants to inveigle their way into the business, or outright frauds. Toria will quickly uncover that you have not done this sort of work before, but she may be flattered into giving a first-time location scout pointers on choosing a site. My advice to you would be to play up your novice status and appeal to her professionalism."

Will made a face. "Why is it that I have never considered Toria Albi as a professional?"

"You should have. She may not be the world's greatest actor, but she's a seasoned star and has produced some recognized work both as a comedienne and as a dramatic actress. Her films may not be to your or my taste, but she has a certain degree of success that cannot be overlooked. Female actors with her physical features cannot make it on anatomy alone. She's probably more intelligent than her directors wish to show on the screen. Therefore I suggest that you tell her how pleased you are that Mandy has made her acquaintance because you really would like to have her opinion on the site. I'll bet she takes the bait."

"I'll try," he said, not convinced he could succeed.

"Will, use your sex appeal."

"Sex appeal? I don't . . ."

"Ask Mandy if you do or don't. I think she will be straight with you."

Leaving Elspeth's suite with more confidence than when he first came in, Will went to find Mandy. He considered Elspeth's ploy and, since he could think of no other way to handle the situation, decided to adopt it.

*

Just before two o'clock, Amanda Bell made her way to the business center and, finding it empty, logged on to one of the computers and checked her email. Her mother had sent her a photograph of her father, his long legs straddling a donkey. Mandy was chuckling over it when Vittoria Albi entered the room. In delight, Mandy motioned to Toria and showed her the image.

Toria's face, behind the large sunglasses, broke into one of her famous smiles. "*Cara*, you love your father, yes?"

"Yes. He's a marvelous person."

Toria took off her glasses, shoved them in one of the pockets of her Burberry and put her hand up to a large, dewy eye. Mandy could not decide if this was a practiced gesture or genuine one.

Toria's voice cracked. "My father died when I was eighteen, but I loved him too. He was full of life and loved every minute of every day. He was killed when the brakes on his car failed on the Amalfi Drive. Do you know it?"

"I've driven it. What a gorgeous road. My passenger, however, was a bit perturbed by the curves and was quite impolite about my driving skills." Mandy did not concede that perhaps her passenger had a point.

Toria seated herself with dramatic grace in the chair next to Mandy, turned her head up in a slow twisting motion and sighed. "It's one of the most beautiful but dangerous roads in Italy. My father, like you, loved its challenge. They said afterwards someone had tampered with the brakes of his car, but no one could ever prove it. My mother blamed one of his lovers. That was unkind, but my mother is a very jealous woman. When he died, my father and she were living apart, so why should she have cared?"

"I'm sorry," Mandy said, swiveling around and looking into the sadness in the eyes behind the exquisitely applied mascara on Vittoria's lashes. "It must have been very hard for you."

Toria nodded. "*Sì*. My mother and father always fought about me before Mamma left him. My mother wanted me to be a film star; my father wanted me to be happy." This time Toria's tears were real.

Mandy leaned over and put her hand on the one Toria had stretched out along the arm of a nearby chair. "Have you ever felt happiness, being a film star I mean?" she asked.

Toria's face brightened, and she brushed the tears off her cheek. "Of course. I should not complain as much as I do. Being a film star is glorious most of the time. I am sad because I have been alone for many days with my mother in the same rooms here at this hotel, and I don't like being divorced and in hiding."

Mandy saw her opening and took it. "Then you must escape. Come with us this afternoon to Villa Taranto—with Will, my boss, and me. He thinks it will be a wonderful place for a film, and certainly you will be as good a judge as anyone as to how right he is. Your mother can't object if we're careful about it."

Vittoria Albi smiled again but with the joy of a small girl who has been offered a trip to the ice cream shop. "I would like that, yes, very much. When do we leave?"

"As soon as we can. Now." Mandy checked her watch. "Will is waiting for me and will be delighted to have you along. *Andiamo*, let's go."

La Toria pushed back her magnificently coiffed head and giggled like a schoolgirl. "Let me get my scarf, so no one will recognize me." Saying this, she made her exit.

Mandy brought the BMW around under the portecochère, where she saw Will and Vittoria waiting just outside the door and chatting with each other. The doorman stood at attention like a wooden soldier, but his eyes were round with admiration for the much-concealed film star. Seeing Mandy's car come round the bend, he jumped into action and swept open the door for Toria. She smiled as she would have to a fan and lowered herself with studied elegance into the front bucket seat. Mandy leaned over to Vittoria, pulled the seat belt around her, and gave her a kiss on the cheek. Will opened the back door without assistance and arranged his long body as comfortably as he could. The doorman closed the car door behind him and gave them a little salute.

"I see you have met Will," Mandy said in Italian.

"He's very charming. I already like him!" Vittoria responded in English.

In her rearview mirror Mandy could see Will blush and straighten his tie. "*Signorina*, I . . ." he started.

"You must call me Vittoria. My friends call me that, and, Mr. Will, I think you will be my friend."

Mandy chuckled to herself to see him react to Vittoria's seduction. All for the best, she thought. With great exuberance, Mandy steered the car out on to the narrow street and hummed a happy, tuneless tune. Careening down the hill toward the town center, she cried, "Let us escape from the walls of our captive hotel and see what real delights we can find."

She turned around to look at Will and heard a gasp from both her passengers. She focused her attention back on the road and dodged a delivery van parked halfway up the curb.

"Why would he park in such an idiotic place as that," she said nonchalantly. "Will, I can guarantee that Villa Taranto is one of the most beautiful spots in Italy and will not disappoint you. It was one of my favorite places when I was a child."

Vittoria stretched out her hand and clutched the handle on the dashboard. She turned to Will. "Mr. Will, tell me about your film. Does it need a female star?"

"I bow to you, Toria Albi," he said. "I will tell the producer that you have helped me on my search for the perfect spot for the film. I don't know if he's selected the cast as yet."

Toria was not sidetracked, even when Mandy made a sudden left turn in front of an oncoming car. "Tell me more," Toria begged

"The producer told me he has a script about an intrigue in the papal court during the Renaissance that involves one of the Borromeo cardinals. He has asked me to visit the Borromean Islands but also to find a spot where the cardinal can meet his co-conspirators."

Mandy brought the car into line and broke in. "Vittoria, I know Villa Taranto would be perfect for the film. I am so glad you have come along to tell us what spots there will really work." Mandy hoped Toria had forgotten what Mandy had said about the film being set in the Second World War.

Toria relaxed slightly but kept her grip on the handle. "My mother has shut me up in our rooms for at least the last hundred days. It's wonderful to get out in the open. Once or twice I tiptoed out of the hotel room when my mother was having her nap after lunch, but she found out and was very angry with me. Mr. Will, my mother is . . . oh, never mind. It's just glorious to be out. Amanda, look at the hat on that woman. It is *bellissimo*. Pull over. I must ask her where she got it."

Mandy put her foot on the accelerator and swiveled around the next corner at breakneck speed. "Vittoria, we must keep a low profile. We don't want anyone to recognize you."

"Bah, Amanda. No one cares but my mother if I am recognized," Toria said.

Will broke in. "*Signorina* Vittoria, I hope we can go through the villa without being noticed because I don't want anyone to know what we are doing. If word got out that the famous Toria Albi was visiting the gardens with a Hollywood scout, we should not have a moment's peace."

"OK, *va bene*. You two are almost as bad as my mother, but I give in." Toria smiled her most photogenic grin, but she pulled up her scarf so that it hid more of her face. "Now you'll say I'm safe. I haven't felt safe for a long, long time."

Mandy negotiated the road out of Stresa with much derring-do. Vittoria was exhilarated but Will wary.

"After I became famous," said the star, "my mother would not let me drive. She said I must always protect myself, and she and *il duca*, my stepfather, always made sure someone was with me when I went out. That's why being married to Marco was so much fun. He drives, drove, like you and my father, Amanda. Every curve and intersection was a chance to show his skill. I loved the way Marco handled a car. It made me laugh, but I hung on until my knuckles became white. Is that how you say it?"

"Something like that," Will said. His hand was clutching the handle on the door in the backseat, and his knuckles had gone white.

Soon they all were laughing, enjoying an outing that had the air of an escape for all of them and sharing outrageous stories. Will told about riding on a wavering cart in India while trying to photograph water buffalo; Mandy told of a hideous encounter between her father's Land Rover and an asp on an Egyptian desert road; and Toria topped them all, recounting a tale of an ex-president of Italy who, standing in an open van during a hunting excursion at her stepfather's estate, was victim of an unexpected accident when her mother shot a grouse that fell on his head with the most unfortunate consequences.

A Scandal in Stresa

Will said he had called ahead and requested a private tour of the gardens, thus dispensing with having to buy tickets at the entry. When Will told the guard at the gate to the gardens who he was, the three of them passed through with an elegant *"prego"* on the part of the man. On the other side they found their guide, a professorial type who obviously had no idea who Toria Albi was nor had any curiosity as to why one of the people on his tour was so elegantly shrouded. Will was grateful for this and took both Toria and Mandy's arms as they ventured along the cobblestone avenue into the gardens. The *professore,* as they dubbed him, began his discourse on the gardens, speaking in Italian in a monotone uncharacteristic of that language. Mandy translated desultorily.

All three of his charges ceased listening and wandered to and fro among the complexity of the villa's gardens. They admired the fountains, the great trees that lined the formal layout of manicured grass, and the lush beds of begonias and impatiens. Mandy felt a dreamlike trance had covered them, as if they were taken up in the garden's spell and transported back to another time, where fame, murder, and overbearing mothers did not exist. The *professore* stopped his historical anecdotes and led them up the hill to places that were more intimate than the larger spaces below. Waterfalls spilled from the high vine-cover stonewalls, and small niches were hidden among the trees.

They came to an enclosed garden that they entered through an arbor covered with gnarled wisteria vines, and Toria expounded on its suitability because of the way a camera could shoot from various vantage points. She loosened her headscarf and showed her profile from several different angles. Suddenly the flash on a camera burst upon them. A voice cried, "It's La Toria!" Two more flashes, then a whole barrage of them.

Bugger! thought Mandy. This cannot be happening. Toria Albi's first reaction was to turn to the camera and flash a dentally perfect smile. Mandy grabbed Toria's arm, lowered her head and rammed through the line of the three photographers.

Will charged at them as well and began shouting, "Go away. Leave us alone." He encircled the two women with his long arms and began to run. Soon they had outdistanced the photographers and found a hiding place in one of the niches they had seen earlier. The *professore* did not follow.

The paparazzi fled down the hill and found no one there. By the time they reversed their course and headed back up the hill, Will lead Mandy and Vittoria into a back part of one of the public buildings and demanded a secluded room until the photographers were gone.

"*Signorina* Vittoria, we must get you out of here without them discovering where we are staying," he pleaded. "Otherwise, none of us will have any peace until they have found you and obtained their story."

"Bah. I hate these paparazzi. They hound me all the time. Don't they know I am grieving for Marco?"

Will was puzzled. "Grieving? I thought you had just divorced him. There's no time for us to discuss this now. We have to get back to the hotel undetected. Mandy, take Vittoria's scarf, glasses, raincoat, and handbag and run for the car. Head for any nearby hotel and leave you car with the valet parking attendant. Go into the hotel, shed your disguise, and have a cup of tea. When the paparazzi arrive, I fear they will be puzzled at seeing a tall Englishwoman enjoying a cuppa and teacakes. When you feel that you have been discarded by the paparazzi, come back to the hotel in Stresa by a roundabout route. Give me your jacket and hat for Vittoria. She and I are going to take a taxi in the other direction."

Mandy laughed as she jumped into the BMW and waved at the paparazzi, whose heads turned and cameras flashed. She sped off and soon saw they were in hot pursuit. Let them try to catch me, she thought. She sped through the late afternoon toward Verbania, remembering her aunt's favorite hotel where she had gone to have hot chocolate as a child. The clouds darkened, and she turned on her headlights. First the sky was filled with the sound of thunder, and then the rain began. Mandy turned on her wipers but did not slow her pace. The rain, now punctuated by flashes of lightning, became intense. Mandy cursed that she was not driving her own car, whose every subtle move she understood. The sky was now almost black and the rain coming down so densely that visibility decreased to almost nothing.

Mandy suddenly saw a three-wheeler in front of her and threw on her breaks. The ABS engaged but not soon enough. The BMW skidded and plowed into the wall that held back the hill from the lake. The car spun around and hit the guardrail on the other side of the road. Mandy's last recollection of what happened was her wondering how the paparazzi would report La Toria's demise.

20

Sandro Liu lifted Silvia Trucco carefully out of her chair and, in a well-balanced move, stepped over the side of the launch and deposited her on one of the cushioned seats at the stern. Then he reached up and brought her chair on board, folded it and put it by her side. He took her lap rug, shook it out and laid it across her knees, while trying not to touch her stick-like legs. He expected her to be grateful when she looked up at him, but, instead, he saw the same look of compassion Father Pietro had when he found the young Chinese boy huddled under the table not far from his parents' bodies twenty years before in Burma.

"Sandro," she said, "you have the touch of an angel. Thank you."

To hide his discomfort, he leaned over and made a final adjustment to the rug around her knees.

"*Signora.*" He could think of nothing more to say to her, sitting there with complete composure, as if their manner of boarding the launch were a daily activity in which they both took part. Carlo Bartelli had come aboard before them and was sitting under the canopy at the boat's controls and was watching Sandro tend to Silvia. When Silvia was settled, Carlo rose.

"Let me take the wheel, Sandro," he said, a command not a request. "I have done a bit of sailing in my time, and this launch looks tame enough."

Sandro knew the launch was easy to maneuver and therefore made no objection. Although clouds hugged the mountains, and there had been showers earlier, the wind had died down and the lake was calm. Carlo navigated the launch away from the jetty and set his course to the northeast. Sandro stowed the lines and joined Silvia.

"You must forgive Carlo for being brusque," she said as Sandro sat down next to her. "He has a great deal on his mind right now. He's going to Switzerland on important family business, and piloting the boat will help him concentrate on the task ahead."

Sandro looked up at Silvia Trucco and saw her finely wrought aristocratic features. Her gaze toward Carlo held softness, stillness, and caring that reminded Sandro of his own mother. When the families in his village were preparing for the onslaught by the Burmese military forces, she looked this way when she went from family to family, helping them as far as she could. Hiding while his mother was tending to others, Sandro was the only one to survive the massacre. He wondered why he remembered these events as they crossed the lake. What was there about this seemingly benign trip across Lake Maggiore that brought back those days in Burma? He was not sure.

The launch cut through the water with an even speed. Sandro could see Carlo was a skilled sailor. A slight wind rose, increasing the choppiness on the lake, but the launch's motor was powerful, and their progression across the lake was steady and uneventful. Only an occasional gust caught them sideways and caused a momentary shudder, but Carlo righted the craft without difficulty.

Silvia confessed to Sandro that she had sailed little and found the voyage thrilling. Strands of her hair blew across her forehead, and she laughed as she tried to contain them.

Sandro had made arrangements for docking in Locarno, and a berth was waiting for them. He lifted Silvia out of the boat with gentle care, and Carlo had her chair ready for her. Carlo said that, because they were early, they had enough time for lunch at a restaurant overlooking the lake. While eating, Silvia watched the activity in the marina with growing interest. "Carlo, you must get your own launch!" she cried. "I shall learn to assist you. Sandro will teach me."

After they finished lunch and were on their way to the city center by taxi, the mood among them changed. Carlo addressed Sandro. "I want Silvia and you to stay in the waiting room off the lobby of the bank. When I return from my meeting, I will be carrying a large amount of cash. The bank will be providing a guard to accompany me back to the launch. I will travel with the guard, and you and Silvia can take a taxi. Please talk to no one about our plans." His staccato orders left no room for doubt.

The bank manager greeted Carlo with a bear hug and challenged him. "Are you up to your old tricks again? When will we know what the great find will be this time? Come in. I will order some coffee for you and your young friend, *Signora* Silvia. You can wait for us down here."

Seeing that Silvia was comfortable, Sandro pulled up a chair near her. "He must come here often," he observed.

"*Sì*. Carlo is one of the true geniuses of our age at finding undiscovered masterpieces of art. The Lakes Region is famous for its art dealers, and, when they have a good piece, they call Carlo first because he pays them fairly and usually in cash. The bank manager is quite used to Carlo coming here and asking for large sums," she whispered.

"*Signora*, why do I feel that this time it's not a piece of art that Carlo is buying?"

Silvia smiled at him and put a long, manicured finger to her lips. "You are wise for someone so young." She did not say anymore.

A bank employee brought coffee on a silver tray and then left them alone. The coffee was made strong in the Italian way and served with fresh Swiss cream. They sipped it slowly, but, as the minutes went by, Sandro began to feel Silvia's nervousness.

"I've been instructed by Elspeth Duff to help *il signor* Bartelli and you in any way you need," he said, laying down his empty cup.

"Sandro, Carlo Bartelli is a man of many resources. The transaction he is about to make has serious consequences for him and for his family. In his dealings in the art world, he has always kept his plans under wraps. Occasionally he will share these plans with me, but usually he does not. You and I must wait until he asks for our assistance."

Sandro had been warned in Stresa that weather in the autumn on Lago Maggiore has sudden shifting moods that often catch the uninitiated sailor by surprise. By the time Carlo, Silvia and Sandro met at the launch, the winds had picked up, and the cloud cover had lowered. The Alps were no longer visible. Fog crept across the lake and greeted the passengers on the pier near the Kennington launch in forbidding silence.

"It looks like we may have some bad weather on the way back," Sandro said casually, although he was concerned. "No worry. The launch is equipped to handle the sudden storms that often come up on the lake, but it will take me about fifteen minutes to prepare for it. Will you, *signore e signora*, come on board while I do so, or would you prefer to wait at the marina station?"

Carlo had already dismissed the guard from the bank and looked anxious. He glared under his dark brows at Sandro and let out a grunt. "No, we must get on the boat immediately."

Sandro flinched at Carlo's tone and stood at attention. He swallowed hard and stared into space, as if anticipating another demand. None came.

Sandro stepped forward to carry Silvia into the boat. Again he was amazed at the lightness of her body and her soft touch when she put both her arms around his neck. He wanted to embrace her, the way he had his mother when he was a child, but held back as Carlo urged him to hurry. On Sandro's recommendation Silvia opted to take her seat in the cabin below to avoid the oncoming rain. Sandro lifted her down the few steps to the cabin and placed her fragile body in one of the armchairs that gave full view of the prow of the ship and the water beyond. Carlo followed them below, bringing a metal case with him.

"Silvia, I put this in your charge. Guard it well for Constanza. May the Virgin protect her—and us," he said.

"*Sì*, Carlo. Do you suppose she is near us now?"

Carlo shook his head and closed his eyes. "If God is with us, she will be looking out a window, will see us and will know we are here to protect her."

Sandro did not understand the meaning of these words but had the wit to ask nothing.

Carlo and Sandro left Silvia and climbed back to the deck. Silvia insisted they leave the door into the cabin open so she could see and hear them. The boat continued to rock steadily but with more agitation. Carlo drew in his breath and uttered a whispered prayer.

"Sandro, have you sailed in bad weather on this lake before?"

"No, *Signor* Bartelli, but I was raised on the sea and have sailed through many gales. I don't think a rainstorm on the lake could present any challenges I haven't met before."

"Then prepare the boat as quickly as possible before we leave. I am uncomfortable being up here and leaving Silvia alone with the case."

By the time Sandro had unrolled and secured the canvas flaps over the aft deck and checked all the hatches to make sure they were tightly closed, a steady rain had begun, and the wind was blowing relentlessly from the west.

"Are you sure, *signore*, that you do not want to remain in Locarno until the storm passes?" Sandro asked as he took the wheel.

"Is there any reason to?"

"Only for *la signora* Trucco's comfort. The sail back to Stresa will be rough."

Silvia must have overheard the conversation from below and called out her own opinion. "Sandro, I have always tried to make sure that my disability never hampered the smooth functioning of any activity in which Carlo is involved. I cannot imagine that a rainstorm on Lake Maggiore could cause me any harm. I suggest I remain below, and my wheelchair be stowed so that it will not roll about. I have never suffered from seasickness and don't intend to begin now."

Sandro smiled at her pluck but looked to Carlo Bartelli for affirmation.

"The lady has spoken," Carlo said. "Sandro, let's leave as quickly as possible. I am looking forward to another dinner at the hotel and do not want to be delayed. Hold on tightly, Silvia; we may hit a few waves." His words sounded more optimistic than their tone. Carlo spread his legs and held on to the rail near the wheel.

The motion of the lake was rougher than Sandro expected, and the rain was increasing as they headed out of the marina. Soon the visibility was close to zero. The navigation equipment on the launch was minimal because, under normal circumstances, the shore was always visible and the launch used only for day trips. Sandro steadied himself, and the launch, though tossing about, made a straight path toward Stresa.

Sandro did not like the lightning. It came from three different directions in random intervals, and the angry sound of the thunder roared across the lake. Sandro counted the seconds it took the thunder to reach the boat in order to see how far away the lightning strikes were. His counts were short.

Sandro spoke to Carlo over the wind. "Is *la signora* Trucco all right inside?"

"I will go and see," Carlo said.

Carlo disappeared into the cabin and after a few moments reappeared. "Bless, Silvia. She says she is enjoying the adventure. She is firmly ensconced in the armchair and is cradling the case like a newborn baby." Carlo laughed without humor.

Sandro bit his lip so tightly that he drew blood and held on to the wheel, which was now becoming unruly. "If anything happens, can she swim?"

Carlo shouted to be heard. "Probably better than you or I. She swims for exercise everyday, and her arms are incredibly powerful."

"I feel relieved then, *signore*. I can't imagine anything will happen, but, just in case, I think we all should put on life jackets. Will that frighten *la signora*?"

"She suggested the same thing herself and probably is now putting on one. Silvia likes to be prepared for all possibilities." Carlo reached for two life jackets that hung on the wall of the cockpit.

Sandro felt the strength of the man beside him. They stood silently next to each other as the launch made its way through the growing roughness of the waters. Another stroke of lightening hit close by and illuminated a small island in front of them. Sandro turned the wheel, and the launch hummed on into the growing darkness. Carlo handed him a life jacket and took the wheel as Sandro struggled into it.

The next stroke of lighting, however, came from nowhere and, with a blast of incredible intensity, struck the launch. After several seconds of sudden blackness and eerie silence, Sandro smelled acrid smoke coming from the engine compartment. Carlo flung open the hatch, and they saw tiny licks of fire.

"Take the wheel," Sandro yelled to Carlo. Sandro grabbed the fire extinguisher, aiming it into the engine compartment and showered the fire as best he could. It stubbornly refused to die down until the contents of the extinguisher were exhausted. Sandro threw the empty canister overboard with a grunt of frustration. One of the canvas flaps came loose, and he was doused with a wall of rain, which had caught the chill of the mountains above. Wiping the rain from his face and from his short-cropped hair, he skewed around to see if Carlo had any control at the wheel. When Sandro did so, his mobile phone fell from his pocket, went skidding across the deck rail and plunged into the lake.

"Try to keep steady," Sandro shouted to Carlo and bolted into the compartment below. Silvia was sitting upright in her chair with her life vest firmly tied around her torso. Her long fingers, now white with fear, were grasping the case that Carlo had brought from the bank.

"Sandro," she called out to him, "if the launch goes down, try to save this."

Sandro lurched forward as the launch plunged to one side and grabbed Silvia and the case. "I think you should come out of the cabin. The engine's been struck by lightning, and we may lose control. We need to be able to evacuate quickly. Bring your mobile."

The cabin was dark, illuminated now only by the flashes of lightning.

"It is in my handbag," Silvia cried over the moan of the wind, "but I can't reach it. I put it in one of the compartments below the bunks."

"Come outside then. We can get it later." He lifted her and the case and carried her above deck, putting her on a bench only slightly protected from the gale.

"Hang on" he cried out.

The wind battered the flaps, which were still lowered around the aft deck. Carlo struggled with the wheel. "We have lost our power assist and without the engine . . ." Carlo's words were blown away with a strong gust of wind.

"*Signore*, can you find the control for the flood lights? Next to the ignition switch?" Sandro yelled hoarsely.

Carlo fumbled and found them.

"Put them on if you can. They're on a battery pack." The lights came on, but the engine was still. The only sound was of the howling wind, the rain beating on the canvas and deck, the slapping of the waves on the hull, and the crack of the thunder, now receding. From what little Sandro could see at each flash of lightning, they were clear of the island and only the turbulent lake lay ahead.

"I can send a flare," Sandro shouted, fumbling with the latch of a toolbox under one of the benches.

"No," said Carlo. "We don't want to attract attention." He gave no reason for saying this. "Silvia, do you have the case?"

"*Sì*, Carlo, here."

She now was drenched in rain and made no pretense at enjoying the adventure. Her hair was wet, and her clothes clung to her body. Her jaw was set and her eyes fiery when she was not clenching them closed against the rain. Water ran off her nose, and rivulets of rain cascaded down her cheeks.

Carlo called at the top of his voice through the wind, "Silvia, hold on to it for Constanza's sake. Mother of God, be with us. I swear we are going to ride this out!"

He turned his own rain-drenched face back to the task of trying to wrench control out of the incontrollable wheel. Without an engine, the launch began to drift erratically.

Sandro grabbed the wheel from Carlo, but the boat turned into the waves. Sandro knew he was powerless. He let go of the wheel. Suddenly through a break in the rain, Sandro saw what looked like a large fishing trawler. It cut through the sheets of water and was heading directly toward them. Sandro hurriedly raised one of the flaps, so the pilot of the boat could see their emergency lights. Sandro began waving his arms and shouting, although his voice was lost in the riot of the wind. He could hear the surging engines of the boat charging at them relentlessly. It did not appear to see the launch. Carlo muttered an *Ave Maria*, and Silvia, mouthing a prayer, grasped the case as if to fuse it to her chest. Sandro prayed to the ghosts of his parents to keep them all from harm. He doubted that any of their supplications would save them now.

21

After Will left Elspeth for Villa Taranto, Elspeth double checked to see that the launch was ready for Carlo and Silvia, confirmed Biddy was lingering at a table in the dining room where the duchess could easily see her if she decided on a late lunch in public and watched from her window as Mandy pulled the BMW around under the porte-cochère. Elspeth then glanced over at her half-finished cup of coffee and decided she no longer had any interest in it.

The players were in place and now she only could hope that they would carry out the tasks she had assigned them. For the next few hours she would have no control, and she felt suddenly depleted. Glancing at her face in the mirror, she saw the familiar sharp features and also the circles around her eyes and small wrinkles that always appeared when she was stressed. Should she have accompanied Sandro, Silvia, and Carlo? She was not a sailor and could probably not have added any help. Besides she was prone to seasickness. Should she have found a reason to accompany the party to Villa Taranto? She thought it would have alerted Toria Albi that the excursion was not completely spontaneous. Should she have joined Biddy for a better lunch than the coffee that lay on the sideboard? No, that might deter the duchess if she appeared.

The frustration of inaction overtook her. She had made no preparations for the arrival of Richard Munro, although she had not forgotten that he was due in Stresa that evening.

She rang Air Malta and found out that their afternoon flight arrived in Milan at half past five. With any luck, Richard should be at the hotel in time for dinner. She would order the meal to be brought to her room, so that she could talk to him without interruption.

Elspeth, even as a child, had the ability to look at herself from a distance, which she did now. She saw a middle-aged woman filled with independence and self-assurance, at least on the surface, but who at this very moment was looking forward to taking succor from a man who had been in and out of her life for many years. He was hopelessly old-fashioned and had all the endearing and infuriating qualities of male "protectivism", if there was such a word. Then Elspeth laughed at herself and felt enormous relief. Richard's life and hers were woven together despite their divergent paths, first as teenagers, then as friends and recently as something more. This "something more" was becoming increasingly persistent and both warmed and frightened Elspeth. Would it take away her hard-fought freedom?

*

The duchess did not appear at lunch, and Biddy Baillie Shaw spent much of the early afternoon in the lobby reading *Strong Poison*, which did not distract her as she had read it many times before. Having watched various parties of guests leave for afternoon excursions, she was feeling idle and bored and hoped that before her assignment here was completed she would have the opportunity to venture beyond the walls of the hotel. She had expected to spend more time with her cousin but sensed that Elspeth was distracted by other matters and would be impatient that Biddy had not been successful in meeting with the duchess. Finally at four she decided to go up to the tearoom.

The tearoom was on the third floor and was said to command one of the best views of the mountains to the east of the hotel, but today a gathering storm greeted tea takers as they entered the room. Biddy was comforted by the rain and thought of her farm on Loch Tay. She hoped the manager Pamela Crumm had found would be caring of a favorite ewe that had a sore on her leg.

Biddy sat by the window and ordered tea and cucumber sandwiches, although she was tempted by some of the Italian pastries displayed on the tea trolley. She had just taken her first sip of tea when the duchess entered the tearoom. Despite her numerous attempts at disguise, she remained recognizable. Biddy looked up and nodded slightly to the waiter, who took the pre-arranged cue and escorted the duchess to a table that gave her full view of Biddy's. After the duchess was seated, Biddy looked up and smiled at the duchess, who turned away despite her earlier acknowledgment in the breakfast room.

"Waiter," Biddy beckoned, raising a finger imperiously and wagging it at the man.

The waiter approached and said respectfully but a little loudly, "Yes, Lady Elisabeth?"

"Please bring me another pot of tea. This one has become quite cold." Biddy projected her most dramatic voice, imitating an Oscar Wilde marchioness in a stentorian tone that would have produced a chuckle at a student play at Blare School for Girls. It caught the duchess's attention.

"Of course, milady. *Mi scusi*. At once." The waiter, who told Biddy he had done amateur theatrics himself, delivered his lines with credible authenticity.

So far the scene was being played as planned.

Biddy turned to the duchess and said in casually haughty tones, "You know the service here isn't quite up to the standard I am used to. I must ring Lord Kennington and tell him when I return to the UK."

Biddy hated her duplicity because she never had received such excellent service in her life and was beholden to Lord Kennington for letting her be at the hotel.

The duchess looked up from the menu, which she clasped with arthritic hands capped by perfectly shaped scarlet nails.

"Yes," said the duchess in accented English, "although the Kennington hotels are better than most."

"I quite agree," she said. "Have you stayed at the Kennington San Francisco? It's quite my favorite."

Biddy hoped that the duchess had not been there because Biddy had never been to San Francisco or even to America.

"No, it is unfortunate. My daughter, who is . . ." the duchess stopped abruptly and rephrased her thought, "who is here with me, stayed there. She said the hotel is very comfortable."

Biddy congratulated herself on breaking the ice with the duchess and proceeded onward.

"I am visiting from Scotland. This is my first time in the Lakes Region although my father, the earl, came here frequently. The king sent him here after the war to help with the reconstruction." Biddy felt now at her theatrical best. If only her father could have heard of his exalted relationship with royalty. The closest her father had ever come to King George VI was to be seated in a reviewing stand at a war memorial dedication in Edinburgh. The king at that point was in frail health, incapable of acknowledging the lesser Scottish nobility, and would die several months later.

Biddy became bolder. "Do come and join me. Waiter, bring another pot of tea and some of those pastries."

The duchess looked at Biddy for several seconds without accepting, but finally relented. She smiled and said, "It is my pleasure."

Biddy had not anticipated the duchess's appearance or manner. Her immaculate but somber dress, carefully dyed and set hair, and exquisite jewelry belied her humble origins. Her facial bones were broad, and her nose had obviously gone under the surgeon's knife at a time when nose jobs were more radical than in the present day. Her body, however, was small and slender, probably the result of rigorous dieting and hours of strenuous exercise rather than nature. What Biddy had not expected were the duchess's gracious manners and deportment. Pamela Crumm's description of Toria Albi's mother had not prepared Biddy for this. The woman took her seat across from Biddy with great poise, extended her red-tipped hand and said quietly, "I am the Duchess of Astonino." Biddy noted that the duchess gave her title in English.

"How do you do. I am Elisabeth Baillie Shaw." Biddy left off her title, which already had been announced to the duchess.

Biddy had a choice of two courses of action: one, to try to get the duchess to talk about herself or, two, to regale the duchess with tales of the aristocracy in Scotland, and thus further establish her credentials. She chose the latter.

Biddy looked out the window at the gathering clouds and found an opening topic. "In Scotland, you know, we get a great deal of rain, but I never expected to spend my time away from the manor watching rainstorms, which happen frequently on our loch."

The duchess relaxed her guard. She accepted the delicate china teacup from the waiter, who poured out her tea. She sipped the hot liquid tentatively. While waiting for the duchess to respond to her comment, which was rather inane, Biddy took some milk and stirred it in slow circles into her tea.

Finally the duchess answered. "It is the mountains here. They catch the rain. In Astonino, which is on the plain, we have less rain. In truth, we have very good weather there. The duke always said it was the best in Italy."

"Oh, marvelous," Biddy said drawing out her vowels. "Is the duke here with you?" she asked, although she already knew the answer.

The duchess's face shut down in a look of pain. "Oh, no. He died two years ago, quite tragic. He ate something that gave him poison. It was the fish. No one else ate it, you see."

"How dreadful. I'm frightfully sorry for you. My husband died recently, of cancer. I miss him terribly. He would have loved it here, even with the rain. He adored storms," Biddy said.

Since the topic of the weather was now growing vacuous, Biddy asked, "Have you been here before?"

"*Sì*. Many times."

"Then you must tell me what I should see and do. I've only just arrived and took it quite easy today to recover from my trip. It's my first excursion abroad alone. My cousin Elspeth insisted that time away from Scotland would do me quite a bit of good. She thinks that I mope about too much. Luckily, I have a good steward at the manor and can feel comfortable being away."

Biddy congratulated herself on how easily exaggerations of the truth came to her mind.

The duchess smiled sympathetically and took another sip of her tea. Soon the two women were talking about the best shopping in the area and whether it was better to shop in Switzerland or Italy. Biddy, who had had limited funds all of her life, imagined what it would be like to have the kind of money to buy all the items the duchess thought were appropriate to purchase in Stresa rather than in Rome or Milan. They ate all of the pastries the waiter brought and drank several cups of the Kennington signature Darjeeling tea.

"You must show me the shops here in Stresa, duchess."

"I do not go out these days, but perhaps, in this case, I may."

"Then shall we meet in the morning, say at eleven?"

Having made the arrangements, Biddy took her leave and charged unannounced and whooping into Elspeth's suite to proclaim her success.

"You know 'Peth, she isn't the dragon lady that Pamela Crumm seems to think she is. In fact she's quite presentable. I've hopelessly deceived her about the farm and about the vastness of both my acreage and wealth. She was quite taken in."

"Congratulations, but do be careful. The duchess may expect you to buy some of those expensive items on your shopping trip," Elspeth warned.

Biddy considered this and sighed. "Then I must be in a muddle over several items and be quite unable to decide. That way I won't have to purchase a thing."

22

As the Air Malta flight circled for its landing in Milan, Richard could see the lightning in the mountains. He had taken the precaution to hire both a car and driver to take him to Stresa, and he hoped the storm would not delay his arrival time. Elspeth had told him that she was ordering dinner for the two of them, and he looked forward to this with nervous anticipation.

He remembered Elspeth as she was when he had first visited Loch Tay with his Oxford pal, Johnnie. "Come meet my bratty, brainy cousin," the young earl had said, "who is coming to lunch to see what I have dragged up from university." Then across the pasture Richard saw her, clad in an old kilt, a moth-eaten pullover, schoolboy socks and muddy shoes. Her long, light brown hair was blowing in the wind, and she made no attempt to tame its unruliness. On closer observation, he saw that her nose was sharp and fine, her jaw a little too pronounced for beauty, and her brow too wide, but it was her eyes that immediately caught Richard's attention. They were piercing deep cobalt blue and filled with laughter, intelligence and high spirits. When he first looked into those eyes staring boldly out under her eyebrows, he fell in love with her.

"Elspeth, meet Dickie. Dickie Munro, Elspeth Duff, native of the Highlands and local mischief maker," her cousin Johnnie had said, introducing her.

"Welcome to Perthshire, Dickie Munro, a place where parsimony precludes penury. I hope Johnnie is treating you well. If not, I shall put thistles in his bed."

"That's not an idle threat," Johnnie said. "She's done it before."

"An act that was soundly revenged," Elspeth said ruefully. "I'll need to hide my tracks more completely the next time. Come, my laddies, Grandmother Tay will be waiting for us," she said, taking both of their arms and leading them into a spacious kitchen filled with the chaos that was the center of activity at Tay Farm.

Richard had returned to the Highlands multiple times during his years at Oxford and found many excuses to march across the braes and through the forests with Elspeth and Johnnie, but, each time he left, he could think of no way to approach her to let her know his feelings. Over the next two summers with an innocent happiness none of them would know again, the three of them had fished, swam, cheated at cards late into the night and explored the countryside together in Johnnie's old and battered Austin Mini.

When Elspeth entered Cambridge, Richard had moved on to the Foreign and Commonwealth Office for training and traveled to Cambridge to see her on occasion, but then Elspeth had met Malcolm Buchanan and fallen in love with him in that smothering kind of way that lets no one else in. Elspeth had shared her passion with Richard, who silently withdrew. When Malcolm was murdered, Elspeth asked for Richard's support as she would a brother's. Richard was there for her, but she never understood why.

Over the intervening years, Richard married Lady Marjorie, and Elspeth eloped to Hollywood with Alistair Craig. They met, as couples, many times. Richard watched the slow dissolving of Elspeth's marriage but could offer no solace, nor did she ask for any. After the long, dark year when Marjorie had become ill and died, he had returned to the FCO and asked for a quiet posting. The high commissioner's post in Malta was vacant, and he had taken up that position as a way to cope with Marjorie's absence. Last April Elspeth had come to Malta, working on a case at the Kennington Valletta hotel, and they had met again. Every feeling he had for her came flooding back, and he fell in love with her even more passionately than before. She seemed pleased at his attention, but he still did not know how to tell her how he felt. She had changed from the young girl in Scotland. She was now graceful, beautifully dressed, and filled with the confidence of a successful middle-aged career woman. Her eyes still challenged him, and on a rare occasion he saw the ragtag girl who came across the pasture many years before. How could he break through the safe distance she always maintained when they were together? He cursed his own shyness.

His thoughts were broken as the car had started up from the plain and they first encountered the rain. A call came over his driver's radio that there had been an accident outside of Verbania. The driver assured Richard this was beyond Stresa and explained that vehicles on the roads through the Italian Alps frequently had mishaps. Richard thought no more about it and was grateful that his driver was familiar with the local roads.

*

Elspeth had taken special pains with the menu for dinner with Richard, despite her earlier uncertainty about his coming to Stresa. She had requested a small table be set up in her suite's sitting room. She gave a final brushing across the tablecloth, although it was without wrinkles, and she straightened the silver cutlery, even though no pieces were out of line. She adjusted the flowers, although they were perfectly arranged. Finally she looked over the preparations and was satisfied. She glanced at her watch, but it was still too early for Richard to arrive.

She walked to the glass doors to her balcony and watched the lightning. To her amazement, it came from three different directions, like a clash of the forces of nature randomly throwing electrically charged bolts at each other. The rain had temporarily ceased, although she knew it would resume soon. In the hiatus, she stepped outside to watch the display. Far off the thunder rumbled and then echoed down the lake with the bravado of a concerto for percussion only. "May all sailors be home safe from the sea tonight," her father had always said, although to her knowledge he had never been to sea other than an occasional crossing of the Channel to France and a visit to his brother on Malta during the Second World War.

She wondered about the tension she was feeling in anticipation of Richard's arrival. They had met many times since their re-acquaintance in Malta, and each occasion was filled with warmth and laughter. Often Richard and she had been in London at the same time, and she once had been able to take a weekend trip to Malta, where they had stayed on Gozo with Magdalena Cassar, her Maltese aunt. Tonight was the first time since they had been involved in Conan FitzRoy's death in Malta that he would be seeing her when she was working. The nature of her role investigating Marco Celli's murder, the help she was providing surrounding Constanza Bartelli's kidnapping, and the backup security force she had at the hotel should have given her a sense of calmness that she did not feel. Elspeth had learned over the years to follow her intuition, what her cousin Johnnie and Richard jokingly called her "Scottish sensibility." Tonight was no exception, and she cursed that uncomfortable side of her being. She wanted this evening to capture the more pleasant times with Richard. He might serve as a sounding post for her ideas about the casings on the rooftop. Yet she had a premonition that these things would not be so.

Elspeth turned back into her sitting room and closed the balcony doors. She had not heard from Will or Mandy, and Sandro had not called since leaving Locarno. Elspeth assumed that if anything had gone awry she would have heard.

The ring of her phone broke through her thoughts, and Will Tuttle brought the first bad news, confirming Elspeth's forebodings. Mandy Bell's car had gone off the road near Verbania, and Mandy had been taken to hospital unconscious and with a broken leg. The hired car was irreparably damaged. Will was on the way to the hospital and was calling on his mobile to let Elspeth know.

"Poor Mandy. But what about Toria? Was she in the car too?" Elspeth asked.

"No, she and I came back to the hotel by taxi while Mandy was diverting the paparazzi. She, Toria that is, is with her mother."

Elspeth choked. "Paparazzi?"

"Toria was spotted by some photographers while we were at Villa Taranto. Mandy borrowed Toria's outer clothing and was attempting to decoy the photographers by driving away from the villa while Toria and I hid in one of the back rooms. Mandy must have gone off the road and hit the wall during the chase. I just had a call on my mobile from the local police in Verbania."

Elspeth's mind was now racing. "If Mandy is unconscious, how did they know to call you?"

"Mandy had her mobile with her. The police checked the last number she had dialed. Since this was the first clue they had as to Mandy's identity, they rang the number. Since they reached me on my mobile, they don't know where I am staying."

"Good. Please keep it that way, and, Will, stay in touch. As soon as you know more about Mandy, ring me back."

The second call came from Franca Donatello, who informed her that Carlo Bartelli, Silvia Trucco, and Sandro Liu had not yet returned to the hotel nor was the launch at its dock.

Suddenly the rains hit the hotel, beating down with fury on the balcony and whirling in the force of the wind. The windows of her suite protested at the violence.

*

When Richard knocked, Elspeth opened the door, her eyes filled with distress. He took Elspeth into her arms and spoke tenderly in her ear.

"Elspeth, my dear. I seem to have arrived at an awkward moment."

"Oh, Dickie, I am so glad you are here. Everything that could go wrong has just gone wrong." She buried her face in his chest and let out a sound that was somewhere between a wail and a groan. "I planned such a lovely, quiet evening for us."

The disappointment in her voice flooded over him. He looked down at the top of Elspeth's head, closed his eyes and found great pleasure in the firmness and femininity of her body against his.

"Then let me help," he said.

23

The evening had evolved from happy anticipation to crisis mode. Richard and Elspeth had left behind the meal that she had planned, and Richard persuaded his driver, who had not left the hotel, to take them to *Ospedale Castelli*, the hospital in Verbania where Mandy lay uncommunicative. Before leaving the hotel, Richard and Elspeth had met with Franca Donatello in her office and heard from her the official report from the harbormaster in Locarno.

Before leaving Locarno, Sandro Liu had filed the appropriate papers with the harbormaster for departure, despite his warnings of an upcoming storm. Sandro assured the harbormaster that he was capable of handling the launch in choppy waters and that his passengers were anxious to return to Stresa that evening. The harbormaster told Franca that he considered stopping them, but the older man, who seemed to be in charge on the launch, had brushed him aside. The harbormaster had watched the craft slide out of the harbor and head south. Nothing had been heard from the *MV Kennington Lago Maggiore* after that time.

Richard, being a keen sailor, asked Franca to contact the harbormaster in Locarno once again. Franca put the phone on speaker mode, so that they all could hear.

"I am not familiar with Lake Maggiore. Are these storms frequent?" Richard asked.

The harbormaster, who had trained with the British navy and spoke passable English, responded to the command in Richard's voice. "*Sì*. Lago Maggiore is a mountain lake, very deep, long, and narrow, and the weather is always changing. Normally we can see the boat traffic across the lake. Even in storms, the boats have flares and can be spotted from the shore. That is why we are concerned. If the *Kennington Lago Maggiore* had problems, why they did not send a distress signal?"

"What is the visibility on the lake?"

"Right now? Zero meters. Even with the heavy rain, we probably would be able to see a flare."

"Harbormaster, keep me informed. Call me here at the Kennington Stresa." Richard rang off and bobbed his head as if dismissing a subordinate.

Elspeth turned to Franca and said, "We are going to the *Ospedale Castelli* in Verbania. Please have the night staff watch the duchess's suite. If Toria Albi or the duchess comes out into the public areas of the hotel, have the staff note where they go and what they do. If they leave the building, ring me immediately." Elspeth was not sure what she could do if she were in Verbania, but she would think of something if it came to that. Uncharacteristically Franca complied with her request meekly. Sir Richard Munro's presence must have made the difference.

*

Will Tuttle held Amanda Bell's hand, but she gave no response. He willed a healing force from his hand to Mandy's. In the last two days his emotions had been engaged in many ways that he had not expected. Mandy always amused him, sometimes terrified him but never bored him. When he woke in the morning, he looked forward to the surprises she might bring to the day. In contrast, Vittoria Albi awaked in him more physical reactions, which both embarrassed and excited him. The willowy, free-limbed, auburn haired girl's young enthusiasm was in a strange juxtaposition with the cultivated sexuality of a thirty-something international film star. Will was amazed, however, that they both had a quality of innocence that he found captivating.

He faced the dilemma these two women presented. Having watched La Toria when faced with the paparazzi at Villa Taranto, Will felt ambivalent about her instinctive response. Before Amanda had struck up her friendship with Toria, Will had planned to follow Toria if she left the hotel. In his strategy sessions with Elspeth, she had said she suspected that Marco Celli's presence in Stresa was directly connected to Toria's, that Toria had initiated the assignations at the Umberto Primo Hotel, and that the duchess, not Toria, had wanted to have Toria stay out of sight. He knew that the dynamic between the duchess and Toria worried Elspeth. The daughter, it appeared, was devious. Will considered his own feelings toward Toria and expected his reactions were common to many men who came in personal contact with her. A woman like Toria, to Will's mind, would always have to be chary about men's reactions to her and their real meaning.

Mandy stirred but did not regain consciousness. The doctors had assured Will that the fracture of her lower leg was a simple one and that the concussion would leave no major damage other than a black eye or two. They also said they were reluctant to sedate her fully until she gained consciousness, when they could assess fully the extent of her head injury.

How much help could Mandy be to him now? When he had entered the hospital, he recognized one of the photographers from earlier in the day at Villa Taranto. The man, who sat dozing on one of the chairs near the entrance, looked up as Will came in and frowned in puzzlement at Will's familiar face. Will was carrying flowers supplied by the hotel and asked loudly which room his "mother" Amanda Bell was in. The receptionist looked at him oddly, but the ruse worked because photographer lost interest and nodded off again. Will knew he could not carry on this deception forever. He suspected that Toria would want to visit her new friend the following day. If the paparazzi had as much patience as he had heard, Toria's entrance into the hospital would cause a sensation.

Will caressed Mandy's hand with its practical, shortcut nails and speculated what she might say to his gesture had she been awake. The thought of her indignity made him grin.

Toria, of course, did not know his real function at the hotel. He might approach her in the morning but on what pretext? Could he make demands on Toria that she not appear in public, so that she would not be traced back to the hotel? Or should he leave this task to Elspeth? Will wished that Toria did not affect him the way she did. If he had to approach her, he would have difficulty being blunt with her. He decided he would leave the confrontation to Elspeth, as someone older, more experienced, and a woman.

Unable to resolve his dilemma, he dozed off, still clutching Mandy's hand. He remembered their walk along the waterfront promenade and thought how much he really cared for her. Elspeth and Richard's entry into the room jolted him back to reality.

After introducing Richard to Will and hearing Amanda's prognosis, Elspeth must have sensed Will's problem and took control.

"Will, Mandy will probably be released tomorrow, if the doctors find the concussion is mild, but I suspect she will need to stay close to the hotel for the next few days. It would be best for you to return to the hotel with Richard and me, and we call back here in the morning."

Will was reluctant to leave Mandy, but he acquiesced.

*

Returning from her tea with Lady Elisabeth, *la duchessa d'Astonino* watched the lightning from the window of her suite. One could view the storm as a beautiful thing, the balancing of the electric particles in the sky in a fiery display of nature wanting to neutralize its inequities, or as an angry thing, the way ancients saw storms, as a battle for control among the gods. She saw the lightning, flashing above three different mountains, as a mirror of her life, the uncertainty of her childhood in Sicily in the decade after the war, the years of clashes with Giancarlo over his infidelities during her first marriage, and the knowledge that her second husband lusted for her daughter more than for her. How could she convince her daughter that she was safer away from men and under the protection of her mother? The duchess knew that her daughter strayed often and that she had met with Marco here in Stresa. The little girl, Maria Gotti, had cried; the young woman had despised Toria's father; and the older woman had hated *il duca*, although he was rich and gave her a title and position among the Italian elite. Yes, her life was like this storm, but all storms ended and, if one sheltered oneself, the sun would come out again. "Holy Mother," the duchess whispered, "in your grace keep, my daughter and me safe."

She heard Toria in the bathroom, splashing in the marble tub with the gold faucets. How many times had she told Toria that it was a bad thing to have a bath during an electric storm?

Lightning could strike the pipes and be carried through the water, causing instant electrocution.

"Vittoria, will you be done soon? I want to order dinner."

"*Sì, Mamma. Uno momento*. I got wet in the rain and want to warm up."

"Where were you this afternoon?"

"I went for a walk. The rain came before I got back to the hotel, and I forgot my umbrella."

"Who was the man with you when you returned?"

"Man?"

"The one that came in with you?"

"I don't know. He was coming in the door at the same time I was."

The duchess knew that Vittoria's lies flowed easily, as they always had.

"You spoke to him."

"Just a few words. He was concerned that I was wet."

"Nothing more."

"No nothing. Have some wine, Mamma. I'll be out soon, and we can order dinner."

*

Toria slipped deeper under the hot water and wondered what it would be like to be Amanda Bell, who loved her parents and walked freely around the world with people only looking at her because she was inordinately tall and had a mass of dark red hair. No one knew her name or cared, except her mother and father who loved her in return, the way parents should. Money and fame couldn't buy that. Amanda made her laugh, and Will was funny as well. He was trying hard to sound like a seasoned scout, but he really knew nothing about films. He must be the son of a friend of a big producer or director. Whenever she smiled at Will or showed a bit of her body, his face would flush. This made her giggle because of the way his face filled with embarrassment rather than lust. She had not laughed so much, she thought, since she was a child with her father. She wondered where Amanda was now and if she had convinced the paparazzi that she was the famous La Toria. Amanda would be thrilled that she had deceived them, and Toria looked forward to hearing the story in the morning. When she rose from the tub and wrapped herself in the luxurious bath sheet that she took off the heated towel rack, she was filled with happiness and forgot she was mourning for Marco Celli. He had never made her happy the way Amanda and Will had that afternoon. Warmth filled her heart as well as her body when she emerged from the bathroom. She looked across at her mother, who held a glass filled with red wine in her hand and was staring blankly out the window.

*

When Elspeth finally got to bed that evening, she was aware she had not told Richard about the bullets, neither the one at the base of the tree in the park nor the casings on the rooftop. In light of the events of the evening, that seemed like an insignificant oversight, but she regretted that she had not been able to get his advice.

24

Sandro looked pleadingly at Carlo, as the fishing trawler continued in a direct line toward them, its bow cutting through the roughness of the water.

"*Signore*, we must send up a flare."

Carlo shouted back, "*Va bene*, Sandro, OK. Just one."

Sandro flung open the box by the wheel and dug for a flare.

The local boat slowed as the flare hurled its light in the air. Sandro blew out a lungful of air and threw the spent stump into the tossing lake, where it fizzled to nothingness. A sailor in bright yellow oilskins appeared at the rail of the fishing boat. He gestured wildly, pointing to the launch. Sandro assumed that he was being asked if he was all right and shook his head vigorously. Lightning struck again close by, eerily lighting up the area that was still shrouded in the blanket of rain. The wind allowed no sound except for muffled thunder to penetrate the dense cover. Sandro waved his arms, beckoning the boat to come along side. As the trawler came closer to the launch, Sandro could see the powerful engines reverse. The boat swung to and hovered along side. The sailor threw a line and then jumped on to the aft deck of the launch.

Spitting out the rivulets of water that poured down his face and into his mouth, Sandro shouted across the wind,

A Scandal in Stresa

"Our engine has been struck by lightning, and we have lost control. Can you tow us?"

Crossing the deck to the pilothouse, the sailor shook his head and put a large hand to his ear. He steadied himself as he came up to Sandro, grabbed the wheel and tested the maneuverability of the launch. He looked at Sandro and then Carlo and finally Silvia. She was sitting on one of the side benches, clinging to the rail with one hand and grasping the case with the other. Her head was thrown back, her hair flying, and her face was flushed with terror.

Carlo took command. "Can you tow us to the nearest harbor? I will make it worth your while." His words were blown out into the turbulent air.

The sailor, a rough looking man well into middle age, looked at the launch's three passengers and yelled back, "We don't need your money. We always help boats in distress. I can't take you back to Stresa or Verbania tonight. We'll put you into the harbor where we come from."

He raised his hand and motioned toward his crew. With the assistance of one of his men, he secured the lines between the two boats. The sailor motioned to Sandro, Carlo, and Silvia, indicating they should board his boat. Sandro hesitated and then went over to Silvia. As tired as he was and as wet, he had no hesitation. He scoped her into his arms and called at the top of his voice to the sailor, "*La signora* cannot walk. Help me get her across to your boat."

The tarp covering Silvia's legs fell to the deck. The sailor approached, leaned down and gently took her from Sandro's arms, as if she were weightless. Silvia smiled up at him with thanks and called out, "Carlo, here, take the case."

Carlo leaped forward and tried to grasp the case when the launch lurched and the case dropped out of Silvia's hand

and went slithering across the deck. Sandro was faster than Carlo and dove for the case; he rescued it before it slipped over the rail.

Carlo watched in fear; Silvia whooped, "*Bravo*, Sandro."

The sailor bent down and spoke directly into Silvia's ear. "If we go over, don't let go. I can swim for us both," he shouted.

Carlo yelled to Sandro over the wind and the roar of the fishing boat's engines, "Hold that case with your life. It means the safety of my daughter, who means everything to me—and to Silvia."

Sandro sensed the desperate tone in Carlo's voice, and, as a precaution, found a free line, which he lashed around the case and then around his waist.

"With my life," Sandro shouted back, hoping fervently that this would not be so.

Lightning struck the lake again, but this time it was farther away. The fishing boat held fast, and a hand on board, seeing that there were passengers to transfer, pulled the launch as close to the boat as the turgid conditions allowed. The sailor, with Silvia clinging to him, flung himself across the gap between the boats and caught the net that hung over the side. He skittered up the net, as if it were mere child's play, and deposited Silvia into the arms of a waiting seaman.

Carlo was next. The sailor threw a line to him and reached across the breach to grab his outstretched hand. Carlo faltered. The sailor climbed back down the net and pulled Carlo aboard.

Sandro, knowing it was his turn, took stock of the launch and wondered if his responsibility was to the launch or to its passengers. The Kennington Organisation would not look kindly if he abandoned the *MV Kennington Lago*

Maggiore. He lingered a moment, debating how he could save Carlo and Silvia and rescue the boat as well. The case Carlo had entrusted to him hung heavily on his body, and he remembered Carlo's admonishment. Making his decision, Sandro grabbed the launch's main line and motioned to the sailor that he was ready to come over. As the sailor leaned over to aid him, Sandro threw him the line.

Sandro screamed into the wind, "Secure the launch!"

The sailor howled something back at him, which Sandro did not hear. "Secure the launch," he yelled again.

This time the sailor understood and tied the launch's main line to the gunwales of the fishing boat.

Carlo, now safely aboard the fishing boat, beckoned Sandro over. Sandro took a leap toward the fishing vessel. It lurched. He fell into the void between the boats. Even with his life jacket, he sank below the surface. It took him a moment to adjust to the weight of his clothes, shoes and the case. He surfaced in great fear that the two boats would crash together while he was between them. Then he saw the sailor with a pole holding the two boats apart. Sandro reached up his arm and gave in to the sailor's greater strength. The sailor dragged Sandro up on the deck of the fishing boat. Sandro lay there, wet, frightened and feeling a sense of disgrace at his own ineptitude, but the case was safe and the launch secure, at least for the moment.

Inside the cabin, the fishing boat crew wrapped Silvia, Carlo, and Sandro in blankets and handed them each a mug of hot coffee. The brew was bitter and strong, but they drank greedily and gave thanks for their deliverance.

Carlo spoke first. "Will you take us to a safe harbor?"

The large sailor, who identified himself as the captain, replied, "*Sì, signore,* our boat is out of Zenna. It is a small village near the Swiss border but in Italy. There we can give you a place to stay tonight and in the morning can have a look at your boat to see if it can be repaired. If not, we can try to get a tow back to your own marina."

Sandro looked at his watch. It was only six o'clock, although he felt that it was well into the night. Sandro heard Carlo praying. "Blessed Virgin, keep my daughter safe, and let us find a way to hand over the money tomorrow, so that she will come home to us."

Part 2

After the Storm

25

Elspeth's thoughts were as tossed as the wind, and once again she slept fitfully. At last the rain ceased. Her clock read 02:37, and an eerie silence surrounded her. Elspeth rose, opened her balcony door and stepped with bare feet on the cold, wet tiles. A quarter moon was darting in and out of the clouds, casting reflections randomly on the surface of the lake. Other than the wet leaves and twigs on her balcony and the crisp, clean smell of the air, Elspeth could find no lingering sign of the storm. The black lake looked serene. She wondered where Sandro, Carlo, and Silvia were, and dreaded that the lake had swallowed the launch with all passengers on board and then glassed over to hide the evil deed. A chilling wind bit at her, and she stepped back into her room. Suddenly she wished she were on Gozo in Malta with Richard, listening to her aunt Magdelena Cassar play Chopin in her great room that opened out to the Mediterranean beyond. She imagined Richard saying, "Listen to the music and the sea, Elspeth. It is there for us." Why was she imagining this? It must be the low barometer. She closed the doors to the balcony, shutting out her thoughts, brewed herself a cup of steaming chamomile tea, wrapped herself in the throw on the sofa and sat sipping the scalding liquid until she finally knew she could sleep.

*

Biddy Baillie Shaw slept peacefully, imbued with a sense of fulfilled duty in making contact with the duchess, the comfort of an overly generous Italian meal in the dining room where she struck up an acquaintance with a widow from Aberdeen, and the after effects of a fair amount of *vino rosso* of a particularly fine variety. As she snuggled down in her bed and lay in the last throes of awareness, she was rankled by the fact that Elspeth had not shared that Richard Munro was arriving that evening. Biddy had chanced to see him in the lobby as he was checking in. Feeling a bit tipsy at that moment, she decided not to make her presence known, but she was sure that Richard was here to see Elspeth and not for any other reason. She wondered if Elspeth knew that Richard had visited the Duff home on Loch Rannoch several months before. She had met him unexpectedly in Pitlochry, and she had reminded him of their acquaintance many years before.

*

Filled with thoughts of Elspeth, Richard Munro tucked into bed. He could feel her inner anxiety in a way only an old friend would. He also thought of his wife Marjorie, of her calm manner, devotion to him and his career, and quiet dignity even in death. He was well aware that Elspeth could never fill Marjorie's place at his side, but this did not daunt him. He wondered if there were any way to combine his life with Elspeth's and, on that thought, drifted off into the contented sleep of travelers who have voyaged all day and finally reached their destination.

*

Vittoria Albi went to bed without any desire to sleep. Once again her mother confronted her about her wayward ways. Toria did not tell her mother of the private stroll in the gardens of Villa Taranto with two English innocents whom she wanted to be her friends. Her mother, as usual, saw only depravity in her slipping away from the hotel. The duchess, with all her meanness of spirit, had admonished Toria for being a slut, a slave to men, and a disappointment to her family. What family? She has never had any real family but me, and she had spent every moment of her life telling me how bad I am, Toria thought. How I wish her dead! Then Toria crossed herself and, as she went to sleep, decided she would find a way to see Amanda and Will in the morning.

*

Mandy woke from her coma just after midnight and moaned. Her head felt shattered, and her back was stiff. Her leg itched in the temporary splint, and her mouth and tongue felt like sandpaper. The room was dark and smelled of antiseptic, but the door to the corridor stood open, revealing a row of trolleys in the hospital corridor outside. At least I am alive, she thought, but then again her head might feel better if she were dead. Her next challenge was to rouse the attending nurse. Mandy had never been in hospital before except for day treatment of a snakebite in Egypt in a makeshift tent set up by the British doctor on the dig. She remembered from watching telly that there must be a call button, so she fumbled around the area of her pillow and found a device that met that description. She pressed the button hoping it would not elevate her bed but rather summon the nurse. She must have done the right thing because a nurse, dressed in the traditional habit of a nun, appeared at the door.

"Sister, can you tell me where I am?"

The nun turned up the lights and came to Mandy's bedside. "You were in a car accident. The police brought you here earlier this evening. You must rest now."

"Does anyone know I am here?"

"*Sì, signorina,* a young man, English I think, and an older British couple."

Will and . . . ? Mandy was puzzled. Her parents could not be here so soon. They were in the Valley of Kings.

"You must rest, s*ignorina*. You have a broken leg, which for a young person like you will heal soon, and you have a concussion. The Blessed Virgin will watch over you, and you should not be here long." The nun made the sign of the cross and glided from the room.

*

The light woke Sandro, and he turned uncomfortably on the mat on the floor in the fisherman's home. The bed above him creaked, and he heard grumbling. Sandro peered up at Carlo, who was looking down at him. Sandro said through dry lips, "This certainly isn't a Kennington hotel, is it."

"Last night it seemed grander than the Taj Mahal. This morning, however, I have doubts. But, Sandro, is the case safe?"

Sandro raised his blanket and exposed the metal case, which he had bound to his wrist. "I have it here. It makes an uneasy sleeping companion."

Carlo did not react to his humor, saying only, "*Sì*. How was *la signora* Silvia when you got here? They told me she was asleep when I returned from making arrangements for our stay."

"The sailor carried her into the next room. I think it is his wife's and his bedroom. His wife attended to her physical requirements, and then the sailor laid her in the bed. Then they retired to a back room."

"Sandro, do you have any sense of where we are?"

"I think we are in a small village, perhaps the one the captain mentioned last night, but I can't remember the name.

I was rather beaten up by my fall into the lake and was not too clear-headed last night. The sun is coming in the window now, and I see no lake between us and the sunrise, so I assume we are on the east side of the lake."

"We must get back to the launch and get Silvia's mobile." Carlo looked at his watch. "Half past six. That means I have six and a half hours before I must be at the Borromeo Palace on Isola Bella. We need to get back to Stresa and find a way to get there. The launch must be brought back into service without delay, unless the hotel has another launch."

"No, not that I am aware of, but the hotel manager, I am certain, can find one for us to use. Perhaps there's a phone here." Sandro rolled up from his position on the floor with the ease of a master in martial arts.

"No, I don't want anyone on the telephone line to know we are here," Carlo said. "See what you can do to get Silvia's phone if it is still on the launch. And get her chair too. It pains me to see her so dependent on others."

Sandro washed his face, checked his chin, thankful that he did not have much of a beard, and pulled on his clothing, which he had hung on a clothes peg on the bedroom door but were still damp. He did not relish going out into the cold but could find no excuse to delay his departure. The problem lay in finding the sailor from the night before and getting back on to the launch.

He went out into the alley by the house and followed the broken asphalt of the lane down to the dock. The morning light stabbed red arrows through the clouds that clustered over the Alps, and the lake below caught the light and broke it into a myriad pieces. Several gulls greeted him raucously, but he found no signs of human life along the lakeshore. Walking out on the pier, he gazed across the narrow harbor and saw the Kennington launch moored at the farthest buoy. His body began to shiver from the clamminess of his clothes and from the wind off the mountains. He sat down on the deck of the pier and imagined what breakfast would be like at the Kennington Stresa and how warming a cup of steamed coffee and hot milk with a touch of cinnamon would be. The thoughts brought no comfort.

*

Long after dawn Elspeth went downstairs and found Biddy and Richard in the breakfast room. Richard had just been seated, and Biddy was crossing the room in his direction. He rose and greeted her. Elspeth could hear him.

"Biddy, my dear, it is lovely to see you again. Elspeth told me you would be here." He put his arms around her and asked her to join him.

"How nice to see you again, Dickie," Biddy cried. "Why it seems like only yesterday that we met in Scotland."

Elspeth drew up short. Her heart gave a jump and her face blanched. Clearing her throat, she stopped and spoke to the waiter, asking an inane question. He looked at her strangely, and she replied offhandedly, "It's not important." She moved with calculated grace towards the table. She wished Biddy and Richard both good morning. She hoped her voice did not sound brittle, but she feared it did.

Richard rose again and took her hands in his. No hug, Elspeth noted. She did not feel any loving in his touch. She withdrew her hands with slow deliberation and took the seat Richard offered her.

"You met in Scotland?" Elspeth tried to keep her voice neutral and uninvolved. Richard had told Elspeth none of this.

"Late last spring was it, Dickie?" Biddy said with a huge smile.

A Scandal in Stresa

Richard looked annoyed and answered tersely. "Early June, as I remember."

"Yes, the lilacs were still blooming. I love that time of year. Cherry, one of my Border collies, had just had pups. I named one after you. I called him Tay Kennel High Commissioner," Biddy chuckled, "but the lad who bought him called him Bruno. Sorry, Dickie, I tried."

One could not stay unaffected by Biddy's warmth for long, and soon the three of them were chatting like the longtime friends they were.

When Elspeth finished breakfast and retreated into the back rooms of the hotel, however, she wondered about Richard's feelings toward Biddy. Why was Richard in Scotland? It was only a month after the murder in Malta. Why would he have gone there and not told her?

Franca Donatello looked annoyed as Elspeth entered the inner office. Franca nodded at Elspeth without rising and said, "Lord Kennington has been on the phone requiring a report on both Carlo Bartelli and the duchess. I said you would be in momentarily and would ring back. You, of course, will take care of it." The hostility in her voice had returned.

Responding to Franca's displeasure, Elspeth acknowledged her responsibility and retreated to her suite to make the call. Elspeth decided first to ring Pamela Crumm, who was a close friend as well as close confidante in delicate matters dealing with Eric Kennington. Pamela answered Elspeth's call after one ring.

"Elspeth, his high lordship is demanding news." Pamela never called Eric "his high lordship" unless he was in a state of high dudgeon.

"Is he in, or can I filter the latest news through you?"

"He is in the conference room in a meeting with a potential seller of an old hotel in Cairns, Australia, so you are off the hook for the moment. Fill me in, and I will judge his mood once he is free. I can tailor your report accordingly."

"Pamela, you are a gem. Things could not be more unsettled here."

"Fill me in."

"We had a severe storm last night. Sandro Liu, Carlo Bartelli, and his secretary took the launch to Locarno yesterday afternoon. I don't want to go into the details right now, but Carlo went to see his bankers, and it is my understanding he may have withdrawn a great deal of cash."

Pamela kept current on the high profile guests who stayed at the Kennington hotels. "I understand that he is a master at purchasing art pieces in out-of-the-way places and often carried large sums of cash to close the deal," she said.

"It is more complicated than that, Pamela. The modus operandi is the same, but this time his concerns are personal not professional. I need to talk to Eric about this. Can you make sure he calls me on a secure line?"

"Of course, but you sound as if there is a problem."

"Indeed there is. The launch disappeared on the lake last night. I can't rouse Sandro on his mobile. I have rung Carlo's secretary and can't reach her either. I left several messages for them both."

"Are they an item—Carlo Bartelli and Silvia Trucco?" Pamela asked, always curious about the private life of the guests.

"Pamela, you haven't done your usual research well. She is about his age, efficient, intelligent, well groomed, and all business. As you warned me, she is confined to a wheelchair. No, I think their relationship is based on mutual dependence only." Tactfully Elspeth did not add "like Eric and you."

"What happened last night?" Pamela asked.

"The launch must have gone down," Elspeth speculated. "One of my first tasks this morning is to see if that's true."

"Is there anything to report about the duchess and her daughter?" Pamela asked.

Elspeth wanted to say that no everything was just fine. Instead she shared what had transpired the afternoon and evening before.

"Gracious," Pamela said. "How will Eric explain this to Sir Collingwood and Lady Bell?"

"I think, from what Will Tuttle said, that they are well aware of Mandy's driving habits and will not be in the least surprised. More likely they will be relieved that she has not killed herself."

"Where are the duchess and her daughter now?"

"As far as I know, they are in their suite."

"Can the daughter be contained?"

"Hopefully. It was an incredible break that Mandy and Toria hooked up and that Will was included in their excursion. Now that Mandy is out of circulation, I think Will may well be able to keep the connection going."

"Can Lady Elisabeth meet with the duchess today?"

"It's already arranged. Biddy has lured the duchess into a shopping excursion into Stresa, which would give Will time to see the daughter."

"When will Amanda be back at the hotel?"

"Will is ringing the hospital later this morning, and I'll let you know."

"Elspeth, things are not going well for you, are they? Is Lady Elisabeth being a trial? She has a strong personality like yours."

Elspeth considered Pamela one of her closest friends. They had been in league professionally and personally for over five years and had formed a bond that Elspeth had with few other people in the world. Therefore she felt confident that she could speak freely.

"I can manage Biddy. Do have Eric call me when he is free."

Elspeth rang off abruptly. She put down the receiver and wondered why she felt so unequal to coping with the problems at hand. Damn you, Dickie, a pained voice said in her head, why did you hug Biddy this morning and not me?

26

Laura did not see a "Do Not Disturb" sign on the door and knocked gently. Getting no response, she opened the door with her key and saw Toria Albi talking on the house phone. The duchess came into the room. Laura made excuses for her incursion and went as noiselessly as possible about her cleaning. Remembering Elspeth's instructions, Laura paid close attention to what was being said.

"Who did you think would be on the phone? Why were you so eager?" the duchess snapped.

Toria put her palm over the handset and tossed her head defiantly. "No one," she said.

"A man? Don't you understand how dangerous it is for you to meet strange men? Stresa is not a safe place. Look what happened to Marco."

"Mamma, I don't want to think about what happened to Marco. Besides the call is from some lady and is for you."

The duchess spoke briefly into the handset and then turned to Laura, as if suddenly aware of her. "Start with the bathroom first," the duchess said.

Laura did as she was bidden but left the door to the bathroom ajar in order to hear. The duchess and her daughter resumed their bickering.

"You are not an innocent, Vittoria. I brought you here to protect you; why must you defy me?"

"You're not my prison guard."

"I think I must be. You are not cautious. I worry about you all the time because you do not care for your own safety."

"I have nothing to worry about."

"You should worry—all the time. You are too much like your father. He never paid any attention to his cars and drove them too fast. I warned him over and over, and he never paid attention. He died because of his own stupidity at not ever checking his brakes."

"Don't hound me again about my father. I loved him even if you did not."

"*Basta!* Enough!" the duchess screamed.

Laura heard the sound of a smack and a howl from the younger woman. Toria fled into her bedroom and slammed the door.

Laura stood still and waited. Finally she crept back into the sitting room and said quietly, "I need more towels. I come back later." She pushed her trolley back into the hallway, silently closed the door and let out a gasp of relief. She hurried to the service lift and took it down to the back offices of the hotel, where she found Elspeth and related what happened in the duchess's suite.

"Well done, Laura," Elspeth said, remembering to pronounce all the vowels in her name. "Now tell me what the duchess did after Toria Albi left the room."

"She stand still for a long time and look out the window. Her face is like a stone. Then she go into her bedroom, open the wardrobe and touch each one of her things, all in neat row, like she is checking items in a shop."

"Like doing an inventory," Elspeth said.

"*Sì, signora.*"

"You've done well, Laura. Please keep watching."

Laura took the service lift back to the second floor and resumed her duties. Because she had told the duchess she would bring new towels, she knocked again, went into the suite and put her bundle on the towel shelf by the sink. The duchess stood silently with her back to the maid, and Laura retreated as quickly as possible.

Laura then rolled her trolley into the suite next door and began cleaning the rooms, which had been vacated earlier that morning and were in great disarray. She hummed a popular tune to herself. She had plans to meet her boyfriend by the lakeside that evening. Distracted by an invasive ray of sunlight, she looked out the window toward the lake. Something caught the corner of her eye, and she moved so that she could see windows of the suite she had just left. Toria Albi, dressed in jeans, a windbreaker, and trainers, her hair pulled back in a ponytail, slowly emerged from the window of her bedroom and began inching along a ledge of the building. She looked around furtively. Something inside her bedroom window distracted her. A hand appeared in the window and either grabbed at her or pushed her. Laura could not be sure which. Toria took a misstep. With a look of horror in her face, she soared into space. As if in slow motion, she fell three stories to the street below.

Laura screamed, but no one outside the room could have heard because the rooms of the Kennington hotels were heavily insulated against sound transmission.

*

Biddy Baillie Shaw returned to her suite after breakfast. She wondered why Elspeth was out of sorts when she had come into breakfast. As usual Richard had been charming and had left the breakfast room after telling them that he was looking forward to getting access to a friend's sailing boat.

Biddy wondered if Elspeth had had a tiff with Richard the night before, but his cheerfulness belied it.

Now Biddy knew she must focus on the duchess. Buoyed at her success the day before, Biddy reached for the house phone and rang the duchess's suite, the number of which the duchess had shared the day before.

"*Pronto*," a female voice answered with breathy eagerness.

"Lady Elisabeth Baillie Shaw here. I wish to speak to the duchess." Trying to keep to her aristocratic role, Biddy did not add "please."

A hand covered the receiver, and Biddy could hear voices speaking in rapid Italian.

The duchess came on the line. "Lady Elisabeth, such a pleasure to speak with you again."

Biddy confirmed their plans for the shopping expedition, and the duchess agreed to meet her at eleven in the lobby. In the interim Biddy decided that she would make some effort with her appearance, a pastime that seldom occupied her. She went into the wardrobe and chose one of the skirts that Pamela had selected for her that was particularly flattering, one of Elspeth's Parisian scarves, a blue silk blouse that matched her eyes, and one of Elspeth's gold necklaces. She took her finery into the small dressing room off her bedroom and completed her toilet with a great deal of care.

Biddy waited in the lounge impatiently. Having lingered there for many hours the previous day, she no longer was enchanted by the opulence of the furniture, the spectacle of the view, or the attentiveness of the staff, who in the space of ten minutes had twice offered her tea. She checked her watch; it was three minutes past eleven. Promptness was a cardinal virtue in her family, and she grew impatient. At ten minutes past eleven the doors to the lift opened; the duchess, dressed in a shade of violet that reminded Biddy of an aubergine, stepped out, stopped and looked around the lounge. Seeing Biddy, she put up her heavily bejeweled hand, waved and smiled broadly. Biddy rose and went to greet her.

Biddy suggested they walk into the city center, but the duchess was shod in such a fashion that walking other than on heavily carpeted surfaces would prove painful. Her high-heels with sharp toes contrasted to Biddy's lower-heeled shoes, which for her were a stretch toward elegance. Biddy mentioned that she had a car at her disposal that could take them to the shopping area. This pleased the duchess. The receptionist rang down to the car park, and the car came to fetch them five minutes later.

The duchess said she was familiar with all the boutiques both in and out of the five star hotels along the waterfront and the driver indulgently chauffeured them from one to the next, although a few steps on the pavement would have sufficed. Biddy, who considered shopping a necessity and not an art, feigned an interest in some of the gold jewelry at one of the shops. The duchess responded with great enthusiasm and soon had the shop assistant bringing out pieces that were not in the display case. Biddy, knowing she did not have any funds to spare for frivolous luxuries, decided that ambivalence would serve her well.

"All these pieces are so lovely, duchess. I don't know which to pick."

"I will pick for you, Lady Elisabeth. The duke always said I had an eye for beautiful jewelry. Here, I like this one."

The duchess's eye was indeed discerning. She chose a simple, exquisitely-crafted brooch that would have suited Biddy extraordinarily well had her life been led in Edinburgh or London and not on the farm on Loch Tay. The duchess felt

Biddy's hesitation and chose another. This time the brooch was more intricate, equally lovely, and equally unsuitable.

Prevarication was Biddy's last hope. "Oh, duchess, I do like them both, but it's still too soon after my husband's death for me to buy jewelry. My father, the earl, would chastise me if he were to find out." Biddy did not mention that her father had been dead for many years and never cared a whit about what she wore.

The duchess brushed Biddy's protestations aside. "What you must do is have both set aside."

"Extravagance is difficult for a Scotswoman, duchess," Biddy said. She then changed the topic. "Do let's go have some lunch," she suggested. "As excellent as the food is at the hotel, I am in the mood for a change. Does that suit you? We can have the car come back later."

"I know a restaurant where the food is excellent. I have not gone out of the hotel for many days, and they have excellent soup at a restaurant that is famous throughout the region. The duke and I sometimes drove here on a day trip just for the soup alone."

"Is your home far from here?"

"About three hours drive. The duke's estate covers much of one of the most beautiful regions in the Piedmont plain. You come and visit someday. The hunting is the best in Italy. When my husband was young, his family entertained the King at a shooting party there."

Biddy imagined King George VI and then realized the duchess was taking about King Victor Emmanuel. Biddy knew the mention of the small Italian monarch was meant to impress her. Since she could not remember if the Victor Emmanuel had been alive after the Second World War or if he was a Fascist, she pretended that having him hunt on one's land was commendable. Biddy also did not mention that she shot only at foxes that tried to get into her henhouse and had disliked guns ever since a grouse hunter on the moors had killed her favorite dog when she was a child. The duchess rambled on about hunting parties at the estate, and Biddy was glad when they were seated in the restaurant and the conversation turned to food.

As they were finishing their hearty soup and on the verge of ordering from the dessert cart, Biddy was startled when Will Tuttle came in, looking very agitated. He handed the duchess a note, which Biddy saw was addressed in her cousin's hand.

27

Before leaving for the marina in Baveno to claim the use of his friend's runabout, Richard decided to hunt out Elspeth and entice her to join him. He had stepped outside earlier, breathing in the bracing air and savoring the fresh breeze. All in all it was a perfect day for sailing. He expected that the boat would be small, but it would be a change from the seagoing sailing yacht he had at his disposal in Malta.

He found Elspeth in Franca Donatello's office, but, soon after entering the room, he knew something was amiss. Elspeth stood rigidly looking out one of the windows. Franca stood with her back to Elspeth and was holding a telephone handset into which she was speaking rapid Italian. Like many men, his immediate reaction was to retreat, but he sensed Elspeth might need his support. Franca put down the phone and, pleading a problem that demanded her immediate attention, hurried from the room, leaving Richard and Elspeth alone.

"Something has gone wrong, hasn't it." He approached Elspeth, who withdrew so slightly that only a would-be lover would have noticed. "Has anything happened to Mandy Bell?" he asked.

She turned to Richard without acknowledging any reason for her coolness. "Will has gone to the hospital this morning and should be back soon. No, I haven't heard anything else." Elspeth's brow was knit, and her eyes looked away from him.

A Scandal in Stresa

"What is it then?" he asked.

She nodded slowly and looked at him directly. "Dickie, I need to take you into the confidence of a person I promised to protect and whose secret I agreed to keep. I cannot cope without some help from someone I trust completely. Just before coming down here, I heard from Eric Kennington, which is rare for a Saturday and therefore must be important. He instructed me to set right a situation that requires more resources than I have at my command right now."

The seriousness of Elspeth's voice drew Richard to her. "Of course I'll help. Only tell me what I can do."

"Yesterday an ex-minister of the Italian government and his secretary were on the hotel launch to Locarno, the one that we lost contact with last evening. You know about the launch, but there's more. One of our security personnel piloted them across the lake. I have reason to believe that the purpose for the ex-minister's trip to Locarno was to withdraw a large amount of cash from a Swiss bank and bring it back here last evening. I think the launch may have sunk."

"Elspeth, my dearest . . ." he started, but he saw she was not receptive to his endearment.

Elspeth continued, "I am told the great depth of the Italian lakes is the result of glacial activity many eons ago. Boats that go down are often lost in the depths." She drew her arms tightly around her rib cage and puffed out a short burst of air.

He wanted to come closer, but his natural prudence overtook him. "Did you ring the Italian authorities this morning? What about the harbormaster I spoke to last evening?"

"Franca phoned them both. They have heard nothing," Elspeth's voice was emotionless.

Richard walked over to where Elspeth was standing and gently put his hand on her arm.

"Tell me as much as you can," he said. "Of course I will keep your secret."

Elspeth relaxed and went on to explain. "Since his retirement from government, Carlo Bartelli, an ex-Minister of Cultural Affairs, has actively promoted young Italian artists. He's an enormously rich man in his own right but also represents wealthy investors who are looking for bargains that will increase in value over time. Eric Kennington has helped Carlo by buying art from these artists for all his hotels in Italy. Last Friday, Carlo's secretary called Eric and requested rooms here in Stresa. She said Carlo had a personal matter that needed his attention, and later Carlo called and requested the services of a hotel security guard and a launch. Carlo arrived here with his secretary on the day Marco Celli was shot. Hopefully that was a coincidence. The disappearance of the launch is of great concern to Eric. Carlo is a friend and Sandro, our security guard, is a valued employee. Eric does not like mysteries, and he keeps all of us on the security staff on constant alert in order to keep the Kennington hotels free of them."

"When did you last hear from Sandro?" Richard asked.

"He rang me from Locarno at about three yesterday. He said they would be returning to the hotel in time for dinner and asked that arrangements be made to have it served in Carlo and Silvia's suite."

"Did he have a mobile phone with him?"

"Yes, but I can't raise any signal from it. I only got his voice mail."

"Does Carlo also have a mobile?"

"His secretary does. I left several messages on it, but with no reply."

"Did she have it with her on the launch?"

"I would assume so."

"But you don't know."

"No, not for sure." She said this coolly, but Richard saw her body tighten.

"Lake sailing is different from ocean sailing, particularly on a lake like this one. The winds off the mountains can cause unusual conditions. With both the winds and the lightning yesterday evening the launch could have suffered any of a number of problems, sinking being the worst of them. I wouldn't make an assumption that the launch is lost. My first guess would be that it was incapacitated and that both Sandro and Silvia's mobiles were as well," he said, hoping it would calm her."

"That may be why they haven't answered my messages, but if they are on land, they could use a landline to contact me."

"Either they do not have access to a phone or there is a reason they have chosen not to reply."

"Giving us a mystery that's unacceptable to his high lordship," she said blowing out her breath.

"Elspeth, I've never understood your relationship with Eric Kennington."

"It is complicated, I assure you. Ask Pamela sometime."

"I plan to."

"Richard," she said using his proper given name, which she seldom did when they were alone together, "there is another situation I have not shared with you." Her voice cracked. "Something much more complex. It has to do with murder."

She hugged herself more tightly, lowered her head, pressed her eyes closed and clenched her jaw. "You know Marco Celli was murdered outside the hotel last Monday afternoon. I didn't tell you that he might have been the wrong victim."

Richard drew back in surprise. "Are you telling me that the ex-minister may have been the intended one?"

"I don't know for sure, but Eric wants me to find out. He also wants me to keep Carlo's visit here confidential and, particularly, to keep his presence from the police.

Richard had often heard Elspeth speak of her a longstanding respect for the police. "I can see why you're worried," he said.

"I don't like to withhold evidence for long. For a few hours, perhaps, or even a day, but the police will know the Kennington launch disappeared in the storm. I hope they don't come to the hotel to ask questions that Eric does not want me to answer. When Marco was killed outside the hotel, we could deny any involvement, but we can't deny that the hotel launch has gone missing and refuse to answer questions about it."

Richard shook his head in sympathy, but she did not seem to notice.

"There's one more thing I haven't told anyone, but I want to share with you," she began.

The ringing of Elspeth's mobile broke through her words.

"Yes, yes, yes," she shouted into the receiver. "Sandro, where are you?" She looked up at Richard and grinned with relief. "You don't know? Do you have any idea at all? On the eastern shore? Are Carlo and Silvia all right? And the launch? Sandro, give me the number you are calling from. I know of a way to get you back here this morning. First, you must find out exactly where you are."

Elspeth wrote down some figures and rang off.

Richard smiled wryly. "Am I to be your knight in shining rescue craft?"

Elspeth grimaced and laughed. "Yes, please."

"Then I must be off to Baveno to see if the runabout will hold four people and is indeed shining. Is there anything more I should know?"

"I may have neglected to tell you. Silvia, Carlo's secretary, is in a wheelchair, but she is highly mobile. I hope that won't present a problem."

"If the runabout won't do, I'll find something larger. I'll do my best and contact you when I have anything to report. I'll keep my conversations vague. If you don't understand, let me know."

"Thank you, Dickie. This isn't quite the visit you had envisioned, is it."

"The pleasure is being with you, Elspeth. A little adventure along the way just makes things a bit more interesting."

Richard turned to go, but Elspeth stopped him.

Her voice became strained. "Why did you go to Scotland in June to see Biddy?"

Richard remembered Elspeth's distance in the breakfast room earlier. "I went to Loch Rannoch to see your mother and father. I met Biddy in Pitlochry when I was getting petrol, and we chatted briefly. That's when I saw her."

Puzzlement crossed Elspeth's face. "Why did you want to see my parents?"

"There was something I needed to know that only they could tell me. I promise you that one day I will share our conversation but not now. Be patient, Elspeth. Things will happen in their own time."

He took her tenderly by the shoulders and planted a small kiss on her forehead.

*

Will Tuttle strode from the hospital with joy in his heart. Mandy, despite the cast on her leg and developing black eyes, was in excellent spirits, and the hospital's head sister had assured Will that Mandy would be discharged that afternoon. In the meantime, Will decided to find Toria Albi, who he thought would like to know what had happened to Mandy. Seeing that no paparazzi were around, he found a taxi and directed it to the Kennington Stresa. The driver said he had lived in Chicago, and he spoke enough English for them to chat during the trip.

The driver's conversation inevitably turned to Marco Celli's murder. "Marco Celli, he liked the women. La Toria and he marry but she divorces him. The papers they talk about this many weeks. He is very sad and see many women after to, how do you say, console him."

"Do you think one of these women killed him?" Will asked.

"No. It was a man. No woman is possible to shoot like that. One bullet in the eye and *finito*." The driver took his hand off the steering wheel and put his finger to his head.

"A jealous husband?" Will speculated without enlightening the taxi driver that he was involved in investigating the murder.

"*É possibile*, but I think no."

"Why?"

"Because *la polizia* no find clues."

The driver turned his head toward Will in order to make his point and narrowly missed a Fiat van that was delivering several large boxes to a curbside shop.

"Perhaps the police are waiting to have all the clues together before they tell anyone," Will suggested.

"No, *signore*. In Italy the paparazzi are very strong. If the police know anything, the paparazzi find out. Now the murder is already five maybe six days ago, and the paparazzi go home. There are no clues." The driver turned his attention back to the road and accelerated.

"Do you think the murderer will ever be discovered?" Will asked, gripping the sidebar on the door. The driver's method of manipulating a car reminded Will of Mandy's.

"It is possible. He is very clever. When he shoots, he escapes. No one see him. Then he disappears."

"I didn't see the press. Did the paparazzi say what kind of gun was used?"

"*Sì*. The newspapers say powerful rifle. The killer is very accurate."

"The *mafia*?"

"I think no."

"Why?"

"Marco Celli is from Milano not Sicilia."

"Who do you think killed him?"

"*Non lo so*. I don't know. My wife thinks it is Toria Albi." The driver overtook a large lorry on a curve, fortunately without encountering a car coming from the other direction.

Will shuddered.

"Toria Albi isn't a man."

"No, but my wife thinks La Toria is jealous about Marco and the new women."

"Do she think that Toria Albi shot a high power rifle?"

"No. My wife is crazy. A woman with a figure like La Toria cannot shoot any rifle." The driver took his hands off the steering wheel and made a gesture outlining Toria's chest, whistled and began to laugh.

Will was glad when they finally arrived in Stresa. He did not want the taxi driver to know anything about Vittoria Albi, where she was, or how nice she was. He paid the driver and went immediately to the back offices of the hotel, where he met Elspeth. She seemed distracted but came around when he reported the good news about Amanda Bell.

He was on the verge of leaving when Laura burst into the room.

Laura began sobbing uncontrollably. *"Signora, signora.* I see Toria Albi fall from the window. Her body it falls thirty meters, and it hit the pavement, and she not move. I see all this from the room next door. I think she is dead!"

28

Sandro sat on the pier and drew his knees to his chest for warmth. He waited for someone to materialize who might help him. Since most of the moorings were empty, he assumed that many of the boats were already out for the day. He could see across the lake through the clear morning sky but did not know the area well enough to recognize the opposite shore. A gull flew over and squawked at him. As he smiled up at the bird, he noticed an old sailor further down the pier, who was watching him with a blank stare. Sandro rose stiffly and walked over to the man. The short end of a limp cigarette dangled from his unshaven lips.

The old man hardly moved at Sandro's approach but finally turned and gawked at him. *"Non parlo inglese o cinese,"* he growled.

Sandro rose to his full height and responded defensively in Italian, "I'm Italian."

"You look Chinese," the old man said, "or my eyesight is worse than I thought."

"My parents were Chinese, and therefore I look Chinese, but I'm Italian, from Livorno." Sandro was not entirely sure why he shared this last bit of information with the old man. It did not thaw in the man's attitude.

The old man took the cigarette from his mouth and spat into the sea. "Why are you here? This isn't a spot for tourists.

We want to be left alone to do our fishing, not be pestered by foreigners."

Sandro wanted to snap back, but he needed the old man's assistance so refrained. "My boat was struck by lightning last evening and kind members of your village brought us ashore." He stressed the word kind. "My boat's the one out there. The blue launch. Can you take me to it?"

The old man spat again, took a last drag on his cigarette and threw it in the water. "How do I know it's yours? Too fancy for a young man like you."

The man's suspicion startled Sandro, and therefore he had no immediate answer. His mind, as well as his body, was chilled by the brisk air and dampness of his clothing. A gust of wind hit his back, and he grunted from its coldness. Finally he said, "It belongs to my employer. I fell in the lake last evening during the storm when I was trying to return to Stresa. The engine of the launch was struck by lightning, and I lost my phone, which went overboard."

The man shrugged.

"One of my passengers had a phone, but she left it onboard when we were rescued. I need to get that phone so I can call my boss. If you will take me out to the boat, I will tell you where the phone is, and you can go on board and get it for me. I also need one of the passenger's handbag. I'll tell you exactly where to look. I'll give you ten euros to do it." Sandro hoped this incentive was enough.

The sailor rose. His legs were gnarled and his gait unsteady; Sandro wondered if he had been drinking. After a long moment, the man led him over to a battered rowboat. He motioned Sandro to get in the back. The old man rowed with the ease of a lifetime, steering the small craft to the gunwales of the Kennington launch. On Sandro's instruction, the man boarded the boat and disappeared below deck. Emerging with Silvia's bag and mobile, he sourly repeated his requirement that he be paid and wanted ten more euros to take Sandro back to shore. Sandro found twenty euros in Silvia's bag and handed the notes over. The man's grin revealed gaps between rotting teeth. He rowed Sandro back to shore without further comment.

Safely on the cold planks of the pier, Sandro opened Silvia's mobile and dialed Elspeth's number and was relieved when she answered. The old sailor lurked several meters away. Sandro beckoned to him.

"What is the name of this village?"

The sailor mumbled a name that Sandro could barely hear. "Sen?" he asked, repeating the man's sounds as best he could.

"That's what I said." The man grumbled, turned and walked away, rolling two ten-euro notes lovingly between his fingers.

Sandro retraced his steps back to the house where they had spent the night. Sandro entered into the warm embrace of the interior and told Carlo what had happened since he had left. Silvia was sitting in an easy chair by the large wood stove in the kitchen, and the wife of the sailor was pulling fresh bread from the oven. Sandro longed to give in to the tantalizing aromas and linger over breakfast, but Carlo was impatiently looking at his watch. It was now close to nine o'clock, and Sandro could feel the fierceness of Carlo's anxiety. The sailor's wife confirmed that the name of the village was Zenna. Once again Sandro rang Elspeth at the hotel and conveyed the latest information.

*

Richard Munro was having difficulty finding the address in Baveno that he had been given for the location of the runabout. He had his taxi drop him near a large boatyard there. His Italian was limited to asking *dove?* where? and pointing to the address his friend had sent him. Cursing the passing minutes, he found a thin, ragtag boy at his side who could speak some English and offered Richard a tour of the boatyard. He knew that scamps such as the boy could be infinitely useful but always extracted a price. Richard was willing to pay.

Much to Richard's relief, when they found the boat slip, the "runabout" was a twenty-five foot long sloop with a powerful diesel engine and an ample covered deck area. Richard rang Elspeth and awaited her instruction. Elspeth gave him the number of Silvia Trucco's mobile, asked him to take charge of the rescue and bade him to stay in touch.

The boy stood and listened to Richard talk into his phone. When he had finished, the boy approached him.

"*Signore*, I am a good sailor. You take me for today on your boat. OK? Five euros for the whole day. I help you sail."

Looking at the sloop, Richard considered that the boy had done him a good turn and might be of assistance.

"Hop on board, then. What is you name?"

"Sebastiano."

"Sebastiano, you are my first mate," Richard said, holding out his hand to seal the deal.

"First mate. OK." The boy took the outstretched hand, shook it up and down with glee and sported a wide smile with too many big and crooked teeth.

It took Richard several minutes to examine the sloop and get familiar with the controls. In the meantime, he directed Sebastiano to find the charts. Consulting with Sandro by mobile, Richard set his course and sailed out of Baveno harbor shortly before ten. He calculated that it would take him less than an hour under power to reach Zenna. He instructed Sandro to be waiting for him at the pier.

*

After taking a call from Elspeth in which she told him about Richard, Sandro turned to Carlo and Silvia and switched to English, so that the sailor's wife would not understand. Explaining that Richard was on his way, Sandro did not expect Carlo Bartelli's reaction.

"Who is this Richard Munro? How does he know we are here?" Carlo's voice was filled with the anger of one urgently pressed but feeling out of control.

Sandro tried to stay calm, knowing no other way for them to return to the hotel. "I believe the hotel made these arrangements, *signore*. The hotel does not have another launch. Richard Munro, who is staying at the hotel, is a friend of Elspeth Duff. He has use of a boat moored in Baveno. From my conversation with her, I don't think Ms. Duff shared anything with him except for the fact that we are stranded here and need to return to the hotel."

"Did she tell him it was urgent?" Carlo demanded.

"Not that she said."

Carlo became more agitated. "Then are we at the mercy of an English day sailor who may or may not be reliable. I have a great deal at stake here."

The sailor's wife finished her breakfast preparations and left the room to carry on with her other duties. Carlo, Silvia, and Sandro sat alone with their breakfast. Carlo's distress clouded the dark room.

Sandro spoke stiffly to Carlo with less deference than he had used before. "*Signor* Bartelli, Lord Kennington instructed me to be of service to you in every way possible, but that is difficult to do if I don't know what is happening. You keep looking at your watch, which makes me think that something we are doing is very time sensitive. Am I wrong?"

Carlo looked at Sandro for a long time. Finally the older man's face softened.

"They swore me to secrecy, but I am going to trust you, Sandro, since you put your life at risk for us last evening."

Carlo turned to Silvia for affirmation, and she nodded her agreement. Then he spoke directly Sandro, who put down his bread and gave Carlo his full attention.

Carlo spoke without hesitation. "My daughter is being held by a Chinese man who is aiding the Nepalese Maoist terrorists. The man is demanding one million euros in cash, which is what is in the case you have guarded since last evening. I must deposit the money behind a pavilion in the gardens of the Palazzo Borromeo this afternoon at one. If I do not, the man has threatened to behead my daughter."

"Do the police know this?" Sandro asked, hoping his face did not register the horror he was feeling.

"No. I have told Elspeth Duff some of the details, but you are the only person other than *la signora* Trucco who knows the full importance of delivering the money this afternoon."

"What happens after that?" Sandro asked. "Will they release your daughter?"

Carlo frowned. "Once he has the money, he said Constanza would be safe."

Sandro tried to remember his past training. "*Signor* Bartelli, I was an intelligence officer in the Italian navy and have dealt with intimidation before. Please forgive me if I ask some questions. Do you trust the caller? Has he given you proof that he actually has your daughter in custody? Are you sure he is not deceiving you?"

A Scandal in Stresa

Silvia, who had listened intently but silently from her chair, finally broke in, her voice calmer than Carlo's. "Sandro, Constanza Bartelli has an extremely strong will and a relentless personality. Three weeks ago she left Kathmandu and went into the mountains of Nepal to pursue a story about the Maoist rebels and, more particularly, one of their Chinese advisors whose name is Wei Ling-dao. Last Friday Carlo had a phone call from a person with a Chinese accent. He didn't identify himself, but he said that he was holding Constanza and wanted the money in exchange for her safety."

"Do you think the caller was Wei Ling-dao?" Sandro asked.

Carlo responded, "We have no idea. It very well might be either Wei Ling-dao or one of his associates. It doesn't matter as long as Constanza returns to Italy without harm."

Sandro thought back to the steps he had learned in his training, ones that should be used in a case of kidnapping. He was well aware that the hostage's family too often gave in to the kidnappers without establishing if the kidnapper was telling the truth. As intelligent as Carlo Bartelli and Silvia Trucco appeared to be, Sandro suspected they were reacting to their fear for his daughter's wellbeing rather than thinking of ways to facilitate her release without the extortion succeeding.

"The money means nothing to me," Carlo assured him. "I have enough money that it will make only a small dent in my finances."

"Don't you want to recover the money once your daughter is safe?" Sandro, who never had been rich, assumed that this would be the case.

"No, that is not important to me. What is important is Constanza's return."

Sandro was incredulous. "So you plan to leave the money and wait to see if your daughter is safe?"

"Precisely." Carlo raised his head and looked haughtily down his long nose, as if Sandro could not understand what a trifle the ransom money was.

Sandro had an idea, which might be absurd, but he asked anyway. "Has this type of thing happened before?"

Silvia glanced up at Carlo with a worried look, which made Sandro feel that Carlo's answer might be evasive. Carlo chose not to answer. Instead he changed the topic and started planning how to get Silvia's chair from the Kennington launch and all of them down to the lake to meet Richard Munro's boat. They decided that Carlo should go down to the pier and negotiate having Silvia's chair brought to the cottage. This left Sandro able to talk to Silvia alone.

Silvia sat still in the chair by the stove and said nothing.

Sandro fidgeted. Finally he said, "*Signora*, please forgive me if I seemed impertinent just now with *il signore*. When I was a child, extremists in Burma murdered my parents. They were given no mercy. I would not be here today except for the bravery of a priest who sheltered me after the onslaught of those soldiers who must have believed military power was more important than human life. It's not good to give into terrorists, the military or otherwise."

"Constanza would not agree with you about the terrorists, Sandro," Silvia said, her voice hardly audible. "For her the Maoists in Nepal are in the right. She told me that they are heroes who will overthrow the corrupt monarchy in Kathmandu."

Sandro frowned. "Then why are they demanding ransom?"

"We don't know for sure that they think of it as ransom."

Sandro was baffled. "I am not an expert on affairs in Nepal, but the reports in our press would indicate that the Maoists have killed many thousands of people in order to overthrow the legitimate government of Nepal. *Signora*, I want to help you in every way possible, but I find it difficult to have *il signor* Bartelli hand over the money with no assurances they will release his daughter. Aren't you afraid?"

"I, personally? No, the lowest moment of my life came when the Nazi's murdered the nuns in the orphanage where I lived and took the use of my legs from me. Like you, I have lived through the worst and have known the basest depths of inhumanity. Neither one of us can change the past. We can only live for now."

The sadness of Silvia's words dug deep into Sandro's mind. He seldom revisited those last days in Burma. Although on occasion the memories, like maggots, ate into his dreams and awakened him with almost unbearable pain. He looked down on this physically crippled woman, who every day carried the scars of ultimate cruelty, and wondered how she achieved such dignity, beauty, and wisdom. He knelt beside her, but he felt he did not need to speak for her to understand the tears in his eyes.

"Sandro, there are issues here other than the money. I'll share them with you because we have already taken you into our confidence. Carlo and his wife are estranged, and Carlo's only real family is Constanza. Constanza is almost thirty years old now, and, the more protective her father becomes, the more radical she becomes. In my position, I can talk to both of them without taking sides, but they perform an awkward dance around the topic of money. Carlo would spend any amount of money on his daughter, but he wants to control it because he fears she will donate it all to left-wing causes. She, on the other hand, is devilishly clever in finding ways to get the money. As worried as we are about her safety, we don't know if the kidnapping is real or simply another way for her to give away her father's money. We have to face that possibility her abduction is real, but there's some chance that it may just be another of her schemes."

Sandro shook his head on hearing this. "Why does he give in?"

"Because he loves Constanza, and she loves him, and because they have been doing this dance most of her adult life. His wife takes much more of his money, although there is no longer any love there. Carlo is a shrewd businessman, but he doesn't know how to handle the women in his life."

Including you, Sandro thought, because you seem the best of the lot, and he doesn't see that at all.

*

Richard was enjoying the sail and anticipated that they would arrive in the fishing village ahead of schedule. Sebastiano proved a skilled first mate for his small size, and his antics amused Richard. He wished that Elspeth were along, although at times he suspected that she did not enjoy sailing as much as he did.

"Sebastiano, is that the village ahead?"

"*Sì, capitano*. I see people waiting on the pier."

Richard screwed up his eyes and regretted he did not have the perfect eyesight of the young boy. It took several more minutes before he could make out several figures on the pier, including one in a wheelchair.

They soon drew up along the pier. Sandro caught their line, tied it securely and gave a hand to Richard, who instructed Sebastiano to stay with the sloop.

"Aye, aye, *capitano*."

Richard approached the Italian man, held out his hand and introduced himself. "I am Richard Munro." He did not mention his title or rank. "Elspeth Duff is an old friend. She asked me to come and take you back to Stresa."

The man's voice bordered on the impolite. "I am Carlo Bartelli. I may need your services for more than a simple crossing to Stresa. I must be on the Isola Bella before one o'clock. It is now just before eleven. I do not know if there is time to return to Stresa and find another way to get there."

Richard turned back to the boat and called to Sebastiano. "Do you know the way to the Isola Bella?"

"*Sì, capitano.*"

Carlo was obviously not pleased. "Is it necessary to have this urchin along?"

Richard did not let Carlo's ill humor affect him. "He seems to know these waters better than any of us. He has spent his entire short life on them. He tells me that his father is assistant harbormaster in Baveno."

Richard turned to Silvia, again introducing himself by name but not by title. Silvia was more gracious and thanked him for coming.

*

Sandro stood and watched the interplay. He considered staying in the village in order to retrieve the hotel's launch, but his conversation with Silvia had made him curious as to who would come for the ransom. After Carlo left the money, Sandro wondered how long it would be before someone retrieved it. If he could devise a plan to see or even speak to the person who collected the case, he might have a chance to find out if the person was the kidnapper or even possibly to follow him.

Sandro's mind continued to work as he carried Silvia and her chair onto the sloop, took a place next to her and made small talk about their passage across the lake.

29

Elspeth anticipated that the paparazzi would come, but she was surprised at how quickly. After she instructed Laura to take a rest in order to recover from what she had seen, she told Will to find out if Toria Albi's body had been removed from the street. When Will had gone, she found Franca at the reception desk. When she told Franca what had just happened, Franca let out a cry.

"*Non è possibile!* It is not possible! No, not here. Who told you?"

"Laura, the second-floor room attendant."

"Laura? Poor Laura, she is new here and a good worker. Now she will quit. We must alert the other staff. The paparazzi will be here at any minute. The tragedy will not escape their attention long. *Mio Dio!*" Franca flung her arms about, her bracelets knocking together discordantly.

"Franca, we must let the duchess know," Elspeth said. "She's gone into Stresa with Lady Elisabeth. I'll make arrangements to get word to them as soon as possible, certainly before the press find the duchess and tell her of her daughter's death. When Will returns, I'll send him into Stresa to find them. No, better yet, let me get him on his mobile."

Elspeth guided Franca back to her office and left her semi-reclined on one of the sofas that edged the room. Then Elspeth made her way to the front of the hotel and watched a doorman shooing off a man with a video camera.

*

It did not take Will long to find where Toria Albi had fallen. Two of Stresa's police vans and a police car surrounded the scene, but their lights were turned off and sirens quiet. An ambulance was leaving when Will arrived, and he assumed it carried Toria's body. Her shape, which had been chalked on the sidewalk, was contorted, arms flung out, and legs crooked, although the police had, to Will's mind, exaggerated some of her natural curves. Will bowed his head in genuine grief and whispered a farewell to the ill-fated actress, her warmth and voluptuousness now a thing of the past.

Will pulled a camera from his pocket and began shooting. The sky was bright, and no one saw him at first because there was no flash. He moved around to another view, where he could see the hotel and the window above from which Toria must have fallen. The window was on the downhill side of the building, and Will estimated that the fall had been about thirty meters. No one could have survived that. A policeman saw him and began yelling. Will wished Mandy were there to translate, although the policeman's message was clear. Will ran. The policeman lost interest in him and returned to post.

Will raced around the side of the hotel and catapulted himself past the doorman, who luckily recognized him and let him by the guard who was now posted at the main entry to the hotel. Will dashed through the door of Franca's office just as Elspeth was tapping in his number.

"There you are, Will," Elspeth said. "What have you found out?"

"Not a great deal, but I was able to get several shots of the place where Toria fell. Here, let me show you."

He allowed the slide show to run on his viewfinder, which conveyed vividly what was happening where Toria fell.

Franca, still visibly shaken, was the first to ask. "Were there any paparazzi there?"

"No, not yet, although I suspect they will be soon. The police may brush them aside but not with any seriousness."

"Will, were there many onlookers?" Elspeth asked.

"No, just a few shopkeepers and three young boys. The police vans were hidden from the main road, and the ambulance was just pulling out of the alley when I arrived."

Elspeth, remembering Franca's familiarity with the police, asked, "Franca, how would the paparazzi learn what had happened?"

Franca put her head in her hands and said through the many rings on her fingers, "Aldo—*il commissario*—tells me that they drop in the police station several times a day to see if something has happened."

"I see," said Elspeth, trying to imagine the worst possible outcome. "If one of them learns something, do they tell the others?"

Franca shrugged. "It depends. If one thinks he can get an exclusive, he is less likely to share."

Elspeth's thoughts were racing. "That would make sense, and it may buy us a little time. Will, please find the duchess and Lady Elisabeth as soon as you can. They went into Stresa on a shopping expedition and might be at any of the better shops, or even having an early lunch. Here, let me write a note for you to give to the duchess."

Franca calmed down as Elspeth spoke to Will. "*Sì*, Will. Let me give you some places you might try first," Franca said.

With Will dispatched on his errand, Elspeth turned once again to the manager of the hotel and wondered if the two them would be able to cooperate in this crisis. It would not take long for the press to put together Marco Celli's death and Toria Albi's fatal fall. Would they cry suicide? Or worse, murder? At best Toria's fall would be classified a terrible accident. If Elspeth could come up with this many scenarios so instantly, she was sure the lurid minds of the press could devise something more sensational.

Elspeth turned to Franca. She was now seated at her desk and drumming her fingers as if expecting Elspeth to solve their dilemma with all due haste.

"We need to discuss what we do now, Elspetta," Franca said, stressing Elspeth's name but making no suggestions.

Elspeth was annoyed but hid her reaction as well as she could. "How will your staff react to the paparazzi?" she asked.

"There will be no problems. We have many famous people staying here, and there are procedures in place. What I am worried about is the reaction of the duchess. I fear now that Toria and Marco are dead, she no longer will want to remain incognita."

Elspeth had already arrived at that conclusion. "Let's hope that Will finds her quickly," she said, "and he can bring her back to the hotel before there is a crowd to greet her. My cousin will be of great use, I think. Sometimes she appears to be quite scatty but, in a crisis, she can take matters in hand and offer support when others are floundering about. It probably comes from having been raised on a working farm. She's quite extraordinary at the birth of an animal or when one is injured. I am truly glad that Biddy is here."

Franca rose from her desk and, in a reflexive gesture, she touched a small but exquisite statue of the Virgin on one of the shelves of the built-in bookcases. Franca's lips moved in a silent evocation.

"We have a doctor on call," Franca said finally. "He is retired, but we retain him because he is kind and speaks several languages. Most guests do not need any high level of medical care. I will call him now and see if he can be here when Will brings Lady Elisabeth and *la duchessa* back. I do not know how the duchess will react to the news, but at least *il medico* can give her something to sooth her or even sedate her."

"Do that, Franca. I'll call Lord Kennington. He will not be pleased."

Elspeth turned and stalked from the room, later regretting her petty reaction to Franca. Was it because she could think of no good way to keep the situation at the hotel in hand? Or was it simply that she was perplexed that she was unable establish a good working relationship with Franca?

*

Biddy and the duchess were at the point of ordering their desserts when Will found them. He handed Elspeth's note to the duchess and said quietly, "I'm sorry."

The duchess wiped the edges of her mouth on her napkin, took the note, and read it. Showing no reaction at all, she folded the piece of paper and then looked around the table, as if there was something she wanted to find there but did not. Finally, in a low voice, said, "Take me back to the hotel."

Biddy was perplexed, looking first at Will and then back to the duchess.

The duchess handed her the paper and said, "*Ecco.* Here."

Biddy took the paper and read what Elspeth had written.

A Scandal in Stresa

Dear Duchess,

It is my sad duty to tell you that your daughter fell from the window of her hotel room earlier this morning. The police have informed us that she must have died instantly, although I know that will be small comfort to you. Will Tuttle, who brings this note, will help you in any way possible. I extend my deepest sympathy.

Elspeth Duff

Biddy stared down at the note, written on heavy hotel notepaper emblazoned with the Kennington coat of arms and inscribed *Comfort and Service*. Sadness filled her, as if the tragedy were her own. Biddy could not fathom how she would feel if the note had been directed to her.

"Your car is outside, Lady Elisabeth. I have settled the bill. Will you help me take the duchess to the car?" Will said.

They found the car on a side street, and Will handed the duchess into the backseat. Biddy thought that only large men have such gentility.

The duchess brushed away Will's attentiveness. "I do not need your assistance," she said.

Her voice was so sharp that Will drew in his breath. He said he would ride in front and leave her alone with Biddy in the rear. He took out his mobile, rang Elspeth and made arrangements for the car to enter the hotel through the underground car park.

The duchess sat rigidly in the back. Her eyes were unseeing, and she seemed unaware of the others in the car. Biddy was reminded of photographs and films she had seen of Queen Mary at the funerals of her relations: stoic, dignified, detached, and seemingly unkind. The duchess was not royally born, and Biddy wondered why the imitation.

Biddy took the duchess's hand and held it as the car took them back to the hotel. The duchess's hand was so cold that it made Biddy shiver. Neither of them spoke.

Franca Donatello was standing by the lift when the car entered the car park. She opened the back door of the taxi and spoke to the duchess. "My sympathies, duchess," she said in English. Biddy wondered if it was for her benefit.

The duchess emerged from the car without acknowledging Franca's presence and said in the same language to no one in particular, "I want to go to my room."

Franca extended her hand to the duchess. "*Duchessa, il medico* Franchetti is here if you would like to see him."

"I want to go to my room. I do not need a doctor. I need to go to my room."

At first Biddy wondered why the duchess wanted to go back to the rooms where Toria Albi had last been, but, having lived in the country all of her life, Biddy had helped many friends and neighbors through the first moments of grief and understood that some people needed to face the death of a loved one in solitude. She bid the duchess goodbye and invited her to call for support if needed.

*

Amanda Bell's return to the hotel could not have been more poorly timed. She eschewed the wheelchair recommended by the doctor and insisted on leaving the hospital with only the assistance of crutches. She wanted to surprise Will with her mobility, but, because she was conscious that her black eyes might not be appealing, she put on Vittoria's large sunglasses. After having looked in the mirror at the hospital, Mandy suspected her university friends would have described her face as "sunset over Kashmir." She promised herself that, when she returned to university, she would find a better crowd of friends.

Along with the sunglasses, the hospital had given her Toria's handbag, which had been recovered from the crash, and, which to Mandy's delight, contained enough cash for her to hire a taxi that was large enough to accommodate both her cast and her crutches.

The taxi driver grinned at the tall, auburn haired young woman who insisted that she ride in front with her broken leg outstretched.

"Andiamo. Let's go," Mandy demanded "Faster. This road is impossibly slow."

"Signorina, I do not want to attract the attention of *la polizia.*"

"Rubbish," Mandy said in English.

The taxi driver laughed. *"Va bene, signorina*, but you pay the fine."

"Davvero. Of course. I'll tell them that I must see my lover after my accident, and they will let you off."

The taxi driver increased his speed but not sufficiently to satisfy Mandy. "Can't you go any faster?"

"Signorina, what is your rush?"

"My lover is waiting for me."

"Amore?"

"Sì. Amore." She sighed deeply.

What she was not prepared for was the paparazzi outside the hotel. The doormen, now numbering four rather than one, were standing guard and had cordoned off the pavement at the entry. Mandy estimated that twenty or so photographers and men carrying imposing video cameras lined the edges of the barricade. When her taxi pulled up, they jostled for position and watched her awkward descent from the car. One of the doormen came to her assistance and positioned her crutches for her, so that she could stand and make her way up the stairs to the entrance of the hotel. She did not respond to the questions the newsmen threw at her, but, when she arrived in the lobby, she realized she had been shaken by the experience. At the reception desk she asked for Elspeth and Will. Neither answered the call, but Franca Donatello appeared and escorted her to the back rooms before telling her about Toria Albi.

Mandy shook her head in disbelief. "No. That's not possible. Yesterday she was so full of life. We all had a wonderful time at Villa Taranto, and she was so amused when I went off pretending to be her."

Franca put her hand Mandy's arm and spoke softly to her. "We have sent Will to collect the duchess and Lady Elisabeth. He should be returning shortly. Elspeth Duff and I have been trying to decide what would be best for us all to do now. It is difficult because we do not know how the duchess will react or what she will require. First and foremost, she is a guest here, and we must be of service to her in anyway possible in this tragedy. When Will gets back, we may need you and him to help. Why don't you go up to your room and make yourself as comfortable as possible. After your stay in hospital I am sure that you will want to change your clothes. Can you do this without assistance?"

"I think so." Mandy looked down at the cast on her leg, a concoction of plastic, cloth, and Velcro in an unbecoming shade of green. It reached to her ankle but, in order to hide it, she could easily wear a skirt, one of the longer, more modest ones that she had taken to Egypt.

Mandy hobbled her way out to the lobby, where the concierge stopped her and handed her an envelope.

"*Signorina* Bell, this was left for you this morning," he said.

A Scandal in Stresa

Mandy put the note in her pocket and took the lift to her room. She was about to throw the envelope on the sideboard in the entryway when she looked at the address, which read "Amanda Bell, Room 208" in large and unformed Italian script. Mandy tore open the envelope and read its contents, which were written in Italian and heavily underlined:

> *Mia cara Amanda. Let's escape again today. Can I meet you and il signor Will, and we can find another garden to visit? My mother is going out at eleven, so I can leave after that without her knowing where I have gone. Telephone me after eleven and let me know. Or I will come to your room and knock on the door. Ciao, Vittoria.*

The childishness of the note touched Mandy deeply. From its innocence, one would not have guessed a famous film star such as Toria Albi had written it. After their time together, Mandy felt fame was not an easy thing for Toria.

While Mandy was dressing, her room phone rang. It was Will.

"Oh, Will. What a terrible thing! Do you know how she fell?"

"No one does yet. We may never know. Franca thinks it may be suicide from a broken heart because of Marco Celli."

"That can't be true. I received a note written by Toria this morning. It doesn't sound suicidal. On the contrary, it is filled with mischief."

"What? Say that again."

"I had a note from Toria . . ."

"Yes, I heard that, but 'mischief?' Mandy, I'll be right there. Don't go anywhere. Above all, don't show the note to anyone but Elspeth or me."

"I'll be here. I'm hardly able to run away." Mandy said.

30

Sandro watched Sebastiano stand on the prow of the sloop and wave his thin arms in the air with the joy of youth. The wind had picked up and the lake was choppier than it had been earlier, but the boat, with its high-powered engine, cut through the water with a steady purr. Carlo Bartelli had asked to take the tiller, and Richard Munro let him do so without comment. They stood near each other but hardly spoke. Sebastiano directed them toward a small group of islands to the west and occasionally motioned them to the port or to the starboard as if conducting a large symphony. Richard smiled at the boy's antics, but Carlo Bartelli made the corrections without any visible sign of emotion.

Silvia sat on one of the benches and watched the two men. She turned and spoke to Sandro, who was at her side.

"Carlo is seldom so quiet," she confided. "Usually I can sense his mood but not now. I would feel better if we had heard directly from Constanza, which we usually do when she is up to one of her schemes. Constanza's lack of communication is worrisome."

Puzzled, Sandro turned to Silvia. "*Signora*, why did *il signor* Bartelli give in so easily to the demands?"

Silvia shook her head and sighed. "I'm not sure, but it's probably because he believes Constanza will be safe. Still, I don't know why he is so silent."

Sandro bit his lip. "After he leaves the money, will he try to discover who comes to pick it up?"

Silvia gave a crocked smile and shook her head. "There's no one to do that."

Sandro thought for a moment. "I could do it. If I were let off the boat before we find a berth on the island, I could circle round and watch the drop-off location. No one would associate me with *il signor* Bartelli."

Silvia leaned over and put her hand on Sandro's. "I don't think he would want you to be put in any danger."

The warmth of Silvia's hand did not quell the enthusiasm of the young man. "What danger could there be? I was trained to follow people when I was in naval intelligence. Besides, Lord Kennington assigned your care to me."

"Care for Carlo and me, yes, but not Constanza. If the kidnappers suspected you at all, they might harm her."

Sandro shook his head in disagreement. "How could they suspect?"

Silvia's face filled with anxiety. "We know nothing of the kidnappers or Constanza's cooperation with them, and, most of all, we don't know how much she is threatened."

Sandro frowned. "Do you think Constanza planned all this?"

"*Sì e no*. To me, this time feels different from the other times. Carlo is acting as if thinks so too, not by anything he has said but how he is acting. I'm worried, Sandro, that the abduction may be real, and the people who have Constanza will not be satisfied with our case full of euros. Yet, I don't want you to do anything to harm us—or you."

Sandro smiled back and said nothing.

*

Richard Munro's graying hair was cut short and carefully barbered because he thought of himself as a sailor despite the fact that his entire career had been in the diplomatic corps serving Her Majesty's Government in the Commonwealth. But, on those dark and humid evenings in Africa or Southeast Asia, he had avidly read sea stories and the historical adventures by Conan FitzRoy and others like him. Richard imagined himself the hero of those books. Today he felt the same way.

Carlo Bartelli had chosen to exclude Richard from his plans when they reached Isola Bella, but the daring of today's events opened Richard's imagination to the possibility of real adventure. The freshness of the wind and Sebastiano's liveliness heighten Richard's anticipation. It took great effort for Richard to stand looking blandly sympathetic to what was happening around him.

They approached the island at speed. The pier in front of the looming Baroque façade of the Palazzo Borromeo offered a spot to offload passengers. Sebastiano jumped from the boat to the docking ramp and pulled the line with a practiced hand.

Navigating the sloop closer to the ramp, Carlo motioned to Sandro. "I want you to take *la signora* Trucco's chair off the boat to the top of the stairs. Then come back, carry her up the stairs and place her in the chair. I will need you inside, as there are several flights of stairs and no lift," he said.

Richard saw Sandro set his jaw slightly as if he had other intentions than following Carlo's orders.

When they reached the top of the stairs, Carlo Bartelli took hold of Silvia's chair; the case was firmly in her grip. Sandro followed closely. Carlo wheeled the chair over the rough decorative pattern of the stones of the plaza to the ticket window. He purchased three tickets and then proceeded to the gate where he surrendered them. The dark entryway of the palace engulfed Carlo, Silvia, and Sandro.

Richard waited as they disappeared from view. He knew he must act swiftly if he were to follow them. He turned to Sebastiano. "First mate, can you watch the boat if I go ashore?"

"Aye, aye, *capitano*." The boy saluted and straightened his back. His open shirt fluttered in the wind showing a thin, hairless chest.

Richard leaped from the boat and scaled the stone steps two at a time, arriving in the plaza just as a public ferry disgorged its passengers. They flooded the space, which made Richard curse his luck as he queued for a ticket. Five precious minutes were wasted before he handed his ticket to the dour ticket collector at the entrance to the palazzo.

Richard was thankful that the security gates that were beginning to appear in many public places were not present here. It took a moment for his eyes to adjust to the gloom of the entry room. He followed the crowd up the regal staircase and into one of the grand staterooms of the palace.

Richard and his wife had visited the palace several years before Marjorie had become ill, and he knew signs directed the crowd through the grand reception areas and bedrooms on the ground floor, down into a depressing grotto below, and then back up to the main rooms of the palace before leading visitors out to the gardens. He suspected that if Carlo were meeting someone at the palace, he would more likely set the meeting for a secluded spot somewhere in the garden. Richard looked for a guard and finding none, he stepped over the cordon put up to divert the general public and hastened into the long gallery that opened to the gardens. He was alone when he reached the end of the room. Glass doors, which at first seemed locked, opened automatically.

A steep stairway led up the gardens. No wonder Carlo had instructed Sandro to help with Silvia and her chair. Richard took these stairs cautiously, knowing that there was the distinct possibility Carlo and Silvia might see him. He nearly reached the top, when he saw Sandro coming from the path signposted "WC." Richard intercepted him there.

"Sandro, I must speak to you. Has Carlo Bartelli gone into the garden?"

Sandro was reluctant to share information at first and said haltingly, "Yes, he had me carry *la signora* up to the main garden above. He asked me to stay with her, but I pleaded urgency."

"Is he with her up there now?"

Sandro nodded. "Yes, and they have the case with them. She had it hidden under the blanket around her knees as we went through the palace. *Signor* Munro, I am not at liberty to tell you what is in the case, but it is very important. *La signora* Silvia is worried about *il signor* Bartelli and about his daughter. The case has something to do with her."

Richard was excited. "Do you think the two of them are in danger, Sandro?"

"Personally, I think not. The people who want the case are probably more concerned with what is in it than they are with *la signora* Trucco or *il signor* Bartelli."

"Then let's see what we can do," Richard said. "Let's go up into the gardens and find out what Carlo Bartelli plans to do with the case. He may deliver it to someone but more likely he will leave it somewhere. If he does leave it, you keep your eyes on the case and find out who comes to fetch it. I'll follow Carlo. Do you have a camera?"

Sandro shook his head. "No, I lost everything in the storm last night except my money belt."

"Bother," Richard said, thinking what to suggest next. "Do you have a good eye for faces?"

"Yes, we were taught that when I was in intelligence in the navy. They made us learn a series of facial recognition types and characteristics, the kind you see in a police identification sketch."

Richard smiled at the young man's confidence and liked him better for it. Together they marched up the last of the stairs.

Carlo and Silvia were sitting near an enormous tree at the entrance to the gardens, and were in deep conversation. Finally Silvia drew the case from under her blanket and handed it to Carlo.

Screened by a hedge, Richard and Sandro watched Carlo take leave of Silvia and go off down one of the paths. This left Richard and Sandro in an awkward situation. If they entered the gardens, Silvia would see them; if they didn't, they would lose Carlo.

At Richard's behest, Sandro skirted behind Silvia. Richard suspected that Silvia would watch Carlo, and his assumption proved correct. Sandro sidled behind a row of bushes without Silvia turning around.

In the meantime, Richard consulted the map he had bought at the ticket window and tried to devise a way to follow Carlo without Silvia seeing him. The tourists from the ferry had just come out from the labyrinth of the palace, which solved his predicament. Richard joined the group. He followed a large woman with a broad-brimmed hat and kept behind her as they entered the gardens. Silvia was distracted by the sound of the new tourists and turned toward them. Richard hunched down and hoped she would not pick him out in the crowd.

Richard caught a glimpse of Carlo slipping down a path. Having studied the map, Richard knew of an alternate route. He hurried along it. The insistent pungency of the smell of the box hedges made him want to sneeze, so he drew out his handkerchief, which also served as a mask.

Richard lost Carlo and cursed his bad luck. As Richard rounded a corner, he found himself on a long landscaped balcony that overlooked most of the gardens. In the distance he caught sight of Carlo, who was turning down a path that led to the eastern edge of the gardens. Richard consulted his map again and saw that Carlo was heading toward a small building labeled "The Aviary." Just beyond where Richard was standing, steps led down from the main gardens. He dashed down the steps as swiftly as possible without breaking into an actual run. Reaching the bottom of the staircase he saw Carlo again, this time hurrying down the path that led away from the aviary. Carlo was no longer carrying the case. Richard hoped Sandro had been close enough behind Carlo to see where the case had been left.

*

Sandro Liu faced a hard decision that pulled at conflicting loyalties. As an employee of the Kennington Organisation, he was committed to keeping Carlo Bartelli and Silvia Trucco safe, but over the last twenty-four hours his sympathy with their dilemma had stretched the meaning of that protection. The security office at the Kennington Organisation in London had trained him that his assignments should not extend beyond the bounds of the hotel itself. Exception was made for a hotel vehicle, the launch being considered one of them. Sandro's having accompanied Carlo and Silvia to the Isola Bella was on the verge of violating the security office's directive, but, because Sandro felt his task was to keep Carlo and Silvia free from harm, he had no qualms as to what he was about to do. Silvia's genuine concern for Constanza had affected Sandro, and he had also picked up on Richard Munro's zeal for following Carlo into the gardens. Sandro cursed the loss of his mobile and his inability to call Elspeth Duff, but, on second thought, this might be an excuse he could use to disobey her orders. With defiance, he followed Carlo Bartelli down the path toward the aviary.

Sandro kept a long distance between himself and Carlo. When he saw Carlo go toward an ornately striped and corniced building with bulging glass cages, he found a thick hedge flanking an opulent stone urn, where he took cover. He could see through the bushes and could retreat behind the statuary if anyone came up the path. He watched Carlo take the case to the side of the building and then almost immediately emerge empty-handed on to the balustrade-lined gravel path.

At first Sandro considered going to retrieve the case. That would allow him to wait and identify who might come to get it. Before he could act on this rash plan, he saw an angular, weather-beaten Asian man in a dark athletic jacket, with a rucksack slung loosely over his shoulder, coming down the path toward the birdcages. Sandro remained immobile. Was this a chance tourist?

As Sandro peered from behind the shrubbery, he felt too vulnerable to move from his hiding place to get a better view of what the man was doing. Sandro's growing suspicion that the man was here to collect the case was confirmed when the man slipped into the alleyway alongside the building and reappeared a short time later with a now heavily-loaded rucksack strapped to his back.

What next? The money had been collected, and Carlo and Silvia would now have to wait to see if their daughter would be freed. There were no guarantees. Both the money and Constanza Bartelli could disappear, leaving Carlo and Silvia bereft. All of Sandro's training told him to let things lie; all of the compassion he had felt for Silvia over the last day told him to find out where the man was going because that would lead to Constanza. Before the man left the gardens, Sandro would have to make that choice.

*

Richard saw Carlo Bartelli hastening up the path toward Silvia. Richard, a fan of spy stories, said to himself that the drop had been successful. He wondered where Sandro was and if he had been able to follow Carlo to the drop-off point. Richard thought he would call Sandro's mobile but realized Sandro had lost this in the lake the night before.

Carlo proceeded up the wide path into the lower part of the garden and hastened past the intricate box hedge mazes and lily ponds. Richard circled around on the ornate balcony and, in doing so, disturbed the white peahens and their chicks that were grazing there. They gave a harsh call and fluttered off. Carlo did not turn toward the noise, but, instead, mounted the steps from the lower gardens and hurried along to the main tier of the gardens to the spot where Silvia was waiting in her chair. He approached her to her visible relief. He sat down beside her and took her hand in a caress that was intimate but not sexual. Silvia looked at him with a trust and friendship that reminded Richard of his late wife Marjorie.

From a distance Richard stood watching them and hoped that Sandro would join Carlo and Silvia soon with an explanation of why he had been gone for so long. Richard surveyed both the stairs up from the aviary and the spot where Silvia and Carlo sat. Carlo seemed to be asking the whereabouts of Sandro.

A Scandal in Stresa

After several minutes Carlo rose and began to wheel Silvia toward the path marked for the exit. Richard wondered how they would manage the stairs but did not take the time to find out. He hurried toward the exit, let himself out through a turnstile and was well down the hill and out of sight before Carlo and Silvia had a chance to appear..

Twenty minutes later, when Carlo wheeled Silvia into the plaza at the entry of the palazzo, Richard was standing near the boat landing-area with Sebastiano at his side. Richard took Silvia's chair as Carlo lifted her into the sloop. Then he welcomed them back aboard.

"Where is Sandro?" Richard asked, feigning innocence.

"He did not come back after he left me," Silvia said.

"He should have stayed with Silvia," Carlo said, distinctly irritated at Sandro's behavior. "Now he can make his own way back to Stresa. I shall have to speak to Eric Kennington about his insubordination."

Without consulting the others, Carlo Bartelli once again took the tiller. Richard chose to sit beside Silvia, out of earshot of Carlo.

Silvia spoke first. "Do you think Sandro went to see who was coming to collect the case?"

"I am not sure," he replied. "He may have."

31

The police *commissario*, Aldo Ponchetti, strutted into Franca Donatello's office. His short, wedge-shaped legs were encased in tight fitting trousers, and his police tunic was complete with a row of medals. His unnaturally black hair was kept in place by stiff gel and was undisturbed when he took off his high-crowned hat. Elspeth, who was with Franca, wondered at the display because earlier Franca had said that she had invited him to come to her office without ceremony through the underground car park. Elspeth hoped no one had seen him enter, particularly the paparazzi snooping around the outside of the hotel.

"Franca," he said as he entered the door of her office and gave her a caress, which she did not reciprocate, "I cannot let our friendship interfere with my investigation." He turned and acknowledged Elspeth with a mini-bow, hand to his round stomach. "*Signora* Duff, I know you wish to have everything covered up so that the paparazzi will go away. I am convinced I have found out the truth. Soon they will know it as well and leave you alone."

Plainly Franca had dressed with more than her usual care, and Elspeth could detect the smell of attar of roses rising from the layers of her scarves. Franca had ordered lunch from the kitchen, a delicate fettuccini with goat cheese and herbs followed by a bed of arugula smothered with a Tunisian-style tagine of lamb with apricots, almonds, and saffron. From the wine cellars she had chosen a local *barbera*. Not the hotel's most expensive wine but better than a policeman could expect, Elspeth thought. At the back of the manager's office the luncheon table was set in the Kennington style. Franca motioned her guests to the table, placed Elspeth and the *commissario* next to each other, and took her place opposite the policeman.

Elspeth suspected that by design no waiter was in attendance. Franca poured the *commissario* a glass of wine. "*Mangia*, Aldo. Isn't this better than a sandwich at your desk?"

The *commissario* held up his glass and turned it in the midday sunlight coming through the large windows. "I feel you have set up a plot," he said. "What information, Franca, are you trying to get from me?"

Franca smiled wickedly, although Elspeth thought it was feigned. "Am I so obvious?" asked Franca.

The little policeman beamed. "I have known you too many years to think otherwise. *Signora* Duff, Franca has been able to, how do you say in English, twist me around her fingers since we are children." He laughed at his own joke.

Elspeth could not decide whether to smile or look disapproving, so she took a bite of fettuccini instead and chewed slowly.

The *commissario* took up his fork eagerly but, before sampling his first course, he spoke seriously. "Suicide in a Catholic country like Italy, *signora*, is a serious matter. Although many Italians are no longer religious, the Church is very firm about not allowing people who take their own lives to be buried in the churchyard. This is not so important in England, I understand."

Franca's swift gesture might have been the sign of the cross, although it was so brief a one that Elspeth could not be sure.

"No," Elspeth said, "it's no longer that important to most people in the UK. Why are you bringing this up this, *commissario*? Do you think Toria Albi committed suicide?"

The *commissario* puffed out his chest, his medals pulling apart. "Almost definitely because, ladies, I think she murdered Marco Celli and was filled with so much sorrow that she did not want to live any longer!" He took a bite of the pasta and rolled it around on this tongue in clear appreciation.

Elspeth watched him curiously and took a sip of wine, while thinking how to respond.

"I appreciate your thinking. Tell us what brought you to that conclusion?" she asked. She tried not to sound irritated, although she was.

He put down his fork and raised two fingers on his left hand. "There can be only two reasons. First, we know that Marco Celli had a woman come to his room many times at his hotel. If it was La Toria, and we think it was, he then came here to make another meeting with her, but she is tired of him and wants to keep him away. Or, second, maybe she sees him with another woman and kills him because she is jealous. *Ha!*"

Elspeth put down her wine glass. She tried to follow the policeman's logic but could not. "Are you saying she was seeing the man she had just divorced, killed him and then jumped from her window? Is there any evidence?"

The *commissario* looked triumphant. "At the hotel where he was staying they saw the woman come in through the back door."

Elspeth looked directly at the *commissario*, but he averted his eyes. "Did someone there identify the woman as Toria Albi?" Elspeth chose not to share what Mandy had learned from the concierge at the Umberto Primo Hotel.

"Perhaps." His eyes narrowed like a cat's, and a silly, thin-lipped grin crossed his face under his small mustache.

"Tell me how Toria Albi committed the murder," Elspeth said. "It definitely impacts the security of our hotel," she added, justifying her request.

"*Naturalmente*, she shot him."

"I see," said Elspeth, although she did not. She remembered the casings from the bullets that Will had found on the roof.

"It is very simple," the *commissario* said, looking down his nose and staring at her, although he had to lift his head to do so, which spoiled the effect. "She told him to come to the hotel, and, when he arrived, she opened the window and fired the rifle at him."

"Then she must have planned everything beforehand. I mean, why would she have the rifle?" Elspeth asked.

The *commissario* smiled the way a parent would in response to a naive question from a child. "*Signora*, you must understand about Italy. Our famous people are not safe. They always carry protection."

Elspeth did not want to say "a hunting rifle?" so only nodded at him. "Are you so positive that you have decided to end the investigation?"

"*Sì, signora*. Like your Hercule Poirot, I use the *piccoli* brain cells *grigio*. We have no, how do you say, loose ends," the *commissario* continued. "Toria Albi is the murderer, and she committed suicide because she was filled with sadness at her sin. I shall write up my report when get back to my office and send it to Milano." The *commissario* put his hand to his stomach, smoothed over the wrinkles at his non-existent waistline and smiled. "Franca, this meal is delicious. Now that

I have solved the case, the paparazzi will go away, and you, Franca, will be happy."

*

Knowing there was little more she could do for the duchess, Biddy returned to her rooms and rang Elspeth.

When Biddy had finished telling Elspeth what had transpired that morning, Elspeth said, "Biddy, I talked to Will Tuttle a moment ago, and he has just left to fetch Mandy who is back from the hospital. I want to talk to them about something that happened this morning before Toria fell from the window. I would like you to join us as well. I expect Mandy and Will to arrive at any moment, and I'll ring you when they get here. I also will have room service bring up some coffee."

*

While waiting for the others, Elspeth went to the writing desk in her suite and on hotel stationery penned a note to Richard Munro.

My dear Dickie,

Your helping out this morning has proved more invaluable than I could have imagined. By the time you receive this, you will have seen the hungry press at the door and wonder what it is all about. Toria Albi fell from her hotel room this morning and died on impact with the street below. Franca Donatello and I had a maddening interview with the police, who are insinuating that Toria committed suicide after murdering Marco Celli. The duchess has retreated to her room, and the doormen are keeping the paparazzi at bay for the moment I hope.

> *Your sound advice would be sorely appreciated. I have something to tell you that I discovered yesterday and that I think may be important, although I have not yet shared this with anyone other than Will Tuttle. Besides, I want to hear what happened on the lake this morning.*
>
> *Please ring me when you get this.*

Elspeth thought a long time about a fitting valediction: *with love, best, warmest regards, fondly*? None seemed quite right, so she simply signed it boldly *Elspeth*.

She was finishing her note when room service arrived. The waiter wheeled in a tray with coffee, tea and some small cakes and fresh fruit. Elspeth gave him the note and asked him to leave it for Richard at the reception desk.

*

At Will's knock, Mandy called out that the door was unlocked. He found Mandy sitting up in the chair by her window. She was clad in fresh, brightly colored clothing and was sporting a captivating smile. The hideous green cast was only partially covered by her skirt. He tried not to show his rush of pleasure at seeing her.

"We have been summoned by Elspeth Duff and need to show her your note from Vittoria. She said the police are now convinced Vittoria took her own life," he said.

Mandy's face filled with horror. "Will, I only knew Vittoria for a short time, but my take on her the last few days was that she had no suicidal tendencies. I don't believe that she was really grieving for Marco Celli. I think it all was an act."

Will nodded. "I agree. Now we need to tell that to Elspeth. She said the lunch she just had with the police verged on the ridiculous, and she did not agree with the conclusions they reached. The letter from Vittoria confirms her suspicions." Will looked down at Mandy. "Are you able to walk up to Elspeth Duff's rooms?"

"I have become a real wizard with these crutches. Just watch me!"

Will laughed. "Mandy, you are incorrigible."

*

Biddy arrived in Elspeth's suite before Mandy and Will and, therefore, had a moment to sit with her cousin before they arrived. She accepted Elspeth's offer of a cup of coffee and a small cake, lowered herself into a chair and let out her breath.

Looking exasperated, Biddy crossed her arms across her chest. "This holiday is not turning out as I expected. You should have warned me, 'Peth, that terrible things might happen, the way it always did when we were children, only worse."

Elspeth eyed her cousin and smiled. "I think as a child I always knew we would get into mischief, but you always were willing to come along, as I remember. I had no such designs for you this week, and I truly am sorry about Toria Albi for her own sake, as well as her mother's. By now you probably are beginning to understand why my job with the Kennington Organisation, for all its perks, is not an easy one. Eric never sends me on an assignment that is devoid of difficulty, believe me. He says he leaves that to lesser beings."

"I hope he pays you well."

"He does, and that is one of the reasons I continue working for him. But, Biddy, more importantly, I need you to give me your opinion of the duchess. You said she isn't quite the dragon lady that Pamela Crumm makes her out to be. Why?"

Biddy sipped her coffee before answering. "You know, I quite like her. Somewhere in her life she's developed good manners that, in my short acquaintance with her, certainly covers any hardness. Before Will came with the bad news, we were having a very enjoyable excursion. She, of course, has traveled a great deal more than I and chatted easily about her life and views on the world. I almost forgot that I was supposed to be the jaded traveler and should not have been entranced by what she said."

"Tell me a bit more about her reaction when Will gave her my note."

"At first she looked annoyed when Will came up to our table. He was deferential and made his care feel real. He had our car waiting for us at the back of the restaurant. Franca Donatello met us in the hotel car park and escorted the duchess up to her suite without our having to face the press, which I saw outside when I crossed the lobby later."

"Yes, Will is a treasure," Elspeth agreed. "Biddy, tell me how did the duchess react emotionally at the note?"

"She froze."

"Froze? What do you mean?"

"How can I describe it, 'Peth. It was as if everything stopped for her, even the warmth in her body. I took her hand on the way back in the taxi. It felt like a dead chicken's foot. I know it's a terrible comparison, but that's what it was like. It had no life. She spoke only the most necessary words, and those were so hushed that I hardly could hear them."

"Did she seem surprised?" Elspeth asked.

"Surprised? Now that you ask, no."

"I find that unusual, don't you?"

"Why?" Biddy looked perplexed.

"Put yourself in her situation. If someone told you that your Mary had fallen to her death, wouldn't you cry out in disbelief?"

"Good heavens, what a terrible thought. Of course I would. What mother wouldn't?"

Frowning, Elspeth said, "Yet the duchess did not, but perhaps that is neither here nor there. We all react differently to bad news."

A soft tap came at the door. Elspeth called for Will and Mandy to come in.

"Let's hear what Will and Mandy have to say about Toria Albi," Elspeth said. "They may shed some light on the matter of her so-called suicide for us."

After hearing Mandy's news, Elspeth asked, "Do you have Toria Albi's note with you?"

Mandy pulled the note from a pocket in her jacket. "Toria wrote this note this morning asking to, as she put it, escape with Will and me for the day. Yesterday Will, Toria, and I went to Villa Taranto and had a wonderfully abandoned time. Have you been there? It's worth a trip. Vittoria—Toria—acted completely light-hearted all afternoon. I think she suffered terribly under her mother's constant eye and did, indeed, need to escape."

"Mandy's right," Will added. "Vittoria seemed so happy to be with us and thought it a great lark when Mandy drove off impersonating her. The sad thing is that Toria never knew that Mandy was hurt on her behalf. One has a feeling Toria would have gushed with sympathy."

"Did she mention Marco Celli's death?" Elspeth asked

"Only that she had loved him and was grieving. I took that as pure dramatics on her part," Mandy said. "It seemed rather odd to me, particularly as she seemed so happy all afternoon."

Will agreed. "Somehow she acted like a gleeful child most of the time, almost as if Mario's death hadn't happened."

"Then we have a dilemma here," Elspeth said. "From what we know, we must assume that Toria Albi didn't kill Marco. But, at lunch the *commissario* said he was convinced she shot Marco and took her own life in despair over what she had done. He's closing the investigation. Unfortunately, if Toria didn't kill Marco, the killer is still out there, and we still don't know if the real target was Marco Celli. Will, Biddy, and Mandy, I think that your jobs just got harder. Biddy, stay in touch with the duchess. She may have valuable information for us and can tell us what Toria's mood was this morning. Toria may have been subject to mood swings; the duchess will know. Mandy, I need you to be about the hotel. Watch and listen, and tell me anything you see. Will, I have several tasks for you but want to discuss them with you later, when I have a little more time to formulate a plan. Let's all meet here later."

When Elspeth was alone, in order to preoccupy herself until Richard called, she opened her laptop and logged on to the internet. She was not sure what she was looking for, but she began by Googling "Toria Albi." A knock came at the door after she had read through several fan websites and had found a more serious site that addressed Toria's life and films.

Richard was grinning when he came in the room. Still in his windbreaker and boating shoes, he took Elspeth in his arms and kissed her on the cheek. Elspeth had forgotten how comforting a man's embrace could be when times were troublesome, and she did not shrink away.

He stood still, keeping Elspeth in his arms. "I came as soon as I retrieved your note from the reception desk. What a fuss at the front door of the hotel. Is that what you want to talk to me about?"

Elspeth released herself from his embrace. "Dickie, I need a wise person to talk to right now. I fear that things are getting overly complicated."

Richard led her to the sofa and sat down next to her, taking her hand in his. "My dear Elspeth, I am afraid I am about to make them more complicated yet."

Elspeth sat bolt upright. "Has something happened to Carlo or Silvia?"

"No, they are here and quite recovered from their ordeal on the lake last night and are comfortably settled back in their rooms, but I am afraid I have lost Sandro Liu."

Elspeth jerked herself around and faced Richard. "Lost? Did he drown? I thought he was safe."

"He was safe, but now he's disappeared. It's a long story."

Elspeth freed her hand from Richard's and rose. She walked over to her desk and placed both hands on the back of its chair. "I thought things were bad, and now they are definitely worse," she cried out. "Good heavens, what will I tell Eric?"

Richard rose and went over to Elspeth. "First, you must tell me what is going on here. Then, let me share what happened on the lake. Together we can decide what to tell London and what we will keep to ourselves."

Elspeth leaned her forehead against his shoulder and closed her eyes. "Oh, Dickie, I am so glad you are here," she whispered.

32

Knowing he was committing an act in violation of the conditions of his employment, Sandro Liu made the decision to follow the man who has picked up the case rather than returning to Richard Munro's boat. Yesterday he would not have made this decision, but now, having taken to heart the confidences that Silvia Trucco had shared that morning, he could think of no other option. Silvia had struck a chord in him that went so deep that he no longer cared about his contract with the Kennington Organisation. As he lifted her in and out of her chair, he saw the bones that were her legs and envisioned again and again the horrors she had suffered as a child at the hands of the Nazis. These visions regurgitated his own memories of his mother and father being beaten to death. Following the man with the case became tantamount to his seeking revenge for both brutal acts. If he could find Carlo Bartelli's daughter by tracking the man, he would be able to give Silvia the gift of the safety of someone she loved dearly. He wanted to do this above all other things.

Looking neither right nor left, the man with the case in his rucksack walked with purpose from behind the aviary. He seemed focused on getting out of the garden as rapidly as possible without attracting attention. Sandro had no trouble following him. The man left the gardens by the main exit, struggling for a moment to get his heavy rucksack through the turnstile. Freed from the gate, he hurried down the stone path to the ferry landing.

Sandro followed the man as closely he dared. The man asked the guard at the gate when the next ferry was due to go to Locarno. The guard explained he would have to return to Stresa and could take the next ferry from there. Good, thought Sandro, he is going to Switzerland.

Sandro watched the man find a seat just outside a food kiosk. Noting the schedule posted beside the dock, Sandro saw that the next ferry to Stresa was due in thirty minutes. He withdrew to the men's room and took a hundred euros out of the money belt that had survived last night's storm. He was grateful that his stepfather, a man of the sea, had insisted that his money belt be waterproof. At times the extra plastic layer made Sandro sweat, but his plunge in the lake did not damaged his cash, credit card, or his identity papers inside.

Sandro's next problem was disguise. Like the man with the case, Sandro's East Asian appearance might be noted. He still was wearing the clothes he had put on that morning and the morning before that at the Kennington Stresa. Although now dry, they were wrinkled, and he felt soiled all over. Sighting a gift shop near the ferry gate, he went inside to see if they had any clothes that would change his appearance. He selected a black windbreaker emblazoned with gothic letters in white saying *humilitas*, the motto of the extravagantly rich and sometimes corrupt Borromini family, and a grey baseball cap with *ITALIA* written in multicolored letters across its crown. He also purchased a pair of wraparound sunglasses.

As they boarded the ferry, Sandro kept well behind the man, whom Silvia had called Wei. Wei moved up to the uncovered seats in the front; Sandro chose a seat in the back near the diesel engine that exuded rank-smelling fumes and made him slightly seasick. When the gangplank was lowered at Stresa, Sandro bolted from the ferry and ran to the ticket office, so that, if Wei spotted him, it would seem that Sandro was choosing his destination before knowing Wei's. The man seemed more intent on his own voyage than Sandro's, much to Sandro's relief.

At the designated time, they boarded the large hydrofoil that crisscrossed from one side of Lago Maggiore to the other before finally heading toward Switzerland. Sandro positioned himself behind Wei in the queue of boarding passengers. Again Wei went forward. Sandro held back and found a seat between the two gangplanks, one on each side of the wide boat, in case Wei decided to leave the ferry before Locarno. During the first part of the voyage, Sandro debated whether to approach Wei and try to speak to him or to try to disappear behind his baseball cap and sunglasses. He chose the latter course for fear Wei might attack him or make a run for it.

From his seat Sandro could see Wei. He stood absolutely still near the windows at the side of the boat, slightly hunched in what Sandro knew to be the wu chi position in tai chi chuan. If he had to confront Wei later, Sandro would need to be prepared. Sandro's throat tightened. At any minute he might have to face a master of the martial arts. He wished he had stayed more in practice with his training in tai chi.

Wei's bulging rucksack was leaning against the wall of staircase that led to seating below. Wei kept his eyes on it and did not look around.

The ferry made its way slowly up the lake, stopping at port after port. Sometimes the ferry simply unloaded and loaded passengers quickly, but, at other places, the stops felt interminable. Sandro watched the passengers around him in order to get his mind off Silvia and Constanza Bartelli. It being late in the tourist season, most of the travelers were local, and Sandro was glad of their ordinariness. He wondered if they realized that they had a kidnapper among them, a man who was carrying a million euros ransom in cash in a case, not handcuffed to his wrist but thrown casually by the bulkhead. Sandro doubted that few of the passengers had ever contemplated what two thousand carefully bundled five-hundred-euro notes would look like.

Sandro's ticket allowed him to board and alight from the ferry as many times as he wished. He wanted to be prepared if the man checked to see if he was being followed by jumping off the boat and then jumping back on just before departure. Had Sandro been in Wei's position he might have employed this tactic, but Wei just stood in the front section of the hydrofoil and maintained the wu chi position from port to port, an ability only a master could achieve. Sandro admired his strength, but he also was scared by it.

The ferry loudspeaker announced that they were now entering Swiss territory. The man did not move when the other passengers prepared to disembark. Sandro decided that he should get off the ferry as speedily as possible, clear the gate and wait for Wei outside of the disembarkation area. That way, he could follow Wei and not be trapped in the crowds that had stopped in the shops along the quay.

The man crossed the dock with purpose, setting out on foot. Sandro followed, trying to remember all the surveillance techniques he had used in navy intelligence. Stay close, but not too close. If you think the person you are following has spotted you, go past them and then double back. Stay as inconspicuous as possible. Change your outward appearance, so that the casual observer won't associate you with someone they have just seen behind them. If you are confronted, say you are lost and leave immediately.

The man seemed intent on his destination and showed no signs that he knew someone was following him. His pace was swift, but Sandro kept up with him. Sandro's heart began pounding from anxiety as they crossed the large plaza in the center of Locarno.

Although doused by a passing shower, the man stuck to the open. Sandro thought of darting under the wide arcade along the edge of the plaza but was afraid he might lose Wei if he did. Wei turned up a narrow street and hurried up the steep slope out of the plaza. He entered through the low doorway into an inconspicuous hotel and was gone from sight. After an hour he still had not reappeared.

Sandro had to make a quick decision. Seeing no shops nearby, he dashed back down the hill to the plaza, where he purchased a rucksack, some underwear, a pair of jeans, two differently colored tee shirts, another windbreaker and baseball cap, a razor and toothbrush, and a pair of pajamas. Armed with "luggage," he felt more comfortable asking for a hotel room. Sandro produced a credit card and his passport and hoped the Kennington Organisation would approve the cost.

After showering and changing clothes, Sandro went downstairs to the hotel's dining room, which offered simple fare: pastas, ordinary second courses, and fruit or ice cream for dessert. Sandro was hungry enough that he did not care. He ordered frugally, hoping that his transgression from the terms of his employment would not force him to pay for his own keep.

Wei appeared halfway through Sandro's meal. Two other men, both Chinese, accompanied him. They spoke quietly in Cantonese together. Sandro caught snatches of their conversation, which was commonplace.

Wei ordered for them all in stiff, stylized English. The waiter took the order and disappeared into the kitchen. Sandro, sitting with his back to the men, picked up the gist of their conversation.

"What now, comrade? What about the woman?"

"I'll handle her."

"And the money?"

Sandro could not hear all of the response, but Wei gave the name of a bank to his comrades. Sandro only caught the word "Suisse."

When they were served, the men ate in silence. Sandro did as well. When the men rose, Sandro at first thought he should follow them but decided he might be noticed. He sat still as they exited the dining room. The waiter came to offer dessert, and Sandro ordered coffee and ice cream. Sandro asked the waiter in Italian what he knew about the men. The waiter was willing to chat, especially after Sandro gave him a ten-euro tip.

"They came four or five days ago, from Asia, I think, or at least their clothes were badly cut, as if copied by someone who did not understand European tailoring."

Sandro noticed that the waiter was smartly dressed, even though he only wore a white shirt and black trousers, and that his shoes looked expensive. Sandro wondered what the waiter must think of his hastily acquired jeans and tee shirt. No matter, Sandro thought, he wants to talk, which is fine with me.

The waiter continued, "They stay very close to the hotel and are here for most meals. The leader goes out once or twice a day and stays away for an hour or two. Except the leader, they stay in the lounge, smoke a lot and watch the television, although they do not appear to understand Italian, French or German."

"They are speaking Chinese. I can understand a little," Sandro said, "because my parents were Chinese, although I grew up in Livorno. Do you know what nationality they are?"

"I don't, but my girlfriend works at the reception desk. I could find out for you."

Sandro drew two more ten-euro notes from his pocket and gave them to the waiter. "One of these is for you and one for your girlfriend. If you could find out the name of the leader, I would appreciate it."

"Oh, you are a detective. That explains it."

"Explains what?"

The waiter looked embarrassed. "My girlfriend wondered why you checked in with a rucksack you had just bought in one of the shops in the plaza."

"Was I that obvious?" Sandro asked, responding to the waiter's curiosity.

"No, it's just that my girlfriend has a vivid imagination and likes to think that all the guests are . . ." the waiter paused, looked for a word and then laughed, "are mysterious."

"When I first came in, I would have described myself as rumpled, not mysterious. I took a spill in the lake last night."

"Oh." The waiter sounded doubtful.

"What is your girlfriend's name?"

"Isabella. And she is *bella*. I am going to ask her to marry me soon, when I have enough money saved. Are you married?"

Sandro laughed. "No. I don't even have a steady girlfriend."

"How sad. Girlfriends are delicious." He kissed his fingers and released the kiss into the air.

"I met someone recently, however, an older woman, who epitomizes everything wonderful in a woman. She has stolen my heart, I'm afraid." Sandro warmed inside as he thought of Silvia Trucco.

"Is she married?" the waiter asked.

"To her boss, but in spirit only, not in the church."

"Then all is not lost. Is she rich?"

"I don't know, but in the short time I've known her she has changed my life. That is why I fell in the lake and why I'm here."

The waiter clapped his hands together with joy. "Then you do have a romantic story. When you finish your coffee and *gelato*, why don't you join us at the café around the corner and tell us everything."

Sandro decided the waiter and his girlfriend might prove valuable sources of information. He accepted the invitation, although he could feel fatigue overtake him.

The café was filled with smoke, which bothered Sandro, who had never smoked and had become accustomed to the new smoking ban in Italy. His two companions ordered beer, Sandro a glass of red wine. They found a table in the corner and, after they were settled, Isabella turned to Sandro with enormous excitement. "Ricco tells me you threw yourself in the lake over love for an older woman. Is it true?"

Sandro laughed at how quickly his remarks had become distorted. "Only partly. We were out in the storm last night. After our boat was struck by lightning, I fell in the water trying to help her on to the boat that rescued us. I was soaked and lost my mobile, but no one was hurt."

"Do you love her terribly?"

"Deeply as one would a mother but not terribly as one would a lover. She's the wisest woman I have ever met, both complex and caring. A dunk in the lake was a small price to pay for her safe return to shore."

Ricco looked up at Sandro. "I don't think I love my mother that way; do you, Sandro?"

"My mother was killed by terrorists when I was very young, so I don't know." Sandro could not hide the hurt.

"Oh, I'm so sorry, Sandro," Isabella said with real pity in her voice. "Ricco, you are a brute."

The moment passed, and Sandro decided to find out about the Chinese guests at the hotel. "Isabella, do you get many Asian guests at the hotel?"

"No, not many. Sometimes we have some Japanese tourists, but this is the first time I remember any Chinese ones—first the group of them and now you.

"Are they Chinese?"

"They all have Hong Kong passports."

"Hong Kong is part of China, Isabella. Don't be silly." Ricco took her hand and kissed it.

Isabella stood her ground. "No, they were Hong Kong passports. I know for sure. When we return to the hotel, I'll show you."

Sandro saw the opportunity. "I think, Isabella, that you are right. When the British left Hong Kong, they did not give British passports to the people born there. There was enormous controversy at the time, as Hong Kong passports issued by the British were considered second class. I'm not sure if these passports are still valid, but I would love to see one. Did you make copies?"

"Yes, the manager insisted because they didn't look genuine. When we go back to the hotel, I'll show you," she said again.

"That group does seem a strange lot," Sandro said.

"Perhaps they're spies!" Isabella sounded ecstatic at the idea.

Ricco rebuked her. "Too obvious," he said.

"No," said Sandro, "Isabella may have a point. What makes you think they are spies?"

"The leader, whose name is Lyndon Wey, creeps in and out of the hotel like a spy. He never says a word of greeting and seems uncomfortable being in the hotel. We may not be a fancy hotel like the Kennington Stresa, but we provide comfortable accommodations, so most of our guests say."

Sandro sensed that she was beginning to feel the effects of the beer and could be plied for more information.

"Does this Lyndon Wey go out the night?"

"Not that I know of. He usually leaves just before noon and comes back in an hour or two and again goes out at about five and comes back for dinner."

"It sounds like he is meeting a contact." Sandro hoped that his voice implied the shady nature of Wey's activities.

At that point a group of young people came into the café and, seeing Ricco and Isabella, came rushing to their table. Sandro, having slept the night before on the floor of the fisherman's cottage, sorely wanted to retreat to the comforts of the hotel but feared that Isabella might have second thoughts about showing him Lyndon Wey's passport the next day. He ordered a cup of espresso and prepared for a long night of reveling.

33

After Richard had retreated to his room to change his clothes, Elspeth went out on her balcony and watched the reflection of the sun on the Alps. The fresh air did not alleviate her dilemma, and soon she returned to her sitting room. She rang Biddy and Will and invited them back to her suite. Richard had promised to return shortly. She wanted to talk to them all before she approached Franca Donatello or rang Eric Kennington.

While waiting for them, she began to formulate the outlines of a plan. She felt that the key to the mystery was the duchess, who was the only person in the hotel still alive who had known Marco personally. Biddy was Elspeth's best hope in dealing with the duchess.

Next Elspeth considered how to use Will. She wondered how far she could relax the rules against searching guest's rooms without disregarding Eric Kennington's dictates. Such an invasion of privacy normally was done only in instances where the police had to be brought in, although there had been many occasions where Elspeth had asked members of the hotel staff, such as Laura, to be vigilant when cleaning a room or delivering room service items. Will's skill with a camera might help here as well.

She smiled as she came to her task for Richard. Was she letting down her guard? Be sensible, Elspeth, she thought.

Protect your independence, whispered a small voice that she could not ignore. Richard would be most useful in making the arrangements for the return of the hotel launch. He had mentioned a small boy who had served as his first mate earlier that day and whose father was the assistant harbormaster in Baveno. The boys' father might be at the marina in the morning and able to find help to restore the launch's engine.

Next was the issue of Sandro Liu. Where was he? Was he in some sort of trouble? Why hadn't he returned to Richard's boat? What, if anything, had lured him away? Then Elspeth had the worst thought of all. What if the money in the case Carlo had left behind in the gardens had been too enticing to Sandro, and he had run off with it? That would be a huge problem.

When her three guests arrived, she laid out the rudiments of her plan, but she did not mention the idea that Sandro might have stolen the case. She expected Biddy to be the most resistant to her assigned role but was surprised at her reaction.

"I feel rather like Miss Marple," her cousin said. "The duchess reminds me of Jean MacTavish, who lives in the village near the farm," Biddy explained. "When her son was killed in Iraq, she retreated into her cottage and locked the front door to all her family and friends. Like the duchess, Jean showed no emotion at all when she had the news. Finally, her daughter, who worked on the farm, came to me and asked me if I could do anything for her mother. Rather than knocking at the front door, I went round to the back of the cottage, opened the kitchen door and found Jean at the kitchen table staring into the cold hearth. When I went to her and put my arms around her, she started to cry. Her grief was such that until another human being found a way to approach her, she could not weep. When I came in, she began to sob and talk about her son. By the time I left two hours later, she had rebuilt her fire, unlocked the front door, and let in her family and friends."

"Are you suggesting that the duchess is not as unapproachable as she seemed coming back from the restaurant, Biddy?" Elspeth asked.

"Not if I can find a way into her suite by the kitchen door, so to speak. Let me think how I might do that."

Will nodded his head sympathetically. "When two of my closest friends were killed in a riot in India, I would have liked someone coming through a kitchen door to hold me."

Elspeth was surprised at Will's sensitivity but in the past had frequently found this quality in men of Will's size. They did not need to prove their toughness the way men of smaller proportions often did. Gentle giants, Elspeth thought, and liked Will better for his openness.

Richard remained silent through this discussion. Elspeth wondered if he was thinking of his wife's death. Lady Marjorie would always be a part of Richard, a part that Elspeth could not replace. Did she want to?

Putting these musings aside, Elspeth turned to Will. "I have been trying to think of ways for you to access to the duchess's suite when she is not there. If Lady Elisabeth invited the duchess to her rooms, that would give you time to get into the duchess's suite."

"What are you expecting I'll find there?" Will asked.

"I'm not sure. Anything that might link Toria with Marco Celli or would establish any connection between the duchess and Marco's murder. If you find nothing, the shots from the roof were possibly meant for some else. From what the room attendant who cleaned their suite had told me, Toria and her mother did not see eye to eye on the merits of Toria's ex-husband. The police have already decided there is a link between the murder and, as they are calling it, the suicide. I need to be convinced."

Will set his jaw. "Vittoria Albi was not suicidal."

"She fell from the window," Richard added in, "and there must be a reason why."

Elspeth concurred. "Exactly. Franca Donatello assured me that all the windows in the hotel are usually kept sealed for the comfort of the guests. Therefore, why was Toria's window open? The police assume that Toria shot Marco from the window of her suite. Evidence Will found on the roof yesterday contradicts that fact. If Lady Elisabeth keeps the duchess away from her suite for an hour or so, Will should be able to go through everything thoroughly. I only hope Lord Kennington doesn't discover what we are doing. I've no idea what you will find, Will, in either the duchess's or Toria Albi's space. In her current state of grief, the duchess probably hasn't touched Toria's things. Wouldn't you all agree?"

All nodded except Biddy, who frowned slightly. "Either that or she spent the afternoon getting rid of anything to do with Toria."

Elspeth glanced at Biddy and said, "That's what Will will try to discover. Take your camera, Will, and record everything that seems even slightly important. Can you control the flash?"

"Yes, I can override it."

"Do that and get the pictures back to me as soon as possible," Elspeth said.

Elspeth turned to Richard and addressed him formally. "Richard, I would like you to get the launch back to Stresa as soon as possible. I doubt there is much you can do this evening, but I would appreciate it if you would try."

"I expect that most of the boats are off the lake by now, but I can drop round the marina in Baveno in the morning and see if I can find Sebastiano. Elspeth, can you lend me a hotel car? That will make my task a lot easier."

"Yes, of course. I suggest we all go our separate ways now. Biddy, please let us know as soon as you make contact with the duchess. Call room service and order Galliano cocktails. That will be your code for saying the duchess is in your suite. If she says she has to leave, call room service again and cancel the order. I'll arrange for room service to call me about these orders as soon as they come in and will let you know, Will, when it is safe for you to go to the duchess's suite. Let's all meet back here after dinner, say at half past nine—unless something happens to change our plans."

After Biddy and Richard left the room, Elspeth motioned to Will to stay. She picked up the room phone and rang down to Franca Donatello's office.

"Franca, Elspeth here. Has the room attendant on the second floor, Laura, left the hotel yet?"

"No, Elspetta."

"Good. Ask her to come to the conference room near your office. Assure her that her diligence will be favorably reported to London."

Will and Elspeth found Laura waiting downstairs. She was dressed in black jeans and a tight tank top, and her hair was loose, which made her look, to Elspeth's eyes, audaciously flirtatious. Will smiled widely at her, and she smiled back without any sign of deference. Elspeth hardly recognized the demure room attendant she had spoken to earlier in the day.

Elspeth spoke first. "Thank you for staying, Laura. It looks like you have plans for the evening."

"Nothing special, *signora*. I meet with friends at the café, but there is no hurry." Her tone was polite, echoing the way she had spoken earlier.

"Laura, Mr. Tuttle is working with me to try to find out more about the tragedy of Toria Albi's accident. When you cleaned her suite this morning, did you notice anything out of the ordinary?"

Laura screwed up her young and now heavily made-up face. "They fight, but everyday they fight. The *signora* asked me to get more towels for her bath. I have no extra towels on my trolley, so I go down to the linen storage on the ground floor to get more. When I come back, I knock on the door. The *signora*, she asks me to come in with the towels. The door to *la signorina*'s room is open a bit, and it feels like there is a wind in there. I start to go to see why, but *la signora* tells me to take the towels to the bathroom. She closes the door to *la signorina*'s room before I see in."

"Did you see the *signorina*?" Elspeth asked.

"No, the door is not much open," Laura said.

"Did you hear anyone in the *signorina*'s room?"

"No. There is no noise."

"How did the *signora* act?" Will asked.

"She seem in a hurry."

"In a hurry?"

"How do you say? *Impaziente*."

"I see. Impatient. Thank you, Laura. You have been very helpful. Enjoy your evening," Elspeth said.

"*Grazie, signora—e signore*," she said, reserving her grin for Will.

When Laura left, Elspeth was puzzled. "Will, what do you make of Laura's account, particularly the bit about the door to Toria's room?"

"Damning."

"Damning? Why?"

"It sounds like the window was already open at that point. This is just a guess, but could Toria have been trying to escape by the window and the duchess knew she was out on the ledge?"

Elspeth frowned at his words. She stood, walked toward the window and looked out. The whiteness of the grotesque outline made by the police chalk was still visible. She turned to face Will. "When you told Lady Elisabeth and the duchess about Toria, did the duchess seem surprised?"

Will considered. "Startled rather," he said.

"How is that different?"

"Surprised is when you don't expect something. Startled is when you know something and don't expect the other person to know it."

Elspeth looked at Will for a long moment. "I've never made that distinction. Follow your thought, Will. Where does it go?"

Will lowered his sandy head and shook it back and forth for a long time, frowning. "I'm trying to think what might have happened. If the duchess knew the window was open and Toria had climbed out of it, the duchess didn't want Laura to see."

Elspeth bit her lower lip. "That sounds rather sinister. If Toria was already outside the window, perhaps threatening to jump, then the duchess was shielding Laura from what might happen. The duchess would not be aware that Laura went to the next room, where she saw Toria fall."

"If the duchess saw Toria fall," Will said, "why did she go off with Lady Elisabeth as if nothing had happened?"

Elspeth tried to imagine the sequence of events. "If I were Toria and in the midst of a fight with my mother, I would try to escape. If *la mamma* blocked the way out, as it seemed she did, using the window ledge would be a possible alternative."

"Do you think the fall was an accident or something worse?" Will asked.

"I would prefer to think the whole thing was an accident not the alternative," Elspeth said. "When you get into the duchess's suite, explore both possibilities. I'm not overly optimistic that the mystery will be unraveled by your search, but we can only hope."

After Will had left the office, Elspeth sought out Franca, who was in the dining room inspecting the setup for dinner. Elspeth drew Franca aside to a secluded corner.

"It's been a long day, Franca, and not an easy one for the hotel staff. I appreciate all the work they have done to keep the paparazzi at bay and allow privacy for the duchess and the ex-minister." Elspeth was careful not to use Carlo Bartelli's name. "Will you be here this evening or will you entrust your duties to a night manager?"

"Paolo is a very capable night manager and will be handling the normal duties, but, considering all that has taken place here today, I will be staying on as well. What are your plans, Elspetta, for the rest of the evening?"

"How I wish I could stay and enjoy the end product of the delicious odors that are coming from the kitchen, but first I must speak with the ex-minister. I will keep in touch."

"*Va bene*. I will tell the night staff to take instructions from you."

*

As he was coming back to his room, Will met Mandy, who was piloting a hotel wheelchair along the hallway. She had abandoned her crutches in favor of this more rapid means of transport. All at once, he was glad for her forthrightness. Mandy had no wiles, or at least none that were apparent to him.

"Have you had tea?" he asked.

"Pots. I'm swimming in it, and I ate one too many of those orange scones. I couldn't stay on this assignment forever as I would be as big as a tree, but I will miss all this good food when I get back to university."

Will tried but could not imagine Mandy in the form of a large tree.

"Come down to the back rooms with me. I need to get your advice on something from the female point of view," he said, trying to stay with the business at hand.

"Your feelings about Vittoria yesterday?" Mandy guessed.

Will reddened. "Well, actually, yes, but not what you think."

"I don't think anything, Will." Mandy looked up from her chair and smiled impishly.

"Liar," he said. He was relieved by her sanity. "Mandy, you are a treasure!"

She said unabashedly, "I've always tried to be. In light of my father's profession, however, this was often overlooked for more ancient relics."

Will guffawed. "Come along, goose," he said. "We have things to talk about."

Franca's office was empty when they arrived, but the night manager, who recognized Will, allowed him to use the conference room where Elspeth and he had interviewed Laura. Will hoped Mandy would not look out the window and see the area cordoned off by the police.

Will and Mandy sat across the table from each other.

"What's your opinion of Vittoria's mother?" Will asked.

"Britches," said Mandy. "My father always made us modify impolite words when I was a child," she added as if in explanation.

"Why?"

"Because he thought he could fool my mother, who was Italian. She would say, '*Pantaloni, pantaloni*? Don't you mean *cagne*?' which literally means female dogs. Then we would all laugh."

Will was delighted. "You do love your mother and father!"

"With all my heart, Will. They're the most wonderful people in the world."

"What a relief," said Will.

"It's my turn to ask why."

"Because I thought for a moment there was no such thing as normal."

Mandy chuckled at this, reached across the table and placed her hand on top of Will's. "If you had met my parents, you would not use the word normal. They are eccentric to a fault."

"I love you, Mandy."

"Will, this is so sudden," she said. If she caught his meaning, she flaunted it.

They both laughed with a merriment Will had not known for a long time. Despite her impetuous driving, Mandy represented a sane world rather than an insane one. Will thought this a blessed panacea.

"Seriously, tell me what you think about the duchess," Will said, trying to look serious.

"In ancient cultures, postmenopausal women were both powerful and frightening because they held the responsibility for propagation of the tribal myths but also had the ultimate power to dictate matters of life and death. When male-dominated religions came along, these women were branded as witches and marginalized, and, in reality, think about what that meant. In India, widows were burned on their husband's funeral pyre. In the modern European world, however, widows retire genteelly to the country and are expected to do so-called good works. Go to a posh social event in the Counties and see if you can find any aging widows there. Unless they are very rich, very well-connected, or titled, you will find their absence instead."

"What does that have to do with the duchess?"

"She represents a fall back to ancient times."

"A person who ultimately decides matters of life and death?"

"Exactly."

"Didn't Vittoria tell us that her mother was often indisposed in the afternoon? One would think she was just an old woman who drank too much wine at lunch."

"The old women of the tribal past used many herbs and potions, thus the witch legends. Perhaps alcoholism is only a modern manifestation of that."

Will looked across at Amanda and smiled. Her sophomoric intensity charmed him but also gave him some reason for thought. Did the duchess really have the power of life and death? He would have to think more about this, but right now he was just enjoying being with Mandy.

34

Once again Elspeth walked out onto the balcony of her suite and braced herself against the Alpine air. She rested her hand on the cold stone of the balcony rail, but that did not help steady her thoughts. She needed time to think about how to approach Carlo and Silvia after their ordeal on the lake and on the island. She went over everything that Richard had told her and tried to make sense of the events of the day and Sandro's disappearance. The safety of Carlo Bartelli's daughter was the key issue. Sometimes a direct approach with people in distress worked, but sometimes it had the opposite effect. She decided she would let her instinct guide her after she arrived at Carlo and Silvia's suite.

She knocked at their door and saw Carlo's eye come into the peephole. He unchained the door and let her in. The furrows in his brow had deepened and dark circles surrounded his eyes.

"*Signora* Duff, I want to thank you for offering Sir Richard's assistance today," he said rather stiffly after she had entered and he had re-chained the door. "I had no idea we were in such distinguished company until we returned to the hotel, and Silvia logged on to the internet. None of us has any privacy anymore. One need only to go to a computer and all one's past is revealed." He gave a hollow chuckle.

Elspeth smiled perfunctorily. "*Signor* Bartelli, I hear that you have had a very stressful two days. I apologize that we haven't given you better service."

"The Kennington Stresa cannot be blamed for lightning hitting the launch, *signora*," a voice said.

Silvia was sitting in her chair behind the sofa, but, as she spoke, she wheeled herself into full view. Her shocking pink terrycloth robe set off her high complexion but also the deep shadows under her eyes.

Elspeth continued with caution. "Richard has been a friend since I was young, and we have maintained a friendship for many years. He has been a source of stability and wisdom for me many times. I'm glad to hear that he was of help to you today."

Carlo nodded. "He assisted us in a way that we cannot repay. Do sit down, *signora*."

Elspeth took a place on the sofa and waited for a moment. Silence fell between them. Finally she ventured, "I'm concerned about Sandro Liu."

Silvia looked up at Elspeth. "Sandro was of great comfort to us throughout the last two days. We too became anxious when he didn't return to Sir Richard's boat after we had stopped on Isola Bella."

Carlo turned to Silvia with what Elspeth perceived to be a warning.

Despite his look, Silvia continued. "Sandro is a remarkable young man. I don't know if you know his background, but he survived a terrible incident in his youth when he watched his parents be killed by military forces in Burma. *Signora*, I know from personal experience how much such a thing has an effect on one for the rest of one's life. Sandro and I had had several talks over the last two days, and I fear that he has taken it upon himself to correct what he considers a great injustice. He ignored my pleadings to him that issues with which Carlo and I were dealing were not his. I cannot tell you why he didn't come back to the boat, but I can guess that it had to do with his own feelings, not with anything that Carlo and I asked him to do."

"Young men can be impetuous, *Signora* Trucco. I have a son in America who also has a sense of what is morally right and has often acted on it when he should have shown restraint. I appreciate what sensibilities Sandro may have been feeling. Unfortunately, Lord Kennington may not share the same view." Elspeth hoped she sounded empathetic.

Carlo broke in. His voice was harsh. "*Signora* Duff, you must realize that, if Sandro Liu did go off to right what he thought was wrong, he is putting my daughter in grave danger."

Elspeth saw fear in Carlo's eyes and decided to broach the subject most on her mind. "*Signor* Bartelli, do you think it *was* your daughter's abductors who retrieved the money today?"

Carlo's lips tightened, and he continued to stand rigidly by one of the armchairs. "I would prefer . . ." he began.

Silvia interrupted. "Carlo, I have never overridden you before, but now I think I shall. You may fire me if you wish. I have quite a lot of money saved and can quite easily live on my own. When the launch was hit by lightning last evening, it was Sandro who saved the case with the money. *Signora* Duff, Carlo delivered it today just as demanded. We believe that Sandro followed Carlo when he left the case and may be chasing the person who collected it. That would explain his not returning to the boat."

Silvia clearly had more faith in Sandro's actions than Elspeth had. Elspeth did not bring up her suspicion that Sandro might have stolen the case.

Carlo glared at Silvia but addressed Elspeth. "I would have preferred that Sandro had stayed out of this." His voice was angry. "If he decides to demand the money's return, the rebels may think the money was left as a trap. Do you see my dilemma?"

Elspeth had not imagined this scenario. "What a terrible situation. I agree. Sandro is only making it worse."

Silvia looked startled. *"Signora*, you must not be so severe. Perhaps my talking with him about his parents and my own situation during the war brought back memories that . . ." she paused, "that fueled old fires of injustice. I am an old woman and will take responsibility for making Sandro remember his old wounds. I don't think he knew that both Carlo and I have lived through this type of situation with Constanza before."

Elspeth watched the two people with her in the room. She wondered about their own relationship and their intensity. Elspeth did not know how to respond to them compassionately. Her Scottish upbringing, despite her many years in California, made her uneasy with invading people's privacy. Consequently she decided on a more formal way to respond, one that allowed her some degree of comfort.

"I regret that Sandro seems to have acted inappropriately," she said. "It's a matter of grave concern to the hotel management, and we will act accordingly. I know it's a difficult moment for you both. Have you heard anything from Constanza?"

"No, not yet," Carlo said. His voice was flat.

Elspeth could not read his reaction. She cleared her throat. "There is another rather unfortunate matter that I must bring up. You both were outside the hotel when the bullets were fired that killed Marco Celli. Today Marco's ex-wife fell from the window of her room here in the hotel and was killed on impact with the street. The local police are calling the death a suicide, but there's the possibility the *carabiniere* will become involved, and they may come and question our guests. I know how sensitive your stay is. The hotel's greatest obligation to you is to keep your presence here confidential. I hate to add to your burdens, but I'll need your cooperation on another matter. We want to keep the police out of the hotel at all costs."

At that moment Elspeth hated her role in the Kennington Organisation. She was imposing the needs of the hotel over the needs of Silvia and Carlo. The complexity of the situation overwhelmed Elspeth, and she knew Eric Kennington would expect her to make everything smooth again. Had it only been the murder of Marco Celli, or only the death of Toria Albi, or only the confidential matters of Carlo Bartelli, or only the defection of Sandro Liu, she would have shifted into problem-solving mode and in all likelihood come up with a neat solution. The possible interconnection of all these things, if any, baffled her, and she could find no straightforward answers.

She continued, "This afternoon I went down to the underground car park and found your car parked there. Although it is out of the way of the traffic along the route to the lift and is covered, any person entering the car park could, if they were looking for it, find the bullet hole in the windscreen. There has been some speculation in the press that the bullet that killed Marco Celli came from the large car at the scene, which we know is not true. If the police or any member of the press corps find your car and record the number plate, I fear you will lose your anonymity as guests here. Is there any way that you can have your car moved? I know it seems a minor issue, but it may become an important one."

"Our driver has made arrangements with a local auto shop to have the windscreen replaced on Monday," Silvia said.

"He told the shop that a stone hit the it. It would have been replaced yesterday, but the shop did not have that specific one in their inventory and had to order one from Milano."

Carlo nodded. "I will telephone the driver and have him move the car. He has family near here, and I am sure that he can find a place to conceal the car until Monday."

Elspeth shook her head. "I recommend that you have your driver cancel the appointment with the repair shop and have him drive the car to Milan or Rome tonight. I'm not suggesting that we interfere with any police investigation. If necessary, you can come forward later, but, for the moment, I think you can plead innocence, saying you have been involved in your own matters and were unaware that there was a police investigation going on. We can discuss what you will say to the police only if that becomes necessary."

Carlo turned on Elspeth. "I have no intention of lying to the police." His tone softened. "I frequently take trips throughout Italy making art purchases. When I travel, I am often unaware of the more sensational news, so my lack of knowledge of the murder would not be unusual."

Silvia sat quietly for a moment and then added, "Unfortunately, here in Italy, politicians and public figures are frequently the target of shootings. We were frightened when the car was hit by the bullet, but we can say honestly we were so preoccupied with Carlo's business that we paid little more attention to it."

Elspeth was appreciative. "You can count on my assistance in any way you need it. As for the problem with Sandro, there's another member of our security staff here in the hotel. He's otherwise occupied this evening, but in the morning I'll send him out to see if he can find Sandro before there is any more trouble."

35

Lady Elisabeth Baillie Shaw and *la duchessa d'Astonino* sat sipping the second of their Galliano cocktails. Both were tipsy. Biddy, who was used to single malt whiskey, was the more sober of the two and later was able to remember most of what the duchess said to her.

Biddy did not find it difficult to come in the "kitchen door." She ordered a bouquet of flowers to be sent to the duchess's suite with a handwritten note.

> *My dear Maria,*
>
> *Since coming back to the hotel, my heart has been filled with the sadness of your loss. Do come up to my suite, if you feel up to it. I would like to help ease your sorrow in any way I can.*
>
> *With deepest sympathy,*
> *Elisabeth Baillie Shaw*

Biddy had calculated that using their given names without the formality of their titles would have lure to the duchess. She was correct. The duchess phoned Biddy, addressed her as Elisabeth and accepted an invitation to cocktails.

The duchess's tongue loosened with drink, and her English deteriorated. "Marco is bad for Vittoria. She always says he is a simple, strong man who forgets his power, but I see often the bruises. Her make-up does not cover them."

The duchess touched her jeweled hand to her reconstructed nose and sniffed in her sorrow. "Always I tell her that she is a star and does not need a man like Marco. She says she loves him."

"I loved my husband too." The irrelevance of Biddy's statement did not seem to register with the duchess.

The duchess took a large swallow of the yellow liquid in her tall glass. "I think I love my first husband. We wait many years for Vittoria and finally she come, and I am very happy. Then I find he have another woman. I love him no longer and only love Vittoria."

"I am sorry," said Biddy. She was thankful Ivor had not strayed in their many years of marriage.

"He die when Vittoria just about to become a star. He never knows. I do not care."

Biddy almost expected the duchess to bare her canines because of the intense look of hatred on her face, but the fangs did not appear.

Biddy stopped sipping her cocktail in order to keep her head clear enough to elicit more from the duchess.

"Did you love the duke?" Biddy asked, trying to sound innocent.

The duchess began slurring her words. "He ish a very old man, but he love Vittoria not me, and he want to protect ush. Thish ish a good arrangement."

"So you did not love him." Biddy hoped she sounded matter of fact.

"No, but he help ush. We give him beauty and young life. He give ush the villa and money and, how do you shay, status." The duchess had a hard time with this last word and finally let it go after three tries. "When he die, he shtill love

Vittoria, but I think he ish no longer happy when she ish away, and he want her to shtop being a film shtar and come live only at the villa. I think thish ish not good for ush."

"You're a practical woman, Maria." Biddy said, taking the duchess's talon-like hand.

"*Sì*. I musht always protect Vittoria. She ish—wash—the mosht beautiful, but she ish—wash—not the most, how do you shay, practical. She believe she love Marco." The duchess shook her head back and forth quickly, her long earrings swishing to and fro.

"How sad," Biddy said, suddenly sorry for the duchess.

The duchess finished her drink and poured herself another. She took a long swallow.

Biddy set her own glass aside. "Were you afraid of Marco?" she asked.

The duchess snorted in an inelegant way. "No. Marco no frighten me. He ish, how do you shay, a bully, *sì*, but he ish a bully who runs away when shomeone say pffff." The last word came out more as spittle than anything else. The duchess's English was getting more obscure, but Biddy followed the gist.

"If you were not afraid of him, why did you come here to Stresa?"

"Because Vittoria try to run back to him from the villa."

"How did he find out you were in Stresa?" Biddy's mind now had begun to clear despite the two strong cocktails she had imbibed.

"I think she tell him. *Stupida!*" The duchess no longer seemed to be able to contain her emotions within her command of the English language.

"You must have been very glad when someone murdered him." Biddy said blandly, as if it were a simple statement.

A Scandal in Stresa

"*Sì*. It ish the besht day. Vittoria cry; I celebrate." The duchess raised both her hands and crooked her fingers like claws.

The gesture frightened Biddy. "Do you know who killed him?"

"*Io?* Me? No. But, if I know that person, I give him much money. He ish my hero." She smiled gleefully, if somewhat lopsidedly.

"Do you think it was a man?" Biddy asked, now fascinated in a ghoulish way.

"*Sì*. A hushband. The women all love him. Sometimes he cannot shay no to them."

Biddy could not follow the duchess's last bit of reasoning but ventured on. "I wonder if the police have any real clues."

"*La polizia* are shtupid."

"Oh, why do you think so?" Biddy did not share what Elspeth had told her about the *commissario*'s conclusions.

The duchess could no longer sit straight and fell slightly to her side, bracing herself with one hand. She put up her other hand to her heavily sprayed hair and, in doing so, disarrayed it so that tuffs stuck out in an odd manner.

"They think that Vittoria kill him, but they not shay so because she ish a beautiful film star." The contempt in the duchess's voice was chilling. "She ish too shtupid to kill him. She just say she love him, and she cry all the time when he ish dead. Shtupid girl!"

The duchess rocked back and forth in her chair and then began to emit an eerie sound that Biddy thought might either be a laugh or cry of anger or something in between.

The duchess continued to screech. "The men are all alike. They think they are sho, how do you shay, attractive to the women and so shmart. They think the women will not find out about the other women. Intellish . . . intelligent women always know. I think Vittoria ish like her pappa. She believe Marco love her. I know he doesh not. He ish a pig. He deserves to die. The others, they deserve to die too."

Suddenly the duchess stopped and looked at Biddy and, with conspiracy in her voice, she said, "I kill him like the others if I have the chance." She raised her hand and began stabbing the air.

Biddy was confused. The duchess' meaning was as dark as the hatred in her eyes. Not knowing what to say, Biddy remained quiet but could feel cold terror run down her back.

The duchess took another drink. "I go now." She put down her glass, rose unsteadily and then slid slowly backwards on to the sofa. The noise from her lips ceased. She had passed out.

Biddy later described the scene to Elspeth and Richard. "She sent shivers down my spine. I've never heard such hatred. I felt that she wasn't describing Marco Celli or the police but rather other men in her life."

"Where is the duchess now?" her cousin asked.

"I tried to wake her up, but she was completely unconscious. She was sprawled on my sofa, so I stretched her out as best I could. I never realized how floppy drunk people get. Luckily I had no trouble because she's not much larger then some of my ewes at home. Then I covered her up with a shawl and came up here. She's probably still down there."

Biddy was shaken. Any hint of fuzziness in her mind vanished when the duchess began to laugh. Biddy never wanted to taste the sweet stickiness of Galliano again because it now rose from her stomach and turned sour in her throat.

"Do you think the duchess had anything to do with the deaths of either of her husbands, Dickie?" Elspeth asked.

He sniffed. "I wouldn't be surprised. At the very least she despised them before they died. I expect the duchess had some of Toria's beauty when she was younger, but her vitriolic nature must have taken over years ago. The ferocity of her need to protect her daughter must have become so consuming that she could think of little else."

Biddy was horrified. "How awful that must have been for Toria. If she ever saw even the least of what I saw just now, she would have been terrified of her mother. It makes one wonder if she really did commit suicide."

"She couldn't escape her mother," Elspeth added. "Can you imagine the mixed messages she got from her father, from her stepfather, and from men in general, who responded so passionately to her beauty but at the same time from her mother, who poured acid in her ear?"

Elspeth rose from her chair and went over to where Biddy was huddled on the sofa. Her hand was on her head.

"Thank you, Biddy, for taking on the duchess. Not a pleasant task nor is the duchess a pleasant woman. Elspeth said.

"When her mother took over, I can assure you, that would be poison to any man," Richard said. He sounded as if he knew.

Biddy looked at them and blew out her breath. "I should have hated such a mother, especially one who criticized every move in your life. Thank goodness Mother and Daddy never were that way. What are we going to do now?" she asked.

The phone rang. Elspeth picked it up and listened. "Yes, we'll bring one," she said.

Elspeth turned to Biddy and Richard. "That was Will," she explained. "He was able to get into the duchess's suite when she was with you, Biddy, and reports that he has made an important discovery, but, before he tells me what he saw, we must tend to the duchess. Dickie, perhaps you can go up with us and help Will lift the duchess into a wheelchair and take her back to her rooms. Biddy and I will come along, in case she comes to consciousness."

"If she is anything like Cook at my great-aunt's house in Edinburgh, I would guess that she won't be aware of much until the morning," Biddy explained that this cook had fascinated her when she was a child because her great-aunt had always left the dinner table before the others to see "if Cook was all right." Biddy had followed her aunt one night and had seen her drag Cook away from the cooking sherry and into her bed. Cook, even if not fully recovered in the morning, presented breakfast without fail.

Armed with a hotel wheelchair for the duchess's limp body, they met Will outside Biddy's suite. The limp body offered no resistance. The service lift was only a short distance away, and they met no one as they descended to the floor below. They left the duchess unconscious on her own bed.

Elspeth thanked Biddy for her work and let her return to her rooms. Biddy slid into bed after nibbling at a bit of toast and sipping some broth, which she had ordered from room service. Before falling off to sleep, she cursed the effects of the strong cocktails she had shared with the duchess. From now on she would stick to single malt whiskey.

*

As they left the duchess's suite, Will drew Elspeth aside and requested a private conference with her. Richard made his apologies, and Elspeth and Will retreated to her suite. She could feel that Will was excited.

A Scandal in Stresa

"You won't believe what I found in the duchess's wardrobe," he said. "She's an incredibly neat person, so I almost missed it because it was so cleverly hidden."

"For heaven sakes, Will, what was it?"

"A hunting rifle."

"A hunting rifle?"

"With a telescopic lens."

"Tell me more."

"Vittoria's room was in a state of havoc, and I didn't have time to go through the extreme clutter. When I got to the duchess's bedroom, everything was in such incredible order that I wondered if it was even worth searching. Her clothes were neatly hung, dresses together, jackets together, blouses together; you can see the picture. She'd put four large cases at the bottom of the wardrobe. I examined them, but they appeared to be empty. I almost left, but I wasn't quite satisfied. One case was heavier than the rest and, unlike the others, was locked."

"You broke the lock?"

"No, I picked it."

"I didn't know you had that talent, but go on, Will."

Will looked bashful. "I took the heavier case over to the bed and, using techniques that Lord Kennington might not approve of, opened the case with, if I might say so, skilled ease."

Elspeth was amused by Will's euphemism. "And?"

"Inside a flat box was fitted tightly into the bottom of the case. It looked as if the case had been designed for it. The box was also locked, but again I was able to get inside." Will's eyes twinkled.

"And you found the gun."

"Mmm hmm. I'd thought to bring latex gloves, which I wore throughout the search, so I took a chance at removing the gun from the box and taking extensive photographs of it."

"Do you have any idea what type it is?"

"No, I don't know much about rifles, but the pictures should help. I downloaded the photographs to my computer and also sent them to my secure email address in case there were any problems."

"Will, are you thinking what I am thinking?"

"That the duchess was the one that fired the rifle that killed Marco Celli?"

"There is that possibility," Elspeth said.

"How can we prove that the duchess used it? The duchess can still remove the box, if she thinks someone has tampered with it, and then we have no evidence that she brought the rifle here. Do the police have the bullet that killed Marco Celli?"

"They must. But wait. There were three bullets, but only two shots were heard. I think the third was fired as a test earlier and, consequently, the murder must have been premeditated," Elspeth said.

"Do the police know about the casings I found on the roof?"

"Thank heavens, no. The *commissario* thinks he has solved the case, and, so far, hasn't demanded to search the hotel. I think he found a plausible but incorrect solution in what they are calling Toria's suicide and did not want to bring in higher authorities. Toria's throwing herself from the window does offer an easy solution."

"She didn't do it, Elspeth. You saw the note."

"I did but the *commissario* didn't. He brushed off any suggestion that didn't support his theory."

Will suddenly looked worried. "Will we be tampering with evidence if we don't tell him about the casings, the rifle, and the note?"

"The most that could happen would be that we would be accused of not being forthcoming. Quickly, bring your camera. Let's go do something that Lord Kennington might find unforgivable but may give us another piece of evidence."

At that moment Elspeth was glad that she had not told Richard about the bullet at the base of the tree or the casings on the roof.

It was now dusk, but Will thought there was enough light for him to take photographs without the use of a flash. They crossed in front of the hotel and made their way into the park. A sign on the gate indicated that the gates were closed at sunset, but no one had done so. Elspeth looked around to see if any paparazzi were lingering outside the hotel, but none were to be seen.

Elspeth led Will to the tree where she had discovered the bullet and pointed to what she had found the day before. The bullet was still lodged in the trunk of the tree, which was in shade.

"I can try to get a picture but no guarantees," Will said after judging the light. "Or we can try a technique I use frequently, particularly when I am taking photographs in places I am not supposed to be. We'll pretend I'm taking your photograph. You stand near the bullet hole, and I'll get both in the picture."

Elspeth smiled sweetly and posed. Will took several photographs using his flash and then asked her to shift positions. She glued on her smile again and did as Will asked. No one appeared to be paying attention to them, although it would be difficult to know if anyone was looking out from a window.

"You already have photographed the third bullet," she said. "In the car park."

He grinned.

They returned to the hotel and went to their respective rooms. Elspeth waited ten minutes before Will arrived at her suite with his laptop in tow. Frame by frame they went over the photographs in the car park, in the garden, and on the roof. Elspeth was amazed at the skill he used in each of the photographs. Not only were all of them informative, but they also were artistically brilliant.

"Will, don't share these with anyone for now. Perhaps we are withholding evidence, but the *commissario* here is a bit slow and will not know there is evidence until we point it out to him. Somehow I doubt he will ask."

Elspeth made two personal calls before she took on her final task for the day. The first call was to Biddy, who pleaded a fierce headache, and the second was to Richard, who invited her to dinner. She accepted gratefully.

She turned back to the phone and rang Carlo Bartelli's suite.

"I have one more request for you and *la signora*," she said to Carlo, who answered the phone. "I know how tired and distressed you must be, but I also am worried about your anonymity here at the hotel. May I come up again first thing in the morning and tell you my plan? It can wait until the morning. Today has been an long day for us all, and I do not want to trouble you further tonight." She did not yet know that, in the morning, Carlo and Silvia would have graver concerns on their mind.

36

Richard brought flowers to Elspeth's room. It was a quaint gesture, particularly at a hotel that daily provided flowers in abundance to all the rooms. He produced two perfect yellow roses that had the slightest blush of red at their edges. He knew these roses were Elspeth's favorite. As she leaned over to smell the flowers, he noticed with appreciation that she had shed her severe business attire and was dressed simply in an exquisitely cut, blue woolen frock and a multi-color shawl thrown with casual elegance around her shoulders.

When they left her suite, he folded her arm into his. As they entered the lift, he said, "Should we have invited Biddy tonight?"

Elspeth shook her head. "She is nursing a bad headache. Besides, Dickie, I wanted us to be alone."

He warmed all over. His courtship with Elspeth was slow, but he sensed not hopeless.

As the doors of the lift closed in on them, Richard squeezed her arm to his side. "I have been neglecting you, my dearest Elspeth. I know that Eric demands twenty-four hour diligence from you when you are on assignment. What a pleasure that you actually have agreed to leave the hotel and dine with me."

Elspeth cocked an eyebrow. "He pays me well to stay attentive when I am on a job."

"Despite his dictates, I'm going to see that you have a real break from duty tonight," Richard said. "There is little else you can do until morning, and an evening at an excellent restaurant away from the hotel will do you more good than harm. Ring Franca, if you must, and tell her I have booked a table for us at the *Lombarda,* which I've been assured serves the best food in Stresa. Let's walk, shall we? The night is new, and we once were young." He took her hand possessively, and she made no attempt withdraw it.

They strolled companionably down the hill, walked across a small plaza and found the restaurant in an alley off of it. Richard had requested that their table be as private as possible and had arranged that they not be disturbed during their dinner other than by the waiter. When with Elspeth, he seldom used his title, but this evening he gave it pompously to the maître d'. He had found in the past that a title attached to a name was often more effective than monetary remuneration to insure preferential treatment.

As they were seated, Richard said, "Elspeth, I have taken the liberty of ordering for us because I did not want this precious time to be interrupted by negotiations over the minutia of the menu. Forgive me if I have presumed, but this may be the only time we have together alone all weekend."

"I'm extraordinary grateful that, for a short time anyway, someone else can make some decisions for me. For the next few hours I don't want to be responsible for a single thing and want to be totally indulged."

"Your wish, my dear, is hereby granted."

Champagne arrived without bidding and shortly afterwards a first course of pasta covered with a sauce of fresh tomatoes, basil and olive oil.

Elspeth leaned back in her chair and stretched her arms, placing her hands on the white damask tablecloth. She sighed. "Dickie, this is the first moment I have unbent since Eric Kennington gave me lunch in London, so many days ago that I've lost count. What a ride. I expect you to make me forget all about the murder and its consequences until after our dinner is done. Tell me how things are in Malta."

"What a lovely nation, Elspeth, as you know."

"It seems to suit you. You look marvelously well. And how is Aunt Magdelena?"

"My favorite person in Malta. She invites me to Gozo occasionally, and I accept whenever I can tear myself from official duties. She doesn't seem to change with age other than that she has announced that she will no longer play contemporary music."

Elspeth laughed. "Does she still have monthly soirées?" she asked.

Richard shook his head. "Not monthly. Now the soirées happen when she wants them to, always to celebrate some wonderful happening: a baptism, the acceptance of a poem or an artwork by a friend, or someone's birthday or anniversary."

"Does she still practice shamelessly with her window open?"

"Shamelessly."

"I do miss Malta."

"Then when this is all over, come visit us."

"Perhaps I shall, if I can find time. I always feel so at home there. Since my parents are not listening, I will say that Aunt Mag has been the greatest gift in my life. Staying with her is like a holiday treat."

The second course came at that moment. The waiter explained it was slices of a whole boned chicken with artichokes and black olives.

Elspeth savored her first bite and leaned back with a sigh. "Oh, Dickie, thank you for rescuing me this evening."

He looked across at her. His heart was full, but, when he was with Elspeth, he never felt that she was completely with him.

"Elspeth, why do you continue to be such a conundrum to me? Your heart seems so loving toward your family and yet, besides them, who . . ."

He let his sentence hang unfinished and rotated the stem of his wine glass for a long moment.

"I think any lessons I learned about loving were from the steadfastness of my mother and father and the never-ending warmth of Aunt Magdelena. I also adore my children even at a distance. I've been lucky to have these people for my family."

Richard waited, but she did not address the second part of his sentence. He thought of the men she had chosen to love in her life, the brilliant and quixotic Malcolm Buchanan and the flamboyant and egotistical Alistair Craig. Richard wondered how much these two men had wounded Elspeth. He found this troubling.

Elspeth looked down at her food and then up at him. She frowned slightly and then changed the subject.

"It's odd, Dickie, that you never speak of your family, even though I have known you for almost forty years."

Richard stiffened. His memories were not fond ones. "They gave me all the privilege of my lineage but, sadly, were incapable of granting me anything else. Both my parents died just before I entered Oxford and left me just enough income to live on but little else. The family title went to my older brother.

A Scandal in Stresa

When my parents died, their funerals were conducted with all the proper pomp, with many friends and acquaintances attending, but nobody cried." A muscle in his jaw tightened.

Elspeth reached out and took his hand. "I'm so sorry," she said.

"One reason, I think," he continued, "that I always loved coming to Tay Farm when I was at Oxford was the sheer exuberance of love that surrounded your family. It wasn't that they were effusive; love just was their state of being."

"Speaking of my family, why did you go to Scotland in June?" she asked.

"I will tell you, Elspeth, but not until your assignment here is over. Come to Malta then. In the meantime, please trust that my reasons are honorable."

They finished their meal on safer topics and with a dessert of lemon ice and wild strawberries. Afterwards they strolled down the promenade along the lake and watched the crescent moon rise over the mountains. When they arrived at the door of her suite, he kissed her lightly on the cheek. She smiled warmly, took his hand in hers and thanked him but did not return the kiss.

37

Sandro Liu woke up with a headache and a blurred idea of the ending of the last night's festivities at the pub. He did remember, however, that Isabella had been good to her promise and had shown him the Hong Kong passports after the end of party. He recognized them not as the old passports issued by the British but rather as the new one's issued by the Chinese government for the special Hong Kong administrative region. He was particularly interested in the one issued for Lyndon Wei and recognized the Chinese characters for his name—Wei Ling-dao. So it had been Wei who had picked up the case on the Isola Bella.

He felt vindicated that he had followed Wei the day before. If he could track Wei today, he probably would find Constanza, but he was alone and did not have a mobile phone or human backup. Sandro did not know the layout of Locarno and, if Wei wanted to elude him, he undoubtedly could do so in a few minutes. Sandro's only hope was that Wei would not suspect anyone knew where he was or what he was doing, but that hope was small.

Through the mustiness of his mind, Sandro recalled that Ricco had told him that Wei went out twice a day, at noon and then in the evening. It was now nine o'clock, which gave Sandro a few hours to plan his surveillance. He took a long, hot shower, although he had done the same thing the night before, and shaved off the whiskers he had accumulated over the last two days. He decided to eat outside the hotel, even though breakfast was included in the price of the room. He found a coffee bar near the hotel and ordered a cappuccino and pastry to take with him. He then went in search of a shop that might offer him at least the modicum of disguises, which was a hard mission to fulfill because it was Sunday morning. He found clothing vendors in kiosks along the shopping arcade, but electronics shops, where he might have bought a new mobile phone, were closed. He cursed himself for not getting one the afternoon before, but he had been too intent on following Wei.

Sandro returned to the hotel before eleven. A new receptionist stood behind the desk. In order to establish that he was a guest, Sandro asked her if he had any messages. He found a dark corner of the lobby, where he transferred his new acquisitions into the pockets of the black anorak he had just purchased. The receptionist lost interest in him and put on some headphones. Her body began to gyrate to some inaudible tune.

Wei came down the lift just before noon. He did not look at either the receptionist or Liu but hurried out of the hotel. Sandro tried to appear uninterested in Wei's departure, and the receptionist was contorting her body in such a way that Wei's actions could not have been of any importance to her.

Sandro emerged into the street just in time to see Wei turn down the side street and set off at a fast pace to the main city plaza. Wei made his way toward the ferry dock. Sandro heard him buy a ticket to Ascona. Sandro waited for Wei to walk out to the quay before buying a similar one. From the map on the wall of the ticket office Sandro saw that Ascona was a suburb southwest of Locarno. Sandro became increasingly certain that Wei was too focused on his destination to notice he was being followed.

After the ferry docked at Ascona, Wei made his way along the waterfront, and Sandro followed as closely as he dared. Soon they were in a residential neighborhood, which made Sandro's presence more noticeable, but Wei did not turn around. Sandro noticed that Wei was becoming agitated. He was talking to himself and kept checking under his coat. Was Wei carrying a firearm?

Sandro drew back because he could see Wei from a long distance, the streets being straight in orderly Swiss fashion. He saw Wei stop and look around him. The hedge-lined street was empty, so Sandro hastily retreated into a nearby entryway. Wei squared his shoulders and approached a house that Sandro noted was the seventh one on the left-hand side of the street. Wei inserted a key into the lock of the iron gate and disappeared from Sandro's view.

The street was now deserted. Sandro considered what his best approach to the house might be. He had not affected any disguise up to this point, but now he pulled on a duckbilled cap and his new anorak. He walked nonchalantly along the street and arrived at the entrance to the house where Wei had disappeared. He peered through the iron bars. Seeing nothing, he went up to the gate, which Wei had left unlocked. Cautiously Sandro opened it. No one was about, which emboldened him. He slipped into the garden beyond. That was the last thing he remembered other than an acute pain radiating through his skull.

Sandro slowly came to through a throbbing haze and became aware of a gun pointed at his temple. The voice behind the gun spoke in Chinese and asked his name.

"I am called Liu," he answered automatically, the way he had been taught as a child. He looked up and saw Wei.

"Why are you here?"

Sandro had difficulty grasping the question and even more difficulty in answering it without telling the truth.

"I'm looking for Constanza Bartelli," he said, since he could think of no other excuse.

"Has her father sent you?"

Sandro put his hand to the back of his head, where he had been struck. "No, I came on my own."

Wei put both hands on the gun. "He sent you, I know. To get his money back."

Sandro became aware of another person in the room, but his eyes would not focus at first. Soon he made out a woman and saw that she was European.

"Are you Constanza?" His voice was little more than a croak.

The woman nodded. "Did my father send you?" she echoed, this time in Italian.

"No, truthfully he did not," he said in the same language.

"Speak English!" Wei demanded.

Constanza spoke in English this time. "Do not worry, Comrade Wei. I only asked him again if my father sent him."

Sandro was beginning to make her out clearly. She walked around the room freely, so Sandro guessed that she might, as Silvia had feared, be in collaboration with Wei.

"Take the gun away from his head, comrade. Let me talk to him," Constanza said.

Wei nodded curtly at her and did as she asked, but he made no attempt to put the pistol in the sheath under his coat.

Constanza's tone was angry. "If my father didn't ask you to come, why did you come?"

"Because I talked to Silvia."

"Silvia worries too much. Can't you see that I'm well?"

Sandro thought she not only looked well but also anger heightened her color. "*Davvero, signorina.*"

"English!" shouted Wei, and he raised his gun.

Constanza nodded and turned back to Sandro. "Don't you understand that my father and Silvia are overly protective? I've been on my own for a long time. I don't need them."

"Was it you who demanded the money? Silvia expected it might be."

"My father won't miss the money. Do you know what the money will do for the poor people in Nepal? A hundred euros can keep a family of four for a long time. My mother once spent a million euros on a necklace that is too valuable for her to wear, and my father agreed to pay for it. Don't you see something wrong in this picture?"

Sandro smiled at her passion. "Silvia warned me that you were an idealist."

Constanza snorted at him.

"Is that all you get out of this—a sense of altruism?" Sandro asked.

"And a damn good story."

Wei drew himself up to full height and looked into Constanza's dark eyes, which were on a level with his. He switched to broken English. His tone was commanding.

"I want you keep Liu hele until I come back tonight," Wei growled at Constanza. "You do that? Or I get man come help you?"

"One of the men with you at your hotel?" she spat out. "You told me I wouldn't have to deal with them again."

Wei's look did not waiver. "I afraid this man take you back to fat-ha." Then he turned to Sandro. "Is that plan?"

A Scandal in Stresa

Sandro felt that his head was cracking open and was slow to realize that Constanza and Wei Ling-dao had a different relationship than he had thought at first. Silvia had spoken so lovingly of Constanza that he had expected her to be more docile than she was. Sandro's self-made mission was to find Constanza, and he presumed that she would be glad to be rescued. Yet, now, she was acting in strange concert with Wei Ling-dao, as an ally and not a captive. Sandro began to wonder if he had been foolish to follow Wei off of Isola Bella. He was disheartened when Wei spoke to Constanza. What was the best course of action for him now?

"In Nepal I see you shoot lifle, Constanza. You also use pistol?" Wei asked.

"Not as skillfully, perhaps, but my father insisted that I learn to handle a handgun sufficiently for self-defense. Daughters with a father like mine in Italy are often targets of thieves and kidnappers," she said, although Sandro did not know for whose benefit. "For many years I carried a pistol, a very pretty one that my father gave me. Although it was supposed to be deadly, I never used it other than to practice shooting at the police station where they showed me how to use it."

"If you not want my man come, then I leave gun with you. I tie him up," Wei said pointing to Sandro.

Mio Dio e Santa Maria, thought Sandro, repeating the expression he had learned from his Italian family. She is on their side, not ours.

Constanza turned and looked at Sandro. There was no kindness in her eyes.

"You don't need to worry, comrade. I have dealt with much more dangerous men than this one, who seems to be a lunatic fueled by my father's secretary's sentimentality," she said to Wei.

"Lock dool. Not let him go out. He only go back to you fat-ha."

After Wei left, Constanza invited Sandro into a modern-looking kitchen and indicated he should sit at a small table in the corner. She spent several moments preparing coffee in an espresso maker without consulting him as to whether he wanted a cup or not.

Finally she turned to him and spoke to him in Italian. Her voice was harsh. "What did you think you would find here?"

"The person Silvia described."

"You speak Italian like a native. Were you born there?"

"No. When I was young, my parents were brutally murdered by the ruling military, in my case in Burma. An Italian priest saved me and brought me to Livorno where his family raised me." He wanted to add that he did not have to carry a pistol because his family in Livorno was not rich, but he sensed that would only antagonize her further.

Constanza stopped and looked at him for a very long time. Finally she said, "You have lived in Asia. You know what real poverty can be."

"Yes. Although I did not live in poverty when I was young, I was surrounded by it."

"Why were your parents killed?"

"Because they were in Burma to help those in poverty; they were aid workers for an international agency."

"Why were they killed then?"

"Because they spoke out against the government."

Constanza did not respond directly. "Will you have some coffee?" she asked instead.

"Please. Do you have milk? I don't like sugar."

A Scandal in Stresa

Constanza took some time to fill his cup and her own. She took a container of milk from the refrigerator and sat down across the table from him.

"Do you have a name other than Liu?"

"In Italy I am called Sandro. To my adoptive family it sounded like my Chinese given name."

She blew over the top of her cup and took a sip of her coffee. "Did my father hire you to come here?"

"No, I was honest when I told you that. I work for the Kennington hotel chain. When your father and Silvia came to stay at our hotel in Stresa, I was sent to ferry them across the lake to Locarno and to be of service to them in any way they asked."

Constanza stood up and, waving her cup out in the air, challenged him. "Then why, for God's sake, are you here now?"

"Did you hear last night's storm?"

"Of course. One would have to be deaf and blind to have missed it."

Sandro related the story of the launch's failure and the subsequent happenings of the night.

"You just described my actions as being, how did you put it, sentimentalist," Sandro ended. "Will you allow me to refute your argument?"

"Go on," she said.

"*Signorina* . . ."

"Oh, *per l'amore de Dio*, call me Constanza."

"OK. Constanza. From the short time I've known you, I've come to perhaps a hasty conclusion that your mission in the world is righting the wrong of economic poverty by any means. Am I correct?"

"Poverty does the greatest harm in the world. It subjugates millions and gives them no hope."

"Consider poverty not as an economic condition but as a human one. It appears that you think of Comrade Wei as a liberator. Is that so?" Sandro said, ignoring his coffee.

"Of course," she responded. "The current regime in Kathmandu is noted for its corruption and despotism."

"I don't know a great deal about Nepalese politics. It's only occasionally reported in the Italian press, but, when I was a child, I lived under a repressive regime. I knew, even then, that my parents believed that the real poverty of a society is the curtailment of free speech and movement."

"As is the case in Nepal."

Sandro felt he had finally engaged Constanza and therefore confronted her. "Does Comrade Wei allow free speech in his ideology, or is the structure of the Maoist resistance in Nepal militaristic and hierarchical?"

Constanza bristled. "Aggressive resistance to an oppressive regime must be both."

"Would Gandhi have said so? Or Martin Luther King? Or Jesus Christ? Did those men ask for money for armaments or did they passively resist without weapons in order to enrich the spirit of the people?"

"They all were killed by people who disagreed with them. What good did that do?" she said.

"You tell me."

He waited, but she said nothing. Instead she lifted her coffee cup to her lips and took a long swallow, while looking at him with curiosity and wariness.

Sandro could feel himself getting heated. "Your father cares nothing for a million euros if giving it to Comrade Wei guarantees your safety, but Silvia does care. As you know, she's often on the internet, and, since receiving Wei's call, she read all she could about him. He may have convinced you that his mission in Nepal is relieving the suffering of the people, but Silvia is convinced that the million euros will be used for the purchase of arms. Any victim of military oppression can tell you that neither the use of arms nor violent death does anything to relieve the poverty of the human spirit. In fact, it reduces the real essence of humanity to the power one person has over the other's body and mind."

"You sound like a priest."

"Do I? I am sorry you think so. Do you prefer the philosophy of Comrade Wei?"

"He is fighting for the Nepalese people."

"Is he? How many of them has he killed? How many more will he kill with guns bought with the million euros your father gave to him? Constanza, you asked if your father had sent me? The answer is no. I came because I personally could not bear to see those million euros spent for more military or paramilitary aggression. I came knowing that my job with the Kennington Organisation will probably be terminated once I return to Stresa. I also came because I didn't want to be a part of facilitating something that would kill more innocent people like the nuns in Silvia's orphanage and my parents."

Constanza snapped back, "So who is the idealist now?"

"Rest assured, I am." Sandro eyes met hers with defiance.

Until he met Silvia Trucco the day before he would not have thought that this was true. He knew now it was, and what he was doing was a way to avenge the nuns and his parents' deaths.

38

Elspeth regretted that the major Sunday morning papers blared out the tragedy of Toria Albi's death. There no longer was any way to keep the crowds of the curious, both from the public and press, away from the environs of the hotel. Video cameras were already shooting footage of the main entrance.

Looking out Franca's office window Elspeth noticed a police guard near the spot where Toria's body landed and several passers-by who brought flowers and laid them on the pavement. A television camera crew videoed the street scene, the flowers, and the façade of the hotel beyond. Soon, along with showing this footage, the studios in Milan were reporting that Toria Albi had thrown herself off the top of the tower of the Kennington Stresa in an apparent act of suicide. One society reporter stated that it was caused by La Toria's grief over the death of her recently-divorced husband; another speculated that she might have been the person who shot him and then killed herself in fear and remorse. Soon the masses of onlookers grew in front of the hotel, and Franca had to mobilize as much of her staff as she could spare to keep them away from the porte-cochère and main doors.

Being late in the season, the hotel was sparsely occupied, but many of the guests asked if they could depart immediately and without penalty and left by the entrance to the car park. Three of the hotel staff were posted at the entry there to insure that the press and public would not use this as a way to get into the hotel. A mood of hushed chaos began to fill the hotel.

Elspeth was on the phone to Pamela Crumm soon after the first broadcasts were aired. A half-hour later Lord Kennington called Elspeth back.

She saw Eric's number flash on her mobile and sat down on the sofa in her sitting room, looked out at the lake, and wondered if she could find another job easily. On the third ring she answered, "Elspeth Duff here."

"Of course it's you, Elspeth, and you know it's me. This is no time for posturing. I need every bit of your talent, which I have always found considerable. That's what I pay you for, not your charm." Elspeth winced, remembering her flippancy in their earlier phone call. "Here are my instructions."

"Let me get something to write on." Elspeth opened her leather notepad, which was at her side.

"Four items need your attention. I want you to handle them in this order."

Elspeth wanted to snap "Yes, sir," but instead she said, "Of course."

"First, you must handle the press attention over Toria Albi's fall. I want you to call a press conference. I'm compiling a statement for you to read."

"When will I have it?"

"In about an hour."

"Shall I get an Italian interpreter?"

"No, get a written translation. You can find that more easily in Italy than I can here. Use Amanda Bell."

"Consider it done."

"Secondly, find Sandro Liu. Use Will Tuttle to do so."

"I'll let him know."

"Call me as soon as possible with your plan for him."

"I will."

"Thirdly, get the duchess out of the hotel immediately. I've paid a lot of money to get your cousin involved in this affair, so use her if you can."

Elspeth had once heard Pamela Crumm say that Eric's mind ticked when he was thinking. She could almost hear it now.

"Yes, Eric. Biddy has already established a relationship with the duchess, so there shouldn't be a problem."

"Fourthly, do not let the police into the duchess's suite unless they insist on it. After she leaves the hotel, lock the suite up and let no one in, not even the cleaning staff. If the police demand access, I want you to go with them into the rooms, make note of everything they look at and report back to me when they leave."

Elspeth looked down at the four points on her pad. "Is there anything else?"

"Yes, have Sir Richard get the launch towed back to Stresa. I'll have any mechanical difficulties taken care of later, so you won't have to worry about it once it is back in its berth."

Elspeth scribbled down the last item and drew in her breath. "I'll get on it," she said.

"Oh, and Elspeth, you can't be held responsible for what happened there. Just make it right."

"I'll do my best," she said and allowed herself to breath out.

"I knew I could count on you. Call me when things are in place."

He rang off abruptly before she could ask him about Carlo and Silvia. On that matter, she thought, he must trust my judgment. After all, she had already planned most the things he had just directed her to do, except the press conference.

A Scandal in Stresa

The easiest of Lord Kennington's tasks was the first one. Elspeth informed Franca that she would be setting up the press conference and had decided it would be best performed outside of the hotel under the porte-cochère. Next she stepped out of the front door and turned to the people who were standing pressed to the cordon that the doormen had set up.

She spoke in English. "I hope you can understand me. The Kennington Organisation is deeply saddened by the death of Toria Albi, and we would like to speak to you about it at two o'clock this afternoon. We will be providing translations for those of you who do not speak English. Please return here then." She heard mumbling among the crowd, but they slowly began to disperse.

Satisfied that she had suppressed the hoards at least temporarily, she returned to the hotel and called Will and Mandy to the small conference room. As Elspeth waited she was filled with doubts. Sandro could be anywhere and the million euros with him. "Find Sandro," Lord Kennington had said. Why would Eric be so concerned about a lesser member of the security staff? Why now was Sandro's wellbeing second on her list of priorities? She wished she could read Eric's mind, but even Pamela Crumm had admitted she could not.

Will knocked boldly at the door, and Mandy, in a wheelchair, slid in silently beside him. Elspeth greeted them without a smile.

"Will and Mandy, I have just spoken to Lord Kennington, and he has asked me to give you a new assignment that does not involve Toria Albi. As before, you both must keep what I tell you strictly confidential. You must trust no one outside of this room. First, Mandy, I will need your translation skills."

Both Will and Mandy looked puzzled at the grimness of Elspeth's tone but assented with a nod.

"Will, do you know Sandro Liu?" Elspeth asked.

"Yes, he's the other security chap here. We worked together once in Rome, but I only know him slightly," Will said.

"Good, then you will recognize him if you see him. Let me fill the two of you in. Yesterday afternoon, while taking care of two of our guests, Sandro disappeared. The guests returned to the hotel without incident, but Sandro did not. Lord Kennington wants you to find Sandro. I plan to introduce you to the guests and hope they can give us some clues about Sandro's whereabouts. In the meantime, I want you both to be prepared to leave the hotel at a moment's notice."

"But my leg?" Mandy pleaded.

"It may be an advantage, but I don't yet know how. Bear with me, and keep your mobiles active, both of you."

After they left her rooms, Elspeth made her way down to Biddy's suite. Biddy was lying on her chaise lounge and looked miserable.

"Damn, 'Peth, I had no idea those cocktails were so potent. My head feels like the inside of a cuckoo clock when the hour is striking twelve."

"Surely, Biddy, there is some local Highland cure?"

"Probably two stiff drinks of whiskey, but, as I have not had this problem with Galliano before, I expect the Italians have a better solution. Besides, even the thought of two stiff drinks, even of whiskey, revolts me."

"Biddy, you are brilliant." Elspeth beamed for the first time since Lord Kennington's phone call.

"I am? How?"

"I needed a way for you to contact the duchess. You just have provided one."

"She drank a lot more than I did." Biddy sounded defensive.

"It doesn't matter how much you drank last night. What matters is that you see her as soon as possible. Lord Kennington has instructed me to find a way to get the duchess out of the hotel. Since you had been hired by him to be our contact with the duchess, this newest assignment goes to you."

"You mean I have to work in this condition?" Biddy put her hands to her temples.

"Precisely."

"Oh, 'Peth. You always were cruel at the end of a caper."

"This isn't a caper," Elspeth said with annoyance. "The duchess is, at least peripherally, involved in the deaths of Mario and Toria. The paparazzi already are straining at their leads outside. We do not need to give them any further incentive."

"It's rather like old times, isn't it. I seem to be in deeper trouble than I imagined I would be, and you are expecting me to extricate myself." Biddy looked pained.

"This time, Biddy, you have the entire staff of the Kennington Stresa at your disposal. Here's what I propose. Ring the duchess and grumble into her ear about your headache. Suggest that she might recommend a cure. From what we know of her, hangovers must be an almost daily occurrence. If you can lure her away from her suite, all the better. Then tell her that we are planning a press conference."

Biddy moaned. "A press conference? About what?"

"The newspapers this morning splashed the news of La Toria's fall and possible reasons for it across Italy and probably the rest of Europe. One speculation is that she committed suicide because of grief over her divorce; another is that she shot Marco Celli in anger and then took her own life."

"Do you believe either?" Biddy asked.

"No, I don't, but that's not the issue. Lord Kennington wants the whole affair moved away from the Kennington Stresa. We're trying to get the hotel out of the news."

Even hung over, Biddy made a suggestion. "Why not have Maria at the press conference? Wouldn't attention be focused on her and not the hotel?"

Impressed with Biddy's thinking, Elspeth asked, "Do you think you could persuade her to speak to the press?"

"I can try. Nothing ventured . . ."

"Biddy, sometimes I totally underestimate you. Call me when you make contact with the duchess."

Elspeth knew that Eric Kennington's command to lock up the duchess's suite might follow if Biddy were successful.

First she called Richard, who accepted his task with alacrity. Then she decided to approach Carlo, although she feared that he would prefer not to speak to her again after Sandro's defection. Silvia answered the call and invited Elspeth to their suite.

As she made her way to Carlo and Silvia's guestrooms, Elspeth tried to formulate the best way to approach them about getting Mandy and Will involved in the search for Sandro. Finally she decided on the direct approach.

Carlo was standing by the window as Silvia escorted Elspeth into their suite.

Silvia spoke softly. "Carlo, *la signora* Duff is here. She wants to speak to us about Sandro," she said.

Carlo turned, irritation crossing his face. "I trusted Lord Kennington to provide me with protection, and what happens? This young Galahad decides to disobey every request I made of him and to take matters into his own hands. I am intensely angry with him because I believe that his recklessness will directly endanger my daughter. Have you anything to say?"

Elspeth drew back, not expecting this reaction. "I cannot defend Sandro, *signore*. I spoke with Lord Kennington a few moments ago, and he's as concerned as you are. He instructed me to find Sandro Liu using every resource I have available. He believes that if we find Sandro, we also will find your daughter."

Carlo glared at Elspeth. "In what condition does he advise that you will find them? Dead?"

Elspeth had learned over the years how to deal with verbal attacks aimed at either the hotels or her personally. She steadied herself in order to take the abuse and stay above it.

"Eric is proposing that I send two of our security staff to find Sandro. Since we assume that Sandro may be searching for Constanza, I don't want to proceed without your concurrence."

Carlo thought for a moment. "As worried as I am, I trust Eric's judgment. You have my agreement. I want to hear no more about it until you tell me Constanza is safe. Make any arrangements you want with Silvia." He fled from the sitting room.

Silvia motioned to Elspeth to take a seat by her. Elspeth sat down with as much composure as she could muster after Carlo's attack.

"Please, *signora*, do not mind Carlo's words. We have had many instances similar to this, but this is the first time that Constanza has not responded in any fashion. That's why Carlo is tense. Unfortunately when he is troubled, he always sounds angry."

Elspeth spoke quietly. "I don't want to intrude on his welcome anymore. Would you be willing to come down to the hotel offices and speak with the two people who will be trying to find Sandro?"

"Carlo has asked me to handle this, and I will. I'm as anxious as he is but not as emotionally upset. Tell me when to come."

"Is now possible?"

"Yes. Now is best."

Elspeth escorted Silvia to the service lift and down to the conference room by Franca's office. Silvia chatted mundanely as the machine lowered them to the ground floor and said she was curious about seeing the back rooms of the hotel.

"I had no idea of the complexity of the hotel operations. As a guest one always assumes that the running of the hotel ends with the reception desk."

Elspeth laughed. "That's what we want everyone to believe. Lord Kennington pounds into us daily that the workings of the hotel should appear to be seamless to every guest. We always put on our best face."

Silvia wheeled past the security screens, briefly commenting, "Are we so well watched?"

"The idea is to provide you with every means of protection as well as comfort."

Will and Mandy were waiting for them. Silvia's eyes lit up when she saw Mandy sitting in a wheelchair on a level with her own. "*Buongiorno, signorina*, I see we are both bound to furniture."

Mandy grinned in response to Silvia's irreverence.

"My car crashed into an embankment last night," Mandy explained. "Fortunately I'm in better condition than it is. They have not declared me beyond repair."

With a beautiful smile Silvia turned toward Will. He blushed.

Elspeth made the introductions. Silvia shook Will's outstretched hand. "*Signor* Tuttle, I understand from *la signora* Duff that you are a member of Lord Kennington's security staff. You should understand that two days ago we entrusted our safety to another of your security staff. We are upset that he's now disappeared. We fear he's chasing someone who may harm my employer's daughter, and his pursuit will put her in grave danger."

Will nodded to her sympathetically.

Silvia went on, "*La signora* Duff assures me that you can find Sandro and, one hopes, Carlo's daughter."

"I will try my best. I don't speak Italian, but Amanda has agreed to accompany me as my interpreter."

Silvia looked over to Mandy. "Can you do that from your chair?"

Mandy made an awkward attempt at a vehicular pirouette in the wheelchair the hotel had provided.

Silvia snorted. "That relic will do nothing for you. I've been in a wheelchair since I was young and have learned that chairs are like shoes. If you are to accompany *il signor* Tuttle to find Sandro, you must have a chair that suits your purpose. I always travel with several chairs, as other women travel with shoes. I'll have my *chair à la sport,* as the salesman called it, delivered to you immediately. You can do proper turns in it on a moment's notice. I think it can be adjusted to someone your size."

Mandy thanked Silvia. "I'll look forward to perfecting my turns," she laughed.

After asking Silvia to explain the events of the last few days, Elspeth continued. "Will and Mandy, with *la signora* Trucco's permission, I want you to go to the Palazzo Borromeo gardens and try to find where Sandro went. It shouldn't be difficult. Although there undoubtedly are many groups of Asian tourists who visit the gardens, single Asian men are probably more unusual."

Silvia broke in. "Two in one day must have been particularly notable. Carlo and I speculate that the person who picked up the case was Wei Ling-dao, whom Constanza mentioned in her email. However unassuming Wei Ling-dao and Sandro tried to be, their presence in one afternoon would probably have been noticed by someone."

"Where do you think Wei Ling-dao would take the case?" Will asked.

Silvia responded readily. "We think he took the money into Switzerland. That would be a logical place for him to transfer it either into a bank account or to an organization that could facilitate its transfer to Nepal."

"I see," Will said. "Please be assured, *Signora* Trucco, that we will do everything in our power to find Sandro Liu and Constanza Bartelli and return them to Stresa intact and well."

"*Prego*. I hope so," Silvia said and bowed her head.

39

The mechanics of setting up a press conference, Elspeth discovered, were relatively simple. She had the London office contact the major Italian media networks and request that they set up their own links in front of the hotel porte-cochère. Franca Donatello had her staff rope off the area. By half past one, the area was humming with activity. Elspeth watched from a window and saw that not only was the Italian media represented but also the French, German, and British, and CNN as well. So much for protecting the sanctity of the Kennington Stresa, she thought. She wondered how Biddy was doing in luring the duchess into appearing at the event.

*

Biddy was not sure that she was up to her task. Not for the first time in the last few days, she longed to be back at her farm on Loch Tay. Her head pounded, not so much from the effects of the Galliano cocktail as from being asked to interface with a person whom she had once liked but who, at a moment's notice, might act like a screaming harpy. With a muzzy head, or even without one, Biddy found her assignment a daunting prospect. The call to the duchess had been easier than she thought. The duchess invited Biddy to her rooms and, when Biddy arrived, the duchess appeared to be clear-headed, despite her comatose state the evening before. She offered no excuse or apology for passing out on Biddy's sofa.

Biddy wondered at this lack of acknowledgement. Either the duchess remembered nothing, or she was so frequently in this condition she no longer felt it necessary to comment on it.

Biddy decided on a dramatic approach. "I am destitute. I know I drank far too many cocktails last evening, and my head resembles the timpani section of a Verdi opera." Biddy thought the analogy clever, but it was lost on the duchess.

Biddy tried again. "Maria, do you have a cure for this sort of headache? I never tried Galliano cocktails before. They're much less forgiving than single malt whiskey."

She let out a groan, one that would have brought laughter at a Blare School for Girls' theatric production. Maria was oblivious to its emotiveness. She blankly stared at Biddy.

Finally the duchess said, "My dear Elisabeth, the effects of Galliano cocktails vary from person to person, I fear. I feel nothing this morning, except I only grieve for my daughter. Possibly that pain is so great that there is nothing else to feel."

Feeling a little foolish, Biddy went on. "Maria, what can one say? Your daughter was so beautiful and so alive."

"And now dead." The duchess's voice was flat. Biddy noticed that the duchess's eyes were dry.

Biddy tried another approach, one that might lead to the duchess to the press conference. "Your daughter was loved by the public."

"*Sì*. Everybody loves her. She is a great star."

Although not agreeing with the duchess' assessment of her daughter's fame, Biddy persisted. "This morning I spoke with the manager of the hotel, who told me that there would be a press conference to answer questions about your daughter's accident." She stressed the last word purposely.

The duchess glared at Biddy. "The hotel is trying to protect itself. Who protects Vittoria?"

A Scandal in Stresa

The duchess was about to fall into the trap Biddy had set, but Biddy continued cautiously. "I don't know for sure, but I suspect it will be a member of the Kennington Organisation from London who will speak."

"*Ha!* What does he know? Not the truth." The duchess's eyes flashed black.

"Does anyone know the truth, Maria?"

"I do!"

"Then why don't you address the press?"

"Me? Why?" The duchess looked uncertain.

Biddy took advantage of the question and interjected what she hoped sounded like a spur-of-the-moment idea, not one she had rehearsed all the way down to the duchess's suite. "I think that if you did speak at the press conference, you will clear up any misunderstandings about your daughter's fall." Then Biddy drove her point home, hoping her voice was filled with sympathy, not triumph. "If you tell them the truth, then I think you may be left alone to grieve without the paparazzi hunting you down."

The duchess sat bolt upright. "Do they know I am here? Who told them?"

Elspeth earlier shared with Biddy that the duchess's existence in the hotel had been withheld from anyone beyond the immediate staff. Therefore Biddy could answer truthfully. "No one that I know of."

"I will think about this," the duchess said. She paused before going on. "What would you do if your daughter throws herself from the window?"

Biddy waited before answering. "I believe I would go to the press if my daughter was a star." Her words were slow and deliberate, and she hoped they sounded noble.

"Then I consider it."

Biddy did not breath an audible sigh of relief, although she would have liked to. "I think you are quite brave, Maria."

The duchess instinctively brushed her hand across her rigid hair. "Tell me who I talk to about this."

"I will find out and ring you."

Biddy rose from her seat.

Maria reached out her cold hand and clasped Biddy's. "*Va bene*. OK. It is decided. What time is the press conference?"

Biddy inwardly gasped at the strength of the duchess's grip. "I don't know, but I'll get all the information for you."

"Are *la polizia* there?" The duchess sounded offhanded, but Biddy was perceptive enough to wonder if the duchess really was so collected inside.

"I understand that many people gathered on the street outside your daughter's window after she fell. The police are keeping the people away, although several people left flowers."

"*Sì*, many people all over the world love Vittoria. Are there police in the hotel?"

"Not that I have seen. I believe the Kennington Organisation discourages them."

The duchess looked as if she were palliated.

"That is good. It is not necessary to have them here. Now leave me, Elisabeth. If I am to speak to the press, it is necessary that I prepare."

*

The crowd of reporters and onlookers gathered well before two, and they were abuzz with the rumor that Toria Albi's mother would have a statement to make.

At ten minutes to two, Maria, *la duchessa d'Astonino*, without Elspeth's knowledge, made her appearance outside the hotel. Because she was a small woman, she stood on a

A Scandal in Stresa

box provided at the podium and lowered the microphone. She had chosen black clothing, which draped her frail frame, and she had put kohl around her eyes, which exaggerated the darkness of her sorrow. Franca fetched Elspeth and Biddy, and the three of them hurried to the front door of the hotel to watch. They saw the effect the duchess was having on the crowd. She embodied deep mourning.

She spoke in Italian, her rich voice emotive. Franca interpreted for Elspeth and Biddy.

"*Signore e signori*, ladies and gentlemen, I have been asked to make a brief statement. Forgive me if I am unable to take questions afterwards. I have come here today because I feel that you need to know the truth, and, that by my telling the truth, you will allow me to leave here and retire to the privacy of my personal life. Yesterday morning my beloved daughter, the magnificent film star Toria Albi, died as a result of a fall from the roof of this hotel. The only consolation to a grieving mother is that she died instantly. Early this year my daughter filed for divorce from her husband, Marco Celli. He abused her during their marriage, and she needed to protect herself against his violence. Even after their divorce, he continued to follow her. Toria and I came to Stresa to hide from him, but he found out about our presence here. Last week he came to Stresa. My daughter received threatening telephone calls from him, and, unfortunately, she became very agitated. She saw him from our hotel window and could no longer control her fear. Unknown to me, she brought a rifle from our country estate to Stresa. She fetched this rifle from her cases and shot Marco from the roof of the hotel. As you all know, he fell just outside of here."

Her voice grew harder.

"My daughter was a great actor, but, in her fear of Marco Celli, she had grown irrational. After Marco died, she became very depressed. I did not know the reason for this until yesterday morning, when she confessed to me what she had done. I could offer her no consolation. Minutes after she told me that she shot Marco, she ran up to the roof and threw herself off. Suicide is a terrible thing, *signore e signori*. It is against the teachings of our mother church and rips through the families of the deceased with violence that can never be repaired. I beg you, now that I have told you the truth, to leave me alone."

She bowed her head and finished with less bitterness.

"Remember her for her great talents and not for these final deeds of her life."

The duchess's voice cracked at the end. She had tears in her eyes that just escaped falling on to her cheeks. She turned from the lights of the video recorders and flashes from the cameras and, with quiet dignity, withdrew into the hotel.

The press and onlookers remained silent as she left, allowing her to disappear before they departed hastily to file their stories.

The performance was magnificent.

"Balderdash!" Biddy spat out in a most unladylike way. "That was a total lie!"

Will Tuttle, who had come up behind them during the speech, echoed her sentiment less crudely. "She couldn't be telling the truth. Everything Toria said and did on our excursion to the Villa Taranto gardens completely contradicts what the duchess said, and Toria fell from the window not the roof."

Elspeth regarded them both and hesitated before speaking. "How do you propose we dispute what she said?"

"I have my photographs. The ones I took in the duchess's suite last night," Will said.

"What do they show, Will? Can they prove anything?" Elspeth asked.

"That the rifle was in the duchess's wardrobe, not Toria's."

Biddy broke in. "She could contend that she taken the rifle from Toria and stored it away where no one would find it."

Elspeth shook her head at the cleverness of the duchess's statement.

"Do you think the duchess shot Marco then?" Biddy asked.

Elspeth nodded. "Probably, but there is no way I can think of to prove that."

Will swung around and faced Elspeth directly. "I think that the duchess pushed Vittoria from the window."

"In all probability she did," Elspeth said. "I can question Laura again, but she wasn't sure of what she saw. And how do we now present all this to the police?" Elspeth asked. "Let me call London and tell them what has happened. In the meantime, I need Mandy and you to follow up with the other matter we have discussed. Off you go. Good luck."

Will departed after expressing his frustration, and Franca went back into the back rooms of the hotel. Biddy and Elspeth were left alone.

"Do you really believe the duchess is guilty?" Biddy asked.

"Is there any other explanation?"

"What will happen now?"

"I expect the duchess will retreat to Villa d'Astonino, and her statement will preclude any further police investigation into the matter."

"Do you really think that?" Biddy asked.

Elspeth nodded.

"I never knew how sheltered an existence I live on Loch Tay or how much I like it. Your life, 'Peth, seems filled with the dark side of the rich and famous."

"A very rich and very unhappy American billionaire once shared with me that wealth does not change the sorrows of life; it just eases the way. I've thought of that often."

"Now what?" asked Biddy.

"Now we see that the duchess retires from the hotel to her estates, and that the paparazzi leave us alone."

"Have you become so hardened to things like this?" Biddy asked her cousin.

"Most of the time, yes. This time I'm not certain."

40

Mandy waited for Will near the main door to the hotel, which had now been cleared of all vestiges of the press conference. The afternoon was warm for October, but Mandy, taking advantage of her mobilized condition, had packed a small bag with outer clothing and supplies. She had added her passport in case she needed it, a credit card, and as many euros and Swiss francs as she could get from hotel reception. She had also tucked collapsible crutches into the pocket at the side of one of the arms of the chair. While she sat there, she examined Silvia's chair carefully, admired its sleekness, and experimented with Silvia's promise of perfect pirouettes.

Will appeared shortly after half past two, carrying a camera bag, a large folded map of the Lake Maggiore area, wrap around sunglasses, an anorak, and a baseball cap reading *STRESA*. He looked the epitome of a tourist.

"Let's go, Mandy. Are you up for some sleuthing?"

He took the back of her chair and rolled her into the sunlight. The doorman called a taxi for them. On Mandy's request, he directed it to the dock from which the ferry to Isola Bella sailed.

Once they arrived at the Palazzo Borromeo, they had no trouble arousing the memories of the ticket collector for the ferry, probably because Mandy flirted with him outrageously. He remembered that two Asians had both boarded the ferry going back to Stresa the afternoon before. He was convinced one man was shadowing the other.

While waiting for the return ferry, Will and Mandy made their way along the lakeside shops. Inside one they found a small bouquet of white and yellow chrysanthemums. On the way back to Stresa, they threw the flowers overboard in memory of Toria Albi. Mandy was at first amused and then warmed when Will took her hand as they watched their small memorial bob in the wake of the boat and then disappear.

Will and Mandy's main hope was to find Sandro in Switzerland, where Silvia Trucco had speculated Wei would take the money. When back in Stresa, Will bought tickets for the hydrofoil to Locarno.

Finding Sandro in Locarno proved difficult. No one remembered that any Chinese men had come off the ferry the afternoon before, and the taxi drivers waiting for fares proved useless to Will and Mandy's quest. Will finally decided to canvass the hotels near the ferry landing, asking if their "friend" Sandro Liu was staying there. It was almost dusk by the time they found the hotel where Sandro had spent the previous night. Because the hotel had no ramp, Will took charge of the wheel chair, and Mandy hobbled up the stairs on her crutches. Mandy approached the receptionist, whose name badge identified her as Isabella. She spoke to her in Italian.

After looking up and down at Will and Mandy, Isabella asked in English, "Are you Sandro's back-up from his detective agency?"

"Yes, we have come from London, and it is vital that we find him," Mandy prevaricated. "We have important new information, and we fear his life may be in danger."

Isabella looked doubtful. "What is the name of your agency?"

"The Kennington Organisation," Will blurted out on a guess.

Isabella ignored Mandy and smiled sweetly at Will. "Then you are OK," she said and went over to the mailboxes from which she pulled out a letter addressed to "Agent from the Kennington Organisation."

Will tore open the letter and skimmed its contents. Then he handed it to Mandy, who read it more slowly.

> *I expect ED will have sent someone out to find me, and I can use your help. I am following WLD and if I can find a phone I will call back to the hotel when I have an address of where CB might be. If Isabella is there at the desk, she will tell you more about the man I am following. She helped me find out his name last night. Swear her to secrecy. (She will like that.) If you can, send this information on to ED so she can let CB and ST know. – Sandro*

"*Signorina,*" Will said, "please keep this confidential. Did my colleague leave an address of where he was going?"

Isabella shook her head. "No, nothing."

"Did he tell you where he was going?"

"He was following Lyndon Wey." Isabella shifted her eyes back and forth conspiratorially.

Will laughed. "Oh? Who is Lyndon Wei?" he asked.

"The man who is staying here with the two other men from Hong Kong."

"Other men? Who are these men?"

"I don't know, *signore*. They stay in the hotel all day long."

"Do they ever go out?"

"No, not until today."

Will's deep voice cracked. "And today?"

"They had a phone call on their mobile about an hour ago. One of them went out about half an hour before you came."

"Which way did he go? Or did he take a taxi?"

"No, he was walking. The man gave me a piece of paper with *Via dei Giardini* written on it. That's very strange because that is where my grandmother lives. It is outside of the center of town. I showed him on the map."

"Was there a house number?"

"*Sì*. Number 15. I remember because my grandmother's house is number 51."

Will was excited now. He pulled his map from his pocket and spread it out in front of Isabella. "Show me where."

"Signore, it is not on your map."

"Do you have a map that shows it?"

"*Sì*. Because it is in the suburbs, most Locarno tourist maps do not show it, but I cannot give you my map."

Mandy followed the conversation and finally, in Italian, she said, "Isabella, my boss can be demanding. Tell me where to go and I will make sure he will find it."

Isabella looked at Mandy and said, "Do you love him?"

"Very much, and I want to protect him."

Isabella smiled wistfully and in rapid Italian gave Mandy directions. Later Mandy told Will that she used a trick her father had taught her many years before. As Isabella rattled off the directions, she mentally imagined the way and memorized the moves she would have to take to get there.

Isabella ended her instructions and chuckled. "Take care of him. I like his blond hair, but I think he is a bit of a . . ." She did not finish her sentence, but Mandy smiled in understanding.

A Scandal in Stresa

Will and Mandy found the house in Ascona when twilight was in its final stages. The air was now crisp, and the waning moon had risen. It shed just enough light on the street to make the house numbers readable.

Mandy put on a black pullover and Will his navy anorak. They moved through the impeding night unobserved. No neighbor ventured out into the darkness as they walked along the line of heavy hedges along the street.

After having found number fifteen, they withdrew into the shadow of the hedge nearby to assess their next move. They could see lights through the gate, but no sound came from the interior.

Will leaned down and whispered to Mandy in her chair. "Let me go ahead and see how to get into the house. There appears to be a garden at the side beyond the main entrance. You stay here until I get back."

Mandy demurred but silently thought otherwise. She already was planning her own foray into the grounds. Will was willing to leave her here in the safety of the shadows, but that was not what she had in mind. Her father would have recognized Mandy's headstrongness, but Will did not.

*

Will made his foray across the street. He had learned many years before to carry his large frame on soundless feet, and he arrived silently at the gate. He tested it; it was not latched and easily swung open. He stepped inside and closed the gate noiselessly behind him. No reaction came from the house.

Will crept toward a window that was cracked to the night air. The room beyond was dark, and he could hear nothing. As he neared the window, however, he could see a light though a door that was ajar at the far end of the room. Will wondered if he should try to lift the lower portion of the window and crawl in, but he doubted his ability to do this without arousing the occupants of the house. He hesitated. Someone came into the room and switched on the light. Will drew back into the gloom of the garden. He could see the man who entered and recognized him from the photograph Will had found on the web after speaking to Silvia. It was Wei Ling-dao.

Wei was addressing someone beyond the door in a language that Will did not recognize, but he assumed it was Chinese. Wei's voice was level and conveyed no urgency; in fact, he seemed to be joking. This calmed Will, but, when the man came to the window, his tone changed.

Wei suddenly turned, drew up the sash and said in English, "Who are you outside? I see you." Wei spoke to someone in another room, and floodlights immediately filled the garden. Will was silhouetted against a trellis of ivy.

Will began to run. A figure leaped from the window and followed in rapid pursuit. Will made for the gate, but another figure was waiting with arms crossed. Will turned toward his pursuer. The man raised his fist and shoved two bent fingers into the soft underside of Will's jaw. Will collapsed on ground, shook his head and gurgled in pain. The two men grabbed Will by the arms and dragged him inside.

*

After Will had been gone for a few minutes, Mandy emerged from the shadows and moved noiselessly across the street. As easy as the chair was to use, she wondered how Silvia managed without recourse to working legs.

As Mandy approached the gate, she heard the commotion. She stopped, hoping she had not been seen. She heard running footsteps, followed by the shuffling of feet and then a thud and a cry of pain. She could not see beyond the gate. She decided to postpone her entrance into the house until she discovered the reason for the sounds. Was Will in trouble?

Then there was the noise of something heavy being dragged along the path and the slam of a door.

Mandy waited, checking her illuminated watch. She decided to stay still for ten minutes, but she imagined what might be happening to Will. She moved forward again after five minutes had elapsed. She approached the gate, which was slightly ajar. The garden was now inky, and blinds obscured the view through the windows at the front of the house.

Her eyes by this time were well adjusted to the dark. She wheeled slowly around the perimeter of the house. A staircase led up to the front door, but the door at the back had only one step. Mandy knew she could negotiate this with careful maneuvering. The step had a low rail at each side. Using these, she propped herself up and lifted Silvia's chair on to the porch. The space was crowded with large wooden crates, which offered Mandy protection if she were heard. She shifted the wheelchair behind the boxes and settled herself into it.

Before she could take further note of her surroundings, the door opened and an Asian man stepped out and lit a cigarette. Mandy rolled back farther, making no noise as she did so.

The man stood for a long time, inhaling the smoke from the foul-smelling tobacco. Mandy could not see the man, but she doubted it was Wei Ling-dao. She suspected that this was the man who had left the hotel in Locarno just before she and Will had arrived. The man finished his cigarette and went back into the house. Mandy noticed that the door made no sound. The man did not turn on the light inside and passed into the next room. She counted to one hundred and then rolled her chair out, opened the door and slid into a darkened kitchen. Through a crack in the door at the end of the room Mandy could see light and hear voices. She could distinguish three people speaking. Their common language appeared to be English, although a man and a woman occasionally spoke to each other in Italian. When they did, the third voice, speaking with a heavy Asian accent, demanded they speak English. Mandy found a spot behind the door where she could fit her chair and which afforded her limited vision into the room beyond. She sat still and listened.

The woman's voice was angry. "Comrade, we have come a long way together. I didn't expect you to go back on your agreement."

The Asian answered, "I make no agreement."

The woman, whom Mandy now assumed was Constanza Bartelli, burst out. "Damn you, comrade! What's the money for?"

"For the opplessed people of Nepal. You said you help cause."

"And in return?"

"In leturn for what?"

"Have you forgotten?"

"I folget nothing, Constanza."

"You promised me an interview!"

The man's voice became non-committal. "It not wise."

"I brought you thousands of kilometers and got you one million euros for that interview." Constanza was now in a full rage.

The man remained adamant. "It not wise."

"*Bastardo!*"

"English!"

"Bastard!"

"I not know word."

Another voice broke in. Mandy guessed it was Sandro Liu. "Wei, perhaps you and *la signorina* Bartelli can reach a compromise."

"No complomise."

"Then why did you take the money?" Sandro asked.

Wei screamed out. "She say she give for my people. Not wise anyone to know I come Switzeland or to know whele I go in Nepal."

The man who Mandy suspected was Sandro lowered his voice and began to speak in Chinese. Mandy could not understand the words, but she understood the meaning. Wei's reply reflected the same refusal as his English words did.

In Italian Constanza demanded, "What's he saying, Sandro?"

Sandro responded in English, but Mandy suspected that he purposely made his words complex, "His recalcitrance is untenable. He categorically renounces any previous concordance between the two of you. My prognostication is that he will remain obtusely adamant." Mandy wondered at his erudition.

"English!" Wei shouted.

Constanza blazed out, "We are speaking English."

Wei's response was harsh. "Sit down, Constanza, and you, Liu. I not want to shoot you, but I shoot if you not talk English."

Alarmed, Mandy wheeled her chair about slightly, so she could see more clearly through the crack. She noticed that the kitchen door was the kind that pivoted in two directions. Wei stood with his back to the door. Sandro and Constanza were facing Wei, and consequently Mandy. Wei had a revolver in his hand, and he was screwing on a silencer.

"Bastard!" Constanza shouted again. "You deceived me!

As Wei raised his gun, Mandy lunged forward. She flung the door open, throwing Wei to his knees. The revolver slid across the floor toward Constanza. She bent over, lifted it and pointed it directly at Liu. "Bastard!" she said one more time, this time with a sob.

Wei Ling-dao spat out something in Chinese.

Sandro responded by yelling at Constanza, "The other man!"

The man who Mandy had seen on the porch swung open the door behind Constanza and pointed a gun directly at her.

"Watch Wei!" Sandro commanded, and he turned to the Chinese in the doorway. With his head down Sandro charged the man.

Wei sprang to his feet and lunged toward Constanza. Seeing him coming, she raised the gun and aimed at his heart. With her eyes wide open, she pulled the trigger.

Before Sandro could tackle the man at the door, another shot rang out. The man fell in an agonized twist, clutching his leg and rattling off a stream of Chinese words that Sandro refused to translate later.

Mandy lowered the small pistol she had brought from Egypt and tucked in the pocket of Silvia's wheelchair and thanked her father's foresight in teaching her to disable an attacker and not kill him.

The room was filled with flashing lights. Will, who now stood in the doorway, recorded the event so precisely that later his photographs were some of the main pieces of evidence in the Swiss court of law.

Epilogue

Warm winds came off the Mediterranean, which was unusual for November. Richard and Elspeth wandered out onto the balcony of Magdelena Cassar's home in Gozo to savor the last bars of the grande dame's private recital for them. They stood and let the notes linger and breathed in the fragrance of the damp air that came through the darkness.

Finally Richard spoke. "Did Eric Kennington ever acknowledge how well you handled the situation in Stresa?"

"No, but that's not unusual. My return to London was not comfortable. Eric didn't like the publicity around the duchess's volatile press conference. He pointed out that I could have prevented the whole thing by whisking her away from the hotel before the paparazzi converged on the spot."

"Elspeth, my dear, why do you put up with that man?"

"Actually, although he is a martinet, I am quite fond of him, and of course I would do anything for Pamela Crumm."

Richard reached over and lightly touched her cheek. She smiled up at him.

"What did happen to the duchess?" he asked. "Did she finally depart without any further fuss?'

The memories of Stresa filled Elspeth's mind. "Shortly after the press conference, she left the hotel under our protective wing and returned to Villa d'Astonino. I wish it had ended there. When she had arrived at the hotel, she gave assurance to Eric that her bank in Milan would cover the bill, but, after she left, the hotel was told that the duchess had no funds available."

"Did she default then?"

"Totally. The bank said that they no longer would honor her line of credit. It appears that the Astonino estate was heavily encumbered and had been for many years. The bank had respected the word of the late duke that they would eventually be paid but had less faith in the duchess, particularly since Toria, her source of income, is dead."

Richard raised his eyebrows. "And did Eric Kennington blame you for that?"

Elspeth laughed. "No. Despite his bombastic personality at times, Eric is basically a fair man. It was he, after all, who had given a nod to the duchess's stay at the hotel."

"What about Toria's money? Surely there must be royalties from her films?"

"Toria's will left everything to a shelter for battered women in Naples."

Richard turned, leaned on the parapet and looked out to the dark sea. "Ironic, isn't it. Do you still think the duchess killed Marco Celli?"

"Without a doubt. I'm also certain she killed both of her husbands and pushed her daughter to her death."

"But, my dear, you have no way to prove it."

"No, I never will, but what is the saying, the punishment fits the crime? Where is Maria Gotti Albi d'Astonino now? Living in a villa that is soon to be taken over by the bank, without a husband, or husbands, and, most of all, without her only child. Had she been convicted of any of the murders, her fate could not have been more lonely and empty. Do you think she can sleep at night?"

Richard turned to Elspeth. "No, I cannot imagine living with such ghosts."

Without protest, Elspeth let Richard put his arm around her shoulder and draw her closer.

After a long time he spoke again. "What finally happened in Switzerland?"

The wind caught her hair, and she reached to tame it before she answered.

"Oh, that was a tangle indeed."

Elspeth related the events in Ascona that she learned after Richard left Stresa.

"What an extraordinary story. It strikes me that this is not the sort of thing the Swiss like happening on their soil," Richard said.

"After the shots, Mandy dialed 1-1-7, the Swiss emergency number, and the police arrived within minutes. She also rang me. I immediately contacted Carlo Bartelli. It was he who went to Switzerland to negotiated with the police."

"You are right. What a tangle indeed. Will there be a trial?"

Elspeth shook her head. "That's still to be seen. It clearly was a case of self-defense on Constanza's part, but the Swiss will want to make sure. Carlo made arrangements with the Swiss legal authorities and took Constanza under his own recognizance. Because of his contacts in the Italian government and the Italian embassy in Bern, he was able to keep her out of jail. Constanza, Sandro, and Silvia are now in residence at the home of one of Carlo's bankers in Locarno and are awaiting the decision of the Swiss authorities. Carlo and Silvia left the hotel shortly after hearing about the events in Ascona. I must say I was relieved that Carlo's car with the bullet hole in the windscreen was finally out of the car park."

Richard smiled down at Elspeth, who was now resting her head on his shoulder. "Your loyalty is to the hotels, isn't it."

"Yes, I suppose it is. The whole situation in Stresa really was rather bigger than my safeguarding the hotel and its guests. There was only so much I could do."

He nodded with sympathy. "Did you say Sandro Liu is in Switzerland? Did Eric Kennington let him go?"

"Yes. He had overstepped his duties, but, on the fortunate side, Carlo hired him to be a bodyguard for Constanza."

"How did he react to that?"

"It was Silvia who asked him. I think he would have done anything for her."

"And Constanza?"

"Carlo said she was subdued and was relieved at Sandro's intervention in Ascona."

Richard reached up and, with a tender gesture, pushed away a wisp of Elspeth's hair that had blown once more in her face.

"What about Wei's henchman?" he asked.

"When he was shot, he fled from the house. No one has seen or heard of him since. The other men at the hotel in Locarno disappeared the same night and have not surfaced since."

"And the million euros?"

"The Italian Embassies in both Bern and Kathmandu are making enquiries."

Richard shook his head. "Nothing will come of it. That's typical of the twisted ways of diplomacy that have graced my life. What happened to Mandy Bell and Will Tuttle?"

"Mandy is returning to university for the spring term. Because Wei's accomplice disappeared, there could be no charges brought against her. Will accompanied her back to London. They went together to tell Eric and Pamela what happened in Stresa and Locarno. Eric tried to recruit Mandy, who remained firm in her resolve to finish university. She said she might consider his offer after that."

"Your Lord Kennington is manipulative."

"Oh, definitely. Dickie, I want to thank you again for rescuing the launch."

"It was my great pleasure," he said. "Did Franca ever make amends with you?"

"No, but I think she was glad to get rid of us all."

The music from within ended. Magdelena Cassar put her head around the French doors to the terrace and bade them goodnight.

Elspeth went to Magdelena and hugged her, as she had done for so many years of her life. When she did so, Magdalena whispered in her ear. "He is a wonderful man. Don't let him go."

"Oh, Aunt Mag, I am too old for that sort of thing."

"You know, my dear, that you are lying to an old woman who loves you very much." Magdalena swept from the balcony after blowing Richard a kiss.

Elspeth returned to the rail of the balcony. She knew her face had reddened. She hoped the blush was hidden in the darkness of the Mediterranean night.

"You haven't asked about Biddy? Or has she already contacted you?" Elspeth hoped her voice did not sound strained.

Richard gently pulled Elspeth around where he could see her in the borrowed light of Magdalena's great room. "No, my dear Elspeth, I have not seen her or talked to her since I left Stresa."

"But, I thought . . ."

He lightly placed his fingers on each of her cheeks and smiled down at her. "You thought what?"

"That you were fond of her."

"Now I understand. You need not worry, Elspeth, my dearest. I have always preferred her cousin."

Elspeth regretted her jealousy. "Why did you go to Scotland last spring?

"To see your parents and ask them something."

"And that was? You said you would explain." Elspeth tried to keep her voice calm, belying her true feelings.

"Because I needed to talk to them about Malcolm."

"About Malcolm?" Her heart turned. Malcolm, whom she had never ceased to love and whose youth and excitement had been robbed from her by a sniper's bullet on a lonely road outside of her college at Cambridge.

"Because, my dear, you have never let Malcolm go, and I cannot ask you to marry me until he is truly buried and mourned, and you have taken him out your daily thoughts." He took her in his arms and kissed her gently. She did not resist.

Slowly she pulled back from his embrace. "Will you help me, Dickie, if I try to find out what really happened and why he was shot? It's been over thirty-five years. It won't be easy."

He wiped away the tears on her cheeks. "Of course I will, but remember that my motives are selfish."

"I will remember," she said in a hoarse whisper. "Thank you, dear Dickie."

Author's Appreciation

Special thanks go to my brother, David Ingram, MD, a former naval officer and avid sailor. He not only helped me with medical and sailing issues but also was kind enough to come with me to Italy in 2004 to explore all the places described in the book. And, as always, deepest gratitude goes to Ian Crew, my chief supporter and also taskmaster.

I could not have completed this book without the advice of my editor in Dundee, Scotland, Rachel Marsh, M.Phil. She did the daunting task of editing the book in order to ferret out my numerous errors. Any mistakes that remain are entirely my own.

Also appreciation is due to E. V. Fraser, who assisted me with my rusty Italian, and Jocelyn Jenner, who helped me with British English usage.

Apologies are in order to the police in Stresa for the ineptitude of the police *commissario*, Aldo Ponchetti. His character and actions are completely fictional.

Finally, thanks to our gracious hosts at the Hotel du Park in Stresa, whose location I stole for the Kennington Stresa.

Read on for an excerpt from the third Elspeth Duff mystery, *A Secret in Singapore*.

From *A Secret in Singapore:*

In the unusual act of rising unsettled from her mid-afternoon rest, Magdelena Cassar crossed the cavernous room that was at the center of her home, a resplendent converted farmhouse on the island of Gozo in the Republic of Malta. She approached Elspeth Duff. Elspeth was one of the few people in the world who merited any disruption of Magdelena's normal daily routine. When Magdelena retired to her room an hour earlier, Elspeth was sitting on an ornate baroque settee covered in intricate needlepoint that was one of the few pieces of furniture in the great room other than the two back-to-back grand pianos. Magdelena looked at Elspeth with the deep love a mother might have for a child, although Elspeth was not hers.

Always sensitive to her niece's moods, Magdelena spoke to Elspeth. "Even with the cool breeze coming in my window, I couldn't sleep. I tried to study the Chopin nocturne for tomorrow's soirée, but I couldn't lift it up because I could feel the weight of your sadness a room away."

She sat down next to Elspeth with the effort of an aging woman, oversized by modern standards in London and New York although acceptable as venerable in Malta. Magdelena still had the grace of the long-famous but blew her breath through her eagle's nose at the effort of sitting down. She put her hands on Elspeth's.

A Scandal in Stresa

Elspeth had not discernibly moved over the last hour. The set of her sculptured Gaelic jaw, the stiffness of her backbone that was pushed against the hardness of her chosen seat, and the tightness of her lips had not altered. Although her eyes were open, they did not seem to take in her current surroundings but were focused on another place than this, a place of pain rather than beauty. As she had often done as a child, Elspeth laid her head on Magdelena's ample chest and smiled weakly as she negotiated a spot free of the strands of amber beads.

"Elspeth, *mia cara,* where are your thoughts?"

Elspeth turned a sad stare toward Magdelena as if puzzled at her presence and the warmth of her caress. "Sorry, I was far away."

"And not in a good place." Magdelena's rich voice whispered in Elspeth's ear.

"No, not in a good place. Richard says I'm still haunted by those days in Cambridge when Malcolm died. Did you know Richard was there afterwards, after they found Malcolm's body?"

Magdelena remembered those times, when Elspeth had come here to Gozo after Malcolm Buchanan had died. Three decades had long passed, but Magdelena could recall each heart rending day that Elspeth had spent in Gozo at the end of the summer of nineteen sixty-nine, acting as if she were unalive herself. Elspeth stayed under Magdelena's wing for a month. Only at the end of that time could she raise her head and get through a day with the normal gestures of the living. Finally she was able return to Girton College at Cambridge to complete her studies. Caressing Elspeth now, Magdelena knew instinctively that her niece was back in that old place of sorrow.

"My dear one, do you go back to that time often?"

"Dear Aunt Mag, you'd think after all these years I'd have more sense."

Magdelena rose from the settee, to the protest of the aged piece of furniture, and retreated to one of the piano benches, which bore her weight with more fortitude.

Despite her artistic temperament and often passionate rather than rational way of dealing with difficult situations, Magdelena Cassar offered a solution to Elspeth.

"Have you ever gone back, *cara*, with all your great skills and looked for the person who shot Malcolm?"

Magdelena's suggestion roused Elspeth from her torpor. "Go back? But you know the police searched for years and never found anything."

"If you went back now, could you find out what happened?" Magdelena asked.

"Of course I couldn't. How many years has it been? Thirty-five? Trying to find the murder now would be hopeless."

"Would it?"

Elspeth set her jaw stubbornly, "How could I? Lord Kennington relies on me to provide security at his hotels, and I rely on him for my livelihood. I simply can't ring him in London and say, 'Sorry, Eric, I have some old ghosts to exorcise.'"

Magdelena had heard her niece expostulate about her employer often enough to know Lord Kennington was a demanding boss. "Does that scoundrel give you no time off? It seems to me that you have worked for the last year with no break at all."

"That always happens when there are urgent security issues at his hotels. Things have become worse since the recent rise of terrorism."

"Does he ever compensate you for all that time?"

Elspeth avoided the question and posed one of her own.

"What good would it do to go dredging it all up again? Can you imagine my going back to Cambridge and delving into a murder that happened a over a third of a century ago?"

"I can imagine it very well. Elspeth, you must put Malcolm to rest. Surely you have the ability to find the murderer."

"Should I go dig up the old police investigations, if they still exist?"

"No, not at all. I think you should go back to Cambridge as a mature woman and skilled investigator and find Malcolm's murderer on your own."

"How?" Elspeth challenged.

"I do not know, *cara*, I play the piano; I do not investigate crimes. That is what you do."

Elspeth smiled at this.

Magdelena thought of her own past. In her heyday, she had been one of the most famous pianists in Europe. Even now an invitation to her monthly soirées were sought after by those visiting Gozo who remembered her performances that had filled the concert halls and recital rooms for several decades. Magdelena had retired to Gozo, where she lived since before the Second World War, to be with Elspeth's uncle as he aged, and she had remained on after he died. Although Magdelena had never had officially married Frederick Duff, she had been Elspeth's beloved aunt for many years.

"Are you suggesting this ridiculous idea as therapy, Aunt Mag?"

"Of course! You still love Malcolm and won't let go of him. You haven't let him die, *cara*. I'm suggesting that you find his murderer. Then you can bury Malcolm and get on with marrying Richard."

Elspeth's face contorted the way it did when she was a child and was considering whether to be rebellious or not. "I've no intention of marrying Richard," she said. "Where did you get that idea?"

Ann Crew is a former architect and now full time mystery writer who travels the world gathering material for future Elspeth Duff mysteries. Visit *anncrew.com*.